DRAGON SAGA

BOOK TWO

THE SEA STONE

NICOLETTE
ANDREWS

Editing by Katie Crum & Charity Chimni
Case Laminate Art by Lauren Richelieu
Dust Jacket Art by Msriza
Exterior Design & Interior Formatting by Charity Chimni
Interior artwork by Nadica Borshkova

First Edition

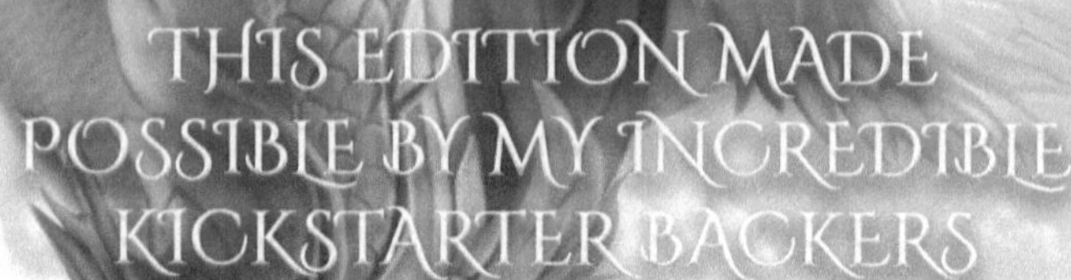

THIS EDITION MADE POSSIBLE BY MY INCREDIBLE KICKSTARTER BACKERS

EXTRA-EXTRA SPECIAL THANKS TO:

ARTHUR DIXON, BUBS MARTINEZ, CHRIS-ANDRÉ PEDERSEN, COURTNEY R. DELGADO, DIANA BRITTON, HEIDI Z., NATASHA WIMMER, SEAMUS SANDS

EXTRA SPECIAL THANKS TO:

AMANDA ESCHMEYER, ASHLEY, AURORE MOREL, CHRISTINE HAAS, DAPHNÉ MELANSON, DR. CHARLES E NORTON III, ELIZABETH FRAZIER, ELVINA PATINO, EMILIE GARNEAU, EMMA FLAWS, FRANCHESCA CARAM, JESSICA JOHANSEN, JOHN CALLAHAN, JONAH PAVLICEK, KAREN BULGARELLI, KASEY OVERSTREET, KASS M., KATHERINE MALLOY, KATIE PAWLIK, KIM HILLMER, LEIA, M W, M. COSGROVE, MARY LIVINGSTON, MOON THEIASDOTTIR, NEREIDA GREEN, NICOLE HAARSTAD, TAYLOR PRINCE

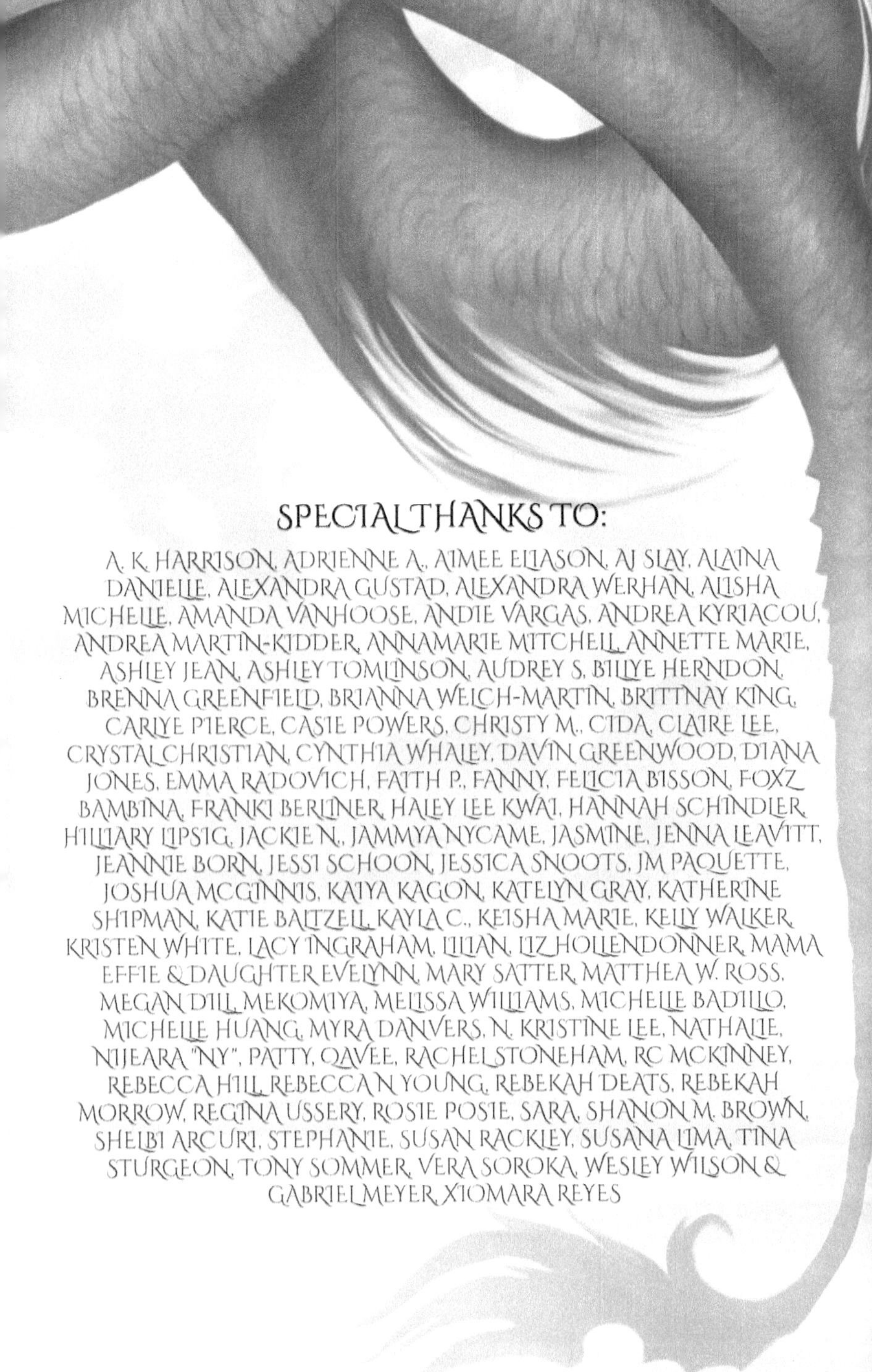

SPECIAL THANKS TO:
A. K. HARRISON, ADRIENNE A., AIMEE ELIASON, AJ SLAY, ALAINA
DANIELLE, ALEXANDRA GUSTAD, ALEXANDRA WERHAN, ALISHA
MICHELLE, AMANDA VANHOOSE, ANDIE VARGAS, ANDREA KYRIACOU,
ANDREA MARTIN-KIDDER, ANNAMARIE MITCHELL, ANNETTE MARIE,
ASHLEY JEAN, ASHLEY TOMLINSON, AUDREY S, BILLYE HERNDON,
BRENNA GREENFIELD, BRIANNA WELCH-MARTIN, BRITTNAY KING,
CARLYE PIERCE, CASIE POWERS, CHRISTY M., CIDA, CLAIRE LEE,
CRYSTAL CHRISTIAN, CYNTHIA WHALEY, DAVIN GREENWOOD, DIANA
JONES, EMMA RADOVICH, FAITH P., FANNY, FELICIA BISSON, FOXZ
BAMBINA, FRANKI BERLINER, HALEY LEE KWAI, HANNAH SCHINDLER,
HILLIARY LIPSIG, JACKIE N., JAMMYA NYCAME, JASMINE, JENNA LEAVITT,
JEANNIE BORN, JESSI SCHOON, JESSICA SNOOTS, JM PAQUETTE,
JOSHUA MCGINNIS, KAIYA KAGON, KATELYN GRAY, KATHERINE
SHIPMAN, KATIE BALTZELL, KAYLA C., KEISHA MARIE, KELLY WALKER,
KRISTEN WHITE, LACY INGRAHAM, LILIAN, LIZ HOLLENDONNER, MAMA
EFFIE & DAUGHTER EVELYNN, MARY SATTER, MATTHEA W. ROSS,
MEGAN DILL, MEKOMIYA, MELISSA WILLIAMS, MICHELLE BADILLO,
MICHELLE HUANG, MYRA DANVERS, N. KRISTINE LEE, NATHALIE,
NIJEARA "NY", PATTY, QAVEE, RACHEL STONEHAM, RC MCKINNEY,
REBECCA HILL, REBECCA N YOUNG, REBEKAH DEATS, REBEKAH
MORROW, REGINA USSERY, ROSIE POSIE, SARA, SHANON M. BROWN,
SHELBI ARCURI, STEPHANIE, SUSAN RACKLEY, SUSANA LIMA, TINA
STURGEON, TONY SOMMER, VERA SOROKA, WESLEY WILSON &
GABRIEL MEYER, XIOMARA REYES

Lord of the
Sea's Palace
Namahane Village
Hidden Temple
Mt. Kitiyama
Akano Forest
Mt. Iwaki
Temple of
Mt. Iwaki
Kaedemori
Clan House
Mountain God's Shrine
Tengu Mountain
White Palace
Sun Temple
Osaka
Kaito's Palace

ONE

A ball of fire zoomed through the air. When it collided with the torii arch, it burst apart in a shower of sparks. The paint on the arch bubbled and peeled, revealing scorched wood beneath.

Tsuki looked over his shoulder, raising an eyebrow as he whistled. "Well, at least you can make a ball of fire. But I think your aim needs some work." He plucked the paper target off the archway just to the left of the smoldering arch. "Do that again, and this time focus on the target."

Suzume huffed as her shoulders sagged, as if that breath was keeping her upright. "Again? But that took forever!" She couldn't keep the whine from her tone.

"With practice, it will come easier," Akira said using her brother's face, not bothering to shift into view. Since the siblings shared a body, they often took turns on who was visible. Whose face you saw correlated to what they were doing usually. Akira handled Suzume's spiritual training, Tsuki her combat training.

"How much practice exactly?" She put her hands on her hips. Just imagining another week or more of staring at her hands, willing flames to appear, made her want to throw herself on the ground and have a proper tantrum. When they first started her training, she thought mastering her powers would be easy, a couple days tops. It had been over a week and today was the first time she had managed to create a fireball. *Making fire is easy, leave me alone with Kaito for five minutes.* Focusing it and harnessing it to attack, that was the not so easy part.

"If you want we can practice with the staff instead." Tsuki grinned with a mischievous glint in his eye. She rubbed the bruise on her shoulder, one of a growing collection given to her by Tsuki during their sparring sessions. *He wants me to admit I'm tired, but I won't give him the satisfaction.*

Suzume glared at him while her arms twitched with the memory of exertion. Even propping them on her hips took a monumental effort. This body wasn't meant for this sort of abuse. It was accustomed to sitting around on cushions and writing poetry about nature while being admired from afar. Up until just recently, she had never even dressed herself. Now she was learning how to defend herself with a weapon, and how to stop the fire from shooting out all over her body.

"Look who's here," Tsuki nodded his head in their newcomer's direction.

There was no point in turning to look, she knew by the sparks dancing along her arms who was joining them. As if keeping up the pretense in front of the conjoined siblings wasn't bad enough, Kaito the dragon, her greatest tormentor, strode into the courtyard. He inserted himself between Tsuki and Suzume, that infernal smirk upon his face.

"Training hard?" Kaito asked as his gaze skimmed over her to the rising tendrils of smoke coming off the burned torii arch, the only evidence of hours of practice. A week's worth of practice, really.

"Yes, now leave, you're distracting," Suzume snapped at him at the same moment her arms gave up and fell like limp noodles at her side.

The hope was the dragon would leave her to gracefully weasel out of any more training today. She was not born lucky however.

"Suzume and I were just about to spar, care to watch?" Tsuki said to Kaito with a sly smile in her direction.

Suzume cursed him internally as she shot him a look that said 'you'll pay for this.'

He only grinned back at her with a look that said, 'you should admit when your beat.'

Two could play this game. "Tsuki was going to let me practice an emergency maneuver." Suzume fluttered her eyelashes in Tsuki's direction, while making a kicking motion in the direction of Tsuki's crotch. He reflexively covered his genitals with both hands.

Akira's husky laughter spilled out of her brother's lips.

"Don't know why you insisted I teach her that," Tsuki mumbled.

Suzume laughed as Tsuki turned his lower body away from her. With narrowed eyes Kaito regarded the pair of them, a hint of ice in his stare. A touch of chill grasped at the back of her neck, eliciting sparks in reaction to his spiritual energy. Whenever Kaito got mad, Suzume was the first to feel it.

"I hope you're behaving." Kaito eyed Tsuki up and down. "I would hate to have to take over Suzume's training. It would really be a bother."

"You wouldn't teach me, you'd just throw me at the nearest yokai and expect me to figure it out," Suzume said.

"That method has worked in the past." Kaito smirked at her.

"If by 'worked' you mean it almost got me killed."

"Well, if you think Tsuki's method is more effective, prove it." Kaito gestured toward Tsuki before plopping down on the ground at the foot of a nearby torii arch. He leaned back and slung his arm over a bended knee. A casual observer would think he was disinterested as his gaze was not focused on her but skimming over the surrounding courtyard, but Suzume knew better. Nothing Kaito did was without motive.

Well there was no getting out of it now.

Tsuki's grin reached from ear to ear. Kaito might take the most pleasure from her discomfort but Tsuki was a close second. In a lot of ways, he reminded her of one of her younger brother, the ones who liked to leave creepy crawly things in her bed.

"Since you're tired, I'll take it easy on you," Tsuki said.

"I'm not tired, I could go for hours more." The lies just kept pouring out of her. *Would you stop already?*

Tsuki covered his mouth with his hand to disguise his smile. "I won't hold back then."

Suzume turned her head away from the others as she silently berated herself for not keeping her mouth shut. A single deep breath helped her regain her composure. But getting into position was harder than she anticipated. Just the mere effort of holding the staff up left her muscles trembling in protest.

Chin cupped in his hand, Tsuki looked her up and down. "Your arms are drooping, bring them up and closer to your chest."

With some difficulty, she did as Tsuki had instructed. But that made her muscles cramp. Pain rippled up her arms as her muscles clenched and spasmed. Suzume had to grit her teeth to keep from crying out. Shaking his head, Tsuki went behind Suzume. From there, he bent her elbows into the angle of his choosing. When she'd first started training with Tsuki being this close to him made her uncomfortable, but she was growing accustomed to it by now. Besides he was one of the few people who didn't bring out the fire in her.

His arms enveloped her, hands moving down her arms, his breath fanned against her skin as he said, "Do you see the dragon's scowl? He's so transparent."

Suzume refused to look in Kaito's direction, mostly because she feared if she stopped focusing on keeping her arms outright they'd betray her, but also because she could feel his displeasure. Her lungs burned from the pressure of his spiritual energy unfurled by his temper. Whenever he was angry the temperature dropped. If Tsuki kept this up she'd have icicles dangling from her nose. Many of her training sessions had been interrupted by the dragon under some pretense or another. But the end result was always him inserting himself between the two of them. Tsuki lingered a moment longer, his hands gliding to her hips pivoting her into the right stance.

"Can we get on with it," Suzume ground out.

Tsuki made one final adjustment to Suzume's legs, his hands sliding down to turn her foot. On stupid impulse, she chanced a glance in the dragon's direction. Kaito looked ready to burst from his skin. Tsuki had taken twice as long as normal to correct her positioning and she wasn't sure if when the practice actually began she'd be able to perform. Tsuki took his place opposite her, his own staff in hand.

Even knowing what was coming she couldn't make her muscles obey. Her entire body felt as if she was trapped in mud, her legs and arms were glued in place. She could do nothing but watch helplessly as Tsuki swung at her. The staff came toward her in slow motion. After an over-long delay, she thrust forward to block, and their staffs met with a clack. The force of his blow knocked her off balance and sent her skidding backward. Tsuki gave her a second to recover before rushing toward her again. Her parry was too low, missing him and his staff entirely, and sent her forward and into Tsuki. He caught her, blocking her fall with his staff, their weapons slammed together and the impact jarred her arms forcing them to seize. Her muscles clenched and she couldn't prepare herself in time for the next swing, which sent her stumbling backward. Suzume lost her balance, or her legs gave out, and she fell to the ground.

She landed on her rear and cursed aloud this time.

Tsuki wasn't even out of breath when he offered her a hand up, "Ready to admit you're tired?"

This was her chance to give up. All she had to do was admit she was tired, she was only human after all.

"If you can't keep up, maybe it's time to quit," Kaito said to her, but there was no mockery in his tone, which only made her angrier.

Kaito held out his hand to help her to her feet, but she knocked it aside, instead using her staff for leverage to hoist herself up. On her feet again, she swayed for a moment as the world spun for a brief second.

Ignoring Kaito she said to Tsuki, "Let's go again."

"You can barely stand, let alone fight. You've done enough," Kaito said, this time irritation crept into his tone as he grabbed her bicep. Where his hand circled around her arm sparks erupted, clashing against the ice which encased his hand.

She shrugged off his grip, and a flurry of sparks danced between them as she turned her back on him. "I think I know my limits better than you," she spat. Then to Tsuki she said, "Let's go."

Tsuki watched their exchange with a frown on his brow. They squared off once more, and the results were not much different than the first time. But this time when she fell to the ground, Kaito practically flew through the air to help her up. Before he could try to help her however, she climbed onto shaking feet.

"I think you've done enough," Kaito said. He was really getting angry now.

Each breath was an uneven wheeze. The combination of Kaito's spiritual pressure and her own fatigue were wearing her down.

"Again," she rasped.

Tsuki looked to Kaito, his expression cautious. He had not resumed his position and his staff remained limp at his side.

"Are you sure?" Tsuki asked her.

"I... said... let's go!" she said between panting breaths. Suzume's form was sloppy, she couldn't hold the staff up all the way, and sweat rolled into her eyes and blurred her vision.

The dragon hovered nearby as Tsuki continued to hesitate, and the two of them shared a look. Since Tsuki was wasting time, Suzume took the offensive and rushed toward Tsuki, her body fueled by her own stubborn will.

Tsuki blocked her half-hearted attack with ease, knocking her backward as easily as knocking down a blade of grass. For a moment, she thought she was going to collapse until she found her balance once more and rushed toward Tsuki again. Though it was more of a half staggering and fumbled attack. Blinded by pride, and fueled by some reserve of adrenaline, Suzume attacked like a cornered animal. She swung at his head, his shoulder, his abdomen, anywhere she might land a blow was fine. Because her movements were so erratic and uncoordinated, Tsuki had to over-compensate, and accidentally struck her across the cheek with the end of his staff as he attempted to block. Flames erupted from where his blow landed, and she spun backward as flickers of flame trailed behind her.

That was the final blow. Her knees buckled beneath her and Suzume crumpled to the ground. Kaito rushed over toward where she lay on the ground with her eyes closed, feeling like a colossal fool. *You idiot, what were you hoping to prove?*

"You idiot," Kaito snarled.

Suzume's eyes flew open as she prepared a retort. Only she could call herself that.

"Don't blame this on me," Tsuki snapped back. "When you're around, she's reckless."

"And you should stop her before she hurts herself."

"Are you really going to talk about me like I am not here?" Suzume interjected.

"You want her to learn, but you don't want her to get hurt. You can't have both." Tsuki crossed his arms over his chest.

"You said you knew how to teach her," Kaito growled.

"How can we teach her to harness her powers with you around? Your spiritual energy overwhelms hers," Akira said, coming to her brother's defense.

"Not to mention you're distracting her," Tsuki added.

"I am not distracted by him," Suzume shouted, trying to cut through the argument.

It worked a little too well because the pair of them swiveled to look at her, as if just remembering she was there. Tsuki, who had maintained control of the body he shared with his sister, had a sly smirk on his face as if this had been his plan all along. Kaito's lips were pulled back in a snarl.

"Then why didn't you stop?"

With a huff, she crossed her arms over her chest. "Why are you even here? Don't you have better things to do?"

"I can't get to more important things until I can be sure you can defend yourself. You're a liability."

"I'm never going to learn if you keep distracting me."

"I thought you said I wasn't distracting you." A slow smirk spread across his face.

From beside Kaito, Tsuki chuckled. At least someone saw the humor in this. Suzume ignored him. Suzume had moved beyond pride and straight into anger.

"Fight me," she said. Drawing on some well of stupid pride, she puffed her chest out as she glared at him. This had to be the stupidest idea she'd ever had. Kaito had just watched Tsuki wipe the floor with her.

The dragon laughed, long and hard, enough where Suzume thought he might run out of air if he didn't stop soon. He wiped a tear from his eye. "You cannot be serious. Why would I do that?"

"You think you can teach me better than Tsuki, well prove it. But when I win you're forbidden from watching me practice."

He crossed his arms over his chest. "And if I win, you have to spend a night with me."

Suzume's stomach flopped. "What sort of request is that?" She stuttered and had to hide a blush that burned across her face.

"You'll find out when I win."

TWO

Morning came too soon. Suzume had spent half the night tossing and turning, alternating between thinking about her impending fight with Kaito and wondering how she could be so stupid. Her blankets were tangled around her as if subconsciously she would rather be strangled to death than have to face Kaito. Suzume exhaled in frustration. Things were so much simpler when she thought he wanted to kill her. Suzume kicked her legs, accidentally tightening the blanket that was wrapped around her. She ripped the blanket off in a temper, and the effort left her panting. *How can I expect to beat him when getting out of bed leaves me winded?*

The coward's way out would be to hide under her sheets. Though if she tried, Kaito would come find her and claim she forfeited, forcing her to give him his humiliating prize. *What did he mean by spend the night with him. He couldn't have meant that...* Suzume shook her head violently. It was better not to even consider it. Kaito was just up to his usual tricks was all. There was no use delaying. She had to face him. Maybe on her way she could come up with a brilliant plan to get out of fighting him. Suzume dressed, albeit slowly, her muscles were sore from the day before. Not a good sign, going into another fight.

Like a woman still half asleep, she stumbled down the hall to the communal room where they shared meals. As Suzume shuffled into the room she spotted a large pot in the center of the room with a stack of bowls next to it. Suzume plopped down beside it before grabbing a bowl, which she filled mechanically. The idea of food made her stomach turn. But maybe food would give her the energy to face Kaito. *Maybe I could postpone, saying I need time to recover.* She shook her head, then she'd have to admit she had gone too far the day before.

"Suzume!" Rin shouted in her ear.

Suzume nearly leaped out of her skin as she dropped her bowl of soup over the front of herself, burning her skin with hot broth. "Why are you shouting?" Suzume snapped as she shook off the soup from her clothes.

Rin tilted her head to the side, a single brow quirked in confusion. "I must have called your name a dozen times. Something bothering you?"

"I'm just sleepy is all. This place is too cold. When are we going to leave anyway?"

"Once Kaito thinks you're ready," Rin said with a smile, which she quickly hid behind the teacup that she sipped from.

"Then we should be leaving tomorrow," Suzume said. "After I beat him in our fight he cannot say I'm not strong enough."

"But if you lose, we may never leave this place."

"Do you think I'm going to lose?" Suzume tried to sound offended but she couldn't quite manage it. Rin was close to Kaito, maybe she could convince him to call off the fight. But that meant admitting to Rin she wasn't up to the challenge.

"If you want, I can talk to him for you."

Suzume glared back at her. "I can handle the dragon. It will be over in a few minutes I'm sure," Suzume said, using her words more to convince herself than the kitsune.

Rin only smiled and nodded her head in agreement. "Of course."

"He probably won't show up. He was just messing with me." The words wouldn't stop coming, she kept talking as if someone had taken a cork out of her.

"Oh, is that so?" said a drawl from behind her.

Suzume felt a chill run down her spine. She turned slowly, cursing internally. Kaito leaned against the doorway, looking well-rested and amused.

"It's not too late to give in," Suzume said, flinging her false bravado like a weapon.

"You don't really think you can win, do you?" He barked a laugh.

Don't let him get into your head. That's what he wants.

"I know I will."

Kaito laughed. "The same way you beat Tsuki yesterday?"

She stood and pretended to be cleaning up her breakfast bowl, though she hadn't eaten a bite. More of it had gotten on her clothes than in her stomach. With hands balled into fists at her side, she marched toward the door.

"I have to get changed," she said as she brushed past Kaito.

"It's not too late to admit I was right," Kaito said to her retreating back. "I won't even make you sleep in my room. All you have to say is: Kaito you are so strong and handsome, please protect me."

This was her chance, she just had to swallow her pride, admit she wasn't strong enough, and this would all go away. *Do you want to get yourself hurt or worse let him make an even bigger fool of you? They're just a few words, say them and this all goes away.*

She couldn't make the vile words pass her lips. Instead Suzume forced a laugh as she turned to face him. "Now you're trying to get out of it? I'm ready for our fight. I can't wait to see your face once I knock you onto your backside."

"So, you want to be on top of me?"

A blush flooded her face without warning and she covered her face with her hands. *Two can play at this game.*

She looked him up and down, and in the same tone she had used to dismiss countless suitors she said, "You couldn't handle me."

"Once we're alone we'll have to see." There was a hunger in his eyes she hadn't seen before, almost predatory, and lacking its usual teasing tone.

Suzume's mouth opened and closed a few times, but she couldn't form a coherent sentence. Surely he meant it as a joke. Her heart thumped in her chest, loud enough she was surprised no one else could hear it.

"Well you'll never get that chance," she snapped before turning and running out of the room before she embarrassed herself further.

Heart slamming into her ribcage, she did a quick change before grabbing her staff and heading to the courtyard where Tsuki and Akira were waiting. Tsuki leaned on the wooden staff, head tilted back as he watched the clouds pass overhead, not a care in the world. Suzume's own staff, strapped across her back, felt like it weighed a million pounds and each step she took was grinding her into the ground until she felt there would be nothing left of her but dust.

"Ready?" Tsuki asked as Suzume approached.

She wanted to shout 'no'. But all she could manage was a feeble, "Yes."

There was no extra time to prepare beyond stretching and chanting over and over in her head. *You can do this.* Kaito swept into the courtyard, looking like he had won already, and Rin followed after him. It looked like they would have an audience to their fight. *That's why he said what he did before. He's trying to get into your head. Just ignore him.*

Not wanting to believe the alternative, she latched onto the idea. It kindled the fire inside her, giving her the motivation she needed to fight through the pain to victory.

She opened her mouth, prepared to make a threat and posture a bit to pump herself up further, when Kaito beat her to it and said, "I hope you're prepared for our second wedding night, my bride."

He grinned at her and her stomach did somersaults. It brought back memories of the time when she had thought Kaito was her ticket back to her place in the world instead of the teasing, infuriating, handsome bastard standing in front of her.

"I am not your bride," Suzume snarled back at him. "And when I win you'll never mention that again."

"Wedding night?" Tsuki asked with a raised brow.

"Only if, when, I win... well, I'll tell you when we're alone." The slow smile and the creeping gaze over her body pricked the flames along her skin. There was no way she was letting him win. The last traces of fear were transmuted into resolve. She would teach him for messing with her mind.

Kaito laughed as he took the staff from Tsuki. Suzume assumed the stance Tsuki had taught her, facing the dragon. Today instead of fatigued muscles, her muscles were too stiff. She felt like a porcelain bowl, just the right strike would leave her in pieces on the ground. *Don't think like that. You can beat him.* It didn't matter that she hadn't even once beaten Tsuki while sparring. Or that Kaito was certain not to go easy on her.

"Ready?" Kaito asked, his position was desirous, he held the staff loose at his side, his shoulders hunched. He looked more like he was prepared for a casual stroll.

That was fine with her. If he wasn't going to take her seriously that would make winning that much easier.

"I cannot wait to see your face when I knock you out," she snarled.

"I hope you're ready for what comes tonight behind closed doors."

Her face felt like it was on fire, and maybe it was, the sparks were running up and down her arms, in response to her anger. And in that moment of hesitation created by that final verbal jab, Kaito rushed toward her. She lifted her staff to parry but he merely glided over the top of her, landing behind her, where he smacked her across the rear with his staff. It was nothing more than a quick pat, like he was chastising a naughty dog. The fire in her gut churned as embarrassment gave way to anger. He wanted to make this into a game to make her look weak, but she wouldn't let him. She spun around, swinging her staff toward him, flames trailing in its wake. A spark of her flame caught the edge of his robe, and burned along the edge of his sleeve. With a quick pat on the flames they were extinguished, he smirked in her direction as if to say 'is that all you got?'

Suzume gripped her staff tighter, the flames running up and down it. Across from her, Kaito encased his staff in ice. Now when their staffs collided, their spiritual energies sparked against one another, fire and ice exploding into steam. Water rolled down her hands dripping onto the ground, and was flung in all directions as they spun around one another, jabbing and dodging. His power unfurled from within him, and the ice in the air burned her lungs. Flames shot from her fingertips and licked along her arms. He did not let out all of his power, but what little he did her own power reacted to it, encasing her in flames as a living moving barrier against his ice. She pushed back, swinging at him and Kaito jumped backward outside the reach of her staff. *He's avoiding my fire so he doesn't get burned.*

"Oh feisty, I like that in a lover."

"Over my dead body." She rushed toward him. Distantly she heard Tsuki shouting to her, probably some suggestion but she was blind to everything but beating Kaito. She was burning with it, literally. Flames raced all over her body, churning in her gut, to where she thought she would burn from the inside out.

She swung the staff back and came down hard, preparing to knock into his head. But before her staff could come down on him, he grabbed a hold of the flaming staff. Where his hand touched it smoked and the flames climbed along his flesh like a forest fire. The ice crept over the burns, and held her fire at bay somewhere along his elbow.

"You can't survive my flames, give up," she said through gritted teeth.

"You rely too much on your fire." He yanked her staff from her grip. And threw it across the clearing. It skidded along before colliding against a torii arch just out of reach.

"That's not fair!" She shouted.

"Who said this was a fair fight?" He swiped at her with his staff.

Suzume leaped out of the way, just in time for a freezing cold staff to graze over the top of her head. The flames dancing along her scalp melted the ice and water dripped into her hair.

If that was how it was going to be, then she wouldn't hold back. While Kaito was coming back from his swing, she launched herself at his middle, using her flaming body as a weapon. The shock sent him tumbling backward and he landed on his back with Suzume straddling his chest. With flaming fingers, she reeled back prepared to slap him with a fiery hand. Maybe if she gave him a perfect scorched handprint he'd know not to play with her the way he had. He writhed beneath her, bucking up and she rode him like the rolling waves trying to hold on. She fell forward and growled, their faces were mere inches apart.

"I was going to wait to have you in this position tonight," he purred in her ear.

The words put her off kilter for a moment and then he pushed back hard, shoving her off him. She flew backward, landing hard on her back, and in a second Kaito was on top of her pinning her to the ground and holding her wrists beneath him. His ice smothered her fire as fast as she could make it, and the unfurling of his full power prevented her from even trying to move.

"What shall we do tonight, my bride?" He grinned down at her.

"You think this is over?" She said through gritted teeth.

"It is. I just won."

Tsuki was coming toward them to call the fight. Suzume arched her back, trying and failing to get out from beneath him. Maybe it had been inevitable from the start.

"You cheated," she snarled.

"I really wanted to win," he whispered into her ear before pulling back a few inches to look her in the eye. It was over. He had her pinned. But his gaze lingered a little too long, and the air between them felt suddenly charged with something more than the tension of a fight. Feeling his muscles in his legs tense that were straddling her hips, and his hands on her wrists, his threats no longer felt empty, and what he had said this morning felt less like a threat and more like a promise.

THREE

Why did I open my big mouth? All I had to do was admit I was tired. Was that so hard? Was it too late to try and run away? Trying to escape down the mountain in the dead of night probably wasn't the smartest idea. She was just as likely to break her neck or fall to her death. Kaito wouldn't try to actually claim his prize, would he? It had to be a joke.

Why am I wasting time even considering it? This is exactly why he had chosen this 'prize', it wasn't so much about getting her alone as it was him trying to get a rise out of her, she was certain. And yet she continued to stare at the sliding door which led into the communal room. The laughter of the others filtered out to her, Kaito's laugh rising above the rest, taunting her. After their fight and her spectacular failure, she'd hidden away in her room too ashamed to face him.

Hunger turned out to be a stronger foe, and the grumbling of her stomach had driven her from her room in search of food. Foolishly, she had hoped no one would be around. But judging from the volume of their voices, they'd broken into the sake again. Suzume smoothed down her hair tucking frayed strands behind her ear. If only there was a mirror to check her appearance. She must have looked disheveled after their fight. Not being able to take a proper bath in ages didn't help either. Suzume lifted up her arm to check if she smelled. She crinkled her nose. There was nothing she could do about it now. *Just open the door.*

Suzume stared at the closed door. The thin layer of rice paper, which she could poke a hole through with her pointer finger, was no great obstacle. But right now, it felt like climbing a mountain.

"Are you going to enter?" A deep voice rumbled behind her.

Suzume leaped in the air, spinning in place. Her shoulders knocked against the door frame as she clutched at the front of her haori. A dark figure remained in the shadows, two swords one on each hip, his face was emotionless like a mask carved from ivory.

"You're back." Suzume squawked. *How can he move so silently?*

The swordsman did not deem her comment worth a try. Of course he was back, why else would he be here?

"Did you find anything out about the missing gods?"

He stared at her without reply. His unblinking gaze was unsettling and Suzume suddenly lost her appetite.

"I just remembered I forgot something in my room. You go in ahead of me." She jabbed her thumb in the direction where she intended to make her exit, when the door slid open behind her.

"You've decided to join us then, my bride." Kaito purred behind her. He wrapped an arm around her waist, pulling her against his chest, preventing any escape.

Her reaction was automatic, she shoved her elbow back into his ribs. Fire rose along her body, clashing with his ice. Kaito spun her around and she had to brace herself against his chest, placing both hands against his pectoral muscles. Though they sparked Kaito was not bothered by it, and instead pulled her closer despite her wiggling away from him and arching her neck backward to get away.

"That eager for our wedding night?" He looked down at her as if he would swoop in for a kiss.

Suzume dodged the almost kiss, dipping below his arms and out of his grasp. "You owe me a rematch! You cheated!" she said once she was free, pointing her finger in his direction.

Kaito placed his hands on his hips, and flashed her that damned smirk. "How could I have cheated when there were no rules?"

Suzume sputtered, unable to come up with a valid counter-argument.

"You don't need worry. I'll be gentle."

Suzume flushed. "It's not going to happen."

"Rin, give her the outfit I picked out for her." Kaito gestured for the kitsune to step forward. In her arms was a fold of blue fabric, in gradient shades of blue starting at the darkest midnight to an almost sky blue. It was embroidered with silver thread along the hems and a pattern that appeared to be the moon and stars.

Though she'd never say so out loud, the fabric was beautiful. She reached for it without thinking, but before Rin could hand it to Suzume however, Naoki snatched it out of her hands. Holding it up, he turned to Kaito.

"Where did you find this?" he asked, his voice sharp. It was the most emotion she had seen out of him since she'd broken Kazue's spell upon him.

Kaito frowned slightly at the swordsman. "It was packed away with a bunch of other kimonos-" he gestured dismissively with his hand.

"These were the goddess of the moon's." His hands bunched around the fabric.

"She can't use them the way she is now." Kaito had already turned away from Naoki, dismissing his protests and returning his attention to Suzume.

Naoki swung a punch toward Kaito which he dodged, but just barely. Another inch and Kaito would have been on his back. He turned to Naoki, anger boiling in his gaze.

"Have you forgotten your place?" Kaito snarled at him.

Naoki's jaw clenched. "Have you forgotten yours?"

The two of them stared at one another, the rise of their spiritual energy stole the breath from Suzume's lungs and she gasped for breath, while her fire sparked to her defense.

Akira inserted herself between them, hands up in a peace-making gesture. "If these belonged to my mother, I would rather you didn't involve them in your games."

Kaito looked from Naoki to Akira then with a shrug he said, "Have it your way then." Then turning toward Suzume he said, "It doesn't matter what she wears because she won't be wearing it for long."

The tension eased and Suzume found she could breathe once again. "It doesn't matter because I am not coming to your room tonight!"

Kaito continued to ignore her and to Rin said, "Can you find something more suitable for my bride to wear? Maybe something red like her temper." He glanced at her out of the corner of his eye before pivoting on his foot, and like a king commanding his kingdom he strolled out of the room.

Suzume stared at his retreating back with more than a few choice words on the tip of her tongue. Naoki had not moved from his spot and was cradling the kimono over his arm, one hand hovering over it, not touching. Akira was watching over him, with a frown on her face.

"Isn't anyone going to stop him?" Suzume swept her arm toward the door. "Now he's stealing from the gods?"

"You did make a bet with him," Rin replied, and there was the ghost of a smile on her face.

Suzume shot her a death look. The kitsune was no help. "I don't care what he says, I'm not going." Suzume snarled at her before marching out.

Out on the veranda that connected the different wings of the palace, there was no barrier to stop the wind. The cold mountain air blew off the mountaintop, cutting right through the thin layers she wore, and her bare feet on the wooden floor felt more like walking on ice. There were no silk slippers here in this desolate mountain palace, just moldy linens, rotting wood, and Naoki who forbade them from touching everything. But it was better than being out there, where yokai lurked and the next day was uncertain. The week they'd spent here had made it feel almost like home.

The full moon in the sky lined everything in silver. They were so high up that the moon looked close enough to touch. Stopping to stare at the moon poking through the wispy clouds, she reached out for it, cupping her hand around the shape of it as if she could hold it in her hand. But like so many things in her life, it was an illusion and beyond her grasp. Sighing, she slid into a crouch, and her gaze moved from the moon to a long-neglected garden. The tree in the center was stripped bare of leaves, the pond emptied of water and fish.

"Don't you think you're taking the joke a bit too far?" Rin asked, her voice carrying into the silent night.

"Who said it was a joke?" Kaito countered.

Their footsteps approached her, and Suzume jumped up and slammed her back against a nearby wall to conceal herself in shadow.

"You don't really mean to sleep with her, do you?"

Kaito laughed. "Of course not, she's a bit of an idiot that needs my protection. I'm teaching her a lesson is all."

There could only be one idiot he was referring to. Suzume raised her fist, considering continuing their argument from before. She'd show him who was an idiot.

"Why do you keep pushing her away?"

He growled low in his throat. His temper washed over Suzume, eliciting sparks along her skin. Afraid the light would draw attention to her Suzume madly patted at her arms to extinguish the flames.

"Are you trying to test my patience? Shouldn't you be more concerned with finding your own mate?"

"Are you offering?" Rin purred.

Suzume's heart thumped in her chest. Rin and Kaito had been lovers once, she knew, but the kitsune insisted that there was nothing between them anymore. *It doesn't matter to me whether there is or not. Maybe he'd stop bothering me as much if he had Rin to distract him.*

Kaito chuckled. "Both of us know that's not a good idea."

Rin laughed along with him and then there was a long silence. *Why don't they move away already?* Or maybe she should take this moment to make her presence known, but she couldn't make her feet obey her commands. With her back pressed against the wall, heart hammering in her chest, she stayed listening to their conversation.

"How did your Hanyou die?" Kaito asked. There was a certain softness to his voice that Suzume never heard when he was speaking with her.

He must really care for Rin. She didn't want to think about why that made her insides twist up and her chest feel tight. Kaito seemed like a different person when he was alone with Rin. *Is that how he was with Kazue as well?* She shoved the thought away, she didn't need to bring her into this mess as well.

Rin didn't answer straight away. *What are they doing in there?* She had an image of the two of them embracing, holding onto one another for comfort over their lost loves.

When Rin did answer her voice was constrained. "A yokai killed him."

Kaito cleared his throat. "I'm sorry."

I didn't even know he was capable of empathy. She scoffed and quickly covered her mouth with her hand, eyes darting to the side hoping they hadn't heard.

The pair of them were too absorbed in their conversation to notice it seemed.

Rin sighed. "We knew our time was limited from the start, or at least we assumed. Not much is known about hanyous."

"Have you met any others?"

"Are you asking to comfort me or for yourself?"

"Forget I asked."

Ice brushed against Suzume's skin, a clear indication he was losing his temper. Kaito's footsteps stomped toward her, and Suzume looked in both directions preparing to flee if necessary. From the corner of her eye, Suzume saw Kaito's shadow coming around the corner. Mere inches separated her hiding space from him and then she would have to explain why she was eavesdropping.

"If you ever wanted to know more about him, I would be happy to tell you," Rin said.

There was a pause, where something unspoken passed between them. Suzume frowned trying to read between the lines of their back and forth exchange.

"What did she name him?" His voice was raspy.

"Takashi."

"She chose well." There was an edge to Kaito's tone, which sent even Suzume's heart fluttering.

"Have you forgiven her at last?"

Kaito moved back toward Rin and Suzume exhaled in relief, then he came back toward her and she sucked in her breath as if the sound of her breathing would give her away. He paced away, only to come back toward her again. *Would you make up your mind already?*

"I made that mistake once, and I learned my lesson. I do not plan on making it again."

"You can't change your heart."

There was a long pause before Kaito answered, "You're right." He said something else but it was barely above a whisper and Suzume couldn't hear him clearly.

Kaito stopped pacing and seemed to have settled further away. Already being this far committed, she inched closer to the corner, just mere millimeters separated her from them.

"What can I do? I'm falling in love with her," Kaito muttered.

"You should tell her how you feel," Rin replied.

Suzume's eyes grew wide. He couldn't possibly be talking about her, could he? She shook her head - it wasn't possible. Kaito could not be in love with her. All he saw her as was a nuisance, a means to an end... or a stand-in for Kazue. The thought didn't sit well at all. *He wouldn't confuse me with Kazue, not after I explained everything, would he?*

"You're right, Suzume might be a complete moron, and bull-headed but my heart belongs to her."

"Who's a moron!" She shouted bursting around the corner without thinking. As soon as she did she collided with his chest, and was almost bowled backward. She was saved from falling on her already bruised rear, by Kaito's arm circling her lower back.

"You know it's terribly rude to listen to other people's conversations."

Suzume tried to push off his chest and escape him. "If you knew I was listening the whole time why didn't you say so sooner?"

"And miss an opportunity to hold you in my arms?"

Suzume's temper flared and with it so did the flames. She pressed against his chest and he jumped away from her to avoid getting burned.

Rin stepped forward as if she was going to protect Kaito from Suzume, which was laughable. Who was there to defend her when he played with her emotions the way he did?

"Do you think that's funny?" She snapped.

"I do, actually." He smirked.

That's all it was, all it had ever been. He never took her seriously, not as a fighter, not as a woman. If he was anyone else, she might have tried forcing a few tears, she could even argue with him if she thought it would do any good. But a sudden realization settled upon her. None of it would make any difference because she was just a joke to him.

"I see," was her reply, and she turned from him without another word spoken.

"Where are you going? Tonight is our wedding night!"

She ignored his jibe, arms swinging as she marched away. *You'll pay for this!*

FOUR

"We're leaving," Kaito announced as he strolled into their communal gathering space.

His announcement had been timed for when everyone was gathered together, allowing him not only a dramatic entry but also providing maximum efficiency to dispense his orders. Of the four people gathered, only Rin looked up to acknowledge him.

"Where are we going?" Rin asked, her fox ears tilted to the side, uncertain.

"That doesn't matter, we've wasted enough time on this mountaintop." His gaze was fixed on Suzume who was staring into the simmering broth in the cook pot at the room's center. It wasn't like her to not have some sort of comment or at least complain at a probable journey to come. *Could it be she is still mad about last night?* He smirked to himself, she certainly could hold a grudge.

"Good morning is the usual greeting, isn't it?" Kaito asked as he squatted down in front of her, forcing himself into her view. Suzume stubbornly refused to look at him and instead scowled into her soup bowl. Dark circles ringed her eyes. It looked as if she hadn't slept at all the night before. *Probably wondering if I was going to come claim my bet after all.*

"Where are we headed?" Rin asked in a failed attempt to steal his focus from Suzume.

Kaito did not bother to look at her, instead focusing his attention on Suzume as he said, "Let me worry about that." Then to Suzume he said, "You're grumpy this morning. Are you mad I didn't visit your room last night?"

Without so much as a twitch, Suzume spooned broth into her mouth as if Kaito was not there at all. *If she wants to play hard to get, I am more than willing to play.* There was nothing like a challenge to wake you up in the morning. Not that he had slept. He'd done enough of that to last centuries.

"Do you have new information about where Kazue hid the artifacts?" Akira asked.

Couldn't they see he was in the middle of teasing the priestess? "That's not necessary." He growled a warning. And then in Suzume's direction he said, "We've been lazing about here too long. And I don't want to spoil my pet too much."

"Then you don't have any leads?" Akira asked, interrupting his game for the final time. The dragon's temper flashed in his gaze as he shot a withering glance in Akira's direction. Akira stared back at him, a serene look on her face.

"You have any better ideas?" his tone burned with acid. He'd been willing to overlook their disrespect but challenging his order was unforgivable.

Akira fixed him with her glare. "If I had any idea, I would not be waiting around here. But heading out into the unknown is reckless."

"We're not going to find the missing artifacts sitting around." He stood up and paced toward Akira. She stood as well, her dark gaze fixed on him unwavering. They stood posturing for a moment, neither willing to give in.

"Hisato is still out there and he wants Suzume. For now she's our only link to Kazue and stopping him. If we leave this holy place you're putting her and all of us at risk. So unless you have a plan, I think we should stay here."

Kaito laughed and then turned away from Akira. "The priestess is good for nothing." He threw the words over his shoulder as he marched over toward the cook fire where Rin and Suzume were seated. The priestess had not so much as raised her head from her bowl the entire time despite his taunting. Kaito reached past her, his arm brushing against her. The only reaction was a few errant sparks that rose from her skin when he got close.

"Suzume hasn't gotten control of her powers yet, with more practice she may be able to connect with Kazue's spirit..." Akira said, her voice droning on in a failed attempt to sway him.

Uninterested in anything his inferior had to say, Kaito made a show of ignoring her by snatching a bowl off the ground. He thrust it toward Rin to fill, and from the corner of his eye watched Suzume for a reaction, but still there was none. *You cannot ignore me forever.*

"The best thing to do is to wait until she's mastered her powers," Akira concluded.

She was expecting a reply and so Kaito tipped back his bowl and drank his soup, forcing Akira to wait for an answer while he drank. When he finished he smacked his lips and said, "We'll be here for a hundred years if we wait until she's gotten control of her powers. And if I remember correctly humans don't live that long." He dropped the bowl, and it was Rin's quick reflex that kept it from shattering on the ground. "I tested her ability yesterday, she's made no improvement. It's time to go." Surely she would say something now. Suzume remained uncharacteristically stoic.

"Then you leave in search of the artifacts while Tsuki and I continue her training."

"You are operating under the assumption that I trust you," he said with a smile that revealed his canines.

A flush rose along Akira's cheeks. "We all share the same goals, we want to bring Kazue's soul back together—"

"I have no desire to see Kazue resurrected." Kaito snarled. "I only want to destroy Hisato and regain my kingdom. Stay here if you desire, I have no use for you. But the priestess is mine and she will be coming with me."

Suzume set her bowl down with a mild thunk and stood up. Now he would get the reaction he was hoping for. Her outburst would diffuse the tension in the room, he and she would bicker and then everyone would agree to search for the artifacts together.

"She doesn't belong to you. Suzume is a person not an object," Akira shouted, a note of hysteria in her normally stoic persona. Kaito hardly noticed as his entire focus was upon Suzume.

"Thank you for the meal," Suzume said before heading toward the door.

"Have you lost your mind at last?" Kaito teased, she was acting strangely. It wasn't like her to not lose control by now.

Again, she acted as if Kaito had not spoken at all. To Akira she said, "I'm going to get ready for practice."

"There's no point, you should be packing to leave. We've got a lot of walking ahead of us. I hope you're prepared," Kaito said, knowing the threat of walking would get a rise out of her.

Once more he was ignored and with it came the rise of his temper. Kaito had enough of these games. As she tried to walk past him, he grabbed a hold of her wrist, stopping her in her tracks. Unlike usual, she did not shout at him to let her go, the only reaction was the sparks along her wrist which were quickly quenched by the ice seeping from his skin. Spiritual power unfurled from within him blanketing the room in a suffocating aura. Because he was so much stronger than the rest of them, his untamed power could kill them all with the mere weight of it.

"Have I not been giving you enough attention, my pet?" he said in a mockingly sweet voice.

Suzume yanked her hand free without a word and continued toward the door. Kaito not one so easily deterred gave chase, but was surprised when Naoki stepped in between them. His expression was unreadable as usual but his hands were resting on his twin blades, making his intentions clear.

"Out of my way, guardian." The swordsman was already on thin ice after his interference the day before, and this was between him and the priestess. If she wanted to play games, then he was more than willing to play.

"She wants to be left alone," Naoki said.

"You speak for her now?" Kaito rumbled.

The swordsman did not respond but when Kaito tried to go around him he held out his arm to stop him.

"Why not let her be?" Rin said as she planted a hand on Kaito's shoulder, trying to be the peacemaker. But Kaito was in no mood.

He shook her off. "We leave as soon as we're packed." His tone final as he attempted to push his way past Naoki, but was knocked back instead.

"Move," Kaito snarled.

Naoki stared at him, his frame taking up the doorway. This was a challenge. One he'd faced over and over throughout his long life. Kaito had risen to his position through blood. If Naoki thought to take control of their group from him, then he was in for a rude awakening. The dragon's power might be diminished but he was still strong enough to take on a mere guardian. Perhaps now was the time to make his position in their group clear. It would make the journey from here that much easier.

Having no need of weapons, Kaito swung a fist encased in ice at the swordsman's jaw. Naoki moved too fast for mortal eyes, and his hand blocked Kaito's punch before it could land. He shoved Kaito backward in one singular movement.

"We do not serve you," Naoki said.

The swordsman's words cut the last thread holding onto Kaito's composure and his power flooded out of him, like a torrential downpour unleashing his spiritual energy, transforming him into something more beast than man. His hands, tipped in hooked claws, balled into fists and his lips pulled back from his rows of pointed teeth in a threatening gesture. When he opened his muzzle, ice poured out of it like a series of deadly arrows which were projected at Naoki in a scatter shot. They pierced the wall behind him, embedding themselves, spreading ice outward from it. Naoki fled, one step ahead of his attack. The edges of the room froze over as his icicles dangled from the ceiling.

Outside the thunder roared, echoing the dragon's displeasure. The swordsman was a fool to challenge him. While the swordsman had been playing nursemaid to the gods, he had bathed in the blood of his enemies. If he thought that they were equals he was wrong. Come to think of it, they were overdue for a rematch. The swordsman had beaten him the last time because Kaito had been weakened, he would not repeat that failure again.

Rin and Akira shouted for them to stop but their voices were nothing but an annoying buzz in his ear. Kaito rushed toward the swordsman, clawing at him, but Naoki was always one step out of the way. Speed was on his side, while Kaito had sheer power. Using the cook fire as a barrier, Naoki thought he could keep Kaito at bay, but the dragon merely leaped over it. The swordsman, not anticipating the maneuver, was caught off guard and Kaito knocked him off his feet at the same time he knocked over the soup pot. Hot broth spilled onto the trail of ice on the ground, sending up clouds of steam around them. Everything else faded away as Kaito looked down at his opponent.

"You lead with anger," Naoki said, unafraid despite being pinned beneath the dragon inches from death.

The audacity of his statement gave Kaito pause and left an opening for Naoki. The swordsman leaned forward head butting Kaito and knocking him backward and giving him room to escape. Kaito snarled as he followed the swordsman out into the hall and to a desolate garden beyond. When they entered the garden, Naoki was waiting for him, twin blades in hand. The pair of them circled one another. The swordsman was the first to attack, rushing Kaito blades twirling like two deadly stars. Kaito pivoted to avoid the first but the second caught him on the forearm, fortunately for Kaito his layer of scales kept him from penetrating the skin and the only casualty was his kosode. But knowing he had been struck only angered him further. It was better to get this over with as quickly as possible.

Kaito swiped upward, feinting from the right, only to follow through on the left. It caught the swordsman off guard and he knocked one of the blades from his hand. It went flying across the garden, coming to rest in the basin of a drained pond.

The swordsman returned to circling once more, favoring the side in which he still had a weapon, his right, leaving his left exposed. Kaito knowing on the ground he could not beat him, took to the air flying above him, and using the clouds for cover he would bide his time.

Naoki turned in slow circles, searching for Kaito. When his back was turned, Kaito dropped from the sky and knocked Naoki down, parting him from his remaining weapon. Standing on his chest, Kaito pressed his foot against Naoki's throat.

"Know your place now?" Kaito snarled.

The swordsman did not miss a beat when he said, "I have never forgotten it."

His flippant attitude broiled at his temper and Kaito considered tearing his head from his shoulders.

"Stop, please!" Akira shouted, she came over grabbing a hold of Kaito's shoulder.

He didn't give a damn what she wanted, he would not have his authority challenged like this. They would obey him or they would perish.

"This is how it shall be, either you bow to me or you leave now."

There was a fire in Akira's eyes which could be dangerous in the future. He had not trusted her from the moment they met but he had let her stay. An enemy you could see was better than one you couldn't. He had a decision to make, kill them all now or let them live. Though he would not admit it out loud, they were making progress in teaching Suzume how to control her power although progress was somewhat slow. *I could find another teacher.* Kaito pressed his foot harder against Naoki's throat.

"What are you doing?" Suzume shouted, she was trailed by Rin. He glared at her.

"Naoki challenged me, this is the price."

"We cannot kill him. He could help us find the pieces of Kazue's soul." Suzume gestured toward Naoki.

He glared at her. He would not be ordered by a mere human. And yet he hesitated. He did not like the idea of killing the guardian in front of Suzume. There was a strange look in her eyes, for the first time she looked truly terrified of him. It was the same look Kazue had given him the first time he had killed to protect her. Their eyes met and for a moment he thought he recognized something in the priestess' gaze that he hadn't seen there before. But he must be imagining things.

"I will not be challenged." Kaito snarled, preparing to make the killing blow despite her protests. Kazue no longer held sway over his heart.

"Kazue is not dead!" Suzume shouted at him.

Kaito looked toward her. "That's not funny."

"It isn't a joke." Suzume clutched something in her hand, the pink fragments of Kazue's heart.

All the air seemed to have been drawn from his lungs as he stared at those shards. It wasn't possible, was it? He had watched her disappear. Kazue had given herself up to save him.

"You're lying," he snarled.

Suzume lifted her head and looked him straight in the eye, "I heard Kazue's voice. I know where we need to go."

Five

He can see right through my lie. I just know it. The dragon was a terrifying sight to behold in that moment, more monster than beast. Gone were the parts of him that made him human. Ice crusted his body, spreading from his feet onto the ground. Power radiated off of him in waves, stealing Suzume's breath and raising sparks along her skin. Never before had the divide between them been more apparent. Though most of the time he seemed human enough, when she saw him in tattered clothes, his clawed foot pressed against the throat of Naoki, and death in his gaze she realized in that moment their worlds were too different for them to ever mix. *This is why Kazue tried to become immortal, to bridge this gap.* Hot on the heels of this thought was another: perhaps blurting out the first thing that came to mind was not the smartest idea.

"What did you say?" Akira said the first to break the silence.

"I heard her voice again," Suzume said looking straight at Kaito. Ready to face him head-on if she had to. Backing down now would be admitting that he was stronger than her. She'd stepped onto this path intent on proving to Kaito that she was not to be messed with and she would see it to the end, no matter how ill-advised her plan was.

"That's not possible," Kaito said, but his tone was saturated with hopeful desperation.

Heart hammering in her chest, she did the only thing she could think to do, continue lying. "She told me to tell you that the day the spider lilies were blooming, she was going to tell you she was pregnant." It was a gamble. Kaito knew Kazue had shared visions of her past with her but just not which ones. The memory of those bright red flowers was burned into Suzume's mind, sometimes even appearing in her dreams. It had not only been significant to Suzume but to Kaito as well. Whether he realized it at the time or not, that was the moment Kazue had decided to become immortal. Suzume knew that without having to be told, as if a bit of Kazue's memory was bleeding into her.

Kaito's reaction was not what she expected. Instead of challenging her and calling her bluff, he looked down at Naoki.

"Will you bow your head to me?"

The swordsman did not react at first and Suzume thought things would take a turn for the worst, but after a few tense moments he nodded his head.

"I'm glad you've learned your place." Kaito snarled, removing his foot from the guardian's throat.

Naoki stood and when he was eye level with Kaito he said, "I never forgot it."

Kaito bared his teeth at him, but gave no further reply. He looked over the assembled group, his gaze suspiciously avoiding resting upon Suzume. "We leave at dawn." Then he turned and walked away, not a word said. As he marched away, Suzume felt as if her knees might give out beneath her and she had to lean against a nearby pillar or else she was going to collapse onto the ground.

Akira rushed over to Suzume, her face alight with excitement. "What else did Kazue say? Where do we go from here?"

Suzume looked at Akira's hopeful face to Naoki's who stood not far away with his arms folded over his chest. Rin remained on the veranda, her expression unreadable, though her ears were tilted in Suzume's direction waiting for her answer. She had not thought much beyond this. *What would Kazue do in this situation?* Grasping for answers, Suzume said the first thing that came to mind.

"We need to go south, to the palace."

Rin frowned, the Kitsune had seen through Suzume's lies, she just knew it. The kitsune knew how much Suzume had wanted to return to her home at the White Palace. It was a stupid answer and if she had more time to craft a better lie she never would have said that. The problem was she was woefully ignorant of the kingdom of Akatsuki, and her entire life had only ever been within the walls of the palace until recently. There was nowhere else she could think of.

"The White Palace?" Akira's dark brows knit together in confusion.

"Why would we go to the white palace?" Tsuki asked, using his sister's face to speak.

Suzume shook her head to deflect their questions and pressed her fingers to her temples. "I'm not sure, I think it has something to do with..." Suzume scrunched her face as if trying to think very hard or listen to a very faint voice. She knew hardly anything about Kazue. But remembering Kaito and Rin's conversation from the night before, she said the only thing she could think of. "It's her son..." she trailed off, not certain any of them would believe it.

"Takashi is at the white palace?" Rin asked, taking a step toward Suzume with an eager look upon her face. Suzume's suspicion was correct: Rin knew Kaito's son.

Hearing the name of Kazue and Kaito's son struck her with a weird feeling of melancholy. Suzume had no real desire to see the physical embodiment of Kazue and Kaito's relationship. Besides it was not like Kaito would ever agree to a search for his long-lost son. She did not see the prospect of a warm family reunion anytime in their future. This lie was getting more and more unruly but she didn't know how to reign it in other than admitting she had lied - and that was something she wasn't prepared to do.

She screwed up her face as if she was concentrating on the imaginary words Kazue was trying to relay. Then after a few moments she shook her head.

"It's gone. But I heard her voice. She wants Kaito to find his son. But how can we convince him?" She shrugged her shoulders in a helpless gesture, perhaps her lie would die here without any pursuit because of Kaito's stubbornness. Everyone knew how adamant he was about never seeing his son.

Akira searched her face as if she was looking for a hint of Kazue there and a snake of guilt slithered around inside her gut. "That's all? Do you have any of her memories, perhaps something that might help separate us?"

Suzume shook her head again. "No, I'm sorry. But maybe she will come back again?" She needed to get away before they started asking more questions and she made this an even bigger mess than it already was. Suzume side stepped away from Akira, but Naoki's unflinching stare held her in place. The swordsman made her nervous in normal circumstances. Right now he was looking at her as if he could see straight into her soul. Or was that just a guilty conscience talking?

Akira covered her mouth with her hand as she looked at nothing in particular, perhaps lost in thought. Meanwhile Naoki had continued to stare at Suzume keeping her from slithering out of the conversation as she wanted to.

"I'll talk to Kaito. I think I can convince him," Rin said.

Suzume's stomach sank, the last thing they needed was to go on a hapless quest in search of Kaito's son - that could only end badly. Either Kaito found out she lied: the worst possible scenario, or they did find his son. And she couldn't even imagine what that would look like. Would he be like Kaito: all arrogance and temper? Or more like Kazue, thoughtful and wise? The thought led to a vision of Kaito as a scholar, which was much too ludicrous to consider. She shook her head to dispel the thoughts.

"Are you sure it's a good idea?" Suzume said, waving her hands in front of her. "You know how he gets when we bring up his son."

Rin nodded. "We thought Kazue was gone, and clearly telling Kaito about his son is important to her. I think it warrants investigating. Maybe he knows where the artifacts are."

"You seem to know a lot about Kaito's son," Suzume countered, trying to distract from her terrible plan.

Rin looked away. "We met once, many years ago."

She's lying.

Before Suzume could expose her and draw attention away from the subject, Akira interrupted. "I think Rin is right. We should convince Kaito, even if we have to leave out some of the details."

"I'll go talk to him. If I can convince him right now, he won't have time to second-guess himself"

"I don't think that's—" but the kitsune had already scurried away, leaving Suzume with Akira and Naoki, and the pair of them were watching her with a strange expression.

"We need to stop her. She's clearly hiding something about Kaito's son." Suzume gestured after the retreating kitsune. Having seen the full extent of Kaito's anger, she was not eager to get in the middle of that conversation. *What have I done? He's going to kill me for sure this time.*

"She's not the only one," Akira said, arms crossed over her chest.

The swordsman continued to stare at her without speaking, further unsettling her. Rather than own up to the lie, Suzume built upon it instead. "When I found Kazue's heart she told me all kinds of things. I didn't think they were all important. Honestly, I think she just wants Kaito to acknowledge her son. I mean, wouldn't you? What is a woman's worth other than bearing sons?"

Akira narrowed her eyes as she looked at Suzume. "You did make it up."

This was her chance, admit she had lied and everything would go back to normal. But a lump formed in her throat, as if her confession had gotten lodged there.

"It's sad that he won't acknowledge his son. If we find him, it might create even more problems than what it would solve. I mean, really, what could he know? He was a baby when Kazue broke her soul apart." The excuses kept pouring out of her.

Akira just stared at Suzume, her expression unreadable.

When Akira didn't respond Suzume burst out, "Would someone say something?"

"I was with Kazue when she gave birth to her son," Naoki spoke up. Suzume turned in his direction, a rock in the pit of her stomach. Why hadn't she thought this through better? She thought for certain she was going to vomit.

"Then you know he's at the White Palace? Did Kazue really give birth to the first emperor like they say?" Suzume laughed, but the others stared back at her with blank expressions.

Naoki ignored her question. "Kazue begged the priest who she entrusted him to to never tell him who his father was."

Suzume deflated a little. "Well maybe she can see he's changed and —" She gave up, she couldn't cover up the lies anymore. "I made it up, alright? Are you happy?" The shame of it left a bitter after taste in her mouth.

"I'm impressed to be honest," Tsuki interjected once again, using his sister's face.

Suzume glared at him in response. *Is this a joke?*

"This is to our advantage, actually." Akira tapped her chin in thought.

"To what advantage? When Rin gets there and tells him we need to look for his son, he's probably going to go on a murderous rampage. *Do they really not see how serious this is?*

"If the dragon thinks you can communicate with Kazue..."

Suzume's stomach did a little flip. She knew that look all too well. It was the face of someone plotting, and she thought Suzume was going to be her pawn. Well she had another thing coming.

"You want me to pretend to be Kazue to get Kaito to do my bidding. I may be desperate but I'm not stupid. You saw what he almost did to Naoki." She threw her arm toward the swordsman.

"And you stopped him."

Perhaps she had brought this upon herself, but her only intention had been to show Kaito he wasn't the only one who could play with other people's emotions. Now she had dug herself a hole too deep to get out of.

"I refuse to pretend to be Kazue," Suzume said, crossing her arms over her chest. It was bad enough that everyone kept mixing them up, she wasn't going to perpetuate the problem.

"You don't have to give up your identity, just make him think that you can speak with Kazue."

She hesitated to agree. She was slow to trust most people. What was their motivation? But on the other hand, Kaito had been throwing his weight around a lot lately. Maybe it was time to turn the tables on him, and let her take control for once.

"And what do you want, to stay here? Because as much as I don't want to be out there, I don't want to grow old trying to master powers here. This mountain palace is worse than an exile."

"Staying here is out of the question at this point. If we want to appease the dragon," Akira said. "But you can influence Kaito as to where we go."

"And where is that?"

"When we were at the monk's shrine we heard rumors of an island north of here, an island guarded by an enormous monster who sank any ship that tried to approach."

Suzume felt a cold shiver up her spine at Akira's words. Shortly after she'd found Kazue's heart, she had dreamed of an island surrounded by ocean. Though she had never seen the ocean before, the place felt familiar to her. It had made reoccurring appearances in her dreams ever since. Perhaps this place Akira had heard about was the same. Considering Kazue had set Naoki to guard her heart, and Akira and Tsuki to protect the staff, maybe she had put some monster to guard the artifacts.

"I get what you're after, but what's in it for him?" She nodded toward Naoki who remained typically stoic in the corner.

"My freedom," he said without inflection.

"No one is keeping you here," Suzume countered, feeling defensive for reasons she could not explain.

"When I left it was with the intention of never returning, but my attempts to escape were unsuccessful."

"Why couldn't you leave?"

"Because I am bound to you."

"I thought you were bound to Kazue's heart?"

"I am."

Suzume looked down at the fragments of Kazue's heart. Strangely enough she had gotten attached to the damn things. She'd been carrying them around as if Kazue really would come back and guide her. But of course that was nonsense.

"Then why don't you just take it from me?" She held out the stone to him.

Naoki shook his head. "That is nothing but a piece of rock. Her power is no longer inside it."

"Then you should be free to go."

"But I am not, because her heart is in you now."

Six

oing down the mountain was much worse than going up. The sheer drops and dizzying heights she'd been able to ignore going up were unavoidable on the way down. Each step she took had to be carefully navigated. At the onset of the journey Kaito had attempted to assign Rin to watch over her on the climb down, but she had loudly protested against it, even threatening to not leave the mountain. As a result, she was left to cling to the smooth rock face and scoot along arm's-width ledges on her own. Cursing herself for her pride, Suzume's gaze slid more than once to the clouds that were beneath her. That had to be against some law of nature. Looking down only made her head spin and she decided she was better off just ignoring it.

The only good thing about being above the clouds was she couldn't see just how far she would plummet if she took a wrong step. That thought inevitably led to her imagining falling forever and anticipating smashing on the ground below. *Don't think about falling, focus on moving one foot in front of the other.* Up ahead, Kaito practically skipped along the narrow ledge, and when they reached a massive break in the path, he sailed over it in a graceful leap.

Suzume got to the end where the gap was and foolishly made the mistake of peaking over the edge. Sheer rock went downward, disappearing into mist and rocks at the bottom. Panic swept over her and she bent over gasping for air. The illusion of bravery was shattered in an instant. There was no getting around asking for help here. She just couldn't jump that far. Without a word, Rin transformed into a massive kitsune and Suzume scrambled onto her back, burying her hands in Rin's thick fur. As they sailed over the gap, Suzume screwed her eyes shut, refusing to look down, but the flying sensation shortly after seeing that drop didn't calm her nerves and her stomach felt like a bubbling bog.

On the other side Suzume slid off the kitsune's back and her legs gave out beneath her. Slumping against the stone wall, she closed her eyes. Her heart was slamming in her chest. The image of the drop was burned into the back of her eyelids. Visions of falling to her death kept replaying in her mind over and over. They had only just started, and she knew there was even more treacherous terrain to come.

"Say the word, and I'll carry you down the mountain," Kaito whispered in her ear so the others couldn't hear.

She hadn't even known he was beside her. His palm was splayed next her head, his face inches from hers. They'd hardly spoken since the day before, just a few perfunctory words as they got on the road. There was a strange look in his eye, this felt like more than his usual teasing. *He didn't really believe me, did he?*

"I don't need you to carry me," she snapped and ducked under his arm to get away from him. A part of her was still afraid he was going to find out. The two of them were caught in this dance, neither willing to admit they had been wrong.

Kaito chuckled behind her.

The remainder of the trek down the mountainside was harrowing and traumatizing. Once they were passed the narrow cliff ledges and the steep stairs, it was back into the forest. The trail was covered in loose gravel and Suzume kept slipping and sliding. Keeping her balance was impossible when her legs were shaking from exertion. More than once she slipped and fell onto her rear. And each time Kaito stopped, turned and looked at her and without words seemed to say: 'offer still stands.' And each time she'd huff, get to her feet, and keep going. He would just love it if she admitted she was too weak to stand on her own two feet. Had it been anyone else, she would have gladly given up on walking, pride be damned.

About mid-day they had been walking for hours without pause. Suzume had pushed herself to the limit, not even allowing herself proper breaks to drink water, instead gulping water as she walked. Hunger frayed her temper. Then a rock jumped out of nowhere and caught her foot. It was several seconds before she realized she was falling. She crashed into the ground, her open water skin spilled onto the ground and splattered her face with flecks of mud.

She shouted a string of curses. Kaito who had been leading the group, while she fell behind, jogged back over to her. "Ready for a break?" he looked down at her with a grin. Not the usual condescending, teasing way he would have said it but almost as if he cared.

Suzume's palms were scraped and she dusted them off on the front of her clothes. "No." *Are you stupid!* She mentally berated herself.

Kaito looked her up and down and gave her a patronizing smile. "I can see your legs shaking from here."

"I know my limits." His concern bothered her, though she couldn't understand why.

The dragon crossed his arms over his chest, and raised a brow that spoke to what he thought of Suzume knowing her limits.

In a show of defiance, she climbed onto said shaking limbs and stormed past him. But instead of making a graceful exit, she slipped in the spilled water from her water skin and slid backward. Before she could hit the ground, Kaito caught her around the waist and pulled her up and to his chest. On impulse, she grabbed onto the front of his shirt and their eyes met.

He chuckled. "What was that about knowing your limits?"

She pushed away from him, angry and embarrassed at her own apparent frailness. Kazue would not keep stumbling over her own feet. "I didn't need you to catch me."

"Apparently you do," he said with that damn smirk again.

She growled low in her throat. Between sore muscles from training, a downhill walk, hunger and thirst, she was at her breaking point.

"Stop treating me like I'm Kazue!"

Her voice echoed through the forest and scared some birds roosting in a nearby tree. They squawked as they took flight. The others turned and stared at the two of them. No one moved. Akira looked in Suzume's direction, her gaze giving her a warning: 'don't expose yourself now.' But what Suzume hadn't considered when she agreed to Akira's plan was that her identity would become even more entangled with Kazue's.

Anger flashed in Kaito's eyes rimmed with blue, storm clouds gathered overhead to indicate his displeasure, and a vein twitched in his jaw as if he was biting down on his words.

"Just because she spoke to me doesn't mean I am her," Suzume said, her anger deflating. Risking the dragon's temper when he found out she lied was much worse than being treated like she might break.

Weighed down by the guilt of her lie, she could not face him. Spinning in place, she stormed off the path and into the forest where she couldn't be seen, where she could compose herself in peace. That's what he would expect anyway: for her to run away.

Suzume stumbled over to a nearby fallen log and sat down to examine the scrapes on her hands. The abrasions were shallow, just scraped skin. It was just one of many wounds upon her hands, arms, and legs. Her skin was getting darker too and her once-plump cheeks were lean and bony from a strict diet and constant movement. Even her arms and legs were firm from growing muscles. Turning her hands over, she examined the callouses forming along her palms. *Did Kazue have scars too? Had she given up on physical beauty in her quest for power?*

Tilting her head back, Suzume sighed. It hadn't been her intention to make a scene. But damn it, it was nice to sit down, just for a minute. The shade was cool, with a light touch of breeze that ruffled her hair and sent a small chill down her spine. Then the chill changed to a prickle. Danger. In the band of her hakama something burned her stomach. Suzume reached in and extracted the fragments of Kazue's heart. She'd forgotten she'd stuffed them there in a rush before leaving the mountain palace. They were glowing faintly and were warm to the touch. *What does this mean?*

Turning the pieces over in her hand, she traced a finger along the cracked edges, and accidentally cut her finger. It was a hair-thin cut but it stung and burned. Shoving the bleeding digit in her mouth, she squinted at the heart fragment. The fragment was throbbing, a stuttering beat. The blood that dripped onto the stone sank into it and a shock ran through her as if she had been struck by lightning straight to her chest. The pain left her doubled over unable to catch her breath.

Gasping, she stood up. Invisible strings had a hold of her, giving her a silent command to follow. It seemed insane but she could not disobey, as if her body was out of her control. *What is going on? Why can I not control my body?* Suzume stood and turned toward a narrow pathway through the forest. At first her steps were faltering but then she was running down the path away from the others, unable to even call out to them. *Kazue is that you?* But there was no response.

Fatigue was inconsequential, her feet moved fueled by unknown power, dragging her further into the forest. Kazue's heart fragments burned in Suzume's grip, the fluttering heartbeat like a small animal in her palm. Until just as suddenly it stopped. Suzume realized she had regained control of her body when she fell to her knees and her body was too weak to stand.

"What was that?" she shouted at the pieces of Kazue's heart. They had returned to hollow pink stones, whose weight was almost nothing, as if they had not temporarily possessed her body.

But the heart did not respond. It was times like this that she wished Kazue hadn't given up her consciousness to save Kaito from Hisato. But maybe this sudden change in the stone meant she wasn't entirely gone. Had her lie not been a lie at all? The thought made her stomach twist in knots. If things were tense with her and Kaito now, how much worse would it be if Kazue could possess her body entirely? She shook her head. It wasn't possible. Kazue was gone. Which meant there was some other nefarious force at work here.

Suzume looked around. She was in the middle of the forest, not sure from which direction she had come. The tingling sensation of danger was gone, but she couldn't help but feel like she was being watched.

"Hello?" Suzume called out.

The only response was the rustle of wind through the trees. Though it was a struggle to do so, she climbed onto her feet and pulled her staff from its sheath on her back.

"I know you brought me here. Show yourself."

To her left the bushes started to rustle, and Suzume's entire body clenched in preparation, waiting for some horrifying creature to burst out and attempt to part her head from her shoulders.

And then it leaped out at Suzume, and she shouted and swung her staff which was knocked from her hand effortlessly. Sparks leaped along her skin and Suzume lunged at her attacker, prepared to use her flaming body as a weapon. But before she could land a blow a hand caught her wrist, stopping her in place.

"If you wanted to practice you could have just asked," Tsuki teased.

Hearing a familiar voice all the fight drained out of her. "Why did you leap out at me?"

"In my defense, you attacked first."

Suzume scoffed and rolled her eyes.

"What are you doing out here anyway?" he asked.

"I need Akira, there's something going on with the heart." She held up the now faded heart in front of her.

"Looks the same to me," Tsuki said as he peered at the pale and empty heart. "I didn't even realize you kept it."

Akira shifted into view, despite her brother's dismissal.

"May I?" Akira asked Suzume, gesturing toward her hand.

Suzume lifted up her hand for Akira's inspection. Her own heartbeat was rattling around in her chest. It felt like she had a hundred ants crawling all over her skin. She felt restless and anxious and had been since they left the palace, as if something horrible was about to happen. Had it really been Kazue's heart that had brought her out here? Akira grabbed Suzume's hand that was holding Kazue's heart and brought it closer to her face. She turned Suzume's hand to examine the heart but did not attempt to pick it up herself.

"It looks the same as before," Akira said a note of disappointment in her tone.

Holding the stone fragments away from her, as if getting too close to them would cause them to take over her body again, Suzume said,

"But it got warm all of the sudden, I cut myself on it and then it sort of absorbed my blood and I lost control of my body for a few minutes."

Akira's brows pulled together in a frown. "I wonder," Akira murmured to herself.

"What?" Suzume said not bothering to disguise her fear.

"We don't know much, but we know you absorbed Kazue's heart when she possessed you. Perhaps the heart is acting as a conduit for Kazue's will," Akira said and she gave Suzume a long thoughtful look.

Suzume's insides squirmed. She didn't like the idea of Kazue using her. It was a hard-enough pill to swallow to think any part of Kazue was inside her, let alone her heart. What would Kaito think if he found out?

The squirming feeling turned to a sick bubbling up inside her gut. Then a pressure rose inside her chest. It was the same feeling she had felt the day she had broken Kaito out of his seal. Something was coming up her throat, and Suzume threw her hand over her mouth to prevent herself from throwing up, or accidentally breaking some other seal nearby. The pain in her stomach was intense as the fragments burned against her skin and the contorting sensation writhed inside her, forcing her to her knees.

"Suzume, what's wrong?" Akira asked.

She looked up at her with a wordless plea for help. Akira reached out a hand to comfort her but flames were racing over her body, forcing Akira to keep her distance.

"The heart," Suzume rasped, hardly able to expel a breath.

"What about the heart?" Akira asked.

Something had a hold of Suzume's heart and was squeezing it. Whatever it was, it was coming closer and with each step the pain increased. She had to let it out or she was going to explode. Suzume's mouth was wrenched open and a burst of light poured out of her body and into the air. With it the pain receded but Suzume collapsed onto her side, curled in the fetal position, panting for breath.

Suzume slowly uncurled from a ball on the ground before reaching for the heart fragments. It pulsed lightly, dark red but fading to pink.

"What just happened?" Akira said.

Before Suzume could explain, a dozen men in black descended from the treetops, surrounding them.

SEVEN

The air crackled with spiritual energy. It clung to her skin and raised the hairs on the back of her neck. Thankfully it no longer left her doubled over feeling like she was about to vomit, but the threat of it still lingered as if something was alive and wriggling inside her stomach. Tsuki took back control of the body he shared with his sister and drew his blade. He stood over Suzume who could not stand, let alone defend herself. The men dressed all in black surrounded them on all sides, but she could see nothing of their faces but a small sliver revealing their eyes. Tsuki held his blade in front of Suzume in a defensive pose as the group crowded in around her.

Their attackers moved as one unit, converging on Tsuki who swung his blade, knocking them back before they could close in and pass him. Until now, she had only seen Tsuki in mock battles, but when he was focused, the humor was gone from his eyes. The blade moved through the air, an extension of his own body, a glittering deadly blur. The masked men moved too fast to be human, and as quick as Tsuki's swing was, they were that much faster. Suzume reached for her staff, though she couldn't imagine what she could do in this condition. Whoever this group was attacking them, they were unrelenting and unafraid of Tsuki and his sword who wandered further and further away from Suzume to pursue their opponents.

In a few heartbeats, Tsuki was no longer guarding her front and she was exposed. One of the masked men saw an opening and slithered behind Tsuki's back, facing Suzume. In his hand he held a single short blade, which he raised above his head, ready to plunge into her chest.

Suzume clutched onto her staff. The fire had died down inside her, as if whatever energy had burst from her had drained her of it all. Holding the staff in front of her like a shield, she prepared for the blade to fall.

But before he could finish the maneuver, a body was inserted between them. There were too many trees surrounding them for Kaito to change into his dragon form, but that didn't stop him from half transforming: his hands tipped with claws, his face was covered in blue scales which caught the light. When he moved the colors refracted and shifted into a rainbow of hues. Power framed his body, his shoulders were wider and he had a muzzle full of razor-sharp teeth. Suzume had never been more entranced and terrified in a single moment. He was both monstrous and beautiful.

"Stand back," Kaito snarled as he stepped in front of Suzume and shielded her from the black-clad men that surrounded them.

Two little words and the spell was broken. "I can take care of myself," she countered as she leaned upon her staff, using it to climb to her feet. She held it up in a defensive pose in front of her.

Kaito did not deem a response necessary, and instead launched himself at their nearby assailants. They moved as one, like the flow of water. Kaito lunged for the nearest one and they jumped out of the way to avoid the dragon's swiping claws. Kaito spun to attack them as the group closed around him. Tsuki joined him, swinging his sword at those along the perimeter. Suzume raised her staff, ready to join the fight when Rin in kitsune form burst from the surrounding brush. She must have been following Kaito, but instead of joining the fight she blocked Suzume's path, keeping her from fighting.

"I can fight!" Suzume shouted at her. She didn't have a reason to argue. It's not like she wanted to fight.

The kitsune in her real form was a head taller than her and covered in white fur, with numerous tails whipping behind her. She turned her head toward Suzume - one golden eye on her, the other on the fight. Though Rin's true form wasn't capable of diverse facial expression,

Suzume sensed a hint of doubt in her gaze. Or maybe that was her own insecurity.

"Kaito ordered me to protect you," Rin said in a voice that was between a growl and a rumble.

A black-clad figure broke from the group surrounding Kaito. In the few moments that Suzume had looked away more had arrived, it was as if they were appearing out of thin air. The man raised his sword, swinging it at Rin who reared back to swipe at him with a massive paw. Teeth bared, Rin attempted to clamp down on the man's shoulder, but before she could get a hold of him, he jumped backward just out of reach. Rin did not pursue and instead stood feet apart in defense of Suzume. The man circled them and Rin's gaze followed him in a slow dance. Staff held in position with trembling arms, Suzume watched the man as he inched closer. It wasn't like Suzume wanted to fight, she knew she was terrible at it but she didn't want to appear weak either.

Tsuki shouted, and Suzume forgot about their stalker for a moment and turned back toward the sound. Naoki had joined the fight, and somehow, he had planted himself in the center of half a dozen of the black-clad warriors, his sword moving in a silver blur. Tsuki had been shouting in premature celebration it seemed, because he was grinning madly as he continued to parry attacks from his own opponents. Naoki struck like a wasp attempting to impale the nearest attacker through the chest. But they moved too quickly. Blink and you would miss it entirely.

The legendary sword reeled backward with fluid grace. Naoki fought like a dancer, controlled and precise. Each strike, however, was evaded as if they disappeared from one place and appeared in another. They buzzed around him - never engaging, only evading. Naoki's gaze was of intense focus, then without warning he spun around and sliced one of the black figures through the middle, severing him in half. But instead of blood and guts, the apparition burst apart in a puff of smoke.

Suzume frowned, wondering if she had been seeing things. At that same moment, the stalker lunged again for them. Rin anticipated his move and clamped down on his shoulder but as her teeth sunk in, he also burst into a puff of smoke.

"It's an illusion!" Rin roared to the others.

Naoki was already swinging his sword, clouds of smoke hallowing his head as the illusions were destroyed one by one. For each one he destroyed two more came out of the shadows to crowd around them. There were perhaps three times as many as when they had first been attacked. Kaito was fighting like a wild animal slashing at his opponents, lunging for jugulars and tearing out imaginary throats with his sharp jaws.

"How is this possible?" Suzume asked not really expecting an answer.

It was difficult to see anything through the smoke. The clang of metal rang out along with the sounds of shouts and grunts. Out of sight, Kaito growled like a wild beast. That same wordless warning rang through Suzume. She spun in time to see two more illusions were stalking around them now, going counter to each other in a slow circle. Rin's golden eyes traced each step they took, but she couldn't keep her eyes on both of them at all times. Suzume's fingertips itched, as sparks danced along her flesh her power was returning. A barrier would be rather convenient but she wasn't sure she had enough energy for that. Akira had taught her how to control it. Even if she could make one now, it would likely take all her energy.

Kaito slashed at a copy with his claws. Smoke spilled from the wound across its chest before it burst into a puff of smoke. The illusions kept on coming. Whatever was making them seemed to have an endless supply.

"We have to find the source," Kaito roared his voice carrying through the haze of smoke.

Five more illusions dropped down from the treetops, above Suzume and Rin. One landed on Rin's back and the other four closed in around them, joining the original two. The kitsune reared backward, large paws swiped at the illusions who were closing in on her, while the other on her back held onto the scruff of her neck, and rode her like she was an unbroken horse. Her numerous flaming tails flickered back and forth as she writhed beneath the rider. Suzume leaped backward to avoid being hit by one her tails.

The five other illusions stepped between Rin and Suzume, blocking her from her defender. They closed around Suzume in a circle and she held her staff in front of her. Though she had little offensive training, Suzume attacked the nearest illusion. The others were distracted fighting their own battles, and she couldn't just keep standing by doing nothing any longer. Even though her body ached and her limbs screamed in protest, Suzume swung her staff with uncoordinated abandon. Her staff collided with the torso of a nearby black-clad figure and it turned on her, and for a moment she thought she had felt flesh but when the fire energy from her body traveled down the staff and hit the copy it burst into a puff of smoke.

Something hit her shoulder and pain seared through her flesh. A dagger stuck to a tree behind her, edged in her blood. The graze on her shoulder burned, and stoked the fire in her gut.

She clutched her bleeding shoulder. "That hurt!"

"They can hurt you even if they're not real," Tsuki said. He'd broken from his own fight to help her and Rin. He made a diagonal cut down the body of another copy. The two halves separated before dissipating.

Suzume swore under her breath as another copy came barreling toward her. The illusions around them had swelled, and it was impossible to say where one skirmish started and another ended. Rin was more focused on her own battle to worry about Suzume and she was free to join the fighting. With a twist of her staff, she smacked it upside the head of a nearby illusion and nearly knocked it off its shoulders.

"Nothing like the real thing to teach." Tsuki smiled before lunging with a forward thrust to impale another illusion nearby.

He wouldn't stand by and defend her. He wanted her to fight. The prospect had her flying high and adrenaline pumped through her body, giving her a second wind. She was drunk off a previously untapped well of spiritual power that coursed through her body, burning her up inside and demanding to be unleashed. It coursed through her body, moving her limbs and guiding her actions. She ran toward the apparitions, slamming into them with her staff. Fighting was a great way to work out your frustrations.

Then once more she felt that electric feeling, it ran up her spine and to the top of her head. She shivered and looked around for the source.

This had to be the person who was making the illusions. The copies were acting the same as before, fighting without regard for their own safety, and everyone had at least four copies to contend with. Everyone but Suzume that was. She tried engaging with a few, but found them easily defeated and then two more would pop up in their place. They never attacked her, just surrounded her.

Whoever was pulling the strings here was after her. *Well if you want me, come and get me.* She scanned the battleground and noticed one copy that stood out from the group. Instead of fighting like a mindless drone, it was moving through the crowd, slipping between fights, heading straight toward her. She assumed the defensive stance and prepared for it to attack. But this one moved differently than the others: it was subtle, a certain ease to the movements that when compared to the others made them look jerky and predictable. This had to be the original. It swung a short blade at her and she raised her staff to block, but when their weapons locked an unseen copy crept up behind her and grabbed her around the middle. It hoisted her over his shoulder and leaped away from the fight, the original following after.

Suzume jabbed the end of the staff into the back of the illusion and it burst into a puff of smoke. Before she could hit the ground, the original caught her in his arms, cradling her. For a second their eyes met, Suzume squinted. Something about those dark eyes seemed very familiar.

"Who are you?" she demanded.

He did not answer and instead ran through the forest, weaving around trees, and leaping over brush.

She wished she could create a ball of fire at will. Luckily her hands were covered in sparks, which were sure to burn him. She placed both hands on his chest and the flames burned through his black clothing to the tan flesh beneath. But as she hit him, the fire ricocheted back at her and she cried out just as he let her go. Contorting midair, she landed on her back. The black-clad stranger stood in front of her, his black clothes torn. Suzume reached for her staff but she had dropped it after she had destroyed the last copy. Instead she jumped to her feet, holding her flaming hands in front of her, staring down at her would-be kidnapper. The stone in the band of her hakama pulsed faintly.

They stared at one another as Suzume matched his stance. Her back throbbed from landing on it, and her front burned in the same place she had grabbed onto her captor. The stranger held a blade in hand which he lowered to his side.

"I know it's you Hisato. Enough games." Suzume touched the place where her attack had been burned into her own skin. She could not attack Hisato without harming herself.

"Who is Hisato?" His voice rang of familiarity. But that was how Hisato worked, he liked to play games.

Suzume forced a laugh, "I'm not falling for that. I know it's you."

"You know me? Who am I?" There was a desperation in his tone, so much unlike Hisato that for a moment she was willing to fall for it. But only for a moment.

"This isn't like you to pretend this long," Suzume said but she felt less certain now.

"Is that why you summoned me? Because you recognized me?"

"I didn't summon you. You're the one who attacked us!" she snapped.

The man took a step closer to her. "I felt a pain, in my chest. Like something had a hold of my heart. I thought you were attacking me..." he said. His eyes were glued to her like a starving man.

This wasn't Hisato, which could only mean one other thing.

"Do you have a piece of Kazue's soul as well?"

EIGHT

She felt like her insides were going to be switched with her outsides. That feeling like something was trying to escape from inside her was overwhelming. And each step he took closer to her, it only got stronger. The man's face was covered with a black mask, just a slit in the fabric revealed his dark, unknowable eyes. Even with so little, Suzume was overcome by this feeling of nostalgia as if she was looking into the eyes of someone she had known her entire life. *I fell for that once with the spider,* she shuddered remembering, *I'm not falling for it again.* If one creature could convince her of a past that didn't exist, she was certain this thing could trick her into thinking he was like her.

She shook her head to break eye contact and took a step back, hands held up between them, a paltry defense. Even her fire barely flickered to protect her, as if hesitant to do so. But her head was spinning. Which way was up and which way was down?

"What are you doing to me?" She snapped.

He sheathed his blade and held up his hands in surrender. That didn't matter if he could make a hundred copies of himself. He might have one sneaking up behind her right now. She didn't want to look away from him, just in case he attacked.

"Who is Kazue? And what does it mean to have her soul inside me? Was that my past life?" he asked.

He kept coming toward her and the closer he got, the more Suzume felt as if her chest was being squeezed by a giant's fist.

"I feel like I'm going to vomit." Her mind was racing. She stumbled backward away from him. What was this feeling? Who was this man? She needed her staff. Chaotic energy was racing all up and down her body, escaping wherever it could along the strands of her hair, along her fingertips and toes.

"What are you?" He stood so still it was eerie. If he stepped back into the shadow of the tree behind him he would have disappeared entirely. Maybe that was the reason for the black mask, it was some sort of camouflage.

There was only one explanation for his strange powers and his odd behavior.

"I'm Princess Suzume, daughter of Izume and the emperor." Her old identity is what came to her quickest, but was that really who she was any longer?

"That is not possible, she was sent to the mountain shrine." His eyes narrowed as he looked at her. Then his gaze flickered away from her. Suzume followed his gaze turning her head before snapping it back to him. No copies surrounded her, no army of darkness. Just the two of them in the middle of the forest, and the wind rustling through the trees was the only sound.

The man reached up as if he was going to throw something. Suzume lifted up her hands as if that would save her. But instead, he pulled down his mask, revealing a handsome face but not one she recognized. He was young, close to her own age. That didn't prove he wasn't Hisato. The darkness of Kazue's soul was a master of disguise, able to shift into any form he chose. He had used the ability before to trick her into thinking he was a priest.

"Do you recognize me?" he asked.

Suzume squinted at him. Clearly this man felt like she should know him but she had never seen him in her life. "If you are trying to trick me, then you should have used a face I do recognize." She looked him up and down once again, just in case. But he looked like just another face in the crowd.

His head jerked to the side, and he reached for a sword at his belt.

Suzume tightened her muscles prepared for the attack. While they were talking she'd been growing a small ball of fire, not much, but enough that if she got close enough it could incapacitate him long enough for her to run. As his attention was elsewhere, she tossed the tiny ball of fire toward him. It sailed right past him. Suzume turned to run, but he gave chase.

She hadn't even gone a few feet before he caught up to her, blocking her path with arms held out.

"Why did you bring me here if you refuse to answer my questions?" he said.

"You're the one who kidnapped me!"

She was certain he wasn't Hisato now. Hisato loved to taunt her with doublespeak and promises of glory. It didn't make this man any less dangerous though.

He stared at her as if she had just declared herself a tree that was in love with the moon.

"I felt you call, I thought..." he trailed off. Then he grabbed Suzume by the wrist and pushed her behind him.

"What are you doing!" She shouted.

A barrier of glimmering green light erupted around them. The man in black stared up at the trees.

"What is going on? Let me out of here," Suzume hissed behind him.

"He's coming," the man whispered.

Suzume felt Kaito's spiritual energy before she saw him, the force of it weighing upon her, the temperature dropping to freezing. Her breath came out in puffs of smoke. And then the trees overhead were pushed back and torn from their roots. The crack of the trunks snapping in half thundered around her, followed by the roar of the dragon.

Kaito had shifted into his dragon form. His large muzzle pushed through the trees, his mouth full of teeth the size of Suzume's forearm that tore the treetops off, exposing a cloudy, gray sky. Lightning flashed behind him as Kaito spit out the branches, and used massive claws to bend back more trees, which groaned before giving way to the force of his anger.

The stupid man. He probably thought he was protecting her from the dragon.

Kaito laughed, his voice like thunder. "You dare take what's mine," he bellowed.

From his pocket the man extracted a piece of paper, on it was a series of markings. When he drew it out, he held it between his palms and chanted under his breath. Though Suzume didn't know the words, the power from them drew the gooseflesh along her arms. The man was imbuing the paper with spiritual power. It was the only thing that could harm Kaito.

She had to stop him before he unleashed it on Kaito. Suzume lunged for his middle, knocking him over, and a blast of green energy was shot off into the forest.

Kaito countered the attempted attack with a spray of ice shot from his open mouth. The tiny shards rained over the pair of them. Lucky for Suzume the man's barrier held and she was not impaled by the razor-sharp fragments.

"I'm down here too, you know," Suzume shouted up to Kaito.

The man grabbed Suzume by the wrist. Fire leaped up to defend her and burned the man's hand. She felt it burning in her own skin and pain radiated outward as if it was coming from inside her.

"We must flee," he said, ignoring the pain he must have been feeling.

Suzume dug in her heels and leaned back to use her weight to keep him from dragging her away.

"I'm not going anywhere," she protested.

Overhead, Kaito was smashing through the branches of the trees, laughing like he was half mad.

"He's about to break through. Come with me before it's too late." It was like he didn't hear anything she was saying. That or he was just ignoring her, thinking she was too stupid to see the danger in front of her.

High above them, Kaito roared. Icicles dangled from nearby trees as he approached them. The man drew another slip of paper out and started to chant once more. Suzume grabbed onto his arm breaking his concentration.

"What are you doing? If you try killing him he's really going to kill you!" she shouted.

"That yokai is one of the most dangerous around, and it is my duty to exterminate him before he wreaks more havoc."

"Let me go and he'll forget all about you."

The man stared at her brows furrowed. "Are you one of them?"

Before she could explain, Kaito's hail of ice sent them both scattering in opposite directions. Suzume leaped for the cover of the trees, and fell hard on her shoulder, and jarred her elbow. Pain shot up and down her arm as she rolled over to her side.

Kaito descended from the sky, caught somewhere between man and dragon. Blue light flickered all around his body and Suzume felt the full weight of his spiritual energy like a stone on her chest. She gasped for a breath, and remembered the training Akira had taught her. She tried to refocus her energy and keep Kaito's from overwhelming her. With a lot of effort, she was able to create a barrier between her and the out-pouring of Kaito's energy and she was able to breathe once again.

The man drew his weapon, seemingly unaffected by Kaito's approach, or so she had thought at first. Until she saw the way his hand trembled and his knees shook.

"Let us go. We don't wish you any harm, dragon."

Kaito threw back his head and laughed. His eyes were an icy blue full of intense rage: something she had never seen before in him, not unleashed like this.

"It's too late for that now."

The man looked to Kaito and looked back at Suzume. He took a step back in Suzume's direction, clearly intending to grab her and make a run for it. Suzume's barrier was not stable and it flickered around her, prepared to collapse under the weight of Kaito's energy at any moment.

Just as he made a dash for her, sword glowing with green energy, Kaito moved in front of him, blocking his attack with a swipe of his clawed hand. The sword was knocked from the man's hand and sent flying into the forest.

The only weapon that remained was his spiritual energy, but Suzume was not certain he could wield it while Kaito was bashing his brains in. Kaito stood between the man and Suzume. It would have been wiser if he ran, but he stood his ground.

"You shouldn't have hesitated, you will regret that," Kaito said, flexing his claws.

Kaito lunged for him, claws extended, preparing for a kill blow. But when his claws were meant to dig into flesh, the person who had been standing there burst into a ball of smoke. Kaito spun in place, searching for the real masked man. He stood on the branch of a tree. He lingered for a moment as if debating making another attempt at his misguided rescue while Kaito snarled and snapped, rushing toward him, preparing another attack. Before Kaito could reach him, he jumped onto the branch of a nearby tree and melted into the shadows. The only sound was the rush of the wind in the trees.

As he disappeared Kaito lost interest in the chase and returned to his more human form before approaching Suzume. The threat gone, she let her barrier fall in a shimmer of sparks.

He held his hand out to help her to her feet. "Are you hurt?" Kaito asked, his eyes raking her up and down.

"I'm fine," she lied, hiding the blistered hand and down-playing the myriad of injuries that were covering her body.

Kaito saw right through her lie and grabbed onto the front of her hakama, which was scorched and exposed the red flesh underneath. He pulled back the cloth unthinking, nearly exposing her breasts in the process.

"I'll kill him for this."

She yanked the fabric out of his hands and covered herself up. "I did this to myself," she snarled, hoping to cover up how her heart was hammering in her chest when he grabbed onto her like that. When had Kaito ever shown a genuine interest in her wellbeing? What had changed in him?

"How could you possibly burn yourself?" Kaito scowled.

She looked away from him, not wanting to say. He grabbed her shoulder again, tugging on her and forcing her to face him.

"Tell me." His expression was softer than usual, more filled with compassion. This had to be a trick.

"Why do you care?" She narrowed her eyes at him.

"Tell me." He growled.

"It doesn't matter." She turned to walk away but he grabbed her by the wrist, preventing her from leaving.

"I won't ask again." His tone was not demanding, but gentle and coaxing. Who was this Kaito? It was a side of him she had never seen before.

She whipped her head to face him - looking him in the eyes, glaring into his soul. She saw real fear reflected there. He had been worried about her but not because he cared about her. No, this was about Kazue, because he thought Kazue was living inside her body. She was nothing but a shell, a vessel to carry around the woman he loved. Suddenly lying to Kaito about having a connection to Kazue seemed like the stupidest idea she had ever had.

Not willing to admit she had lied to him, but also wanting to wound him for the simple fact that he didn't really care about her, she said, "That man has a piece of Kazue's soul inside him. It looks like you'll be reunited with her soon after all."

NINE

Every breath burned, as if her lungs were being stabbed by thousands of tiny needles. The temperature only continued to drop as Suzume and Kaito were caught in a battle of wills. Fire danced along her skin, melting the ice coming from Kaito's stare. Water dripped down her forehead and into her eyes. Suzume accidentally used her injured hand to wipe it away and when the blisters on her hand brushed against her face, it sent pain rippling through her arm and she winced. Bad idea. She'd been trying and failing to pretend her injuries were not bothering her.

"Stop being stubborn. Let me wrap it for you." Kaito reached for Suzume's arm and as he did flames jumped up to defend her forcing him to withdraw before he could get burned.

When Akira had touched Suzume while she was covered in flames, the fire had kept on burning through her and the marks had remained as scars for almost two weeks. Kaito wouldn't risk grabbing a hold of her, even if she hadn't unleashed her fire entirely.

"I'll do it myself," Suzume said and reached for the bandages.

Kaito held the bandages just out of her reach, that damned smirk on his face once more. "Even if you knew what you were doing, how do you plan on doing it single-handedly?"

"I can figure it out." She lunged for the bandages but Kaito merely stepped out of the way. Suzume stumbled but recovered herself before she could become acquainted with the ground.

"Just put out the fire, and stop resisting my help."

"I don't need your help." Suzume placed hands on hips. She'd been sparking non-stop since their encounter with the strange man. Her clothes and bandages were singed probably beyond repair. No one had said anything about the man in black's likely connection to Kazue, as if there was an unspoken understanding among the group not to bring it up in front of Kaito.

"Why can't you control your fire yet? Have they taught you anything?" Kaito shot a glare in Akira's direction.

Akira shrugged as if to say, 'I cannot control her progress.' She and the others were staying well and away from Suzume, perhaps remembering the danger of approaching Suzume when she lost control of her fire. It had been out of control since the masked man, and Kaito testing her temper wasn't helping anything.

"Can't you just concentrate on putting out the fire?" Kaito snapped. The air grew colder and overhead gray storm clouds were gathering. It wasn't a joke anymore.

No one could get close enough to help her even if she wanted help, which she didn't. She knew what this was really about. Kaito wanted to protect the body that held a piece of his beloved Kazue's soul.

"Let it go. You're not touching me."

"Is that a challenge?" He smirked and her stomach churned uncomfortably.

Suzume scuttled backward. "You wouldn't."

He loomed over her, the ice on his breath collided with the flames that were shooting from the tips of her hair, and halos of steam rose up in the air creating vaporous clouds.

"Maybe if you stopped trying to bring on the winter by yourself, my powers wouldn't have to defend me." Suzume said. If she was trying to ease the tension, she was doing a terrible job of it.

"Why do you have to be so stubborn?" He said in a deep rumble as he stalked closer to her.

Her back collided with a tree she hadn't known was there. Kaito was practically on top of her, the air between them crackling as red and blue energy crashed against one another.

"Are you trying to kill me or help me?" She snapped and tried to push him aside, but he slammed his hand against the wide trunk of the tree behind her and leaned in close. Sparks burst as they collided with his icy aura.

Suzume's eyes darted to his face. Having him this close was dangerous, in more ways than one. Kaito had wreathed himself in ice, and where her flames touched the ice melted only to be quickly replaced by more ice. Hot water dripped onto her chest where her flames were melting his ice and it soaked her shirt. They were clouded by steam so thick she could not see beyond it. All she could see was Kaito. Suzume glanced up at his profile, his strong jaw, his dark eyes that were rimmed in blue, indicating his annoyance with her.

"Just let me take care of you." His voice was pitched low, just for her ears.

In moments like this, when she was staring into his dark eyes, the world around them melted away. And all her prejudices went with it. She wasn't jaded over love, there was no Kazue. Just two people with this heat burning between them. The fire inside her transformed from chaotic sparks to a warm glowing burn. Like that time in the temple, their powers swirled together, testing. Red and blue encircled the two of them and was replaced with steam, fire, and ice. Water dripped from the hem of her sleeve and softly thudded on the ground.

"Fine." She sighed. It would be easier to just let him do it.

Kaito thankfully didn't make any smart remarks as they sat on the ground together. Suzume placed herself just close enough to him that they were not touching. It forced Kaito to lean forward to take her hand, which in retrospect might have been worse because that also brought his face much closer to her. Suzume reluctantly held out her hand for him to wrap the burns.

With a surprising gentleness, he cradled her hand in his. Despite having moments before been covered in ice, his hands were not cold. They were warm as he applied a salve to the burns. Her thoughts drifted to the man who had given her the burns, or rather how she had burned herself by attacking him.

It was possible he had been born with a piece of Kazue's soul inside him, just as she had. But it was just as likely it was Hisato in disguise. Though she doubted the latter was true.

"This would have been much easier if you'd just let me help you right away," Kaito said, interrupting the tense silence that had fallen between them.

Suzume glared at him. "I'm only letting you do this because you would have turned me into an icicle otherwise."

He smirked down at his work without replying. When he finished wrapping her hand, he made a twirling motion with his finger. "Now your chest."

Suzume covered her burnt chest with her hands. The spot was still tender, but she was not letting Kaito apply salve there. "I'm not stripping down for you."

"Don't be ridiculous, as if you have anything I haven't seen before."

She shook her head. She had to draw a line somewhere.

"Not going to happen, even I have my limits."

"I could hold you down instead," he said with a grin.

In response the hand he was holding burst into flames. Kaito yanked his hand back just in time to avoid getting burned.

"You better not unless you want to get burned."

"Now you're being just ridiculous," he snapped back, his own patience wearing thin once more.

"We shouldn't waste any more time," Akira interrupted.

Kaito glared at her, perhaps considering a rebuke, but when he saw Suzume flickering like a lit brazier, he seemed to see reason.

"You deal with it then," he snarled.

Suzume thought he would then go and join Rin and Naoki who were hunting the masked man, but instead he leaned against a nearby tree. She should have known he would continue to hover.

Akira came over and looked at Suzume who was sparking faintly. "You're going to need to get that under control if you want me to treat your wounds."

Suzume was still sparking faintly and glaring in Kaito's direction. She took it all back, any positive traits were completely outweighed by his arrogance and mulish personality.

"You're not going to get it under control if you keep stewing," Akira said.

Suzume refocused her attention on Akira. "I am not stewing."

"The sparks say otherwise." She gestured toward Suzume's hair, which was shooting off sparks that fizzled in the air. "Do you remember what I taught you about redirecting the energy? Try that now."

Suzume was still a bit peeved, but she did as she was taught. Closing her eyes, she took a deep breath and imagined the current of energy inside of her body instead of opening and redirecting, as she had been learning to do to harness her power and shoot it out. She imagined closing the door on the multitude of portals from which the fire was spilling out of her, and with it closing down on her feelings about Kaito. It was easier if she wasn't looking at him or arguing with him. If she just ignored him, she might be able to keep it under control.

When she opened her eyes again Akira was smiling, her ruby lips stretched over bright white teeth.

"I knew you could do it."

"If only we could get her to do it in a fight, with Kaito or with a yokai," Tsuki said using his sister's face.

"Easier said than done," Suzume said with her arms crossed. She was still feeling churlish, and wasn't in the mood for Tsuki's teasing. Of course, that only baited him further to try and bring her out of her sour mood.

"Well if you weren't playing hard to get with Kaito," Tsuki said.

"Don't set her off again," Akira chastised her brother gently, as she motioned for Suzume to pull down her haori so she could treat the wound on her chest. "I don't want to get burned."

"Don't you dare peek, Tsuki." Though Suzume wasn't sure if Tsuki could see through his sister's eyes either way. Suzume pulled down the shoulders of her haori to about mid-bicep, exposing her collarbone and the tops of her breasts. "And I am not playing hard to get. I have no interest in Kaito that way."

Akira said nothing but smirked to herself. Suzume got the impression the siblings were silently communicating with one another.

"I hate it when you do that," Suzume said.

Akira dipped her fingers into the salve and then jabbed them lightly into Suzume's wound. "Help you?"

Suzume yelped then grit her teeth and said, "Talk amongst yourselves. I know Tsuki is in there making jokes."

Akira smiled but with much less humor. "We meant no offense," she said before dabbing gently at the burns on Suzume's chest.

"Why do you talk to each other out loud if you can communicate silently?" Suzume asked.

Akira didn't answer straight away, and instead reached around to start wrapping the wounds. Suzume imagined she was weighing her words. "We lived in silence for a very long time. And when we speak inside our mind, it is not so much words as it is a sharing of thoughts and images. Talking aloud makes things clearer."

Akira leaned in, her sleeve brushing against Suzume as she wrapped her torso with bandages. Suzume thought about what Akira had said.

"Do you have a separate consciousness?"

Tsuki laughed, and for a moment his face overlaid his sister's before she took control again.

"Hey!" Suzume shouted and covered her exposed skin before his sister's face came back into view again.

Kaito glanced in their direction with a scowl, but it seemed he had missed the quick peek.

"Yes, we've maintained our individual minds in this form," Akira said, she gestured toward her face, "but as you may have noticed there is a blurring where one of us ends and the other begins." She'd finished wrapping Suzume's wound and Suzume hurried to put her clothes back on.

"And that's how you talk to one another internally. You're thinking together in that middle ground."

"Something like that," Akira conceded. "You're done."

Suzume stretched, testing the limitations of the bandages. It made turning difficult but otherwise it wasn't like she couldn't walk.

When Suzume looked up again, Tsuki was inches from her face. Suzume jerked backward but his hand snaked out to grab the back of her neck and keep her close.

"If you're worried about ever having a private moment with my sister hovering around, you don't have to worry, she likes to watch."

Suzume slapped Tsuki hard on the shoulder and he fell back laughing at her. She glowered at him.

"You're such a lecher," Suzume said but with not as much force.

After training for weeks with them, she'd grown accustomed to Tsuki's antics. He rocked forward and sat cross-legged in front of Suzume, his knees touching hers. She would move away, but she knew him well enough to know that he would only scoot closer to her again.

"Ah, it gets lonely with only your sister for company for centuries." He winked at her. "The offer stands, if you ever give up on your dragon."

"He is not my dragon," Suzume said and turned away from Tsuki. Across the way Kaito was talking to Rin who had returned already. Well, more like Rin was talking at him and the dragon, Kaito, was watching Suzume with Tsuki with his eyes narrowed.

"He's very jealous, but we can use that to our advantage."

Suzume forced a laugh. "He's jealous of you, you mean? Aren't you giving yourself too much credit?"

Tsuki grabbed Suzume's uninjured hand. She tried to pull away but Tsuki had a tight grip on her wrist and wouldn't let her go. She stared as he traced the lines along her palm. It tickled slightly and she squirmed in his grip.

"What are you doing?"

"Have you noticed, the only one your body reacts to is Kaito?" he said and then looked up at her.

His finger paused in the center of her palm. Suzume stared where his finger was planted in the center of her palm. His other hand circled her wrist. She had sparred with Tsuki countless times over the past three weeks and in almost every session it took all her concentration to bring up the flames to use against him in battle and even then, it was weak at best. It was only around Kaito that her flames leaped up without warning.

"It's because he's an ice element and I have too much fire," Suzume said trying to convince even herself.

Tsuki shook his head and leaned in close to Suzume's ear as he whispered, "That's not the real reason and you know it."

His breath was warm against her ear and her skin prickled with goosebumps but nothing else. If Kaito had been this close she would have been shooting off sparks. On impulse she looked over in Kaito's direction. He was coming over, prepared to separate them.

"Deny it all you want, but you can't outrun your heart," Tsuki said just as Kaito came over with a breeze of cold air.

As soon as he was within range the fire rose up inside her as if an internal part of her was trying to prove Tsuki right. He let go of her hand, perhaps sensing that rising flame.

Kaito looked angry and she felt her own self-defense flaring.

"Is there something you want to tell me?" Kaito demanded.

"Don't get the wrong idea, Tsuki was just trying to rile you up," Suzume said, throwing her hands up to defend herself.

"Not about that. The man, you know him. Don't you?" Storm clouds gathered overhead, a sure sign Kaito was really mad.

"What are you talking about?" Suzume scowled back at him.

"That man is working for the emperor."

TEN

Tired and hungry, Suzume crouched in the bushes, flanked on either side by Tsuki and Kaito. The brush was hardly adequate coverage and she kept accidentally brushing against Kaito, which meant sparks kept leaping off her skin like tiny fireworks. Suzume pressed closer into Tsuki, her arms brushing against his.

He looked at her with a smirk, about to make some sly comment, when Kaito yanked her away from him and left her in an uncomfortable position with her knees accidentally brushing against them both. Tsuki gave her a look as if to say, 'see.' She ignored him and looked out at the sea of tents stretched out before them, curls of smoke rose up into the sky as the sun set behind the horizon. The murmur of voices, horses whinnying, and the distant clang of metal could be heard. A flag at the edge of the encampment flapped in the wind. It bore the emperor's crest, a stylized sun rising over the horizon.

"Looks like your lover wants you back," Kaito said teasing Suzume.

Tsuki snickered and Suzume shot him a dirty look before turning to Kaito. "You don't think this might be because *you* attacked the army and threatened to kill the emperor's family... oh and destroyed a temple?"

"I technically only did the first two things."

She rolled her eyes in response.

Seeing the army again left Suzume feeling torn. On one hand Daiki, the general to the emperor's army and her one-time fiancé, represented the life she had once had. But when her mother had been caught having an affair, the emperor had exiled her and all her children. And any marriage or hope for Suzume's future had crumbled to dust. Not long after she had unleashed the dragon, she had been reunited with Daiki and she thought she could salvage that life. But like so many other things in her life, that too had gone awry when she'd been caught by a giant spider on her way to Daiki's palace.

At this point, she would much rather stay clear of Daiki and the army. Not because she had completely divorced herself from the idea of returning to the life she once had, but because this was an awkward cross-section between her lie and real life. She cursed herself once more for saying Kazue wanted them to go to the palace. *Of all the places, that man had to be with the emperor's army?*

Kaito's gaze was focused ahead of him toward the encampment. "I'm going to pay your lover a visit. We have a score to settle." He turned, grinning at Suzume.

"That is not necessary." She threw up her hands to halt this plan in its tracks. She should have known when Kaito had insisted they all investigate, this was what he was thinking. She could see the plot spinning in his head already.

"You said it yourself, Kazue wants us to go to the White Palace. Well it has come to us," he said, gesturing toward the army encampment beyond.

"The palace is not the army," she said, trying to dismiss his train of thought. He was onto her for sure and he would continue turning the screws until she admitted she had lied. What other reason could he want to get mixed up with the army?

"But isn't it strange that you came from the White Palace, and now another person with a piece of Kazue's soul shows up, also with a connection to the palace?" Kaito countered, trying and failing to make her rise to the bait.

Of course it was strange. They didn't know how a piece of Kazue's soul had gotten inside her, and now another person like her shows up seemingly traveling with the emperor's army. She was dying to know more, but they were clearly outnumbered here and she knew when to pick her battles.

"It is a strange coincidence," she said and pretended to examine her broken fingernails as if they were very interesting.

"Then I'll go ask the general about it myself," Kaito said.

Of course his version of asking was attacking the general's army. Suzume took a deep breath to stop herself from giving into an impulsive reaction. *Think before you speak or this will only get worse.* Kaito was trying to get a rise out of her, so surely he wouldn't take that big of a risk for the potential of answers. She doubted Daiki knew anything. He was a bumbling fool given a high position based on family connection. Nothing more.

"For what purpose? This has nothing to do with our quest." She gestured toward the camp.

"This has everything to do with our quest," Kaito said, arms over his chest. "Unless you're not telling me something." He narrowed his eyes as he leaned toward her.

Suzume scoffed and turned away from him. "I just don't think Kazue would want us to waste time here."

"I wasn't talking about that." He grinned.

Suzume spun her head toward him, half caught in a lie. She realized what he had meant was the mystery man who had attacked her. But she'd told him everything she knew - the little she did.

"Why would I lie?"

"That is a good question." He held her gaze for a moment, the two of them locked into a staring match that neither of them would back down from.

Suzume was the first to break the silence, afraid if she had to endure his stare any longer, she'd really cave and confess everything. "You don't know Daiki like I do. He's a pawn. Even if there is some palace connection to Kazue's soul fragments he wouldn't know anything." Suzume flapped her hand at him, dismissing the idea. That's why she had chosen him as a potential husband, because he would be easy to control.

"Then it shouldn't be hard to get information from him," Akira said, interjecting in a smooth tone.

Both Suzume and Kaito swiveled in her direction and shouted in a resounding unison, "Are you insane?"

"If that man does have a piece of Kazue's soul inside him, perhaps we can learn more from him," she said reasonably.

"He didn't seem to know much of anything," Suzume replied as she shot a look at Akira that said 'shut up.' She had her own reasons for wanting to speak with the masked man. But right now Suzume was more concerned about knocking Kaito off the scent of her lie.

"What does Kazue think?" Akira asked with a single arched brow.

Suzume glared at her.

"It would be easier if Suzume went in and spoke to Daiki," Rin said, throwing her opinion into the discussion.

"Easy for all of you." She jabbed a finger in Rin's direction.

Akira added to Rin's idea. "If we go in fighting, we will surely fail. You are the only human among us, and familiar to their leader. If we send you in alone to spy, we have a much higher chance of success."

"But—" Suzume started another protest.

"If she goes in there she'll only get herself killed." Kaito growled at Akira.

Suzume narrowed her eyes at him. As much as she didn't want to go in there, it bothered her even to know Kaito thought her incapable of such a simple task. Espionage was part of the life blood of the White Palace. Suzume had been raised on secrets and betrayal. It would be no trouble to sneak in there, coax Daiki to spill all his darkest secrets, and then escape once again.

"You don't think I could do it?" Suzume challenged Kaito.

He rolled his eyes at her. "You can't even defend yourself. What will you do if things get messy?"

"This is my realm of expertise. I can handle Daiki."

Kaito forced a laugh. "This isn't the palace, Princess. These are warriors, and they know only one thing: the blade."

She shook her head. "You don't know anything about humans. They won't harm me. I'm a princess."

The dragon growled low in his throat. She had inadvertently stumbled on a nerve. "Former princess."

"We can guard her unseen," Naoki said.

Suzume turned her head to look at the swordsman who, up until this point, had been leaning against a nearby tree as if he was not listening at all.

"He's right," Rin said. "Yokai cannot be seen by normal mortals. If we followed her in, we can keep guard."

"These are not just mortals," Kaito countered. "The last time I encountered the general's army he had warrior priests among them. It would be better if I went in alone."

"You're not the only one with something at stake here," Akira said, glaring at Kaito.

Kaito crossed his arms over his chest as he looked back at her.

"Didn't they nearly kill you last time?" Suzume asked.

Kaito narrowed his eyes at Suzume before he let out a huff.

"Fine," Kaito conceded at last. "But the moment things get dangerous, we pull out."

There was no backing out now. If she tried to weasel her way out of this, she'd only look weak in Kaito's eyes. Besides it couldn't be that bad if the others were there with her.

"When do we go, in the morning?" Suzume asked, hoping she'd have more time to mentally prepare.

"There's no time like the present." Kaito grinned at her.

Her gut reaction was to balk at it, but instead she choked down on her fear and said, "Sounds great. "

Kaito watched her, measuring her reaction. Likely waiting for the moment when she gave in and begged for mercy. But she was determined to prove to him she could be just as strong as he was. Besides once she committed to something, no matter how stupid, she was committed. Turning stiffly, she looked at the camp beyond. Pacing along the edge of the perimeter were guards in full armor, complete with masks styled to look like yokai. The masks looked almost child-like in comparison to the real thing. Suzume looked at the others who were waiting for her to make the first move. *No time like the present.* She took a deep breath and forced her unwilling feet to move forward, head held high. She might look like a bedraggled beggar but she would approach with as much dignity as she could muster. She resisted the urge to look back at the others. They would be around, unseen to most. From the corner of her eye she saw Kaito walking beside her. It was comforting to know he was going with her. One of the guards spotted her, and as she approached he swiveled in place before fumbling to grab a hold of a spear he had rested against his shoulder. The soldier pointed the pointed tip at her.

"Stop!" He shouted.

"I should kill him where he stands," Kaito growled under his breath.

Suzume tensed, waiting for the guard's eyes to drift in his direction. But they never did, his gaze was trained on her. Seeing she was a woman he relaxed a bit, loosening his tight grip on his staff, but he did not drop his weapon entirely.

"What do you want, girl?" the warrior asked, his voice echoing from behind his mask.

Suzume made a haughty sound of contempt. If they knew who she was they would regret it. Even if she was exiled, she was still the emperor's daughter. With head high, she declared in her most regal tone, "I am Princess Suzume, daughter of Izume, second wife of the emperor. I demand to speak with General Tsubaki."

Somewhere behind her Tsuki snickered unseen. The man frowned and scanned the forest behind her. Had he heard Tsuki's laughter?

Then his eyes snapped back to her. "You don't look like a princess. You look like a beggar to me." The warrior scoffed. "Away with you peasant."

Suzume had to tamp down on her anger, lest it reveal itself in flames along her body. "If you don't believe me, bring Daiki out here."

A second warrior joined the first and looked dubiously in Suzume's direction.

"What's going on here?" he asked.

"This woman is claiming to be princess Suzume. She's asking to speak with the general." The original warrior made a gesture in Suzume's direction.

"Send her away," said the second.

"Your plan is foiled by incompetent foot soldiers," Kaito grumbled.

While Kaito complained, Akira snuck up unseen behind the man. Wrapping her arms around his neck, she bent her lips close to his ear and whispered something. The man's entire posture relaxed, his shoulders drooped, and his weapon fell to his side.

The second man turned, alerted by his companion's strange behavior.

"What's wrong with you?" he asked as he shook the man's other shoulder, and as he did, Akira went up behind him and whispered in his ear as well. He stopped in place, head cocked to the side listening, a goofy smile spreading across his face.

Then like a puppet on a string, he turned toward Suzume.

"Stay right there, don't move a muscle."

Suzume crossed her arms over her chest, to show her displeasure. But seeing Akira's power over the men made her a little nervous. It occurred to her she really didn't know anything about what the siblings could do. The guard left behind his fellow soldier without a thought. He appeared to be sleeping standing up but his eyes were wide open. Akira sauntered back over toward Suzume.

"What did you do?" Suzume hissed under her breath, eyes darting toward the remaining man.

"Just a little bit of suggestion. It doesn't work on every human. But soldiers are already used to taking orders, so it doesn't take much to break down their defenses."

Suzume wasn't sure if she should be impressed or terrified.

It only took a few minutes for the guard to return with Daiki in tow. As he approached, Suzume assumed her role of demure princess. She lowered her lashes, looked at the ground, hid her hands in opposite sleeves, and pinched herself hard enough to make her eyes water.

"Princess Suzume?" Daiki said.

Kaito growled when the general approached her. Suzume ignored him and looked up at her one time betrothed through her lashes, large fake tears were rolling down her cheeks. "Daiki!" she shouted before running toward him and falling into his arms, as if she had been over-come by emotion at the sight of him.

Suzume clung onto Daiki for a moment longer than was necessary, her breasts pressed against his chest, before she pretended to realize what she was doing, pulled back and lowered her gaze once more.

"I apologize, I'm just so relieved to have found you."

"What happened. We heard you were captured-"

Suzume gave a fake sob and covered her face as to not reveal her lack of tears.

"What am I saying? You should rest first." Then to the guard he said, "Take the princess to my personal tent."

The guard who Akira had influenced moved sluggishly as if he was in a daze, but did as he was commanded. Ushering Suzume toward Daiki's tent. She shot a look to Kaito meant to say 'stay here.' But he shook his head slowly, his scowl pinned on the back of Daiki's head who was shouting commands, and looking at Suzume with a dopey expression. Suzume held her fake smile in place, but she had a terrible feeling this was not going to go to plan.

ELEVEN

aiki's tent was just as she remembered it. Shelves with stacks of scrolls, and maps and other papers spread out along a low table with a single cushion where Daiki likely sat and looked over the documents. The bed tucked into one corner overflowed with pillows and Suzume sighed wistfully, imagining how good a nap would feel. Suzume's body ached from numerous injuries both from scrimmages and from real fights. It seemed an eternity since she'd slept in a real bed. Even a camp bed like Daiki's seemed like a luxury compared to the cold ground she had been sleeping on.

Behind her Daiki cleared his throat and she whipped around to face him, having forgotten for a moment he was there. Kaito loomed behind him, unseen by the general. Yokai had the ability to make themselves invisible to all but those that had a special sight. It was hard to imagine not being able to see the scowl on Kaito's face but she was one of the unfortunate few who could see him. Because she was distracted by Kaito and his glower, Suzume forgot to lower her gaze as she normally would and her eyes met Daiki's. They stared at one another for a moment. She had not felt this the last time she was with him, but she felt very aware of her naked face, her tattered clothes, and tangled hair. At the palace, Daiki would not have seen her without a screen between them or at the very least a fan. Suddenly she felt very exposed.

She lowered her lashes to stare at the ground, not needing to feign embarrassment now. What sort of stories would he tell about her when he returned to the White Palace? The thought made her stomach churn.

"Are you hurt? Would you like something to eat or drink?" Daiki asked, disrupting the awkward silence that had fallen between them. He approached Suzume, twisting his hands together.

Kaito scoffed. "He doesn't really believe this, does he?"

Suzume shot Kaito a look which Daiki misinterpreted as being directed at him and he frowned. "I'm not hurt badly," Suzume said to cover up her oversight and made a show of hiding her injured hands in her sleeves. How did Kaito expect her to learn anything while he was hovering over her like this?

Daiki noticed as she intended and grabbed a hold of her elbow to keep her from hiding it. "What did that monster do to you!"

Suzume pretended to reluctantly let him look at her bandaged hand, while Daiki tutted over it making a show of concern.

"I'll show him a monster," Kaito snarled. Suzume looked over Daiki's lowered head and nodded to the side indicating he should leave.

But he only shook his head and smirked. "I'm staying right here."

Daiki's head popped back up, blocking Suzume's view of the dragon. "I should call someone to check your wounds, and bring you something to eat." Daiki held onto her hand not letting go, however. Not moving to do as he said. He'd grown bolder since their last encounter. Daiki inched closer to her, shrinking the gap and raising the tension in the room. A sudden shiver ran down her spine, and she didn't need to see Kaito to know he was getting annoyed.

A lady would be expected to deny any unflattering feelings like hunger or thirst, but she needed to get Daiki out of here before Kaito did something reckless.

"If it's not too much trouble, I am rather hungry," she said, feigning embarrassment of her own hunger.

"Of course. Right away. Whatever you want I will get for you." He let go of her hand and leaped away from her as if she'd burned him. Which fortunately she hadn't. Her powers never seemed to react to humans.

Daiki practically stumbled over his own feet on his way out the door. "Please have a seat." He gestured toward the low table in the center of the room. Akira was right to send Suzume here, Daiki would do whatever she asked. If she questioned him about the priest, he would probably tell her everything she wanted to know. All that remained now was getting one bothersome dragon out of the way.

Once Daiki's backside disappeared out of the door, she marched over to him.

"What are you doing? You're ruining everything!" she hissed, her eyes darting toward the door, he wouldn't be gone long.

"You two are awfully cozy. Are you sure you're not reconsidering marrying him?"

"Do you want me to find out who that priest is or not?" she snapped.

Kaito ignored her and sauntered over to a nearby desk. Suzume followed after him prepared to argue further when Kaito picked up a diagram that had been lying on the table. It was a painting of a dragon, one that was eerily similar to Kaito. There were small notations written upon it, and Kaito's eyes narrowed.

"It looks like your lover boy knows more than he lets on."

Scattered across the table there were rolled up maps and beneath a pile of parchment a half-written letter. Perhaps Daiki had been in the middle of writing it when Suzume had arrived. Suzume's eyes darted toward the door, she should get away from his desk and get Kaito out before he returned. She didn't need to read through his documents to get what she wanted. Daiki was harmless, it was likely a letter he was writing to his ancient mother. Or a banal account of his day to day life.

"I wonder who he's writing." Kaito nodded toward the letter.

Curiosity getting the better of her, Suzume snatched it up off the table and scanned the beginning of it quickly. It was written in the formal scholar's script. Most women did not know the written word of men. Any court-raised girl knew the informal writing, for poetry and simple correspondence, but her mother had insisted she learn the forbidden characters, though Suzume protested learning it all the way. She was glad of those lessons now. The letter began with unimportant salutations, and blessings upon the emperor to whom she assumed the letter was being written though there was no address placed on it yet.

There is still no further sign of Princess Suzume. It weighs heavy on me to report that we believe she has perished at the hands of yokai, along with my lieutenant who was escorting her, though we found no remains. It was my error to send her away. Had I realized how vital her return was to you, I would have taken more careful action. I will accept any punishment you deem necessary. I beg for your mercy, and that you might forgive your humble servant. Our quest continues, nonetheless. I will not fail you again.

A hundred questions buzzed in her mind. Why was the emperor searching for her when he had exiled her? What was Daiki looking for on the emperor's behalf? Suzume glanced up and Daiki was standing in the doorway. Had he seen her reading his letter? She mentally shook herself. He would likely assume she could not read it. Suzume dropped the paper to the desk without a word as Daiki crossed the tent toward her. A heavy silence fell over the space.

"What were you doing?" he asked, his voice light but she felt a hint of danger in his tone.

"Are you hunting the dragon?" Suzume asked, nodding toward the sketch that Kaito had dropped onto the table when Daiki returned.

He followed her gaze to the sketch and then back to her and frowned. But it was quickly replaced by a smile, one that said he was hiding something. "That's nothing you need to worry about. I'll keep you safe." For the briefest moment, his eyes flickered in Kaito's direction before coming to rest on her once more.

Living in the White Palace had taught her how to hide her true feelings. Outside she appeared unruffled, maybe even relieved. Inside her heart beat faster. She resisted the urge to glance in Kaito's direction. Suzume looked at Daiki once more, his round red face and beady eyes were just as she remembered. He had never seemed like one for politics or subterfuge, and yet she couldn't shake this feeling of unease.

She pressed forward with their plan. "It will be a relief once you find him. I barely escaped this time. I would not want him to come back for me," Suzume said past tight lips.

Daiki sighed and pinched his brow between thumb and forefinger. "If I had known the danger to you, I would have sent one of the warrior priests with you. You must have been terrified." He reached for her, but as he did Kaito growled and Daiki pulled away as if thinking better of it.

Suzume did look at Kaito this time. His eyes were trained on Daiki.

"Something the matter?" Daiki asked sweetly.

Her attention snapped back to Daiki. "You couldn't have known," she said with a melodramatic smile.

Daiki's eyes narrowed for a moment. "You are fortunate he did not devour you."

"He said I was too pretty to eat." She covered her face with her hands as if embarrassed about giving herself a compliment.

Kaito barked a laugh, and Daiki's eyes flickered that way once more. Before he said, "Of course, you are beautiful and I am sure that would-be reason enough to spare your life. But yokai are known for consuming humans with powerful spiritual energy."

"I don't have any spiritual power, though I was sent to a temple to train as a priestess." She forced a laugh as the idea of her having any sort of power was ludicrous.

Kaito was sidling behind Daiki, his hands already half transformed into claws. Though Daiki's body was facing toward her, his eyes were following Kaito as he stalked closer to him. His hand drifted to a sword at his side that Suzume had not seen before. Things were going to get ugly very quickly.

Suzume buried her head in her hands, pretending to be over-whelmed by emotion and let out a fake cry while she figured out what to do next. "It was awful, what he did to that temple, when he took me..." She choked on a pretend sob. When he did not reach out to comfort her, she grabbed his hand from across the table. "That's why I am so glad I found you again and I was able to escape from that monster."

His stare was cold and indifferent. Suzume slowly retracted her hand as his head turned toward where Kaito stood behind him, half monster half man.

"I know you're there dragon, show yourself," he said slowly.

Those who lived at the White Palace were masters of control. They only revealed what they wanted and only presented whatever face suited their purposes. Suzume's mistake had been assuming Daiki was a besotted fool. This was one of the emperor's most trusted men. She thought he reached his position through family connection, but she'd been the one who was played all along.

Kaito lunged for the general, claws bared, slashing into his flesh while Daiki fumbled to draw his blade. Suzume reached for her staff, ready to join the fray, but Kaito shouted at her.

"Don't get in my way!"

Daiki stood spinning in circles, looking for Kaito and tilting his head as if he were a blind man.

"Fight me like a man," Daiki said, squinting in the direction Suzume was facing.

Kaito stalked around him, and Daiki clutched onto his blade unable to see anything.

"You cannot even see me and yet you think you can defeat me?"

"You were a fool to enter here," Daiki said, lunging toward where he had last heard Kaito's voice. But Kaito stepped easily out of the way and Daiki tumbled forward falling onto the ground.

"Enough playing around, let's get the information we wanted and leave."

It was almost painful to watch Kaito taunt Daiki this way. Even though Daiki had used her, the dragon clearly overpowered him.

Kaito grabbed Daiki by the back of his haori, dangling him in front of him, only then revealing his face.

"You are too full of pride, human."

"And you would have done better not to underestimate a human." Daiki smiled and just then vines burst out of the ground, wrapping themselves around Kaito's torso, binding him tightly in place.

Daiki was dropped to the ground. Suzume reached for her staff. As she did, a crowd of masked men poured into the room and grabbed her before she could draw her weapon.

Kaito roared her name as she was dragged out of the tent into the night.

Twelve

As they dragged Suzume out, it only fanned the flames of his rage. It was one thing to draw them into a trap. It was another to take what belonged to him. The general smiled smugly at Kaito, proud of himself for capturing a dragon. The general was a child compared to him, and a fool if he thought these paltry bindings would hold him. The vines that bound his body were already covered in frost. Ice pulsated from his body and turned the vines brittle, and they crumbled as he flexed outward.

The vines crumbled, tinkling to the floor. Shards of ice fell all around him, and ice crept out from his footsteps as he approached the general. The smirk on his face melted like the ice that encrusted everything around him and the general stumbled backward in his haste to escape.

Kaito delighted in seeing him squirm, like the wriggling insect he was. He would enjoy the chase and then he would make the arrogant human suffer for daring to challenge him.

His power was unfurling from within him, unwinding like a coil, forcing the transformation upon him. He assumed his true form, that of a giant serpentine creature, and as the numerous coils of his body grew they pressed against the fabric walls of the tent, causing it to burst apart at the seams, scattering the general's belongs along with it. Papers flew through the air before drifting to the ground. Kaito's storm clouds gathered in the sky pelting the paper. The black ink ran blurring into an unreadable mess.

The general had fallen back, and into his trap. Rin and the others who'd been guarding outside the tent were prepared for him. Kaito was surprised to see that the general had foreseen this as well, and a group of warrior priests were chanting as they shot blessed arrows at Rin, who had assumed her massive kitsune form. Tsuki, blade in hand, was hacking his way closer and closer to them, pushing his way through their ineffectual barriers. Naoki had appeared behind them, and with a swipe of his sword ended the lives of three of the warrior priests. Blood mixed with the rain falling from the sky, turning the mud crimson.

Kaito arrived in time for the fighting to be over and to discover that the general had gotten away. The remaining priests had retreated, but this was only a moment's reprieve. Their battle had only just begun. As soon as he rejoined the others, Rin looked to him waiting for orders. In her true form: a large white fox, feet tipped with flames, red markings on her white fur, and numerous tails whipping behind her, she was quite imposing.

"Should I go and retrieve her, master?" she asked in her rumbling voice. She had changed since he had last known her. The Rin he knew was a trickster, full of smiles. Subservient yes, but not a warrior. She'd grown stronger since he'd been sealed. But he didn't need her assistance. He would retrieve the priestess on his own.

"That won't be necessary," he growled.

Things had changed while he had slept - the world, Rin, and himself. Kaito had never been the type to make these types of errors. How had he not seen the trap for what it was? Before Kazue had sealed him, he had been a master of strategy, always two steps ahead of his enemies. But he had been blinded once again by Kazue. He was so desperate to find out more about the man with a piece of Kazue's soul that he had not considered the general until it was too late. He would not make the same mistake twice.

While Rin had leaped up, ready to fight for him, Tsuki was wiping the blood off of his blade as if Kaito was not there at all. The siblings and Naoki's continued presence near Suzume bothered him. It had been at their insistence that they sent Suzume in. Kaito narrowed his eyes, watching them, but Tsuki was absorbed in cleaning his weapon. Only Naoki met his gaze, but his impassive stare gave nothing away.

When he looked away, Naoki scanned across the camp. His eyes grazed over the nearby tents, perhaps searching for Suzume's spiritual energy. But Kaito could feel her. Like a flickering candle in a dark room, he could spot her anywhere. After a few moments of silent scrutiny, Naoki turned to Kaito. "Something is shielding her energy."

Kaito searched again for Suzume's energy and was surprised to find it had disappeared entirely, as if someone had snuffed out the candle. The thought sent a ripple of momentary fear through him. *She's not that easy to kill, this is all part of their plan.* Kaito was preparing to launch himself into the sky once more, but Tsuki's words stopped him.

"We can find her," Tsuki said to his father.

"You've done enough," Kaito growled.

Tsuki turned toward Kaito as if seeing him for the first time. "And what is that supposed to mean?"

"It was your idea to bring her here. Do you think I could trust you with finding her?"

"Weren't you the one who wanted to go in the first place?"

"And I wanted to go alone." He glared at Tsuki, who held his stare.

There was no use wasting any more time arguing. His annoyance at Tsuki was outweighed by his fear for Suzume.

"I don't need you slowing me down." Kaito snarled, turning he prepared to take off.

Akira's words stopped him. "This happened because you continue to underestimate humanity. That has always been your weakness."

Kaito spun toward her, teeth bared, and lunged for her throat, his jaws just ghosting around her neck. "Do not question me further." He growled again.

Tsuki came back into view and grabbed a hold of the hilt of his blade. "You are not our master."

Rin turned on Tsuki and growled low in her throat like a dog protecting its owner.

Everything was falling apart, and every moment they wasted was another that their larger quest was put at risk. He didn't need them.

"As I said before, either you obey me or you leave." Kaito launched himself into the sky, not bothering to wait for their response.

Kaito slithered through the sky. He did not bother to cloak his spiritual energy, but let the gathering clouds mask him instead. As his temper had risen, so had a storm arrived summoned by his anger, and his need to unleash his wrath. Inside him a storm was raging: over his error in letting Suzume go, his lack of control over the others. They all boiled inside him and were pressing against his skin needing release.

Tents lit up like bonfires in the night courtesy of Rin's fox fire. Despite his order to stand down, she was following along, causing a diversion. Soldiers shouted as they rushed to go and put out the flames and this was his chance to unleash his power upon them. The ice poured out of him like a great sheet. Soldiers running toward the fires could not avoid the deadly shafts of his ice, and were impaled. A few turned and held up shields. Before they could regroup, and attempt a return attack, Kaito flew higher and out of range.

Using the clouds to hide him, Kaito listened for their shouts, trying to detect their positions but his rage had brought unexpected hindrance and the sky burst open with thick sheets of rain that hammered down on his skin and drowned out all other sound. His anger was overwhelming his control, but he reveled in the feeling, having too long held onto his anger at the humans. This was his revenge. Against humanity which had spread like a disease across the land. Against Kazue who had trapped him in stone. In that moment he forgot about Suzume and could only think of unleashing his anger.

He dipped below the clouds and swooped closer to the tents, preparing to unleash another attack. But as he drew closer, a bevy of arrows was fired toward him and Kaito twisted out of the way, his serpentine body coiling in the sky. One stray arrow hit its mark, embedding itself into his underbelly. Fiery pain radiated outward from the wound. The arrow had been imbued with spiritual energy. He had found his missing priests.

Using the clouds as cover once again, he hovered over the camp, spreading out his senses and searching for the priests who had struck him. These were the same damn fools who had tried to ground him the last time he'd come across the general's army. A multitude of mundane human energies attempted to cloud and confuse him. *You cannot run from me.* Kaito waited, weeding through the sheer volume of bodies in his mind's eye until he found them, and there in the middle was a bright beacon of energy, at least twice as powerful as those around him. This had to be the man who held a piece of Kazue's soul inside him.

He would rip Kazue's soul from his chest if that's what it took. He flew lower searching for him. Then just as quickly as he had located the priest, his energy disappeared, masked once more. Kaito dropped even lower. If he could not lock onto his energy, then he would find him visually. But as soon as he appeared from beneath the clouds, more arrows were flying in his direction. They ricocheted off his hide, as if they were nothing at all. The priest had not risked exposing himself to shoot, not while Kaito had him on the run. He had felt Kaito's probing and knew he was after him.

The dragon scanned the camp, searching for him, but the scurrying bodies beneath him all looked the same. He flew higher, half his body coiled in the clouds, and his head peeking out. He would not leave himself vulnerable to attack while he searched. But the arrow that already struck him was throbbing with pain. It felt as if a thousand tiny fingers were creeping through his body, touching on every nerve then alighting with agony. He pushed the pain aside, focusing instead on his task. He would find this man.

Through the crowd, which was rushing one direction or another, he spotted him. One single man dressed from head to toe in black with a quiver of arrows on his back was running away from the fighting. Kaito gave pursuit through the sky, his gaze fixed on the fleeing priest. The pain was becoming more of a distraction, his abdomen was seiz-ing, muscles twitching. Without realizing it, he was flying lower. The priest turned to face him and suddenly all he could see was green eyes flashing in the darkness. Kaito stopped, a wicked grin on his face. He had him now.

The priest drew his bow and shot another arrow before Kaito had time to maneuver. His movements were too slow from the first spiritual arrow's effect. Kaito roared with pain, as the second arrow punctured his shoulder. The sky thundered his displeasure and lightning flashed across the clouds, illuminating the ground below. The man turned and disappeared between a couple of tents out of Kaito's sight once more. Then a group of soldiers scurried out in his place, bows and arrows at the ready.

With his target priest out of the way, there was nothing stopping him from unleashing his power against these fools who attempted to attack him. He showered them in spears of ice. The soldiers were struck by ice but did not stop, they merely burst into puffs of smoke. Kaito roared in frustration just as arrows came flying from every direction all at once.

One of the arrows caught him on the side, and another on one of his legs. The pain doubled and tripled with each strike. Kaito spun for a moment in the sky, thrashing about, trying to remove the arrows that felt as if they were tearing him apart from the inside. This wasn't possible. The other warrior priests shouldn't have been strong enough to hit him. Unless the powerful priest had blessed their arrows. Focusing on anything other than the pain was impossible. When he reached back around to try and remove one of the arrows with his mouth his whiskers brushed against it and they sparked, burned by the holy energy imbued in the wood. He caught a glimpse of an ofuda wrapped around the shaft, and his suspicions were confirmed.

Kaito roared as the energy burned through his flesh, spreading like a disease inside of him. He lost control of his limbs as the spiritual energy of the arrows sapped away all his strength. He lost altitude and then he fell into a cascading tumble to the ground where he slammed into the mud. His limbs were frozen in place, trapped by the power of the arrows.

Kaito raised his head and saw a figure walking toward him. In the gloom of the falling rain it appeared to be a woman. Kaito blinked hard, not willing to believe what he saw as Kazue came closer. But as the figure closed in, Kazue's form melted away, and in her place was a man dressed all in black. His bright green eyes blazing in the gloom.

Kaito resisted the urge to jump up and attack him, and instead laid very still on the ground, waiting for the priest to get close enough. The man approached and when he was within reach Kaito reached out, grabbing him by the ankle and bringing the man tumbling onto the ground. He wrestled with him for just a moment, each taking turns on top before the man got the upper hand. All Kaito could see in the gloom was the glow of his green eyes. As he straddled the dragon, the man suddenly froze.

Kaito took his chance and lunged forward, knocking his head into the other man's head. It knocked him backward where he fell to the ground. Kaito gave pursuit but before he could catch him the priest spoke a quick chant, flinging an ofuda at him, which froze him in place. The man stood just a few feet away panting. His eyes were still glowing that ethereal green. Rain from the storm Kaito had called down fell onto the both of them. Inside Kaito was raging. *I'll tear him limb from limb once I break free.*

The man took a step toward Kaito, raised his bow, and pointed an arrow at his chest. Kaito attempted to unfurl his power to break through the man's spell but the holy energy only bound him tighter, squeezing against his own yokai energy.

Kaito stared into the eyes of his would be killer. Was this how it ended? With an arrow through the heart by a mere human?

Thirteen

They dragged Suzume out of the tent and as she clawed and kicked against her captors, the sound of Kaito's growls echoed through the night. His power flooded out of him, pulsing through her, raising the sparks along her skin in response. Her captors, being mere copies of the original, did not so much as flinch as they carried her away from an angry dragon. She had to get a hold of herself. Looking in control even when you weren't gave you the advantage more than anything else. Losing control meant losing the game, and she only played to win. Suzume took a few deep breaths, calming her mind and giving herself a chance to reassess her situation. But her mind was racing, the world she thought she knew had just come crashing down around her. Daiki had tricked her? The emperor was looking for her? Kaito had fallen into a trap.

Despite the growing panic within her, Suzume steadied her steps and walked without a struggle. The copies brought her to the center of the room, before taking a step back and standing as sentries at the door. She left her expression blank to prepare for Daiki's inevitable arrival. She knew what role she had to play. This was not over and there was still more she could learn. Kaito could take care of himself. Outwardly she might have looked unafraid, unflappable, but inside a hundred different questions crowded to be asked first. *What does Daiki want with me?*

The minutes ticked by and Daiki did not come for her. Her foot tapped of its own volition, and she stopped looking at the blank-eyed copies who did not care if she was fidgeting. *I should just attack them and look for Daiki on my own.* But she did not follow through with that thought, and instead tried to keep herself still by kneeling beside a table at the center of the room. Her fingers drummed on the tabletop, giving away her agitation.

Suddenly the tent flap opened and Daiki walked in. Suzume gave him a withering look as he entered, as if she was not his captive and remained his superior. She would continue to play the part of princess. This role had protected her in a dangerous place like the White Palace and it could protect her here. The only thing that had changed, was she knew Daiki's motives now. Which only gave her the advantage.

"What is the meaning of this? How did the dragon follow me?" She demanded. By speaking first she took control of their conversation.

"Don't worry, you are safe now." He held up his hands in a placating gesture. "I never would have dreamed..." He shook his head before correcting himself, "I never thought... That is, we didn't know he would come after you." He put too much emphasis on the last word, like Suzume was nothing. He too was trying to grasp at a persona that gave him comfort — she doubted she was the first person to fall for this act.

Curiously Daiki continued to stand over her. If she stood now it would lack grace and it would acknowledge his superior position in the room. So she remained sitting but her words were laced with poison as she said, "Are you saying I was bait?"

He waved his hands in front of him to dismiss the accusation. His cheeks were flushed. Either he really was a bumbling idiot, or one of the best actors she'd ever seen. "That is not it, I just thought you were Izume's daughter, nothing more..."

"I thought I meant more to you," she said with a fake pout. She couldn't resist. She was under no illusions about his feelings now. But neither of them were willing to give up the act just yet.

"If I had known you were one of them I would never have let you out of my sight," he snapped, revealing too much in the process.

Suzume's eyes widened as realization dawned on her. Her gaze flickered toward the black-clad clones. Others like her, like the man she had met in the forest. "Like them?" she repeated, fearing she'd be the one to give too much away.

He dropped his hands and stared at her, there was no use pretending anymore. As they stood emotionally bare, they came to a silent understanding.

"Did you really think I would marry you, after your mother was disgraced? Your very paternity has been brought into question. You and all your brother. I cannot marry a girl of questionable birth," he said bluntly.

When last they had met, she did believe that, and that was the sad part. Maybe it had been naive to believe he was in love with her.

"Then what did you want from me?" she asked. Her temper was rising and along with it that tingling feeling, which meant her powers were going haywire.

Daiki shook his head, as if she was an idiot for not seeing it from the start. "You really thought I loved you? I knew you for the snake you were the moment I met you. And had you not fallen so low, you would have made the perfect wife. You're just like your mother."

The insult stung, but Suzume didn't let it show on her face. Instead she sat very still, letting him tighten the noose around his neck.

"All you were ever good for was gaining a connection with your grandfather and his clan. Everyone knew his influence came from your mother's marriage to the emperor." He laughed again at some joke that was meant for him alone.

Suzume grit her teeth and dug her nails into the palm of her hand. *Hold your tongue, let him spill the truth.*

"After your mother shamed your family, your grandfather's star fell. And now it's me who they come begging favors from because I have the powerful connections now."

His belly shook as he laughed at his own joke. Rain hammered on the tent in a sudden downpour. Outside Kaito roared. He had broken free of his bonds it seemed and was searching for her most likely. It wouldn't be long before he came to save her, but before he did, she had to know.

"My grandfather was looking for me?"

"Among others, and now I can see why."

Suzume's hands were suddenly very clammy, she wanted to wipe them on the front of her clothes, but that would not be very princess-like. Not that it really mattered anymore, since she'd been exposed. Daiki knew she was not the shy, innocent girl she had pretended to be, just as he was not the bumbling fool he pretended to be.

"Why is the emperor looking for me?" she asked.

"You know why."

"Because I am looking for you," a voice purred by her ear.

Suzume turned slowly. The room felt as if it was spinning. Even as she turned around she tried to convince herself that this wasn't real, that it was all a dream. Hisato grinned at her as their eyes met. His eyes were dark and bottomless, swirling with chaos and danger. Seeing him here beside Daiki was like finding a bug in your soup. This was a place that held echoes of the person she had been, a life she had been ripped from. But here he was sitting down beside her, a strange juxtaposition of round and red Daiki. Hisato filled the room with his presence, with his insane yet charismatic smile, and his relaxed posture, as if this was exactly where he belonged. She felt like she was tipping sideways and slipping into some form of alternate reality. This could not be real. Daiki and Hisato working together. Hisato and the emperor? Two worlds that had been firmly separate in her mind were suddenly colliding.

"What are you doing here?" Suzume asked, the words flying from her mouth before she could stop them. She could not stop the fire that prickled along her skin, a warning of danger, and a defense she could not use against Hisato, unless she wanted to get burned in return.

"I missed you, Suzume." Hisato leaned across the table, brushing his hand over the back of her hand which was dancing with flames. Suzume felt the pain reflected in her own fingertips where his had touched her, a warning of what would happen if she tried something reckless.

"It is true then, you are a witch," Daiki said, and she heard the note of fear in his voice.

Suzume did not want to take her eyes off Hisato, and said to Daiki without looking at him, "And you were a two-faced liar."

"You wench." Daiki reeled his hand back, smacking her so hard she was knocked backward onto the ground.

The fire inside her could not be contained any longer. It encircled her like a halo of flame, surrounding her as she glared at Daiki. The general loomed over her with hatred and fear in his eyes.

"Even when you've fallen this low, you think to look down on me?"

He stalked closer to her, as if he would strike her again but before he could touch her, something burst from the front of his chest. It glistened with a dark substance, and a stain spread out across his haori. Daiki looked down at the foreign object protruding from his chest. Blood dripped from the tip of it, landing in his upturned hand. Hisato came out from behind Daiki, blocking Suzume's view.

"Why?" Daiki gurgled.

Hisato tilted his head to the side as he regarded Daiki. "You've made too many mistakes, general. And now you threaten me? It cannot be forgiven."

Daiki sputtered, spitting blood onto Hisato's face, which he wiped away with a smirk. Holding out his hand, a ball of black energy formed, then elongated and contorted, turning into a blade dark as midnight, which seemed to absorb all light around it. Hisato held up the blade and plunged it into Daiki with a sick wet noise.

Suzume stared at the lifeless body of her one time betrothed, lying on the ground in a growing pool of his own blood. Sightless eyes stared at her in accusation. Numb with shock, she could not take her eyes off his slack expression or the blood spatter on his face. *Daiki is dead?*

There was no more logical thought left in her. Suzume jumped up and ran for the door, but the copies of the masked man held out their arms, stopping her in her tracks. She spun around searching for another exit, even if she had to cut through the tent walls to do so. But Hisato was there, arms outstretched as if he would invite her into his embrace.

"Don't even think about running," he said as he stalked closer to her. She backed away, her heart ramming against her rib cage as if it would burst out of her chest at any moment. "You cannot run. My soldiers will stop you."

"When I tell them you killed Daiki..."

"But I am right here, Suzume." Hisato shifted forms, taking on the face of Daiki, flushed and breathing heavy. If his corpse hadn't been a few feet away, she would have been convinced he was the real thing.

"Why?" She choked on Daiki's last word. It was mixed with bile at the back of her throat.

"He put something precious to me in danger." Hisato reached out, attempting to place his hand against her cheek, but the flames sparking on her skin kept him away. Suzume could feel the heat of her flames reflected in her skin. As if whatever bond that held them together before had only gotten stronger. It made his point: hurt Suzume and you hurt Hisato. He transformed back into his usual form, smirking at her.

"Now where did we leave off?" He tapped his chin thoughtfully. "Ah, that's right. You played a nasty trick on me back on the mountaintop," he purred.

"I thought you'd enjoy that. You like games, don't you?" she said, but her voice shook as her eyes kept drifting to Daiki's dead body.

Hisato looked to the side, seeing how it was distracting her. He snapped his fingers and a black void opened up beneath Daiki's body. It slid head first into the portal before tumbling into the darkness below. Once he was gone, not even a stain from his blood remained.

Hisato's dark eyes were trained on her. "I've missed your smart mouth, Suzume." He pressed his finger to her lips. "You know I do these things to protect you, don't you?"

"Is this where you say: hurting you hurts me?" She knocked his arms down using a maneuver Tsuki had taught her. She turned and fled for the nearest tent wall, hands aflame. She'd burn her way out if she had to.

But Hisato was there before she could even try, blocking her path. "We're meant to be together, Suzume. I wanted you to come to me but we're running out time."

"What do you mean, running out of time?" Panic suddenly seized her chest but the feeling felt foreign as if it belonged to someone else entirely.

"They know about us. I can protect you from them. If you'll join me."

"And by them you mean the emperor? Is that the lie you told Daiki to get him to your side?"

"It wasn't a lie, Suzume. The emperor knows about your power and he wants it."

She shook her head. "I can take care of myself."

He shook his head mirroring her. "Life cannot be sustained on its own, the fox eats the bird, the bird eats the worm, the worm eats the remains of both the fox and bird. It is vanity that makes you think you can be without me. No one can understand what sleeps inside you but me."

Suzume balled her hand into a fist and looked Hisato in the eye as she said, "Feel free to underestimate me. It will make defeating you so much easier." Suzume focused her energy on her fist, and to her surprise a ball of fire erupted in her hand. She unleashed it toward Hisato, half hoping it would hit its mark and half fearing it would.

He dodged her attack with ease, laughing all the while. "Oh, my dear Suzume, you are so predictable."

She spun around and Hisato was behind her. "I'll do it again." She tried to focus her power to create another ball of flame, but it did not come. She balled her hand into a fist instead.

"You act without thinking, just like your element. You burn with anger, impatience. You embody all of Kazue's impulsiveness."

"I am not Kazue."

"You're correct, but she is in you, waiting to consume you. You took her heart into you and Kazue is greedy. She will not stop until she has all of you. Unless you can learn to harness her power first. Which is what I can teach you." He held out his hand again, as if she would take it and join him.

"You're lying. Kazue is gone. I watched her energy disappear." Even as she said this, she thought back to Naoki, who could not be parted from her because of Kazue's heart.

"You watched the memories of Kazue trapped in that heart burn up. But what made up Kazue continues to live on. She will draw us all to you, until she has reunited her soul and is reborn in you."

A harsh wind blew in through the tent door and rain blew in with it, falling onto the floor as a man entered dressed all in black. He was not another replica like what had been guarding the door, but the original. His eyes were a blazing green, unlike anything she had seen before.

"What perfect timing," he said to the man with a smile. "Suzume there's someone I want to introduce to you." He motioned toward the man who had not moved from the doorway.

Suzume was trapped between the two of them, the man in black, dripping silently on the floor, and Hisato whose laughter was dark and terrible.

"I assume you finished it?" Hisato asked him.

A cold chill ran down her spine. "Finished what?" Suzume asked eyes darting between the two of them.

Hisato smiled at her maniacally. "Killing the dragon."

FOURTEEN

"It is done," the masked man said to Hisato.

Suzume's hands were sparking with flames now, an all-encompassing rage suddenly bubbled up within her. Hisato had tried before to convince Suzume to seal Kaito once more. And it seemed he had manipulated this man into doing his bidding. She strained to listen for the sound of Kaito's roar but heard nothing but the hammering of rain falling on the tent. Now even that was letting up. Was it fading as Kaito's power faded with it?

Hisato looked at Suzume with a grin. "Now there is nothing left for you. Join me."

She was consumed by a sudden urge to destroy. The urge was so powerful she did not even consider her own wellbeing and launched herself in Hisato's direction, slamming her hands into Hisato's chest. The blow knocked Hisato back and the rebound toppled Suzume backward as well, knocking the masked man over in the process. She and the masked man landed on the ground in a pile, and as soon as their bodies collided she felt it: an explosion of fire from deep in her gut bursting out from inside her, and out every inch of her. A bright red stream of her power swirled out of her, and headed straight for the man beneath her, whose every pore was seeping with green energy. Their energies collided together, commingling and becoming something else entirely. An almost humanoid shape hovered above them, like a blob with small appendages for arms and legs.

When Hisato got back to his feet, a trail of blood dribbled from his lip. The energy she and the masked man had created transformed into a shaft, slamming into Hisato's chest and his left shoulder, tearing into his flesh and severing the arm at the joint. Suzume clenched, prepared for the reflection of pain in herself but found nothing. The energy kept moving through Hisato, burning a hole in the cloth wall of the tent and scattering papers everywhere as Hisato crumpled onto the ground like a broken doll.

Hisato's mouth was curled into a smirk. Suzume got up and crept closer, staring down at his tattered corpse. *Is he really dead?* Before she could check his body melted into a pile of black goop, which seeped into the ground and disappeared. Suzume stumbled backward, terrified by what had just happened. All that remained of Hisato was a black stain on the ground.

"Is he dead?" The masked man asked, echoing Suzume's question. He was staring at the place as well with a strange expression, as if he couldn't quite believe what he had seen either.

"What makes you think he survived? There's nothing left of him but a smudge on the ground."

"He wasn't exactly human," the man said without inflection, as if watching someone melt into the ground was normal.

The hairs on Suzume's skin stood on end she felt as if someone was watching her - perhaps Hisato was still here watching over them.

"Come with me. I can take you somewhere you'll be safe," the masked man said, holding out his hand to her.

"I'm not going anywhere with you. You're working for him." She gestured toward the black stain on the ground. She held up her hands in a would-be defensive pose. But it looked less imposing without her staff.

"You have no reason to trust me, I know, but I can take you to someone who can help you."

"I don't need anyone's help."

Suzume's hands were still sparking with flames. She flung her arm at the man, who dipped to the side to avoid getting hit by her fire. And when she was presented with an opening she took it.

Outside was a maze of tents and a thick curtain of mist created by Kaito's power. Along her arms the flames licked up her skin and sparked along the ends of her hair, only to be put out by the moisture in the air, which soaked her clothes and plastered her hair to her face. She refused to believe the dragon was dead. There was no way that one single priest had killed him. She had to find him. Just the thought that Kaito might be dead filled her with an overwhelming rage that only fueled the flames which continued to cover her body.

She ran in what she thought was the direction she'd last heard Kaito's roar. But as she rounded a corner she was confronted with an even greater maze of tents and realized she was hopelessly lost. Shouting was coming from all directions, but somewhere in this labyrinth of tents Kaito and the others were fighting. She could feel it. But she could not discern where the sounds were coming from when they seemed to be coming from everywhere. Picking a direction at random, she ran heedlessly through an alleyway created by the tents, before seeing a pair of armed soldiers running in her direction. It was difficult to say if they were running from a battle or running to a battle.

When they spotted Suzume they shouted for her to stop. Her first impulse was to turn and run in the other direction, but a voice seemed to whisper at the back of her mind. *You can fight them. You have the power.* Instead Suzume stood her ground, letting flames jump off her body, sending flickering shadows onto the ground and tents that surrounded her. As the soldiers approached her and saw the flames they slowed and raised their weapons, closing in on her.

Suzume held her hand in front of her, and a ball of flame leaped into her hand without much effort at all. She stared at it for a moment. Before it had taken hours to create. But ever since she had collided with the masked man she had been feeling different, stronger, more confident.

Suzume and the soldiers stood staring at one another for a few moments, rain falling onto to their faces. It was running down her neck, soaking her to the skin, but now it did not dampen the fire inside her. One of the men drew a bow and arrow, preparing to fire it at Suzume in the same instant she raised her hand about to unleash the ball of fire, when an arrow zipped past her from behind and knocked into the man's shoulder.

The masked man walked up from behind Suzume, bow held at his side.

"Makato, what is the meaning of this?" the uninjured soldier shouted at him.

The masked man, Makato, did not respond to the man's question and instead reached into his sleeve and drew something out. The men drew their swords and rushed toward them. Before Suzume could fling her ball of fire at them, Makato was singing an incantation which illuminated markings on two pieces of rectangular paper. The papers seemed to come to life as he threw them toward the two men. They slammed against both men's foreheads, freezing them in place. It was a neat trick, and if she'd seen it under different circumstances, she would have asked him how it was done.

"Do you think this means I will trust you now?" She asked, staring at him warier than before. She had not let go of the ball of fire and she was considering how she could unleash it and harm him without hurting herself.

"Once you kill a person, there is no turning back."

"Do you expect me to thank you for that?"

"I didn't kill the dragon. I couldn't bring myself to finish it. Something stopped me, and I think you know why."

Suzume narrowed her eyes at him. She had not lowered her defenses just yet. "Do I look stupid to you?"

He frowned. "No?"

She raised her hand up as if she would strike him but she couldn't bring herself to follow through with the action. Hurting him would only hurt her in the end. "Just tell me where the dragon is and I won't burn you to a crisp."

"If I tell you, will you take me with you?"

"Why would I trust you?"

"Keep me as your prisoner if you must. I just have this feeling that you can answer the question I have."

"And what question is that?"

"Who am I?"

"Tell me where the dragon is and I'll answer whatever you want," she lied. As soon as she was reunited with Kaito she would decide what to do with this strange man.

"This way," he motioned for her to follow him. They ran around the frozen bodies of the two warriors, the only part of them that could move was their eyes, which watched them as they snuck past. Suzume glanced at them as she ran by, thinking that if Makato hadn't stopped her she would have killed them both. She dismissed the thought and followed after the priest.

As she ran her feet slid in the mud and her pulse raced with the fire that coursed through her, pushing her harder than she'd ever gone before. Wherever they were going it was close to the fighting because as she drew closer she heard a roar of a great beast coming from her left. *Kaito?* Suzume diverted from the path to follow the sound.

Makato, who was leading the way, chased after her shouting, "That's not the way."

As Suzume came across a fight in progress she discovered not the dragon embroiled in a battle, but Rin. Makato grabbed onto Suzume's arm, trying to drag her away. Soldiers were surrounding Rin from all angles. Rin twisted and snarled as she tore into her enemies, but she was greatly outnumbered. She should help her, but there was still Kaito...

Suzume clenched her hands into fists, the fire was coursing all through her body, an untamed wild animal clawing at her insides. If only she was more powerful she could save them all.

"We have to go," Makato said, urging her to leave.

"She's one of my friends." Suzume gestured toward the kitsune and Makato looked at her properly for the first time. When he did his eyes grew wide.

"Is that a kitsune?" Without waiting for her response, he stepped toward Rin as if in a trance. "Go ahead, I will save the kitsune."

"How do I know you're not going to kill her?"

He looked at Suzume with wide eyes. "I cannot explain it, but I have to save her."

Before Suzume could question him, Makato was already multiplying himself, his numerous copies swarming over the soldiers that surrounded Rin. Suzume hesitated only a moment more. Something in his gaze had convinced her, as if he knew Rin. Perhaps it had something to do with Kazue. Whatever the reason, Suzume was confident Rin could handle herself. It was Kaito who needed her now. She ran in the direction that Makato had indicated and came to a space cleared of tents. There were no soldiers here but the air crackled with spiritual energy. She felt it brush against her skin and recognized it as Makato's energy. The ground was gashed with deep marks and indentations in the mud where Kaito's dragon body had landed on the ground. But what lay on the ground now was not a massive dragon, but a fragile human body.

Suzume approached carefully and as she did, she saw Kaito's body covered in arrows. Blood seeped into the fabric of his haori. At first, she thought he wasn't breathing and that the priest had lied to her, but then she saw the rise and fall of Kaito's chest. The wounds glowed green, and sparked against Kaito's energy. Ice was encrusting his body, as if his spiritual energy was trying to shield him.

"None of us are strong enough to kill him," Hisato whispered in her ear.

Suzume turned, hands held up and flickering with flames. Hisato stood back from her, his eyes glancing at the flame in her hand. For the first time she felt as if she was in control of the situation.

"You'll never be able to kill Kaito, if that's your goal."

"I can see that now. We all share that."

"Share what?"

"Kazue's love for him. It is entwined in our souls."

"I don't love Kaito!" Suzume snapped back.

Hisato threw his head back and laughed. "You can deny it all you like but Kazue's heart is within you. She will sway your thoughts and your heart. She started all of this for him." Hisato gestured toward Kaito.

The anger was boiling up inside her once more. Suzume heard a song whispered in her ear by an unknown singer. Placing her palms together, she concentrated all her energy between her hands, growing the ball of fire with the power of the song. The ball grew to almost the size of her torso, when this collided with Hisato it would kill him for certain, turn his body to ash and then finally she would be free. *And then I will be the most powerful being.*

He smirked. "If you do this we both perish."

There was no hesitation left in her as she raised her arms and prepared to unleash Hisato's destruction.

FIFTEEN

The warriors swarmed around Rin from every direction. No matter where she turned, bodies pressed in upon her, swinging their spears at her. Animal instinct overrode every other thought, and she was nothing more than a series of reactions: biting, snapping, clawing, trying to save her own life. Even with mundane weapons, the warriors were overwhelming her. The numerous wounds all over her body ate up her spiritual power as she healed herself. The ever-shifting group of warriors stole her focus and Rin was lost in a haze of blood and fear.

The centuries had made her stronger, as it did with many of her kind. The longer you could survive, live in this cruel and brutal world, the stronger you became. But despite centuries of power behind her, she was not inexhaustible. After so long in battle, she was testing the limits of her spiritual energy. The long fight had taken its toll on her, and the men who surrounded her knew it. They closed in around her, giving her less room to maneuver, and she thrashed around in the center of them like a fish on a line. With less room to move, the greater the chance of a fatal mistake.

They grew bolder, perhaps smelling the weakness on her. The animal part of her roared, baring teeth, while the logical side of her brain tried to soothe it just for long enough to escape. She could not win this fight, a distant part of herself saw that. But the beast within was focused on survival and could not see beyond the immediate threat in front of her. If she could find a gap, she would flee. With rolling golden eyes, Rin scanned the warriors who surrounded her, searching for the smallest chink in their defense. Just that momentary distraction exposed her, and a warrior lunged forward with his spear pointed at her chest. At the last second, Rin jerked backward, but not soon enough to evade the pointed blade entirely, and it sank into her flank. She twisted away and the shaft of the spear broke off, the blade embedded in her flesh. A howl ripped from her throat as the pain coursed through her veins like fire.

There was little reason left within her as she thrashed about like a wild animal. An impulsive attempt to leap over their heads was cut off by the spears as they stabbed upward toward her belly. She flopped to the side as she canceled the maneuver mid-air. As she fell something struck her hard on the side, sending her careening to the ground. Then burning ropes were tossed over her back, pinning her to the ground. These were no mundane ropes, but fibers woven and blessed for the sole purpose of capturing yokai. Thrashing her head, she snapped and snarled, arching her back to no avail.

As Rin bucked blindly, trying to dislodge the ropes from her back, four warriors held her in place. She had already used up too much of her spiritual energy fighting, and the blessed ropes made it impossible to escape. Eyes rolling in their sockets, the pain blinding her logical brain, Rin continued to fight like an animal in a trap, too dumb to see the hunter approaching. A warrior with a sword marched up to her, and one golden eye focused on him. The reasonable part of her brain told her to pay attention, but the animal part of her was too worried about being trapped and being held down. Rin snapped at him, displaying her pointed canines. It was a final attempt to intimidate him, to stop him, even as he raised up his sword to sever her head from her neck.

Her claws bit into the earth beneath, creating deep hollows as she arched her back, but pushing her flesh into the ropes only made the burning worse. Smoke rose up off her, and the air stank of burning flesh. Her wild gaze met that of her executioner. There was no escaping death. A sudden calm came over her, as the sudden realization struck her: there was no use fighting. It had been such a long pointless struggle. Even before they had captured her, she had been hurting for so long. Perhaps in death she would find peace. Rin closed her eyes as the sword fell, resigned to her fate. *Wait for me Hikaru, I will join you in my next life.*

Metal clanged, followed by a thud. Rin opened her eyes and stared into the blank gaze of her would-be executioner, blood splattered across his face and his expression frozen in shock. The tip of a sword poked through his gut, his hands wrapped around the blade. His head turned down slowly to see where he had been pierced through. His eyes were wide with incredulity. Then he tilted to the side, joining his sword which had already fallen to the ground. Sound rushed over her, as if she had been trapped in a bubble of silence just seconds before. The remaining warriors who had surrounded her now had their backs to her as they fought a multitude of figures dressed all in black.

One of the men holding onto the ropes keeping her in place was attacked by a man in black who had broken through the ring of warriors. The man gave up holding the rope to defend himself. Seeing her chance, Rin threw her weight in that direction and pulled the three remaining warriors along with her. They stumbled forward, unprepared for her sudden escape, and Rin shrugged her way out of the ropes. She turned on the remaining warriors with a growl and a flash of fire from her several tails which whipped around her like a maelstrom. She did not have the energy to shoot fire at them. As it was she could hardly stand up but they didn't know that. When she inched closer toward them, they backed away, spears pointed in front of them.

To her left, whether they had intended it or not, the black warriors had left a space in which she could escape. Rin snarled once more at the warriors before fleeing through her exit. The fox in her wanted to run to the forest, find a hole to hide in, and lick her wounds until the fighting was over.

But once she was out of the thick of the fighting, her head cleared and the animal impulses became distant urges while her logical mind took over. She remembered now why she had been encircled in the first place. They were trying to save Suzume. That had been Kaito's plan. Rin tilted her head back as she searched the sky for the dragon but could not see him anywhere. The storm he had called down was starting to dissipate, the blue sky peeking out from behind the clouds.

The dragon must have gotten Suzume out. *But why hadn't he come for me?*

The stench of blood clung to her fur, her blood and the blood of others. Their plan had failed. And if Rin had fallen into an ambush perhaps the dragon had as well. Fear grabbed her by the throat. She had to find him. Though her spiritual sensitivity was nothing like Kaito's given the circumstances, she should be able to feel his energy. As she spread out her senses, she could not feel Kaito. Something had gone wrong.

Fatigue weighed heavy on her shoulders as she wound her way through the camp. Without being able to sense his spiritual energy, she had to rely on her nose. She caught his scent faintly on the wind. She was not even certain if he was still there, or had been there, but she could not leave not without being certain. As she followed the trail, the scent became stronger but it was weaker than normal. Pushing down the fear, she picked up her pace and ran deeper into the maze of tents.

"What are you doing? You have to get out of here," an unfamiliar voice said from behind her.

Rin spun in place, teeth bared and a growl rumbling in her throat. The man in black stood a few feet behind her, his hands up in surrender.

"Who are you?"

"You need to escape before they see you here."

Rin narrowed her eyes at him. The man was dressed the same as the figures who had saved her, and just the same as the men who had attacked them in the forest. *This is the man who has a piece of Kazue's soul inside him?* He might be an ally, or this might all be an elaborate trap. She wasn't willing to take the risk.

"I'm not leaving without the dragon," Rin rumbled at the man.

"It's too dangerous. Escape while you can."

"Are you trying to stop me?"

"I don't even know why I saved you..." he said after an overlong pause.

"Whatever reason, I thank you but I have to protect my master." There was a twisting feeling in her gut. This wasn't right. Something about him felt very familiar but she couldn't waste time here.

"Do you know me?" he asked her as she turned to leave. His eyes were burrowing into hers.

"Perhaps you knew me in a past life," she said as a way of goodbye before running in the direction of the dragon.

When she found the dragon, he was not alone. On one side of Kaito she saw Hisato, whose arms were outstretched, while on the other Suzume's entire face was illuminated by a massive ball of fire she held in front of herself. The flickering flame she held cast her face into relief giving her an almost manic quality. She could see Suzume's intention written on her face. Rin lunged for the priestess just moments before she unleashed the ball of flame, knocking her aside and sending the ball of fire careening into the sky.

"What do you think you're doing?" Rin growled at Suzume who she had pinned beneath her.

For a moment Suzume's eyes lacked focus. She stared upward without speaking for a few moments before she shook her head.

"Why did you stop me? I was about to end this!" she snarled.

"All you were going to end was your life," Rin growled.

Just then something slammed into her hindquarter, which burned and radiated through her entire body making it pulse with pain. She turned her head to see the masked man, eyes glowing green behind his mask holding an ofuda in his hand.

The sudden change in motive was surprising, but Rin did not hesitate to protect herself. She reared back and opened her mouth. A ball of flame burst from deep in her throat, and it turned the paper ofuda he was throwing at her to ash. As the ball of flame careened toward him, he leaped out of the way, but a stray spark caught on the black hood he wore to conceal his face. The flame caught and spread, forcing him to remove his mask.

He tossed the mask aside and then looked up at Rin. When their eyes met, Rin froze in place. She knew that face, but it could not be possible.

"Even though you failed to do as I asked, Makato, I will share with you a secret from your past," Hisato said, drawing everyone's attention toward him.

Makato, the masked man, was staring at Hisato as if he was a man starved. Everything seemed to have gone very still around them.

Hisato turned toward Rin and smiled, before looking at Makato once more.

"In your past life, you had a wife."

Rin growled a warning. This had to be a trick, this man's face, it was all an illusion perpetrated by this monster before her. She lunged for Hisato, intent on stopping him before he could weave more of his hateful spells.

But as she leaped through the air toward him, dark vines rose up from the ground, wrapping around her body trapping her in place. Rin snarled and looked to the man. It was difficult to look at him, his resemblance so uncanny. He held his hands up, it was his vines which left her suspended in air.

Hisato laughed. "How wonderful. So you recognize him, do you?" Hisato said to Rin. Then to Makato he said, "Makato, Rin is your wife in your past life. I wonder what the dragon will think of this."

"Do you think I am going to fall for that?"

"Don't believe me? Just look into his eyes, look at his abilities."

"That is because he has a piece of Kazue's soul. Suzume has inhuman abilities because of it."

"Ah, but is that really the only reason?" Hisato asked, tapping his chin thoughtfully.

"Enough." Suzume stepped forward, hands burning with flames. "We end this here."

Rin wriggled against the bindings that held her. Her eyes darted around looking for anything she could use to save Suzume from herself. But there was no magic solution that leaped out at her.

"I see you've made your choice. I hope you're happy with your decision," Hisato said to Suzume. Then to Makato, "My gift to you." He nodded toward Rin. "I hope you find the answers your searching for and you remember my offer."

Suzume threw a ball of fire in Hisato's direction but as she did he leaped backward, out of reach. With a wave of his hand he opened a portal and stepped through, leaving not a trace behind.

Sixteen

Something had a hold of Suzume's heart and it was squeezing. The feeling was so foreign for a moment she thought her own power had turned against her and was trying to destroy her from the inside. For a few moments she felt as if she was floating outside her body, completely detached from reality. This couldn't be real. It had to be a nightmare. Had she really almost killed herself to stop Hisato?

Suzume clenched her hand into a fist, pressing it against her chest as if she could contain the fire within her just by sheer force of will. Before today she had only an inkling of the power that dwelled inside her, but what had just overcome her was uncontrolled raw power. The feeling was intoxicating. She was fortunate Hisato had run away, because she might have gone through with it. And what if she had? Would this all be over or would she be dead?

"Are you hurt?"

Suzume blinked. She had been so lost in her own thoughts she had forgotten where she was. The power continued to tingle against her skin but that immense wave of sensation was fading now. Everything seemed dull in its wake, as if colors had lost some of their vibrancy. The world was gray and muted now. All that was left to her was a craving for more of that power. Naoki stood in front of her, absorbing her entire field of vision, his expression devoid of emotion.

"I'm fine." She stumbled over the words, for some reason her tongue felt too big for her mouth. She was a stranger in her own body.

She blinked again and turned her head to take in her surroundings. Tsuki had Makato's arm twisted behind his back and Rin had been freed of Makato's vines. She was kneeling beside Kaito who was still unconscious on the ground. And now she realized she had forgotten all about him.

Suzume's chest constricted as she turned to look at Kaito where he laid on the ground. This couldn't be Kaito. It was not possible for him to be injured, he was supposed to be impervious. *It's a joke. He's going to leap up the moment I show any concern for him and tease me for worrying for him.* But his head lolled unnaturally to the side, and he looked more like a broken doll than a powerful dragon.

"This isn't funny," Suzume shouted at Kaito.

Rin looked at Suzume with a frown. "Do you really think this is a joke?"

Suzume tried to scoff but it was more of a slurred huff. She took one shambling step forward, preparing to prove that Kaito was playing a prank. Her head spun suddenly and the ground circled beneath her feet. Suzume stopped, throwing her arms out to catch her balance. It did no good as her legs buckled beneath her. Naoki caught her before she could complete her fall, and held her upright by propping her against his shoulder. Normally she would have protested this sort of treatment but an overwhelming fatigue halted any argument in its tracks.

Through heavy-lidded eyes she watched as the group gathered together. Fractured conversation floated over her and around her as she struggled to focus on what they were saying.

"This is bad..."

"...do we go?"

"...Protecting her..."

Suzume's eyes fluttered open. She had not even realized she had fallen asleep. Someone's arms were wrapped around her and the wind was blowing through her hair. Kaito had probably given up on his joke and was carrying her away from Daiki's army.

"I don't need you to carry me..." she mumbled, trailing off before sinking into unconsciousness once more.

Suzume woke a few seconds later to an almost uncomfortable heat on her face. Sunlight pressed against her eyelids, trying to claw its way into her eyes. She flung her arm over her face to shield herself from the sun. *I'll just lie here for a few more minutes.*

She lay somewhere between waking and sleeping before jerking awake. The derelict building she found herself in stank of mold and was decorated liberally with spider webs. A few feet away to her right was a broken Komainu, a stone shrine guardian, who was missing a paw. His partner on the left was missing his head, and the base of both pedestals was overgrown with weeds. It would seem this was an abandoned shrine, but being near any shrine building made her uneasy. Suzume had a reputation with shrines. But it was unlikely she'd awaken anything here. This place was in a serious state of decay. The beams of the roof were overgrown with moss, and the support columns were riddled with termite holes.

Head throbbing, Suzume leaned on the creaking support beam and climbed to her feet. She shuffled outside to where Akira and Naoki were standing over a fire speaking in low tones. A few feet behind them Makato was tied to a tree, his head slumped forward.

"Where are we?" Suzume asked, rubbing her aching head.

Akira's head jerked in Suzume's direction. "Oh, you're awake?" There was an odd note to her voice as she scanned Suzume up and down.

Suzume frowned at her but ignored it. "Where's Kaito and Rin?" she asked, resisting the urge to look around for them. *Kaito won't let me live it down that I collapsed after using my power, again.*

Akira and Naoki shared a look before Akira said to Suzume, "We were going to wait to talk to you about that."

Suzume forced a laugh but it sounded more hysterical than anything. "What did he have to give you to play along with this joke?"

"This is serious," Akira said, her ruby lips were pulled into a thin line and Suzume felt her stomach flop.

"Really?" Suzume asked and gave into her impulse to look for Kaito. This had to be a joke. And as much as she didn't want to be the butt of it, she couldn't stop the rising panic from overriding her better judgment.

Akira placed a hand on Suzume's shoulder. "Kaito was seriously injured by the priests. Their holy energy has invaded his body and the wounds will not heal..."

That same fire was building inside her again, bubbling up, coming to the surface unbidden. She thought of what Hisato said. Were these Kazue's feelings trying to consume her? But she pushed that thought away. *I can do something; the power is inside me. I felt it. What if I could heal him?*

"I think it's time we leave the dragon behind," Akira said.

Suzume jerked her shoulder away from Akira's hand. "What are you talking about? I'm not going anywhere," Suzume snarled.

"Look at yourself, you can't even control your power right now because you're worried about him."

"This has nothing to do with the dragon."

Akira shook her head. "We hoped if we could bring you closer together it would awaken Kazue's memories but it seems you're only destined to go down the same path of destruction as Kazue and Kaito."

"I'm not Kazue. I can heal his wounds." Suzume slammed her hand against her chest as if to prove her point.

Akira shook her head. "I don't think that's a very good idea."

"Where is he?" she asked, ignoring Akira's words.

Naoki pointed at a pathway that led behind the building where Suzume had been sleeping, toward the main shrine building. Suzume marched toward it. As she approached the dilapidated shrine building where Kaito was, some of her initial confidence began to wane.

Rin was kneeling beside Kaito on the decaying floorboards that were threaded with weeds poking up from underneath. Shafts of sunlight fell through the holes in the roof onto Kaito's unconscious face. His haori was torn open, and broken shafts of arrows remained embedded in his flesh. Blood soaked the fabric of his clothing and a trickle of blood was oozing from a wound on his shoulder.

Her heart stuttered in her chest and she spoke without thinking. "Why haven't you removed the arrows?" Suzume demanded to the group at large.

Rin looked up, noticing Suzume's approach for the first time. "I can't touch them without getting burned." She upturned her palms to reveal angry red markings on her skin.

Akira had followed Suzume, and surveyed him from a distance.

"The holy energy the priest used will purify any yokai who touches it. While the arrows remain in him, his wounds cannot heal."

"How do we stop it then?" Suzume snapped.

"You remove the arrows and hope it's enough," Akira turned her hands up in a gesture that said 'what can I do.'

Suzume inched closer to Kaito, hovering over him. Several arrow shafts marked his torso, including one dangerously close to his heart. The energy rolling off of him was chaotic, and when she got close the pressure of his spiritual energy weighed down upon her and brought sparks along her skin. One stray spark flew off her and landed on Kaito, singeing his clothing.

She took a step backward. If she wasn't careful, she was going to accidentally burn him. *How can I do this without burning him?*

Suzume looked to Akira, who was staring at her with a mild expression, but she had the feeling she was not going to get any help there. With great trepidation, she knelt down beside Kaito. Being this close to him, she felt the clash of their powers. She had to get it under control before she did more harm. Suzume closed her eyes, remembering Akira's training on visualizing the multitude of damns that controlled her energy. She'd never been very good at it, however, and even after several minutes of focusing she had not managed to shut off all the energy channels.

Figuring it was good enough, she reached for the least threatening arrow shaft. The one on his shoulder. Suzume wrapped her hand around it and pulled. When she did Kaito's eyes flew open, bright and blue as the sky, and they focused on her, pleading without words for her to end his misery. His back arched as he jerked his head away, his entire body moving into convulsions.

Suzume fell backward, accidentally pulling the arrow out with her. But she remained clutching the arrow and panting for breath as the energy in the arrow pulsed against her skin, and she felt that same tingling sensation she had felt when she was fighting Hisato. Kazue's power called to her, luring her with the promise of greater power. She could almost taste it.

Rin held out her hand to help Suzume up.

"Are you ok?" She asked.

Suzume took her offered hand but when they touched something sparked between them and Rin pulled her hand back as if burned.

"What was that?" Suzume asked her.

"You've absorbed some of the spiritual energy in the shaft," Akira said. Her brows were knitted together as she looked at Suzume who continued to cling to the arrow shaft. Suzume tossed it aside, not wanting to seem greedy for power, but her eyes kept drifting toward it.

The next arrow was removed with similar results, but Suzume was prepared for the backlash this time. But with each successful removal, Kaito's power grew stronger and lashed out harder. He roared in pain and ice crept through the building. Fingers of frost crept over everything. Suzume's own fire sparked in response and when she reached for the second to last arrow flames erupted from her hand. It singed the shaft and nearly burned Kaito before she jerked her hand back at the last minute.

Suzume got up to stretch. Kaito was writhing in agony and the constant press of his spiritual power clashing against hers was wearing her thin.

Akira came up next to her. "You don't have to do this," she said.

Suzume glared at her. "Then why don't you do something to help?" Her nerves were frayed.

"I can't. Only someone with Kazue's soul can stop it."

Suzume looked back to Kaito. Two arrows remained, and if she could just tame the fire within her for a little bit longer he would be safe. But the fire kept growing with each arrow she absorbed, giving her more of the spiritual energy within. She should stop, try and find another way. But fighting Hisato had made a craving in her and she was looking for her next fix.

"Then I'm going to finish this."

Suzume went back to Kaito, kneeling at his side. Sweat beaded his forehead and his chest was smeared with blood. The wounds from the other arrows she had removed had not healed yet and continued to bleed. The second to last arrow was embedded in his stomach, she knew it would hurt him but she had to remove it. Suzume wrapped both hands around it, and as soon as she touched it a flood of spiritual energy from the arrow hit her like a punch to the gut. Shortly after that fire exploded out of her and in the same instant Kaito's own energy burst forth to shield him from her flames. The ensuing collision sent Suzume flying backward. She landed hard on the ground a few feet away, hitting her shoulder.

Suzume lay on the ground, covered in sweat and Kaito's blood. Despite it she wanted to continue, though her body was tired, her skin thrummed with the power she absorbed, and she only wanted more.

"You have to stop," Akira said, placing herself in front of Suzume.

"You have to try," Rin said imploring Suzume with her eyes from where she sat kneeling at Kaito's side.

"She's going to kill him at this rate. She cannot even control her spiritual power." Akira pointed at Suzume who was sparking with flames.

"I can do it," Suzume lied, even as the fire increased in power, spreading across her body, turning her into an inferno. When Akira looked at her, her eyes were wide.

"Your aura it's changed..." she said.

"What do you mean?" Suzume asked.

"We don't have time for this. Kaito is running out of time if we don't get those remaining arrows out."

"Just let me try."

"No, Akira is right. You're only going to hurt yourself and him."

"Just watch me." Suzume approached Kaito's body, but as she got closer the fire took on a mind of its own, spreading out tendrils that reached for Kaito and slammed into his body.

He cried out and thrashed, going into convulsions. Suzume stumbled backward and away from Kaito but even as she did, the fire continued to burn him from the inside.

"What did you do?" Rin shouted.

Suzume was staring at Kaito's thrashing body. Trapped inside her own mind she could only watch as her fire continued to burn him, like a wild inferno.

"We need the priest. Only he can save him now."

"How can we trust him?" Tsuki asked, taking control of the body he shared with his sister. "He's the one who made him this way."

"We don't have any other choice."

Seventeen

"I do not have that sort of power," was Makato's reply when they woke him from the sleeping spell Akira had put him under. It had been an impulsive suggestion on Rin's part. A small part of her was holding onto the hope that what Hisato had said was true, and this was the reincarnation of her husband Hikaru. But she also feared letting her own desire lead her into a trap. What were the odds that Hikaru's body had also been reincarnated with a piece of Kazue's soul? Hisato wanted to drive a wedge in their group by sowing doubt among them. Well this particular trick was aimed directly at Rin.

"This is a waste of time," Suzume said, gesturing back in the direction where Kaito's unconscious body remained.

Rin ignored Suzume and knelt down in front of Makato. "If what Hisato says is true and you are the reincarnation of..." she trailed off. She couldn't bring herself to say his name out loud. Not to the face of a man who shared such a striking resemblance to her husband. He looked the same as the last day she had seen him, as if no time had passed at all.

Makato met her gaze with a strange sort of intensity. There was no real recognition there, but a hunger to find the truth as if he could find all the answers to life's mysteries there in her eyes. "And what if I am not him? What happens to me?"

"He doesn't want to do it. We should try something else," Suzume said and took a few steps toward Kaito. Naoki stepped in her way, preventing her from trying again. The fire had not died down, and she continued to flicker faintly. Suzume's power was growing more volatile every day and Rin worried what would happen if they left it unchecked for much longer.

"This is your test. Save the dragon. Prove to me that you are him."

"Why should I help you? How do I know this isn't a trick?" Makato asked, his eyes narrowed at her.

She could only imagine what lies Hisato had told him to lure him into his web. But despite her better judgment she wanted to believe he could save Kaito. If it was his arrows that had done this, then this was his chance at redeeming himself.

"You've been searching to find out who you are," Rin said holding his gaze without flinching.

His eyes were wide as he stared back at her and in an awed whisper he said, "Yes."

"Everything leads back to the dragon. Let him die and you'll never learn the truth."

His eyes drifted past Rin toward the far building where Kaito rested. Distrust was visible in his gaze, but also a hunger, a desperation for the truth.

He deliberated for a moment, and Rin held her breath hoping she had not misjudged him. After a few moments of tense silence, he nodded his head and said, "I'll do it."

Tsuki untied him with a shake of his head. Naoki's hands were resting on the blades of his swords. Neither of them trusted him. But this man had saved her, and if he was Hikaru's reincarnation, then she had to believe he was on their side. Perhaps he had been led astray by Hisato as Suzume almost was, but if he could learn to trust them, then she knew he would become a powerful ally in their fight against Hisato. Suzume took the lead to where the dragon lay.

As they approached Kaito's sleeping place, they found him drenched in sweat and blood. Suzume's footsteps faltered as they got closer, and Makato mirrored her steps as well. He stood for a few moments surveying Kaito's unconscious body.

"If you hurt him, you won't leave here alive," Suzume growled at him, doing her best impression of the dragon.

The dragon's limbs were thrashing as he went into convulsions once more. Rin resisted the urge to grab onto Makato's shoulders and beg him to save her master. This was his chance to prove himself, to the group and to her. If he could save Kaito then she would know for certain that he was Hikaru's reincarnation.

The priest stared down at Kaito for a long moment, as if he was not certain what to do. Then very slowly he sunk onto his knees to kneel beside the dragon. His hands hovered over the Dragon's body, following the flow of his spiritual energy. And then cautiously, he reached for the arrow shaft which was embedded in Kaito's abdomen. With one hand braced on Kaito's stomach and the other around the shaft of the arrow, he pulled.

Kaito's eyes rolled back in his head as he arched his back, screaming in pain. His energy was pouring out of him, strong enough to level even the strongest yokai. Rin threw her arm up to shield herself from the blast, but in the same moment a glowing green light surrounded her and the others, shielding them from the onslaught of Kaito's intense aura.

"Stand back," Makato said before turning his attention back to the dragon. The only arrow that remained was the one inches from Kaito's heart. Makato pressed his hands together and made a quick chant, which weaved around him raising up vines that anchored his body in place before he reached for the final arrow. He yanked but the arrow would not budge at first.

"What is going on?" Suzume shouted. With the unleashing of Kaito's spiritual power, a wind had picked up and a storm was gathering outside, called down by the outpouring of his energy.

Rin did not have a chance to answer. The swirl of energy stole the breath from her lungs and even Makato's barrier could not protect them. Her hair whipped into her face and she had to brush it back to watch as Makato's hands, glowing with green light, laid on Kaito's chest. They almost seemed to sink into his flesh, and suddenly Kaito's entire body was illuminated with green light. Kaito's rolling eyes closed, perhaps losing consciousness once more from the pain. And the final arrow came out.

Makato too was knocked back by the force of this blow, but he was saved from falling by vines that burst from the ground and cradled him. Once the final arrow was out, the wind died and the crushing pressure of Kaito's spiritual energy abated.

Suzume stared at Kaito for a moment, her mouth hung open in shock. Rin crept closer to Kaito. His wounds continued to bleed, but his breathing had returned to a steady rhythm once again.

Makato remained a few feet away, staring at his hands as if they belonged to someone else. As Rin approached him, he raised his head.

"You knew the entire time?" he asked her.

Rin's eyes darted across his face. She had dreamed of this moment so many times since he had been taken from her. When she spoke her voice was thick and cracked. "Hi—Hikaru, had that same ability." She placed a hand over her mouth to prevent a sob from slipping out.

Makato looked to Rin and then back to Kaito. His brow was furrowed in thought. "I know this name. Was that my name before?" he looked back up to Rin, desperation in his eyes. "Who was he?"

"Hikaru was my husband, and I think you're his reincarnation."

He absorbed the information in silence, unlike all of the scenarios she had imagined over the years they were apart. He did not open his arms in instant recognition. Instead he just nodded his head.

"Can you, tell me more about him... me?"

Rin was happy to oblige. She left Kaito to rest, and she and Makato adjourned to a nearby campfire where she spun out their story. Makato listened to the story of Hikaru and Rin's first meeting, which involved a bumbled rescue attempt by Hikaru. Rin laughed, recalling the good times, and grew wistful thinking of the nearly five hundred years she had shared with Hikaru, before he had died suddenly. They had promised one another long ago, that when he died she would find him in the next life and start over together. But she held back from sharing this with Makato. There would be time for that later. He kept his hands folded in his lap, staring into the flames in front of him as she spoke. He did not laugh when Rin told a funny story, nor did he gasp at the exciting parts. When she was finished he did not say anything at all but kept on staring forward.

"Do you have questions?" Rin asked hopefully.

He shook his head slowly. "It's a lot to take in. I've been looking for a long time trying to figure out who I am..."

"But?" she asked before biting her lip to keep herself from saying everything she wanted to say. They would need to take things slow. She had never met any reincarnations before. The closest to a reincarnation she had met had been Suzume, and she hated to be compared to Kazue.

"You seem very nice and you clearly loved your husband a lot, but I don't know..."

Before she could ask him more, Tsuki called out in a sing-song voice, "Morning, sleepy head."

Rin's head perked up and saw the dragon approaching them. He had awoken at last. He was scowling as he approached and there was an odd hobble to his normally powerful, confident stride. *He must be mad that I wasn't there when he woke. I shouldn't have abandoned my post.* But she had been so excited to find Hikaru — correction, Makato — that she'd forgotten all about the dragon.

When he saw Rin analyzing him, the dragon stood up straighter.

Rin stood up to greet him. "Come sit down, your wounds—"

"Where is Suzume?" he snarled, cutting her off before she could finish.

Makato had jumped to his feet, either fearing Kaito still or sensing the tension in the air.

Tsuki looked around, dramatically searching before turning to Kaito with an exaggerated shrug. "Not here."

Kaito balled his hand tighter into a fist. She knew his temper and how protective he was of Suzume, especially after their disastrous mission to get information. He must be worried about her. Not that he would admit that aloud. Rin inserted herself between Tsuki and Kaito holding out her hands to placate the dragon more than anyone else. Before things got out of hand she had to calm the dragon, if only for his own good.

"I can see that," he said through gritted teeth. His words lacked a certain power that Rin could not quite place. His injuries must have taken a greater toll on him than he was letting on. He should be resting rather than snapping orders and making demands.

"I think she went off into the forest," Tsuki said, continuing to press the dragon's buttons.

Rin shot him a quelling look but he only grinned back at her.

"She'll be fine. Naoki is with her I think." At least she hoped. The legendary swordsman was nowhere to be seen either.

What she said did not seem to calm him. It only seemed to agitate him further. And it occurred to her that Kaito had only just recently gotten into a fight with Naoki. Everyone was on Kaito's bad side right now, that was except for her. For now. If she couldn't calm him, she might find herself on the wrong side as well.

"I'll go and look for her then," Rin said in an attempt to appease him. But it seemed nothing would calm the dragon and he turned on Makato.

"Who is this?" Kaito jabbed his chin in his direction.

Makato's eyes drifted to a sword lying on the ground a few feet away.

"Don't even think about it. I'll separate your head from your shoulders before you take your first step."

Makato dropped his arms to his side.

"He's an ally. The one who Suzume found that also has a piece of Kazue's soul inside him."

Kaito stomped over to him and grabbed him by his haori. Normally he would have lifted him off the ground or worse. But Rin suspected that his injuries prevented him from exerting his usual strength.

"So you're the bastard who tried to kill me? I'm glad you're here. It saves me the trouble of having to find you."

Makato grabbed onto Kaito's arms and green light flared under his fingers, scorching Kaito who dropped him and stepped away with a snarl on his lips. Rin threw herself between them, placing her hands on each of their shoulders. Then to Kaito she said, "He saved your life."

"Right after he tried to kill me. How convenient."

The priest seemed unafraid of the dragon. His eyes had shifted color, from brown to green. His confident stance was different than Hikaru's who was more humble and introverted. "You're right, I was the one who sealed you."

Kaito swung around Rin before she could stop him, attempting to land a punch on Makato's jaw, but the priest dodged the strike with ease. Kaito stumbled forward and Rin took a step toward him to help but caught herself at the last moment. Kaito would not want attention drawn to any weakness.

"You should have killed me instead." He attempted to rush Makato again, but the priest moved too quickly for the dragon and he went careening past him. The move exposed his back to Makato who struck him hard, bringing Kaito to his knees.

Rin cried out, but the dragon held his hand up to silence her. She placed her hand over her mouth before any other sound could escape.

Makato stood over him, but instead of another devastating blow, he held out his hand for Kaito to take. This was more like her husband Hikaru. "I tried to kill you but that was before I realized who you are to me," Makato said.

Kaito knocked his hand aside as he climbed to his feet.

"What is the meaning of this," Kaito snarled at Rin.

"He's Hikaru's reincarnation and he has a piece of Kazue's heart inside him."

Kaito shook his head. "Do you take me for a fool? This is clearly one of Hisato's tricks." He gestured toward Makato.

"He has Hikaru's ability to heal. That can't be an illusion."

"You're letting your desire cloud your better judgment. He's not the man you loved." His words stung. Of all people Kaito should understand what it meant to love someone who was mortal. What it meant to have a second chance with the person you loved.

"Just because you cannot forgive Kazue does not mean I have to do the same." She spoke out of anger but the look in Kaito's eyes exposed just how deep her words had hurt. She had always been on his side, but this time she had to draw the line.

"Is that how you feel?" he said in a low growl.

Rin regretted her words almost as soon as she spoke them. She did not want to make an enemy of Kaito. There had to be a way to make him understand. Before she could reply, however, a scream ripped through the air. Tsuki leaped up and Kaito's head swiveled in the direction of the sound.

"That was Suzume."

Eighteen

Suzume retreated into the forest once she knew Kaito was breathing and this entire ordeal was over. She needed her own room to breathe, to sort out everything that had happened. The flames were starting to die down now, but her mind kept wandering back to that feeling, that craving for Makato's energy. While he had been trying to pull the last two arrows out she had felt herself leaning forward as if she could absorb some of that energy by proxy. Even now if she closed her eyes she could imagine that feeling, that rush that sent her spine tingling and her head feeling comfortably numb.

Was this what Kazue felt? If it was, she understood why Kazue had gone to such great lengths to get more of it. The feeling was addictive. Just thinking about the promise of power, her fingers tingled with sensation and flames danced along her fingertips.

As she pushed aside stray branches they caught on fire. Suzume stopped to stare at the dancing flames mesmerized by them. Fire had always had a certain draw to her. But knowing what she could do with that power, the unlocked potential within her it was proving to be an even greater draw than she had imagined. Suzume turned her hands over to stare at her palms. A small candle wick size flame flickered there. Could she gain control over her flame, the way Makato had gained control over his own power?

Maybe I should ask him to teach me? But could she trust him to teach her? No one did anything without a price and considering he had been previously teamed up with Hisato, that meant he had one too.

Suzume pressed on into the forest, searching for a place where she could test out her theory. As she walked she brushed her fingers against brush, leaving smoldering fires in her wake. The more fires she set, the more excited she felt for the potential of her new discovery. There wasn't much time before Kaito or the others came looking for her and she wanted to confirm this alone. Finally she found the spot she was looking for. Far enough away from the shrine that she wouldn't accidentally break any seals, with just enough kindling to not start an out of control blaze. The last thing she needed was to set the forest on fire and trap herself within.

It was a space dominated by boulders, sparse grass, and a few dead trees, previously destroyed by a long-ago forest fire. Suzume climbed onto the largest boulder. It showed signs of past fires, black ash smudged against the granite. This place had called out to her, she wasn't sure how she knew it. But once she perched on the highest part of the boulder she felt as if this was exactly where she should be. Tilting her head back, she let the sun warm her face for a few minutes. *Maybe I should do the breathing exercises Akira taught me.*

Suzume shook her head. She hadn't needed to find her center or focus her energy when she fought against Hisato. It had just happened. Suzume held her hand in front of her. It took little concentration before a flame erupted in the palm of her hand. Suzume smiled to herself, looking at the fire there. *I did it! And it didn't take hours to create.*

Suzume thrust a triumphant fist into the air. She knew the power was in her all along. She couldn't wait to prove to Kaito how powerful she had become. Since she was alone and wanting to practice this new achievement, she hurled the ball of flame at a nearby burnt tree. It collided with the trunk of a tree, splintering the remains of the tree, raining embers on the ground.

Suzume whooped in celebration, she'd even hit her mark. *This is great! I wonder what else I can do...* She looked around the clearing, searching for her next target when she heard a rustling in the bushes nearby.

All her senses were suddenly on high alert. Suzume held up her next ball of flame in front of her, ready to hurl it at whatever yokai was coming her way.

"I know you're there. Show yourself."

To her surprise, it was Naoki who emerged from the shadow of a large tree.

"What are you doing sneaking up on me?" she lowered her ball of flame, but only a little. He claimed he was bound to serve her because of Kazue's heart but that didn't mean he didn't resent her for it and was using this opportunity to solve his predicament.

"If I wanted to sneak up on you I would not have been found," he said before coming to stand before her.

"Why did you follow me out here then?"

He looked at her for a long moment before saying. "Your power is awakening."

"How did you know?"

He pointed to the burning trail she had left in the woods, then to the smoldering trees nearby.

"Alright, you caught me, I was practicing the techniques Akira and Tsuki taught me."

"This does not come from practice."

"Are you saying I'm a liar?" Suzume snapped.

His lack of response had a bigger impact on her than words could. She wanted him to argue or at least call her a liar but he just stared at her.

"What do you want?"

"What I want you are not prepared to give," he said without blinking as he stared back at her.

"Do you ever say what you mean?"

Again her questions were met with silence.

Suzume growled in frustration. "Just leave me alone. You're ruining my good mood."

Naoki turned away from her, staring out at the forest, arms crossed over his chest, making it clear without words that he was not going to leave her alone. Wind blew through the trees, accentuating the silence. She wanted to test the limits of her power, but without knowing what she could do yet she didn't want to make a fool of herself in front of an audience. Albeit a blank and emotionless audience.

"I don't need a bodyguard."

He did not respond.

"As you can see I can control my fire now. I don't need you here."

"That is not what I am here to provide."

"Then tell me why are you here?"

"Kazue found comfort in control. Things she could master brought her peace - I suspect you are much the same."

"One problem: I am not Kazue."

"No, but she is inside you."

Suzume stared at him for a moment before turning back around. She scowled at the back of his head. *What is that supposed to mean?*

"I know everyone expects me to be just like Kazue. But I can choose my own path."

"You must choose it first."

"I am. Isn't that what I just said?" She growled in frustration. Why did everyone have to be so cryptic, everything had to be a lesson to learn or something. She'd made her choice. She was going to get stronger. Finally she was getting a hold of these powers, so couldn't he just be happy for her? Suzume sighed, her fun was spoiled for now and she'd lost interest in practice.

Suzume got to her feet. "Let's head back then."

Naoki followed her lead without comment. She followed the same scorched trail she had made into the forest. Naoki was right, she hadn't exactly hidden herself. The walk, which had seemed to take no time at all on the way in, seemed to take an eternity on the way out.

All that surrounded her were trees in all directions. Her palms itched to burn more, despite her protests otherwise. And she took her frustration out on a nearby rock which she kicked. It skittered across the forest floor before careening into some bushes. The bush shook after she hit it, scaring some forest creature. When the bushes starting rustling, Suzume leaped backward and into Naoki's arms.

Just minutes before she been telling him she didn't need his protection but now all of a sudden, she was clinging to him like a frightened child. Suzume flushed with embarrassment before quickly recovering.

"It's probably a fluffy bunny," Suzume laughed.

Naoki was holding on to the hilt of his sword. The wind whistled through the trees, but other than that there was no sound. A prickling sensation tingled at the back of her neck.

"That is not an animal," Naoki said, pushing Suzume behind him.

In the corner of her eye, something slithered just out of sight between trees. He was right, it definitely was not a bunny rabbit. The flames leaped to her hands, an invitation to prove to the swordsman exactly what choice she had made.

Come and get me then!

The creature burst out from behind a nearby tree and barreled toward them. Its serpentine body twisted around tree trunks, and its hundreds of legs clacked together. Suzume's initial bravery shriveled at seeing her opponent.

Despite her own internal doubts, the blaze of fire she had come to recognize as her laden powers churned in her gut, a small inferno building in her defense. The creature lunged toward them and Naoki blocked it with his sword. But the creature had a long dagger-like stinger on its back end and while Naoki's swords were preoccupied it brought it down, impaling Naoki's shoulder.

He stumbled backward, some sort of poison had come from the creature's stinger and it was eating away at the fabric of his haori. Naoki stumbled and fell face forward onto the ground before the yokai turned back on her, its clacking manacles dripping with an ominous thick green liquid. *Damn it, what do I do?* As the creature inched closer Suzume threw up her arms to shield her face. Its large pincers snapped at her, but before it could clamp down, a shimmering red barrier pushed it back. It reared back, its black head bobbing back and forth, large antennae twitched near the barrier without touching it. *Now let's just hope this barrier holds until I can figure out a way to kill this thing.*

Her built-in defenses, though convenient, gave her little confidence. It was easy to talk a big game when an enemy wasn't around. The barrier encompassed both her and Naoki. She knelt down beside him trying to shake him awake, but he was frozen in place. Whatever poison the centipede used had left him immobile. It was up to her to save them both. She hoped.

Using its long body, the centipede surrounded her. Flames danced along her skin. The combination of her volatile powers and imminent danger turned her into living fire. If she did not get this under control, she would burn away all her energy and then the barrier would fail. Suzume took a few calming breaths, focusing all her energy into creating a ball of flame in her hands. But try as she might, the flames would not do as she ordered them. *Now is not the time. Focus. You can do this.*

The centipede launched itself against the barrier and it flickered beneath the attack. Suzume looked around, desperate for any kind of solution. Her staff was useless against something this big without fire. She knelt down beside Naoki, shaking him.

"Come on, I need you to wake up."

When she touched him, she was struck with an electric feeling, akin to what she had felt when she had fought Hisato with Makato. It didn't knock her off her feet but an idea came into her head. She looked at Naoki, whose blank stare was directed toward a rock on which one of the centipede's back feet rested. Either Naoki was trying to tell her something or she was losing her mind. Because a song rang inside her head, one she'd never heard before but she knew all the words too regardless. *I need something to channel my power into before the song leaves me.* There was no time to question it.

Praying her barrier would hold as she took a desperate leap, she lurched forward pushing her barrier with her, and letting it extend over the rock. The centipede skittered backward as red beams of energy shot off the shield any time it made contact with it. The burst of power was enough to deplete her barrier, which flickered and failed. Swearing under her breath, she jumped over the centipede's body and ran toward a nearby tree with a low hanging branch, rock cradled against her chest.

With a death grip on the rock, she tried focusing on channeling her energy into the stone. She imagined all her flame going into the object, the way Akira had taught her to do with her staff. But redirecting chaotic energy was not that simple when you're being chased by an enormous bug.

She looked over her shoulder to see how close it was and her neck collided with a low hanging branch. Suzume flew backward before landing flat on her back. Gasping for air, she rolled onto her knees and crawled away from her attacker. The centipede caught up, and dozens of legs pattered over the back of her calves. The weight of the giant insect brought her crashing to the ground. Pinned to the ground, the rock trapped beneath her chest, her last hope was to get enough energy into it and somehow direct it at the centipede. Where the centipede touched her, sparks flew and burned its legs, but the creature simply moved a leg out of the way.

With the shifting of the insect's legs however, Suzume managed to roll onto her side, where she came face to face with the dripping mandibles of her attacker. The poison dripping from a fang, fell onto her chest, and burned a hole in the fabric of her haori.

Suzume sang, and even though the words were foreign and her voice was hoarse from running into the tree, she kept on singing. Flames danced over her skin and were redirected to her fingers, coalescing into a burning ball of flame that centered around the stone she had managed to hold onto. As the centipede descended she thrust upward, lodging the burning stone into its mouth. It let out a high-pitched scream as it reared backward and toppled over. Hundreds of spindly legs thrashed about in the air as it attempted and failed to dislodge the stone. The fire spread from its mouth and consumed the creature's entire body. The fire burned bright red, quick and hot and after a few moments all that remained was ash.

Suzume lay where the creature had left her, panting on the ground, massaging her bruised throat. The entire thing had happened in a matter of minutes. Suzume dusted off the ash of the centipede and then crawled over to where Naoki lay.

A voice whispered in her ear. *You've done well.*

"Kazue?" Suzume whispered, her voice croaky but there was no answer.

Nineteen

Footsteps rushed in her direction, but this time they were friendly. To her surprise it wasn't Kaito this time who had led the charge but Tsuki brandishing a sword and a grin. Rin came next, already in her kitsune form, and last followed Kaito.

"We heard you scream..." Tsuki trailed off upon seeing the blackened remains of the centipede. The stone she had used glowed red hot in the smoldering carcass. He dropped his sword to his side and his smile fell.

Kaito pushed his way to the front, and his eyes scanned the area. "Do you have some sort of death wish?"

"I'm fine, thanks for asking," she spat back.

She was right not to worry about him. He was back to his old self again. Maybe he had even faked his injuries to get back at her for lying about being able to talk to Kazue. *Or can I talk to her?* Beyond those three words, Suzume had heard nothing else from Kazue. She mentally shook herself. That was crazy because Kazue was gone. Then she remembered both Naoki and Hisato's warning. Kazue's power would consume her if she let it. *But I am getting control of this power so it shouldn't be a problem, right?*

"What about your arm?" Tsuki nodded toward her. She'd been so focused on survival, she had not realized it when some of the centipede's poison had burned her bicep.

"This is nothing." The last thing she needed was a petty wound to ruin the powerful illusion she was trying to portray. She tried covering it with her hand and winced.

"You call this fine?" Kaito marched over, grabbing her arm and yanking it toward him to inspect it. As he did the fire inside her, which still hadn't quite died away, flared up. Kaito immediately dropped her arm and backed away a step.

"It's nothing," she said, scowling at him.

"And you're a healer now?" He did not reach for her again. Maybe her point was finally getting across. Knowing Kaito though, that likely wasn't the case.

"It could have been worse." Suzume jutted her chin at him and gestured toward the charred remains of her opponent.

"Knowing you, it was probably dumb luck." Kaito crossed his arms over his chest. He didn't even bother to look at the dead yokai.

Suzume prickled at his assumption that she was incapable of taking care of herself. True it hadn't been entirely her own doing. Maybe the only reason she was standing here right now was because Naoki had given her the song she needed to defeat the centipede. And there was the fact that she heard Kazue's voice inside her head again. Which terrified her as well. Not that she was going to tell them that.

"That's what you think! I am getting more powerful all the time."

"You could have fooled me," he said, but it lacked his usual teasing tone. And instead of trying to taunt her into a pointless argument he sounded upset with her. Kaito turned to Rin with a snarl. "Bring her back to camp now."

How can he be mad when he's constantly throwing me into dangerous situations? "I killed that yokai by myself for your information," she shouted after his retreating form, but Kaito did not even bother to look back at her.

Glaring at his retreating back, she thought: *What's wrong with him?*

He had to be in another one of his moods. With his ego, he was likely upset over being injured enough where anyone had to step in. And if Rin had told him Suzume had to help, his pride would have been even more bruised by a human's assistance. Suzume scoffed. *I am getting stronger. He'll see.* They headed back in the direction of the camp. Kaito marched ahead of the rest of them, keeping them at a distance, more than just establishing himself as the leader but more akin to putting a wall between him and the group. *He's definitely in a mood.* In fact, everyone was acting strangely, Rin and Tsuki flanked her on either side, but neither of them were coming very close to her. Perhaps it had something to do with the fact that Suzume continued to flicker with flames. Unlike when she usually used her powers, the fire had not died away this time. Neither had Naoki woken from the poison and he was slung over Rin's back, his blank, staring eyes watching them as they walked. She wished he would wake up, so she could ask him about what had happened to her.

His blank stare made her uneasy and Suzume had to increase her steps to get out of his line of sight. When she arrived back at their makeshift camp at the temple, she saw Makato was once more tied to the tree. At least he was conscious now.

Even though she knew Kaito was in a foul mood, she couldn't let his slight go, and she let her bitterness take the lead. "Why is Makato tied to the tree?"

"Because he cannot be trusted," Kaito snarled with his back still to her.

"He saved your life. Is that how you're going to repay him?" She threw her arm toward Makato dramatically.

"He also tried to kill me. Would you rather I repay him for that?" he half turned but still would not face her entirely.

Perhaps it was petty to argue over a non-issue but she had hoped now that her powers were starting to develop, Kaito would be happy for her at least. But it seemed no matter what she did. He saw her as inferior. "Do you have some sort of problem with humans?"

Kaito turned and rushed toward her, and suddenly he was very close, glaring into her eyes. "Humans cannot be trusted. If you put any faith in them, they will use it against you."

"I'm human. Are you saying you don't trust me?" She met his narrowed gaze.

"Did I ever say I did?"

His words stung more than she thought they would. Without realizing she had been putting a portion of her trust in Kaito. But she should have known better than to put any trust in him.

"Are you going to tie me to that tree next?" she snapped.

"Maybe I should," he said, his voice pitched low and full of intent. If she kept pushing his boundaries, she had no doubt he would.

Something was different about Kaito, though she couldn't put her finger on what. *He isn't blaming me for what happened with Daiki's army is he?*

"Don't even think about it," Suzume raised her sparking hand to show him she was serious.

"Now you're going to challenge me?" he said, baring flat human teeth at her.

"What if I am?" Suzume scowled back at him, she was playing with fire, quite literally. Her power was new and dangerous. She shouldn't be tempting fate by angering the dragon. But it just seemed to be their destiny to continuously butt heads.

Kaito leaned in close to whisper in her ear, "Don't get it twisted. You're nothing to me but a means to an end."

Kaito pulled back, holding her gaze for a moment before he turned on his heel and stalked back toward the shrine building. Suzume stared after him, sputtering.

"You don't mean anything to me either!" A hot blush threatened to climb up her neck but Suzume spun toward Makato and said, "We should untie him, he doesn't deserve to be treated like a dog!" She tossed her hair over her shoulder and resisted the urge to look in Kaito's direction and see if he was listening.

She didn't care what he thought. It wasn't as if she really thought he cared about her. Everything he did was a game meant to make her into the fool. Well she didn't have to listen to *him*.

"Let's see to your wound," Rin said and when she reached for Suzume, the flames flared up in defense and Rin had to jerk her hand away at the last minute to avoid being burned by it.

Rin frowned, looking at Suzume.

Suzume, having no reasonable explanation for why her power was suddenly going haywire decided it was easier to ignore it. "Rin, do you think this is fair?"

Rin looked to Makato and then away, as if it was a crime to just look at him. "It is not my decision."

Suzume growled in frustration. "You can't be serious. This is inhumane."

Suzume looked at Kaito from the corner of her eye. But instead of responding to her, he had disappeared into one of the nearby shrine buildings.

The fire was building now, rising to a crescendo and any moment now she was going to unleash it all and destroy him if she didn't get a hold of it.

"Why do you let him get to you?" Makato asked.

Suzume spun in place, even though she'd almost forgotten he was still tied to the tree. Kaito wasn't watching anymore and her motivation for untying him seemed moot. If she was going to be honest, she didn't trust him either, even if he had saved Kaito's life.

"I don't let him get to me," Suzume scoffed and was preparing to turn away.

"But you're letting your emotions rule your energy. That's dangerous."

Suzume scowled at him. "Are you trying to say you'd know better?"

"I've spent my entire life studying spiritual energy. I think I would know."

Suzume rolled her eyes, pretending his arrogant comment did little to impress her. But she had seen what he was capable of and after what Kaito had said she was more determined than ever to prove to Kaito that she was just as powerful as him, if not more powerful.

"Then maybe you have some idea of how to stop this?" She held up her sparking hands, not really expecting a solution. Akira had tried several different methods to tame Suzume's power and none had worked.

The priest closed his eyes and sang a song under his breath, and the hairs on the back of Suzume's neck raised up on end as power enveloped her like a warm embrace. As his power wrapped around her, she felt the fires that were erupting within her calm for the first time since she'd fought the centipede. Suzume held up her hands, examining them.

"How did you do that?"

"I used my spiritual energy to suppress part of yours," Makato said with a small shrug.

"How is that even possible?"

He looked up at her, a little sheepish "It's an advanced technique, and a bit difficult to explain."

"Try me." She leaned in closer to him, in a way she would have done back at the palace when she was trying to flirt with a would-be suitor or trying to draw information from a reluctant ally. It was somewhat awkward when the object of your flirting was tied to a tree however.

He blushed and his gaze flickered toward Rin who was frowning in their direction. It wasn't the first time Suzume had felt that sort of gaze on her back. There were plenty of jealous woman back at the palace who envied her power and position, many of them Suzume would have called friends to their faces. Whoever Makato was to Rin, it didn't matter to Suzume. Because she could see what sort of asset Makato could be to her now.

Makato cleared his throat and then said, "Well the flow of spiritual energy goes through different gateways that all control different things and..."

Suzume lost interest not long after, and watched Rin from the corner of her eye. The kitsune disappeared in the direction of where Kaito had gone off to pout. Most likely to tell the dragon she was fraternizing with the enemy. As Makato prattled on, Suzume prepared for Kaito to come over in a jealous rage and break them apart. As the minutes ticked by, and Kaito didn't arrive and Rin didn't return, Suzume started to wonder if there really was something wrong with Kaito.

Instead of a charging dragon, Akira approached them after a quick look over her shoulder.

"I couldn't help but overhear what you were telling Suzume," Akira said with a charming smile.

Suzume scowled at Akira, wondering what she was getting at but she held her tongue. Akira had kept her secret from Kaito, she owed her that much at least.

"Would you know how to separate two souls from one another?"

Makato frowned and thought for a moment. "I did not even know it was possible to combine two souls."

Akira gave a delicate shrug. "My brother and I are proof that it is true." For a moment half of Akira's face was taken up by Tsuki's who was grinning out at him.

Makato did not seem surprised by this, only curious, and he leaned closer to inspect them. "Fascinating," he said under his breath.

"If you can help us regain our separate bodies, we can help convince the dragon to untie you."

"You're going to convince Kaito?" Suzume said with raised brows.

Akira smiled at her with a hint of condescension. "Well that's where you come in, Suzume."

Suzume threw up her hands. "We're not exactly on good terms right now."

"We don't need the dragon to make decisions any longer."

"Are you crazy? He'll kill you for saying that," Suzume hissed and glanced over her shoulder in the direction where Kaito was hidden.

"The dragon cannot harm us anymore. His power has been sealed. And I know by whom." Akira turned to look at Makato

The priest stared back at her, unblinking.

"What are you talking about?" She looked between the both of them searching for answers.

"I had to do it to protect him from Hisato. He ordered me to kill him but I could not..."

As if she needed any more proof that Makato had a piece of Kazue's soul inside him, it seemed Kazue's feelings influenced even him.

"Then what you're saying is Kaito is basically mortal?"

Makato nodded. "I can reverse it."

Suzume held up her hand. "No, let's wait on that." *This will teach him for thinking I am not as powerful as him. Let him stew in his own weakness for a while. Then and only then will I let Makato return him to normal.*

TWENTY

Pain wrapped around his torso, like a thorny vine digging into his flesh, compressing his lungs and forcing the air out of him. Kaito had never experienced pain quite like this. No stranger to battle wounds, he had fought humans before and other than priests and priestesses, they were no match for him. Even priests and priestesses had been minor annoyances in his prime. Humans were inferior in all ways. But this pain was far greater than anything he had ever felt before. Even the smallest movement tugged against the tender skin surrounding the numerous wounds he had taken. His skin felt stretched tight over his bones and itched to a maddening degree. *Why have my wounds not healed yet?* They should have healed by now.

Kaito reached for his spiritual energy, thinking to draw upon that deep well of power to speed up the healing process. But just as when he had tried to access it when he first woke up, he felt nothing. It was as if he had been struck blind, mute, and deaf all at once. Because his spiritual energy was more than just power, it was the life force that flowed through all things. The only other time he had felt this disconnection was when Kazue had sealed him. He had sworn to himself that never again would he feel that. He'd rather die.

But his attempt to connect came up with nothing. The ebb and flow of energy, the warmth of life was gone.

The injuries he had sustained must have drained his spiritual energy while healing, that was all. He would be back to normal in no time.

Then why haven't I healed myself? The wounds remained open, though they were no longer bleeding. He reached again for his spiritual core, needing the energy more than ever. He was the dragon, the ruler of Akatsuki. But try as he might, he could never reach that internal river within him, the life blood that made him yokai. He told himself it would return with time, but as almost a day had passed and it had not returned, he was starting to feel an inkling of doubt.

The ground beneath him was covered in boulders, and the trees grew too close together to see beyond much more than a couple feet. As the night crept in so did his field of vision. Before he had been able to see nearly as well in the dark as in the light. But as darkness fell, his feet got caught up in roots and vines that blocked his path. Hisato was out there somewhere, watching him, mocking him. They should not linger here much longer, but before they headed out he had to prove to himself that he was capable of keeping up the speeds he had when he was uninjured.

Though his body demanded rest, he had to keep pushing forward. Showing weakness was not an option. The others could not find out how extensive his injuries were and that they were still not healing.

As he forced his way up the hill, his breath pricked at his lungs, and each footstep was more difficult than the last. The terrain pushed back. Loose gravel made the footing unsteady, and he slid backward. He grasped for a nearby branch to keep from falling onto his backside. The sudden jerking of his torso tugged at his wounds, and sharp pain shot through his entire body.

Kaito clutched onto the branch, it was the only thing keeping him standing as he gasped for breath through the pain. In front of him was a group of large boulders, and just beyond that the crest of a hill where he hoped to get a better view of the surrounding valley and pinpoint the general's location.

Scaling that few feet of rock felt like an insurmountable task. He leaned against the nearby tree and tried to catch his breath as he clutched at what was likely a bleeding wound. Blood seeped through the bandages, mingling with his sweat and making his clothes stick to him. Even the sounds of the twilight forest were diminished by his ragged breathing.

Kaito glanced over his shoulder, back where he had come from. He could not even see the shrine building through the trees due to the growing darkness around him. He could not see anything, could not hear anything. He had been, in essence, made mortal and that fact terrified him. In his very long life he had never felt weak, never helpless, and he wouldn't give into those feelings now.

Kaito turned around, burning with the need to prove his strength. He clawed at the boulders before him, fingers jammed into whatever crevices he could find, half dragging his shaking limbs over the rough surface. Never mind that in his prime he could have leaped up here without a second thought. Never mind that he was leaving a trail of blood on the rocks and the world spun as the air thinned. He was forced to stop halfway up as his trembling legs and arms demanded he stop. But he refused to give in until he had reached the top.

The blood had completely soaked through the bandages and he'd reopened most of his wounds if not all. His clothes would be soaked in blood before the night was through, and if any of them saw they'd know the truth in an instant. And the already shaky ground upon which he had placed his control over the group would crumble beneath him. Even Rin, whose loyalty he thought unwavering, was being called into question. All because of Makato. Host of yet another piece of Kazue's soul.

Kaito sat on the boulder, not bothering with the view. He lay down on the stone, which was still warm from the sun and stared up at the bruised purple of the twilight sky. A few stars had started to push through already. *Is this how you gained immortality, Kazue? You live on in them?* There must be others: if there were two, it was no stretch to believe there were more like them.

Even lying on his back tugged at his wounds and he was forced to roll over into a more comfortable position on his side. The sun held one last toehold on the horizon, just the barest glimpse of golden life lining the mountains in the distance. Gold faded into pink, and then purple. That was how he imagined his own power, stubbornly clinging, hidden, but it would return. The only question that remained was: would the sun rise before anyone found out? How much longer could he carry on this farce before they caught on? Would even Suzume turn on him?

He laughed aloud. "She'd be the first to betray me."

His laughter echoed through the valley around him and came back as if the hills themselves were mocking him for his weakness.

"You're right not to trust her," a voice purred near his ear.

Kaito leaped up, tugging at his wounds. His night-blinded eyes made it impossible to see but he knew that voice.

"I knew you wouldn't be far away," Kaito growled.

"Don't open your wounds on my account," Hisato said from his right.

Kaito spun in that direction. "Ready to finish this now?"

Then from behind Kaito Hisato said, "I cannot stay away from you. That's Kazue's curse I suppose."

Kaito resisted the urge to spin around and chase Hisato's voice. Instead he crossed his arms over his chest and stared forward.

"You're taken in by my sex appeal as well. I can understand it."

Hisato's laughter drifted to his ears like a caress. "Yes, you are irresistible to all of us. But we also resent you, for the child we left behind, for the soul which was destroyed to become your equal," Hisato spat the words.

Hearing mention of the child Kazue had borne pricked at his anger, but he didn't want to reveal that wound to Hisato. If he could find him he would have grabbed him by the throat and destroyed him.

"If you want to fight me, then come out and fight me."

"You know I cannot." A hand brushed against his arm, Kaito reached for it on impulse, stumbled forward and then caught himself.

Hisato's laughter surrounded him. The dragon should have known better than to fall for his tricks.

"You've been trying rather hard to kill me for not being able to."

"That's the problem, isn't it? The echoes of Kazue live on inside us. If only one of us was strong enough to overcome it." There was a long pause as if Hisato was thinking about this. "Suzume has potential."

It was Kaito's turn to laugh. "She will never be Kazue's equal."

"That was always your problem. You underestimate the ability of humanity. It destroyed Kazue and perhaps it will destroy you in the end."

"Do you think you're going to scare me with your cryptic words?"

There was no reply, just silence. Hisato had made his point and left, as was his intention. He had sowed doubt in Kaito's mind. He waited a few more minutes to see if Hisato would return, and when he didn't Kaito decided he had wasted enough time.

Getting back would be difficult. He'd used too much energy on the way up and he could already feel his legs trembling beneath him. But he'd pushed through worse pain and in more dire circumstances before. He reached the ledge that he had just climbed up and carefully lowered himself over the edge, but as he did so he lost grip and slid down several feet before catching his fall on a branch. The result was him landing hard on the ground, blood seeping through his clothes and staining his hands.

He growled low under his breath. *Wonderful.*

"You are in need of assistance?" said a familiar and unexpected voice.

"Stand back," Kaito snarled as he pushed himself into a standing position while he clutched the bleeding stomach wound. Kaito squinted into the darkness, trying to pinpoint the speaker. He bared his teeth in a would-be intimidating posture.

"You can't see me, can you?" The voice held no judgment, just a simple statement of fact.

It seemed all his enemies were going to be visiting him tonight. Kaito spun in place. The voice had moved, now to his right where it had been to the left before. "I can see you just fine." He directed his gaze in the direction the voice had come from.

Naoki tapped him on the shoulder from behind and Kaito swung his fist in his direction, but found nothing but air and almost toppled off the rock before he was yanked backward by a tight grip on his bicep.

"Come for your revenge then?" Kaito snapped as he knocked away the swordsman's grip.

"I harbor no ill will to you," Naoki said, his tone lacking any inflection.

"Why did you follow me?"

"To warn you."

"Of what?"

"Kazue is awakening inside of Suzume."

A chill ran over Kaito's skin. As if the specter of Suzume stood between them, Hisato's words echoed inside his skull, more a real threat than before.

"Are you working for Hisato as well?" Kaito balled his hand into a fist.

"I am bound to the one who knows my true name."

A yokai's hidden name, or true name, had power in it. If another was to learn that name, they could use it to bind that yokai to their will. Kaito had taught Kazue that, though he had never dared give her his hidden name. She had asked about it from time to time. At the time it was a game, that was how she had given him the name Kaito, because he refused to speak his hidden name. Perhaps he would have shared Naoki's fate had Kazue learned it.

"Kazue is dead, so you should no longer have to serve her. Unless you're telling me she is alive somewhere?"

Naoki only stared at him without response. Kaito shook his head. Why did he continue to taunt himself with the idea that Kazue lived on, in any form? Just that one brief moment on the mountaintop had shook his resolve to hate her. It took Hisato to remind him why he could never forgive her. Kazue had ruined his life because she envied his immortality. This was why humans and immortals could never be together. There were some gaps that could not be crossed. His thirst for revenge had been appeased, but he had to let go of Kazue, of the life they could never have together.

"Leave me." Kaito turned away, thinking to dismiss him.

"She is drawing power from others."

Kaito froze in place. It was in Naoki's nature to speak little and only follow commands. He had been created by the Kami to protect and serve. Whether it was Kazue of five hundred years ago or some shade of her that lived now through Suzume and the others. He would not have come here and revealed this much if he had not been ordered.

"Why are you telling me this?"

"Because I was ordered to."

"By whom? Hisato, Suzume, Makato?"

He did not answer straight away. Kaito had to strain through the darkness to even get a glimpse of the silhouette of Naoki's face.

After a few moments he said, "Kazue wanted you to know she is going to return to you."

Kaito hesitated for a few heartbeats, letting the words wash over him. It was a promise that could never be fulfilled. Even if Kazue could somehow come back to life, he would never return to her side.

"Don't say useless things," Kaito growled before hurrying through the darkness.

Naoki followed him all the way back to camp like a ghost, not speaking but his presence known just the same. The subtle snap of a twig, heavy footsteps trailing him when Kaito knew he was capable of moving silently. Kaito allowed it. There was no use fighting him, not in his current condition. There was strength in knowing when there was a battle you could not win.

They were closing in on the camp when something came at him quick from in front of him. On reflex Kaito reached for his spiritual energy but once again came up empty.

"There you are. I've been worried." He recognized Rin's voice before he saw her. The dark had essentially left him blind.

Kaito growled low in his throat in warning. She couldn't have suspected already how weak he was.

Rin ignored his anger as she said, "Suzume has been kidnapped."

TWENTY-ONE

This had to be the stupidest idea she'd ever had. Suzume stomped through the forest, her arms swinging as she walked. But as with most of her less than brilliant ideas, she was committed to this idiotic plan. And if worse came to worst, someone would come to her rescue just like any other time. It might have been in poor judgment to trust the same people who convinced her wandering into yokai infested woods to lure out a said yokai to fight was a good idea. *Not that I'll need their help. I can handle this myself.*

Because the only time her power was effective was when she was in real danger, Tsuki suggested they set up a scenario in which Suzume appeared to be in danger, forcing Kaito to expose his own weakness and allowing Suzume to take control of their group. In theory it made sense, but as with most of her plans nothing ever seemed that simple. Something was bound to go wrong. But here she was, wandering the woods, feeling like an idiot, but she wasn't going to admit it.

All she needed was for some horrid creature to come slithering out of the shadows and challenge her. Then she'd burn it to a crisp and then stand triumphantly over its charred corpse as she gloated to the dragon. Easy.

"Suzume, wait!" Makato shouted from somewhere behind her.

Suzume spun around to face him, grabbing onto her staff but not drawing it. Akira seemed to trust the priest but that didn't necessarily make him trustworthy. Suzume had not even realized Akira had untied him.

"What are you doing here?" she said as she glared at him

He hesitated, standing back from her by a few feet as he rubbed his neck. He wouldn't meet her gaze. "Akira thought it might lure the dragon out if I followed."

"I thought I was the bait."

He cleared his throat and would not look her in the eye. "They're telling Kaito I kidnapped you."

Suzume rolled her eyes. That had to be Tsuki's idea. He had that sort of flare for the dramatic.

"They must really trust you to allow you out here with me. What if you really kidnap me?" She said it jokingly, but she hadn't let go of her staff either.

"You're right not to trust me," Makato said, meeting her gaze at last.

"Is that a warning?" Suzume's grip on her staff tightened.

"Just a way to live by." He shrugged with a slight smirk on his lips.

Suzume gave a false laugh. She had to respect that sort of outlook. But it didn't make her trust him anymore. "Well, you can stay here. I don't need your help."

She turned to go, glancing over her shoulder once she saw Makato had ignored her instructions and continued to follow her. So much for being the group's leader. "What did the dragon do that made you so angry?" he asked her before she could shoo him away again.

"What didn't he do?" Just thinking of Kaito's cold expression while he told her he didn't trust her made her blood boil. As a result, flames leaped higher along her skin and Makato had to jump back to avoid getting burned. "He thinks I'm weak, but I'm going to show him." She balled her hands into fists.

"Why put yourself at risk to prove a point?"

"Do you think I can't do it?" She threw the accusation at him like she would a ball of fire.

Makato looked away from her and it was all the confirmation she needed. That was the real reason they'd sent Makato along. None of them thought she was capable. Well she would show them all.

"I don't need you. Go back to Akira and Tsuki and tell them that." The flames on her body continued to spread outward, no longer confined to her body, but burning along the ground, catching onto bushes and the branches of trees above her. A shower of sparks rained down from above onto her.

Makato looked from her to the burning forest around her, eyes wide and terrified. Something about the priest looking at her like a monster, made something snap inside of her. If anyone should understand where she was coming from it should be him. Weren't they both in the same predicament? He had a piece of Kazue's soul too. But unlike her, he seemed to have complete control over his powers.

"You're not going to prove any points this way," Makato said.

"Just watch me." She flung her arm and a trail of sparks followed.

Makato stumbled in his haste to move out of her way. Suzume stomped past him, anger fueling her movements, and she was no longer certain this was about proving herself or just wreaking as much destruction as possible. Whatever it was, it felt good. She felt powerful.

Stewing on her anger, and walking without destination through the forest for a few more minutes, she felt what she was looking for. A prickle at the back of her neck, a warning of yokai nearby. The unleashed fire had gotten the attention of something living in the forest. All that remained was to stop and let it come to her for a fight. Suzume drew her staff from her holster. The weight of the wood in her hand felt good, it reinforced her decision.

The prickling sensation grew stronger and from behind her Makato said, "Something is coming."

She ignored him, her eyes trained on the direction from which the powerful creature was coming. She felt it too, like a mouthwatering scent, it drew her to it. The power was crying out to her fire which only wanted to consume. She clutched her staff tighter, preparing for a fight. Whatever it was, its footsteps shook the ground, and the forest life was fleeing in the wake of the monster who was quickly approaching.

Then the trees burst apart, a hail of wooden splinters rained down on her as it roared. Suzume threw her arm up to shield herself from the dangerous debris before looking up to see her opponent. A giant chicken swiveled its head from one side to the other, peering down at her with black beady eyes.

Suzume wilted and dropped her staff to her side, the fire dying down as her anger was replaced by incredulity.

"A giant chicken? That's what came to fight me?"

She looked back at Makato to share a look that said, 'can you believe this.'

"Suzume, get away from that thing," Makato hissed behind her.

"What? The chicken? What could it possibly do?"

The chicken was at least three times her height, its head just above the treetops. It moved its head back and forth as it examined her, and the large red wattle on its neck wobbled as it looked at her. Suzume picked her staff up. It wasn't the most terrifying yokai she'd ever seen, but it would have to do.

The chicken made a few more stomping steps toward Suzume.

"Come at me, you main dish," she said as she swung her staff, the flames dancing in front of her, swirling together.

The chicken opened its giant beak and instead of a cluck it roared. The sound shook the ground beneath Suzume's feet and leaves fell from the trees overhead. Out of its beak shot a ball of fire straight at Suzume. She screamed and leaped out of the path of the chicken's fire.

Makato had taken cover behind a nearby tree and was rapid-fire shooting arrows at the giant chicken. It stomped after her shooting fire from its beak like something from a nightmare. In fact, Suzume pinched herself just to make sure this wasn't some sort of insane dream. The pain she felt from the pinch was not reassuring and she and Makato were forced to run through the forest away from the chicken. It was too large to get through the trees without tearing them down, which gave them a few seconds head start to escape.

"Why a giant chicken of all things!" Suzume moaned between panting breaths as they weaved their way through the trees.

"It's a basan. They're attracted to fire. Normally they live deep in the forest and are almost never seen by humans. But they devour fire and burnt things. It must have smelled all the burnt wood and came looking for a meal."

"And it saw me lit up like a brazier and I looked like a rare delicacy." Suzume shook her head. Of all the rotten luck, she drew out a fire-breathing chicken.

"Most likely," Makato said and despite the danger he had a smile ghosting along the edges of his lips.

Suzume rolled her eyes. "How do I kill it? Will fire even work against it?"

"That I don't know..." he trailed off, his tone sounded less than convinced. "I've never seen one before... I've only read about them." He said it almost like a question, as if he could not remember when he had read it or how.

There was no time to question it. The whole reason she had come out here was to fight this thing. What was she running for? She wanted to prove that she was strong enough to protect herself, then that was what she was going to do. Even if she wasn't sure how to defeat it, she'd just have to wing it.

Suzume stopped and turned around to face the basan. She grabbed her staff and gave herself a quick pep-talk. *You can do this. You've fought scarier things than a chicken.*

It was coming up fast, roaring fire. Its wattle swayed as it bobbed its head back and forth, black beady eyes searching for Suzume. With long hooked toes it pushed aside trees, smashing them beneath its feet and taking away the last obstacle between Suzume and it. She concentrated her energy into creating a ball of fire, but the flames would not cooperate, and instead burned out of control all over her body.

She could smell the basan's sulfuric breath as it came within inches of impaling her with its large beak. At the last moment she leaped back-ward. She wasn't making any progress. She should just run and save herself. Behind her Makato shouted her name, but she was too stubborn to give up now. She had the power to stop it if she could just get the fire to cooperate. Makato called to her again, and this time she looked over her shoulder.

He was waving his arms, telling her to run. She started to form a reply when the beak once more came down beside her, almost grazing her shoulder. Suzume slapped her hands against the side of the basan's head in a futile attempt to deter it. But it only roared again, bellowing fire. Suzume looked up and was eye to eye with the massive beak, moments before it was going to shoot fire at her. She threw her hands up, prepared to guard against it, but at the last minute a body was between her and the chicken, grabbing onto its beak and keeping it from unleashing its fiery breath.

Kaito wrestled with the basan and over his shoulder he shouted. "Run, you idiot."

She should have been grateful he'd come to her rescue again. But that was the exact opposite of what she wanted. This was supposed to be her moment.

Instead of running, Suzume used that moment to refocus her energy. And with new resolve, the fire was more willing to bend to her command. It burned brighter and coalesced in her hands forming a perfect sphere of flame.

"Move out of my way, I'm going to destroy this thing," Suzume shouted back at Kaito.

Kaito looked over his shoulder, saw the burning ball, and opened his mouth to say something when the basan took advantage of his momentary distraction and knocked him aside, sending the dragon careening through the air.

It opened its mouth in another powerful, fiery roar. Suzume saw her chance and threw the ball of fire which collided with the basan's fire in fiery sparks that rained down upon her and it. She threw up her arm to shield her face from any stray sparks. At first it seemed it would only be a single explosion, and then Suzume's fire consumed the basan's and traveled back the way its fire had come and into its throat. The basan made a sound more like a squawk than a roar as it swallowed Suzume's flame.

A lump formed in its throat as it swallowed and then it opened its mouth, fire spewing from its gullet. It swung its neck back and forth wildly as it ran in circles before falling to the ground, thrashing about, flapping its wings, and kicking its legs. Fire burst from its mouth and along its body, catching its feathers and feet alight. The basan was being consumed by fire from within, and it gave a pained scream so loud Suzume had to cover her ears to block out the sound.

The sound was cut off as the fire overtook its body, and all that remained was a burning corpse which smelled faintly of cooked chicken. Suzume looked horrified at the dead basan. She thought she would be proud but she was mostly disgusted. At least she had done what she had set out to do. Putting on a triumphant face, she turned to Kaito to brag about her triumph. This ought to show him how powerful she was. But he was still lying where the chicken had flung him, his limbs at odd angles like a broken toy.

A strange sensation overcame her, her chest felt suddenly tight and she could not make her limbs obey her. Rin arrived just then, she looked to Makato, then Suzume, before her eyes went to rest on the motionless Kaito on the ground. The kitsune rushed over to him, and knelt on the ground before tearing open his haori and looking down at his body.

"His wounds have opened up again," she said to Makato who had crouched on the other side of him.

This wasn't what was supposed to happen. She had thought showing Kaito's weakness would make her feel better but she just felt hollow.

"What were you thinking?" Rin turned toward Suzume, but she had no words to explain. She had put Kaito's life in danger for no reason at all. All the gloating triumph was sucked out of her in an instant.

"Why did he even come out here if he was only going to get hurt," she said.

A part of her was hoping he would leap up and tease her for worrying but he hadn't opened his eyes yet.

"You know why he did it," Rin said, her words like a slap across Suzume's face.

Suzume did know: it was all for Kazue.

TWENTY-TWO

Palpable fear had settled on Suzume's shoulders. It made her restless. She couldn't stop pacing and she couldn't focus. She couldn't explain this feeling. For as long as she could remember, Suzume had only ever worried about herself. In a place like the White Palace, you had to look out for yourself because no one was going to watch your back for you. Without meaning to, she had been relying on Kaito to do that for her. And despite actively trying not to, she had started to worry about him too.

Rin and Makato were tending to his wounds, and yet she kept drifting over there hoping to catch a glimpse of him, and find out how he was doing without actually going up and asking if he was ok. *If he finds out I'm worried about him, I'll never hear the end of it.*

A couple more almost casual strolls past and all Suzume could see was the back of Makato's head and Rin standing over him and Kaito. *Was that a bloody rag? Had he bled to death trying to save her from a giant chicken?* Suzume craned her neck to try and see better but to no avail.

Suzume looked around in a way she hoped looked casual. Tsuki and Naoki were sparring nearby. They seemed unconcerned by Kaito's condition. Maybe she was overreacting. This was Kaito after all. He was never seriously hurt for long. *Get it together, he's probably fine. This is probably some elaborate prank and once I buy into it he'll ridicule me for worrying.*

As she was pacing, Suzume did not see Tsuki was coming toward her until she was colliding with his chest.

"Watch where you're going," Suzume snapped at him on impulse.

"I could say the same to you," Tsuki said with a sly grin in the direction of where Kaito was resting.

"Is it time for practice?" Suzume said perhaps a little too eagerly, but she needed the distraction.

Tsuki only shook his head. "We're going on patrol." He gestured toward Naoki who had been silently standing behind him. "Now's your chance to check on Kaito since Rin and Makato went looking for medicinal herbs. It will just be the two of you." Tsuki waggled his eyebrows at her.

"The dragon will be fine on his own," Suzume said. "I'll come with you on patrol maybe you can teach me while we go."

"As much as I like seeing you as an eager student, we need someone to watch over the dragon. In his current condition, he cannot defend himself." He winked.

"The dragon can protect himself." Suzume pointed a finger at Kaito. The reality of the situation refused to sink in.

"You need your rest. You used a lot of your spiritual energy yesterday," Akira said taking control of the body she shared with her brother, "I don't know who is more stubborn, you or the dragon." She sighed.

"Clearly it's him." Suzume gestured toward where Kaito was lying. He had not risen from his bedroll all afternoon.

Akira shook her head. "We'll be back before dark. Don't have too much fun."

She sauntered over to Naoki while Suzume sputtered a series of ineffective defenses. They ignored her excuses and then all that remained behind was Suzume and Kaito. He had to be pretending because as much as she had fantasized about proving she was strong to him, she had not considered the dragon getting hurt. The conflicting emotions left her paralyzed in place.

Rin seemed to think he was badly hurt. Maybe it's serious this time. He hasn't made a scene or anything like he normally would. She shook her head and went to sit on her sleeping roll. She was feeling tired, and a nap might refresh her and give her a clear head. Who knew what new horrors awaited them tomorrow? It would be better to get some rest.

She turned her back to the still form of Kaito sleeping across the camp from her. She'd never really seen him sleep before, or had him be so quiet for so long. It felt surreal. He was supposed to be infallible. *The mighty dragon, brought down by a chicken. Pah. Serves him right for all the humiliation he's put me through.* She peeked over her shoulder. His back remained to her unmoving. *He didn't even yell at me for running off looking for a fight.* She shook her head. *Now I'm wanting to fight him. What is wrong with me?* She lay down and forced her eyes shut, but all she could think about was Kaito and why he wasn't acting like himself. The thought kept nagging at her to the point where she couldn't stand the wondering anymore.

Leaping up, she marched over to where he was lying down. He lay on his side, his back to her. His side rose and fell with each breath, so apparently, he was sleeping. *That's enough. I saw he was breathing, I don't need to be here anymore. What if he wakes up?* But instead of following her own advice, she lowered herself down beside his bedroll, careful not to make a sound, and looked down at his sleeping face. Some of his color had returned. He had looked so pale right after the basan's attack. But there were still dark circles under his eyes that had never been there before.

"Thank you," Kaito said without opening his eyes.

Suzume froze, not sure if this was the precursor to some heavy teasing or if he was talking in his sleep. Whatever it was, it wasn't sincere. Kaito never thanked her for anything.

After a few seconds of waiting for the punchline, she said quietly, "For what...?

"Don't do that." He sighed heavily and opened dark eyes that pinned her in place so she couldn't look away from him. "It's hard enough for me to admit when I'm weak."

The hairs on the back of her neck were rising up on end. He must have been seriously wounded for him to talk like this. *Is he dying?* That feeling of someone grabbing a hold of her heart and squeezing returned.

"It's not like I thought you were invincible. I mean you were sealed by a mere mortal." She cringed at her attempt at teasing. Why had she brought up Kazue now of all times? *I should just go now before I say something else stupid.*

He closed his eyes. "I suppose I deserve that."

Suzume blinked in disbelief at him. "Are you dying?"

He chuckled softly. "No. Just feeling my own mortality is all."

"Are you seriously hurt? What's wrong with you?" she asked her eyes scanning his body. Bandages were wrapped around his bare torso. Normally she would have been embarrassed to look at his bare skin but she was more concerned with his physical health than his physique.

"I'll recover in time."

"Why are you acting like this?" she asked, trying to cover up the panic that had briefly set in.

He wouldn't look at her and instead looked up at the sky overhead. "I'm supposed to protect you. I never should have put you in danger." The last sentence was so low she wasn't sure he meant to say it out loud.

"What was that?" she leaned in close pretending to try and hear him better. Desperately trying to insert some levity into their exchange. The somber mood added a new dimension to their relationship and she wasn't sure she liked it.

He turned his head and their lips were inches from one another. Her heart leaped into her chest. Being this close to Kaito made all the sparks dance along her flesh. As she looked into his eyes Suzume could see something drawing her in.

Love makes you weak. She yanked her head back before she did something stupid.

"Just get better so I don't have to worry about protecting you anymore. It's exhausting," she said with a wave of her hand.

She tried to get up, deciding it was time to put some distance between them before she did something truly stupid. But before she could, his hand darted out and grabbed her by the wrist and yanked her closer to him.

Suzume stared down at him. Her pulse was hammering against his palm. He had to know being close to him made her heart race.

"Don't go, not yet."

This was a Kaito she had never seen before and she didn't exactly hate it. Which scared her almost as much as the idea that he might be dying. Both of which were complex feelings that she wasn't ready to analyze just yet. This might all be a prank after all. But when he looked this vulnerable it was hard to think that was the case. Seeing him like this, it brought out a nurturing part of her she thought herself lacking. *Maybe I should have Makato reverse the spell.*

"I'm not going to play nursemaid to you," she said as she yanked her hand free of his grip.

He grinned. "But you're so good at washing me."

She avoided meeting his gaze, thinking back to when she had done just that brought a blush to her face.

"Then what else do you want from me?" she said with arms crossed over her chest, trying to put a barrier between them, even a flimsy one.

"I don't want to have to keep worrying about you."

"Then stop, I can take care of myself," she replied, chin held up in her haughtiest pose.

"You can't and that's the problem. You have no sense of self-preservation and you keep putting yourself in danger. And knowing I can do nothing to protect you is driving me insane."

"But I can protect myself. Why can't you see that? I'm just as powerful as Kazue!"

Kaito tried to sit up, winced, and lay back down. "Don't try and become Kazue. You're nothing like her."

His words had a powerful sting and any doubts she had about proving herself to Kaito were dashed in that instant.

She scoffed. "What do you expect me to do? Go hide out in some dusty temple and wait for you? I'm not Kazue. You're right. I'm going to become even stronger than her."

She stood up, looming over him. It felt strange to tower over the dragon in this way. It made her feel powerful.

"Don't be an idiot," Kaito growled but Suzume was already storming away from him.

All he cared about was his precious Kazue. Well he would see how much stronger she could be than Kazue. As she was walking away from Kaito, Rin and Makato returned carrying baskets of greens. When Makato saw her, he raised his hands to wave at her but Suzume walked right past him without acknowledgment.

She retreated into the forest, back to the place with the stones she had found the day they had arrived. She plopped down on the rock with an angry thump. The flames were already flickering across her skin as they often did as of late. Suzume held her hand palm up where a small ball of fire erupted, just like the last time she had tried it.

"Need some help?" Makato asked as he approached her.

Suzume did not respond to him and instead focused on making the ball of flame bigger and bigger. The bigger it got the less defined it was and the more it took out of her.

"You can't maintain this sort of energy," Makato said

Suzume's concentration, which was already flimsy, broke and the ball of flame burst apart, flying in several directions all at once. Makato had to duck to avoid getting hit by a stray beam of fire.

Suzume turned to face him. "What do you want?"

He took a few steps toward her, not backing down, even as she grabbed onto her staff holding it in front of her like a shield.

"You're letting your emotions rule you and it's feeding into your spiritual power."

"Thanks," she said sarcastically.

"Fire burns out of control if you let it. And since your soul has an abundance of fire it influences your temper, and you're quicker to anger as a result."

"Great. You can go now." She waved her hand indicating he should leave. She planned on practicing alone.

"I can teach you how to harness your power."

"I don't need your help."

"Try and use your power against me then."

"Are you crazy? If I try to burn you then I get hurt."

"I know, but just humor me."

Since she was in need of some stress release, she decided why not. Once again Suzume created a ball of fire, one smaller than the last no matter how hard she tried to form it large. Makato stood, waiting patiently while she formed it into a ball.

"Ready?" she asked.

He had no weapons or shields but nodded. She really hoped he was going to block her attack before they both got hurt. Just in case, Suzume angled her blow to somewhere that would inflict the least amount of pain on him.

She flung the fire ball at his legs, and then closed her eyes waiting for the recoil. Instead of being struck, she looked up to see a shield surrounding Makato. It was similar to the one that had come to Suzume reflexively.

"Try again," Makato said, dropping the shield.

"I can make a shield too. That's nothing special."

He only smiled and gestured for her to show him. But the shield was one thing she still couldn't manage on her own. Despite her lack of belief in her ability, she tried anyway. She squinted her face hard and tried to visualize a shield around her, but try as she might, nothing appeared.

"I don't want to do it," she said after a few minutes of fruitless effort.

Makato made no comment and then said, "How about you make another fire ball?"

Since she knew she could do that she went to work, but this third one was even smaller than the rest, hardly encompassing her palm. When she flung it at Makato this time it dissipated into a puff of smoke before it ever reached him.

"You're not channeling your power in the most effective way," he said.

"I'll learn eventually."

He shook his head. "You need to learn how to control your spiritual energy first. I can teach you. If you'll allow me."

He held out his hand to her. She still didn't want to trust him, but at the same time Kaito's words haunted her. Telling her to give up on obtaining Kazue's power. Perhaps this was the only way to get what she wanted.

She took Makato's hand. "When do we start?"

Twenty-Three

No person should ever be forced awake before the sun had even risen. But despite this obvious rule, in the dark of the early morning, Suzume was shaken awake.

She grumbled an incoherent rebuke and rolled back over, pulling her blanket tighter around her. Being conscious at this hour should be a crime against humanity.

"Suzume, wake up. It's time for training." Makato nudged her again.

Suzume swatted his hand away. "It's not even morning yet. Besides, Tsuki and Akira know I don't do mornings."

"Your training isn't with Tsuki and Akira."

Suzume grumbled low in her throat once more, before rolling onto her back and staring up at the priest who was grinning down at her. How was it even possible for someone to be this chipper in the morning?

"Who is it with then?" she asked, her voice still thick with sleep.

"With me."

Suzume blinked at him, unable to process what he was trying to say to her.

"I have no idea what you're talking about."

"You want better control over your power, right?"

Suzume groaned. Couldn't he take a hint? "Sure, when the sun is actually up," she mumbled, half asleep.

"The stillness of the early morning is best for what we're going to learn today."

Suzume didn't respond, hoping he would catch the hint and leave. He sat there for a few more moments before she heard his footsteps recede. Just as she sunk into a deep sleep, she was jerked awake with a splash of cold water.

Suzume shot up with an oath and looked over to Makato who was holding a bucket now overturned and empty.

"What was that?"

"In the temple, this is how we woke new recruits who overslept."

"I didn't sign up for this."

"But you do need to learn to control your emotions, and this helps with our first lesson." He grinned.

She did not have an adequate response. Suzume opened and closed her mouth, trying to fight the impulse to shout. "Why does training have to be in the morning, and now wet..." She held up her dripping sleeve and sighed.

On the horizon she could see the faintest glimmer of sunrise, just a smudge of lighter blue against the deep blue of night, giving way to day. The sun wouldn't pass beyond the mountaintops for hours most likely.

"Will you be needing more water to wake?" he asked.

She exhaled heavily. "Are you sure you weren't sent just to torture me?"

He grinned again as he held out his hand for her to take. Suzume sighed and accepted the gesture. He pulled her into a sitting position and she insisted on a change of clothes at least, which meant going into the shrine building and shivering as she exchanged wet clothes for dry ones. She was fully awake by the time she met Makato outside the shrine building, though her mind felt sluggish.

Makato headed toward the edge of the barrier that protected their camp. Suzume looked to Naoki and Rin who were on guard duty. Somehow he had gained an uneasy trust within the group, and they didn't question them as they passed.

As for the dragon, she had not seen anything of him since their last argument. She was simultaneously relieved and concerned. She didn't want another confrontation but Kaito wasn't acting like himself. A part of her wanted to talk to him, but having a rational conversation with Kaito was out of the question. If she even made the smallest inquiry into his wellbeing, he would turn it around on her and accuse her of having feelings for him.

He was the one who was confused. She knew exactly how she felt about him.

"Are you coming?" Makato asked. She had not even realized it but she was staring at the old shrine building.

"Yeah, I thought I had something in my sandal." She marched over to him.

"Do you want to get it out?"

"What?"

"The thing that was in your sandal." Makato nodded toward her feet.

Suzume shook her head. "Oh, no I got it already. Let's go." She half jogged down the path in front of him before he thought to ask her why she had been staring at the building where Kaito was. She had to stop after a couple feet, because she wasn't sure where they were supposed to be going. Makato took the lead instead and led her down a small path directly behind the shrine building. They did not go far before they came upon a ring of stones, each one ringed with a rope and faded folded papers hanging from them, and the ground in the center of the circle had a soft covering of grass illuminated from above by the dim morning light. Orbs of light bobbed up and down in the clearing, spinning around one another in a complicated dance.

There was a break in the canopy of trees overhead and during the day this place would be full of sunlight. But these things moved like enormous fireflies fluttering to and fro. As she approached the space she felt a tingle of energy roll down her spine. Just as she had when she first approached the shrine which held Kaito.

Suzume hesitated at the border of the ring of stones. "What are those?" she asked, staring at the strange moving lights.

"They're hinotama. They're harmless."

"Why did you bring me here?"

"This place was once ruled by a Kami, so it is a holy place. Somewhere you can harness your energy without outside influence."

She did not want to go nearer to it. She had a bad history with magical places. Who knew what she might unleash if she got too close? Maybe those bobbing lights would decide she was delicious and try to strip the flesh from her bones.

"What happened to the Kami?" she asked.

Makato looked around at the space. "I cannot say, but judging from the state of the shrine building, it is likely the worshipers have disappeared, and with it the Kami's power has faded. All that remain are these." He gestured toward the hinotama, which had stopped bobbing and instead were very still. They had no faces but Suzume imagined them staring at her.

"Or maybe someone sealed it..." Suzume thought of the roadside shrine where she had accidentally unleashed the Kami who agreed to grant her wish.

Makato shook his head. "Even if that were the case, it is gone from this place. You do not have to fear it."

"I'm not afraid of this place. I'm afraid of what I might do without meaning to."

He held out his hand to her. "Then this is a good place to start learning. You cannot control something without understanding it first."

"I get the general idea. I focus my energy and then balls of fire come out of my hands." Suzume presented the palms of her hands as if they would burst into flames at any moment.

"To put it simply." He smiled. "But the energy does not only come from within, but the world around you." He gestured to the ring of stones.

"I don't want to use a dead Kami's energy," Suzume said and took a step back. That had to be just as bad, if not worse than what Kazue did when she hunted down and absorbed the energy of yokai and Kami alike.

"You're not going to use that." He laughed, kindly. "Fire can be found even in the rays of the sun as well as the glowing coals of the hearth. Since the sun is less innocuous I thought we could start with trying to harness the sun's power."

Suzume sighed heavily. "What is it I have to do then?"

"First step is coming into the circle."

She looked at the ring of stones as if they would jump up and bite her. She took a deep breath, closed her eyes, and stepped into the middle. The energy along her arms crackled as the fire inside her reacted to whatever residual energy had been left behind by the Kami, or maybe it was the glowing orbs who hovered around the perimeter but did not leave. She stood just on the edge, close enough to leap out in case anything went awry.

She stood there with eyes closed for a few minutes, before peeking out beneath her eyelids to see Makato smiling back at her.

"See, nothing happened."

Suzume released the breath she had been holding and joined Makato at the center of the circle.

"Take a seat." He motioned for her to sit.

Suzume sat facing him, kneeling as she would have back at the palace. Makato took a similar position.

"I talked to Akira, and she explained you had some basic training. You know the different sources of energy in the body?"

"Sure, and you can teach me how to better harness it? Can you teach me how to do that clone trick?"

"In time, but first you need to master the basics. Can you tell me what are the centers of energy?"

"I already know them, why are we wasting time on this?"

"Because it's important." He gestured for her to continue.

She rolled her eyes to stretch out the minute. To be honest she had forgotten most of them. She had only been worried about where her fire would be coming from. "The head, the hands..." She gestured vaguely to the rest of her body. "They're all over."

It was Makato's turn to sigh. "They go like this, head, heart, stomach, hands and feet. They all have their special purpose and meaning and each one is a gateway for your energy."

"Yeah, that was it."

Makato crossed his arms over his chest. "The reason I bring up your energy points is because you need to learn to manually open and close these gateways in order to better channel your power."

Suzume nodded. "I've done that..." sort of. Akira had taught her a method of imagining a series of dams in her body that could be opened and closed to redirect energy from her core to her hands and create fire. But the problem was as soon as she lost her concentration, the dams all opened again. Hence her ability was unreliable at best.

"Show me," Makato said with a wave of his hand. "Draw energy from the sun."

A pale shaft of sunlight was falling on her face and she tipped her head upward. She tried to imagine her face absorbing the energy into her.

"Now breathe in the energy, let it flow through you," Makato said, his voice was low and almost hypnotic.

She sniffed, the only thing she felt was an itch on the tip of her nose. But she did as Makato said and took a few deep breaths. She didn't feel anything. She peeked her eyes open and looked around the clearing. She did feel like her mind was clearer and less tired. Was that the sun's energy? "I think it's working," she said excitedly.

"All energy flows into each other. Being what you are and sitting in this place, your body draws the energy into you."

"Do you draw energy from the sun too?"

He shook his head. "I've always been drawn to the earth and stone. It wasn't until I met you that I realized why."

"Is that why you can make those vine walls?" Her voice echoed back at her in the stillness of the space.

Makato gave a slow smile. "Yes, but that came with years of practice with my spiritual powers."

Suzume crossed her arms over her chest and huffed. She didn't have years to practice, she needed to stop Hisato now.

"For now, let's just focus on finding your center."

Suzume closed her eyes and focused on the energy inside her, she could feel the flame deep within her, that flickering spark that Kazue had given her. If Makato could easily learn to control his power, surely she could too. She was as much a part of Kazue as him.

But before she could even finish focusing on closing even one 'gateway' to make a fireball, she was smacked hard across the back of her skull. Suzume's eyes flashed open and her temper flared. The energy she brushed against rushed to the surface and a burning ball of fire sparked and danced across her skin. The energy around her in the previously peaceful clearing pushed against her fire and she felt it push against her as if trying to repel her from the clearing. But the power was not strong enough to actually force her to move. It felt more like an annoying buzzing insect instead of a real threat.

"What did you do that for?"

"To prove a point. You have no separation from your emotions. Your gateways are wide open."

"I was in the middle of channeling my energy when you hit me!"

"And do you really think your enemy is going to wait for you to finish before attacking you?"

She crossed her arms over her chest in response, "That's why I need you to teach me how to get control of it!"

"Then learn to control your emotions."

"What do you suggest then?" She threw her hands up in exasperation. The energy in the clearing felt like a hive of angry insects now. Her skin prickled as if she was being poked with a needle in a thousand different places.

"First you need to start by letting go of your anger over me hitting you."

"What makes you think I am angry at you?"

He gestured to the flames that danced around her and a cluster of golden lights that were hovering around her. They were nearly transparent in the gray early morning light. If she hadn't been so angry about him hitting her, she might have stopped to admire their beauty. One of the golden flecks of light came over and landed on her arm where she felt a sharp pain like a sting.

"What are they doing?" She swatted at it but her hand just went through it and it floated away.

"Right now they are reacting to your angry energy," he said and held his hand out. One of the specks landed on his finger and transformed from yellow to green and faded into his skin.

"I'm not angry!" As she said this a dozen more lights appeared and buzzed around her.

He was smiling faintly as he gestured toward the collection of dust mote sized lights. "They indicate otherwise."

She ground her teeth together. What did it matter if she was angry or not?

"I want to teach you, but you're going to have to learn to let go."

Suzume rolled her eyes, this was pointless. He obviously couldn't teach her anything.

"This is a waste of time." She marched toward the edge of the stone circle.

The lights flickered and buzzed around her, bumping into her, biting her all over her skin, and her anger only grew. It built up in her like a blaze.

"Suzume, if you'd just listen."

But she couldn't hear him. She was trapped inside a buzz of angry flying lights, which were darting around her and swirling around her, stoking the flame inside her, until it grew larger and larger threatening to consume her. The stone in her pocket warmed up and added to the growing heat. She swatted at the flying lights as if it would make any difference. And then something was bubbling up inside her. She felt it rising and growing inside her before it burst out of her like a blast toward Makato who rolled out of the way just in time to avoid having his head removed from his neck. It collided with a stone at the far side of the clearing, burning through the rope with its folded paper talismans. The flames lit up the stone and a series of arcane markings that had previously been invisible. The flame sank into stone and the markings disappeared.

The stone started to shake and the earth around it split apart, and a long fissure opened in front of it. A long, low cackle emanated from a long hole in the ground, as a clawed hand burst from it.

Twenty-Four

Suzume reached for her staff. With its familiar weight in her hand, she tried to take a step backward out of the ring of stones. But as soon as her feet got close to the edge, energy crackled and sparked against her skin. She leaped away before she could get burned. A shimmering barrier of energy surrounded the ring of stones. The orbs hung above each of the stone lines of energy, connecting them and extending outward to create the barrier. They were not some benign yokai of light, but guardians of this place. Which meant they were there to keep whatever was inside the stone inside.

The maniacal laughter filled the air and rattled through Suzume's skull. She fought the urge to cover her ears to stop the noise, because that would mean letting go of the staff and somehow, she thought it was more important to hold onto it right now. Makato drew his bow and arrow, pointing it at the hole. Something black and gray with oily, black strings dangling from its wrists clawed its way out of the hole. The stone behind it had cracked in half and any sign of the fire Suzume had shot disappeared. All that remained was a smoldering pile of rubble.

The thing, whatever it was, crawled out on all fours. What Suzume had originally mistook for oily string was actually limp hair which fell in a curtain in front of the thing's face. A putrid scent followed it, like long rotten meat.

Makato shot an arrow at the top of its head. It landed in the flesh of the creature with a sick wet noise. But the creature kept crawling toward them, its eerie laughter filling her skull. She grabbed onto the side of her head to try and block out the sound but it seemed to be coming from inside.

"What is that thing?" Suzume asked. Giving up on blocking it out, she held her staff in front of her in the guard position, trying and failing to summon the fire she had just used to free this thing. But it would not come to her; there was not even the faintest spark along her skin. It was as if her energy had been all used up, but she could still feel it churning in her gut, like a small inferno just out of her reach, waiting to be grabbed a hold of and used to vanquish this horrifying creature before her.

The creature stopped its slow progress toward them, and then slowly unbent from all fours to stand and stare at her. It had the general shape of a woman, and was wearing all white. The long black hair was obscuring her face but Suzume could see the molted gray skin beneath.

"It's a yuri," Makato said, not removing his eyes from the creature.

"You're telling me restless spirits are real too?"

It shouldn't have come as that much of a surprise, if Kami and yokai were real, why not the spirits of the dead, trapped on earth because of some unfinished business.

The arrow in the yuri's skull was forced out and it flopped onto the ground in front of it, landing on the grass at her feet. Where ever its feet touched began to rot, spreading outward like an infection, turning green grass at first brown and then black with a mold like decay. The path in which it had crawled out now looked like a slimy black trail.

Makato shot a quick series of arrows into the thing's chest, and it jerked backward with each blow but did not fall. After the last arrow pierced it, the yuri started a slow shuffling progression toward them. The fire was crackling all over her body, and Suzume created a ball of fire, flinging it toward the creature. But when the fire landed on her, it singed her clothes but it did not deter her forward momentum.

Instead of deterring it, she had drawn the creature's attention onto herself and it continued its slow shuffling gait toward her. Suzume backed up, but the barrier behind her was sparking and sputtering as soon as she got close. She stepped away from the barrier, and then hugging the ring of stones, skittered along the edge. Each time she moved, the creature made a jerking motion in her direction to follow. Makato continued to shoot arrows into it to no avail. They only hindered the shuffling footsteps for a moment before it would continue again.

From beneath the curtain of the thing's hair, Suzume could see one eye with a wide, white iris and a flash of pointed teeth as it smiled at her. But it did not speak.

Suzume ran faster than the thing but she couldn't run around this circle forever. She stood in place to lure it closer to her. If she could get closer to Makato perhaps they could make a plan together. The yuri closed the distance despite Makato's attacks. Dispelled arrows were littered on the ground, some snapped under the yuri's foot. Suzume pressed her body against the rock behind her, hands clutching her staff with desperation. Almost. Not yet. Just a second more. She held her breath. And then when it was in striking distance she swung her staff, knocking it upside the head.

The blow landed on decaying flesh, which squished beneath her blow as if it was full of liquid. The head rocked on the neck of the creature, turning almost at an angle and leaving the yuri momentarily stunned. Suzume darted past it to the opposite side of the ring, where Makato was standing ready with his dwindling supply of arrows.

Suzume reached him after her short sprint, panting for breath as she stood behind him. The yuri made a slow uncoordinated turn and resumed its shuffle toward her with much farther to go.

"What is that thing doing in a Kami's place?"

"Someone must have used the holy ground to seal it here."

Suzume smacked him up the backside of his head and when she did she felt a flicker of his power join hers. It felt the same way it had when she'd faced Kaito. Makato shouted an oath before looking back at her with a scowl.

"Why did you do that?"

"I told you my energy unleashed dangerous things and you didn't listen!"

"Is now really the time for 'I told you so'?"

"Well if you hadn't insisted on teaching me here."

The yuri stopped its maniacal laughter, and the silence that followed was worse than the laughter. The two were frozen in place, waiting and watching as it tilted its head from side to side examining them. Suzume's blow seemed to have broken something in its neck because the head wobbled from side to side with each unsteady movement.

The creature was closing in on the two of them now. The entire circle of stones was gray and covered in the creeping slimy filth, which inched up even the rocks and toward the barrier that flickered and sparked against it. She did not want to touch that slime, and feared it was some sort of extension of the creature. Suzume was out of ideas and the thing wasn't stopping no matter what they did.

"We should combine our energy," Suzume said, putting her hand out for Makato to take.

Makato eyed her hand dubiously. "I don't know if that's a good idea."

"Then use your vines or something against it, lift up the stones so we can walk under. Do something, cause my fire alone is not enough."

"When you took energy from me before, I felt something."

"We don't have time to talk about it. This is life and death."

Suzume looked at him, real fear was coiling in her stomach now. How long could they run around in circles before it inevitably caught up with them?

"We have to at least try," Suzume said, grabbing his hand before he could protest further.

When Makato's hand was in hers she felt a rush of power almost immediately. Makato looked at their conjoined hands and then toward the creature. It was almost within arm's reach, and was holding out gray arms as if it would embrace them. The hair fell behind its shoulders and exposed bones protruding from the skin there.

Makato grabbed onto her tighter and with his new commitment the energy pulsing between them grew stronger. Energy shot through Suzume, for a moment stealing her breath. She gasped and her free hand clutched at her chest. It felt as if someone was inside her clawing at her heart. But it went outward from there, passing through each of her centers of energy, igniting them and energy burst from each stream between points in a feeling that was both exhilarating and terrifying.

The inferno that churned inside her gut was spreading through her body, fed by energy that was poured into her from her hand and the contact with Makato. The energy was building beneath her skin, growing and swelling to fill every corner of her before traveling through the hand that connected her and Makato, creating a swirling pathway of energy that coursed through the both of them.

If she closed her eyes she could feel his heart beating in time with hers. It was as if they had become one and part of something larger than the two of them at the same time. She was one with the universe, with every living thing on the planet, connected by a living stream of energy: one every creature drew from and fell into upon their death to feed the living. If she wanted to she could reach into that endless stream and find other hearts beating in time with hers, who must have sensed her call. She felt their answer echoed back at her from miles and miles away.

Makato's hand squeezed hers and brought her back to the present, grounding her in the moment where the thing was nearly upon them, its horrifying gray skin and blackened nails about to grab a hold of her.

Together they took a hold of the staff with their free hands and imbued it with their combined spiritual power. And as if they were two parts of a greater whole, they wielded the energy at the creature. Bright, white, pure energy burst out of them and slammed into the body of the creature.

It stumbled backward a few steps, but did not fall. The energy, instead of burning a hole through it as they intended, hovered in front of the yuri. It clung onto it with clumsy, decaying hands. It caressed the energy, forming it into a ball. The creature's darkness enveloped and shrouded the light until it was nothing more than a pinprick and then gone altogether. When the light was gone and all that remained was a black mass of swirling grays and black, it pressed the energy into its chest. The yuri gasped, its white eyes bulging in the gray sockets as it threw its head back.

Her head snapped forward and she grinned at them. "Fools, you would have been better to be ripped apart than use your energy upon me," she said in a raspy voice.

The energy was still coursing through Suzume and Makato and their thoughts even seemed to be unified. She could not tell where Makato began and she ended. They created a barrier around themselves in a futile attempt to protect their bodies.

Their energy healed the decay of the creature's flesh, bringing her back to a semblance of life. It walked toward them with new pink flesh and a ruby red smile. The yuri closed in, hands reaching, pushing through the barrier as if it was nothing.

Makato was the first to let go, and he shoved Suzume behind him, placing himself in front of the yuri. Suzume felt their shared energy crash into her. Forced inside her by Makato's desperation to protect her, as if he would take refuge within her. Her skin felt too tight, as if she would burst from the energy buzzing inside her. But she was also paralyzed, and lying on the ground she was helpless to act as the yuri grabbed Makato by the front of his haori. She inhaled his energy, which sparked along his skin, the last remnant of the power they had shared together. The yuri then placed her gray lips against his and absorbed his energy through her kiss. Makato was also paralyzed, limp in her hands. The color of his skin faded as she drank in his energy, leaving him pallid and gray.

When the creature was finished she dropped Makato to the ground. She was no longer decayed and stringy, but a woman in shape, with a beautiful face, round eyes, and red cherry lips. She wore a bright white haori and hakama with designs of flowers and insects along the hems. Her eyes had become a golden color and she looked down at Suzume who had fallen to the ground. She was trapped within her own body, paralyzed, and staring at the thing above her.

The woman knelt down.

"I can feel her inside you: that witch who trapped me here for five hundred years. I will have you suffer as I suffered but I will be more merciful and after a time I will kill you. But not yet. There is more to feast on to prepare myself for your punishment."

She looked up at the barrier, and with a wave of her hand she brought it down in a shimmering burst of sparks. She strolled past the ring of stones and the small sparkling lights followed after her as she walked up the trail toward the temple, where the others were unaware of what danger was stalking closer.

In Suzume's limp hand, she held the staff. Just a few feet away, Makato was staring at her, but all he could manage was a slow blink. Suzume closed her eyes. Once again, she was powerless to do anything.

"Lend me your energy, and I can save them."

Suzume's eyes darted around for the voice. But it was inside her.

"Kazue?" she croaked.

Then something deep within her stirred. Similar to the burst of energy when Makato's and her power combined, this felt as if it came from somewhere deeper than that. It reached for Makato's energy and her own which had mixed inside her. Something bloomed inside her, and grew like a fiery flower. Suzume cried out in pain as it burned her from the inside. This was power, this was what she had been looking for all along.

TWENTY-FIVE

The putrid stink of rotted flesh and grave soil hit him like a punch to the face. Kaito reacted without thinking, instinct calling him to defend. Moving too quickly only pulled at his still healing wounds and he had to resist the urge to clutch at the throbbing wound at his side, or one of the others would notice his weakness and exploit it.

They'd all smelled what was coming, and had risen to defend. Naoki drew his sword, eyes trained on the direction from which the horrid smell was coming, his son, Tsuki standing beside him. Rin had transformed into her kitsune form and she leaped in front of Kaito with her back to him, as if to guard.

Kaito scowled at the back of her head. "What are you doing?" he snarled.

"You're still healing, don't pretend like you're not. I can smell the blood on you."

She did not even look behind to him, her numerous fiery tails whipped back and forth. Despite his attempts to hide his weakness, this is what he'd been reduced to.

"Here it comes!" Tsuki shouted.

Kaito looked past Rin to the forest pathway beyond. A lone figure in white approached. It walked slowly, and with each step the ground beneath its feet shriveled up and turned gray and then black. It looked to be a woman in shape, with long dark hair that hung almost to her feet.

"Master, it's a yuri. You should run before it reaches us."

Kaito ignored her comment. "Where is Suzume?" A sudden realization dawned on him. He hadn't seen her in hours. Normally she'd be in the thick of things, squawking her displeasure.

Rin's massive kitsune head flicked across their makeshift camp. "Makato is missing as well." The kitsune half turned as if prepared to go look for them herself.

The Yuri reached Naoki and Tsuki first, who rushed at it with swords drawn. Their swords simply passed through the specter's form and it opened its mouth in a wide parody of a smile as it reached out and grabbed a hold of the legendary swordsman's arm. Its fingers sank into his flesh. Naoki struggled futilely against her grip before she drew him to her and forced her lips against his. Once drained of his energy, she tossed him aside like a rag doll. The yuri had begun to glow with a faint yellow light. Tsuki came up from behind her and swung his weapon but she moved one instant in front of him then behind him. She wrapped her arms around his torso, hands disappearing into his chest and then she lowered her lips to his neck, where she latched onto him. He struggled against her for a moment before going limp in her arms. He too was tossed aside.

This was no mere restless spirit: it was too powerful with an insatiable hunger for power. He could see it glimmering in her eye from a distance. With the energy it had absorbed thus far its body was starting to solidify, but not enough to give it a complete form. There was still a hazy translucent look to her. How was it something this powerful had been here right beneath their noses? When they first arrived, Naoki had swept the area for any potential threat, and he had found nothing. A yuri could not travel far from where it died, which meant this one had likely been sealed until just recently. And he could think of only one person who would accidentally free such a thing.

Where is that idiot priestess? He looked around the camp, Naoki had regained enough energy to stand and was stalking behind the Yuri. Tsuki was shaking his head as he shakily climbed up again. Suzume and Makato were nowhere to be seen. *Damn it. If she got herself hurt...* He wouldn't finish the thought.

Rin growled at the approaching Yuri, any attempts to look for Suzume and Makato were forgotten. The yuri launched itself at Rin, latching onto her shoulder blade. The spirit buried long black nails into the flesh of the kitsune and Rin cried out in pain, thrashing backward and forward trying to dislodge the leech upon her.

Kaito cast his gaze about, looking for some sort of weapon. Naoki and Tsuki both had swords but they were too far away to be of any help. A pile of firewood was nearby. Kaito grabbed a thick log off the stack to use as a bludgeon. It wasn't the most elegant weapon but it would be suitable. He rushed toward the yuri and Rin swinging his make-shift weapon. The yuri had drained Rin of her spiritual energy, and the kitsune was limp in her arms. Her eyes met Kaito's and she let out a small whimper that sounded like a warning.

It did not deter him. The dragon swung his weapon at the yuri, who dropped Rin to the ground without ceremony. His stick slammed into the yuri's shoulder, which had completely solidified with the absorption of Rin's energy. But the spirit did not react at all and simply smiled, revealing pointed canines like a kitsune. She grabbed onto the other end of the wood and yanked it from his hand and tossed it behind her. A trio of ghostly fox tails flickered behind her and a pair of translucent ears were on her head.

Kaito, deprived of a weapon, swung with a fist at her face, but vines rose up from the ground and wrapped themselves around his ankles, trapping him in place. She threw her head back and laughed as he struggled. Her face was something like a cross between Tsuki and Akira, and on her hip was a blade made of golden light. She had absorbed all of their power along with their energy.

"Come to me, lover," she crooned. The vines lifted him up and brought him closer to her.

Kaito pulled his head back away from her as she opened her arms to him in an embrace. There was no fighting the vines as they constricted him, pinning his arms to his sides. As he got closer to her she wrapped her arms around him, her hands sliding into his flesh with no resistance. There was no way of saying where one of them started and the other stopped.

"Do you not recognize me, dragon?" she whispered in his mind, her voice had the edge of an ancient, something powerful.

He searched her face but could only see an ever-shifting visage of his companions: at first Naoki, now Makato, then Rin and finally Akira and Tsuki. Suzume's face was conspicuously absent from the myriad of faces.

"Should I know you?" he growled.

"We were lovers once, before you chose that human woman and forsook your own kind."

Kaito frowned and stared harder at the creature in front of him. He could not remember ever having relations with a yuri, but he was starting to suspect this was not some angry spirit after all.

"That horrible woman. She sealed your power and has kept you like a pet." She shook her head. "I will free you, and then you can never leave me." Her hands sank deeper into his flesh and pain rippled through his body.

"No thanks," he said through gritted teeth. "I've decided to be single for a while."

She only smiled. "You cannot fight me, you belong to me." She dipped in low to give him a kiss. Kaito pulled his head away before she could give him a deadly kiss.

"I'll pass."

Her eyes flashed red and he saw a glimpse of a familiar face. "You would choose that *human* over me? I am the guardian of this forest. You belong with an equal not an insect."

And then he felt it, the echo of the past. A forest guardian who had pursued him relentlessly, making threats against Kazue before she disappeared one day. He had thought nothing of it at the time, but now it was clear what had happened. Kazue had taken care of the problem herself. How had he not seen the signs before? Kazue's desire for power had predated even his sealing.

The one-time forest guardian lifted him up off the ground, holding him in a mockery of an embrace. "I will break this seal and then drink of your lifeblood. It will be days, but you will come to love me for it, and worship me." She removed one hand from his back, and ran it over his chest, caressing and probing until she found the wound on his chest. Her nails plunged into his injury and he cried out from the pain.

She brought her bloody fingers to her lips and licked them clean with a black tongue. She smirked at him. "I will force you to watch as I torture that woman who stole my body from me and sealed my soul, then you will know who it is you are destined for." She sighed wistfully.

The yuri leaned in to press her lips against the dragon's, but before she could something slammed into the back of him. The yuri dropped Kaito and he crumbled to the ground like a rag doll.

The angry spirit turned toward her attacker. Kaito followed her gaze, and was shocked to see Suzume standing in between two trees. Each of her hands burned with balls of flame. But there was something different about her, a new sense of confidence he had never seen before, a certain aura glowed around her. As if she was lined with red light. The fog parted around Suzume's feet as she strode toward them.

The yuri's lips pulled back into a snarl and she glided toward Suzume with hands raised, as if she was going to rip her apart with her bare hands. The yuri opened her mouth filled with sharp teeth and lunged for Suzume who tossed the balls of fire at the creature. The fire collided with her chest and stomach, burning holes through the newly formed flesh and exposing the fog behind her. The yuri paused only for a moment to look at her wounds.

She threw her head back to laugh. "You cannot stop me. I am too powerful now."

Though it was Suzume, it was as if a different person stood before them. An aura emanated from her in a way he had seen back on the mountain when Kazue had used Suzume's body to stop Hisato.

The yuri moved too fast for a human eye to follow. She lunged for Suzume but before she could grab a hold, Suzume leaped out of the way, leaving the yuri to collide with the ground.

It rose up with a hiss and then turned back toward Suzume who had two new balls of fire in each hand. Something Suzume had never been able to do before. The wounds to the yuri's flesh had healed as if she'd never been blown apart by fire. The creature latched onto Suzume's shoulders, clawed hands digging into her flesh, and Suzume, likewise, grabbed onto the yuri's shoulders. The flames caught along the yuri's sleeve and fire spread across her flesh like kindling. At first the yuri only smiled in triumph, but then she threw back her head in a blood-curdling scream, before falling onto the ground convulsing as flames consumed her.

Suzume stood over her burning and writhing corpse. Her expression nothing like Suzume's but not Kazue either. This was the face of a killer. The light from the fire danced in her eyes and Kaito could see the hunger there as well — a consuming desire for power. A song rose from her lips, one that left the hairs along Kaito's neck rising on end. It was a song of binding, one that Suzume had no way of knowing. The same song Kazue had used to seal him in the stone for five hundred years. As the flames died away on the burning creature, all that remained was a single stone. Suzume stooped down to pick it up.

She turned to Kaito, holding the stone in her hand. The flames had died down but the unfamiliar aura around her remained. Their eyes met and Suzume's grew wide.

Her mouth started to form his name, he could see it. Kazue was trying to reach out to him from somewhere deep inside Suzume. He reached out for her, despite how much he wanted to hate her and wanted to put the love they shared behind him. When he saw even the smallest hint of her his resolve crumbled. He crossed the space between them and grabbed her by the shoulders. Already the light was fading from Suzume's eyes, the ghost of Kazue leaving her gaze. He thought about crying out to her, but that might be too revealing. It was too late anyway. Kazue was gone, back to the ether from which she emerged.

Suzume blinked and then stared up at him. Their eyes met and for a moment, he thought she might have been conscious that entire time, perhaps not in control but at least aware. She paused. Her expression shifted from confidence to sudden confusion. She shoved him backward.

"Why are you holding me?" She looked around, in wide-eyed panic. "What am I doing here? Where's that thing?"

The fog was rolling away as if it had never been. Suzume held up her hand as if realizing something was in it for the first time. The stone looked like nothing out of the ordinary, just a rock.

Kaito tried to close the distance, desperate for one more glimpse of Kazue. He grabbed her by the shoulders again. Suzume looked up at him, at once both wary and angry.

"You don't remember?" he asked — there was an unflattering note of desperation in his voice. But he didn't care, he knew what he saw, Kazue was inside her, not gone but living inside her body.

Twenty-Six

"What happened?" Suzume gazed at the smoldering fire that scorched the ground where the balls of fire she had shot had gone astray.

"Kazue took a hold of your body and sealed the yuri." He gestured toward the stone she was holding in her hand. Suzume uncurled her fingers and stared at the rock for a moment before dropping it to the ground as if it burned her.

He should have known once he spoke Kazue's name it would put distance between them. She took a few steps back, and hurt painted her face before it was hidden behind a mask of anger. Flames danced along her body. The heat radiating off her forced him to step back. As he recoiled from her, fearing the damage her flames could do to his already weakened body, her expression hardened further.

The pair of them stared at one another for a moment and distrust warred with desperation within him.

"I'm not Kazue!" Her voice shook through the forest around him. It rippled with power. Power that did not belong to her, but to Kazue.

A new tension settled between them. They'd never completely trusted one another, but they'd had a mutual understanding and a common goal forged by Kazue's influence on both of their lives. Suzume had always been a wild card, lacking control of both her power and her emotion. Now the two were so heavily entwined they reacted together. Before he had been stronger than her and it didn't matter, anything she could throw at him, intentionally or otherwise, he could handle. For the first time, he felt weak. And that made him angry.

"How do you explain the stone? The burns on the ground? You don't have that kind of power yourself. She possessed you!" he snarled. Under normal circumstances he would have felt the rise of his spiritual energy with his temper, but it remained just as dormant as before.

"Why can't you just believe it's my power?" she snapped back.

Her eyes flashed red and for a moment he saw a hint of that same power he had glimpsed when she was sealing the yuri, he felt it roll over his skin. Raw, untamed power. If she attacked now, she would destroy him. He was already losing his grip on their group, and the cracks in his authority were showing. Even Rin suspected his fragility. If he didn't assert his dominance now, he'd lose all control entirely.

"Because you're just a temperamental brat. If you were taking your training seriously you'd have gotten control of this by now." He growled.

"I can control it!" As she said it sparks shot off her hair, nearly catching onto nearby branches.

"That's enough," Akira said, gliding in between them. It seemed she had regained consciousness after the yuri drained her and her brother.

"Don't interfere." Kaito growled at her too.

"You prodding at her is only making things worse," Akira said. Her voice calm and even, which was even more infuriating. Could none of them see what a liability Suzume was?

Kaito glared at her, not wanting to hear reason. "She's a menace. She woke that thing that almost killed us. What are you teaching her? How to become a human torch? Her powers are out of control."

"It's not my fault. It's her heart," Suzume blurted.

They swiveled to look at her. Suzume's face was red and her hands were balled into fists at her side.

"What do you mean it's the heart? Kazue's heart? It shattered into pieces," Kaito said, taking a step toward her unconsciously.

Suzume glared at him. "Are you hoping to bring her back to life?"

"What about the heart?" he ground out, not rising to her bait.

Suzume turned her head away from him to watch Naoki as he approached with Makato leaning heavily on his shoulder. Rin had woken as well and was rushing over to help Makato. Suzume ignored him to pretend to watch Rin fuss over the priest who declined her assistance with a small smile.

The other three joined them and the group settled into a half circle facing Suzume. There was some unspoken understanding that she was dangerous. Perhaps it was the sparks that continued to fly off her at random intervals. Suzume stared back at them defiantly, arms crossed over her chest.

"Do you have to stare? It's rather unnerving."

"Enough stalling," Kaito snapped, short on patience.

Suzume sighed heavily. "Kazue's heart is inside me now."

Kaito laughed, surely this had to be a joke. He'd played along when she pretended she could speak to Kazue.

Suzume scowled in reply.

"Kazue called me too," Makato said.

Kaito's narrowed gaze flickered in his direction. He didn't trust the priest, but he let him stay around because he'd rather have him close where he could watch him than have him with Hisato where he could do more damage.

"What do you mean it called to you?" Rin asked. Her eyes were pinned on him, like a starved woman.

"When I first found Suzume it was as if something was guiding me..."

Suzume gasped. "I felt the same thing."

Makato nodded as if he suspected as much. "And after that, the dreams started."

"What dreams?" Suzume frowned.

"You're saying you haven't dreamed of her?" He looked at her imploringly. Everyone's head swiveled in his direction.

"You have?" Suzume's voice was high and accusatory.

He didn't look directly at anyone but at his feet instead. "It was never anything concrete, but every night since I've met you I see that woman in a field of red spider lilies. She's waiting for someone, I don't know who. Because when they arrive I wake up." He raised his head and his eyes met Kaito's.

The dragon didn't like to think about the fact that a piece of Kazue was also inside the priest. Maybe unconsciously it was another reason he wasn't willing to part from the man. He was another link to Kazue, just like Suzume.

When their eyes met, he swore he saw Kazue staring back at him. He had to look away, even if it made him look weak. Kaito felt like the breath had been stolen from his lungs. The priest was dreaming of the day Kazue sealed him. He was sure of it. Suzume looked from Kaito to Makato and then back to Kaito without saying a word, perhaps she had the same dream. The thought only stoked the fires of his anger, to know these two people shared with him the darkest moment of his life. That moment of her betrayal. The only good thing about learning about the dream, was the cold reminder of what Kazue had done. He could not forgive her, even if she could be brought back to life.

"None of this matters. All that matters is making sure she doesn't kill us all with her fire." He jabbed a finger toward Suzume.

"And how do you suggest I get control of it?" She bristled, their argument resuming once more.

"Maybe we should seal it," Akira suggested with a sly look at him.

Kaito glared back at her. He wouldn't take her bait. He might be weaker than before, but he wasn't going to give in that easily. Whatever her initial motive, it was a logical solution. If Suzume couldn't control her power, perhaps they should take it away.

"What if I get attacked, how will I defend myself?" Suzume said.

"Rin will protect you," he said without conferring with the kitsune. He knew she would obey without question.

"I can teach her how to control it," Makato said, looking at the dragon for permission.

Kaito crossed his arms over his chest and assessed the man standing before him. What was his motive? He didn't want to trust him, but he didn't entirely like the idea of sealing Kazue's power either. But if he did then he might never get a glimpse of Kazue again. And that could either be a bad thing or a good thing. But that was just sentimental crap. He had moved on from his feelings, hadn't he?

"What can you possibly teach her that Akira and Tsuki couldn't?" Kaito replied, his voice dripping with disdain.

"When that thing rose from the ground, our energies were harmonious. If we can learn to balance one another we'll be twice as powerful as we are alone." He looked to Suzume, nodding his head for her to help him.

Suzume nodded her head feverishly. "We were stronger together. It felt like we were connected. You did that, didn't you?" she asked Makato.

He shook his head. "Until recently, I never knew I had control over the earth. You were the same with your flames?" he asked Suzume.

She nodded. "Not until I broke Kaito's seal."

"The pieces of Kazue must have linked up. And then took hold of Suzume's body because she hasn't learned how to channel the power yet. We've seen her unconscious defenses before. Perhaps Kazue drew her energy from Makato's body and used Suzume's body as a vessel," Akira mused, hand tapping on her chin as she thought.

Suzume threw her hands up in a stop motion. "You cannot really think Kazue is possessing me?"

The priest looked pensively at the ground. "I think whatever part of us that is Kazue is starting to wake up."

"Can you try communicating with her again?" Akira asked, she leaned in close to Suzume, peering at her face as if she could see Kazue there. "She may only be able to communicate through images, maybe you've remembered things that never happened to you?"

Suzume's eyes darted in Kaito's direction and their gazes met. He narrowed his eyes, trying to read what she was thinking. But she was a mystery. She scowled and looked away.

"This is crazy. Kazue cannot be alive in me. She ripped her own soul apart."

"How do we know this isn't some plot by Hisato," Kaito said, jabbing a finger in Makato's direction, speaking his doubts aloud for the first time.

Makato stared at him for a long moment. "I can't give you a good reason to trust me. And you may not believe this, but I feel compelled to protect you." He rested his hand on his chest. "You can push me away, but I will defend you and Suzume with my life."

Kaito snorted, this man must think he was an idiot. "You're right, I don't believe you and I don't trust you."

"Well I trust him," Suzume said, lifting her chin in her haughty way. "You can't lock me away in a temple and seal my powers. I refuse."

"I make the decisions here."

"Not anymore," Akira said, coming to stand behind Suzume. She rested a hand on her shoulder, as did Naoki and Makato. The only one left standing between them was Rin who was torn between the two sides. He narrowed his eyes at her, threatening her with his eyes before she joined his side.

"Are you all fools? She'll lead us to our destruction." Kaito gestured toward Suzume.

"Why should we follow someone as weak as you." Suzume nodded her head toward him. She looked down like a queen on her throne. She thought she had won, but she would learn quickly enough that without real loyalty, she could never control this group.

"Fine, you take charge. We'll see where that gets us."

He glared at her. Suzume looked back at him, with a smug, self-satisfied smile. He would only have to keep up this charade just a little longer, then he would return to normal and none of this would matter. Just as long as nothing provoked Suzume's temper they would be safe for now. Which was much easier said than done.

Kaito stalked away from the group, a swirl of emotions churning in his head. Rin hesitated but she eventually followed after the dragon.

She touched his shoulder lightly. "We need to talk," she said.

He shoved aside her touch; he wasn't in the mood. He kept on walking, out of their camp and into the forest beyond. He needed space and time to think. That woman was driving him insane. Couldn't she just trust him to do what was best for her? Even Kazue had not fought him, she understood. Suzume's life had been put at risk time and again and she still insisted on clinging to her damn pride.

Rin chased after him. "You shouldn't be out here, who knows what might be drawn by the power Suzume unleashed just now."

He spun around to face her. "I told you to watch over Suzume."

Rin did not hesitate. "Makato is with her. You need someone to knock some sense into that thick head of yours."

He gripped his hands into fists. Rin had never spoken to him like this before. Was this just a further sign of his crumbling control? She knew how weak he was.

"You forget who you're talking to, kitsune," he said, his voice a low growl.

"You haven't been my master for a long time," she replied, hands on hips as she met his gaze, not as a servant but as an equal. Under different circumstances, he might have been glad to see she had grown stronger, proud even. But right now it only made him angrier.

"Will you betray me next?"

"I've only ever been loyal to you."

"Don't pretend with me. I've seen how you watch that priest. I know where your real loyalty lies."

He swung a fist at her head, which missed when she darted out of the way, his hand collided with the tree behind her. Pain shot up his arm and blood dripped down his knuckles. Another wound to add to his collection. Kaito leaned his head against the rough bark.

"I'll leave you then."

He pulled back and punched the tree several more times, heedless of the injuries he was inflicting on himself. He kept it up until his arm was shaking with the effort, and only then did he lean against the tree, sliding down to the ground with his head bowed forward and buried in his knees.

TWENTY-SEVEN

"Tell me again why Kaito isn't out gathering wood?" Suzume asked Rin for what must have been the hundredth time.

"Because the dragon is still healing," Rin replied without looking back at Suzume, suppressing the urge to sigh in the dramatic way the priestess often did.

Suzume scoffed. "How much more time are we going to waste waiting on him?"

"Don't you think you're being a little hard on him? He nearly died," Rin snapped her patience worn thin by the callous way Suzume talked about the dragon. But also by the dragon who continued to push her and everyone else away. She knew Kaito was worried about his weakness and Suzume's sudden rise to power didn't help things either. Rin could see it even if Kaito wouldn't admit it.

Rin glared over her shoulder in Suzume's direction. She understood Kaito wanting to protect Suzume, because she felt the same way about Makato, but couldn't Suzume at least acknowledge Kaito's efforts?

The priestess just rolled her eyes. "If our positions were reversed, and I was mortally wounded then he would have had me marching down the road in the middle of the night. We shouldn't be wasting time here, who knows when Hisato will return."

Rin took a deep breath. She knew this was just Suzume's way of hiding her feelings. In fact when they'd gone off to collect firewood, she caught Suzume looking around for Kaito.

Calm once more, Rin said, "He isn't like that. When you were unconscious after finding Kazue's heart, he snapped at everyone and couldn't sit still for more than a few seconds. He wouldn't say it out loud but he was worried sick about you."

Suzume laughed insincerely. "He just wants to use me as a proxy for Kazue, that's who he really cares about."

"You can try and deny the truth, but he cares about you. Just like I know that you're trying to pretend like you aren't worried about him when I saw you check on him before we left." Rin gave her a sly smile.

Suzume huffed again and shuffled off a few more feet to pick up a bundle of sticks rather than acknowledge her comments. Rin smirked, the priestess' silence was as good as a confirmation as she would get. And so she persisted.

"If you need help finding time to be alone I can arrange something." The kitsune waggled her eyebrows. Maybe if the two of them could talk it would improve the dragon's mood.

Suzume sputtered. "I don't want to be alone with him!"

"How long are you going to deny your feelings? You're destined to be together."

"Just because I have Kazue's soul inside me doesn't mean I am destined to be with Kaito. Do you think Makato is destined to be with you just because he's your husband's reincarnation?" Suzume shot back.

The kitsune's vulpine ears flattened against her skull. The comment had caught her off guard. "I had hoped..." she trailed off.

Suzume shook her head in disgust. "Have you even asked him what he wants? Or are you just assuming he'll want to pick up right where his last life left off?"

The twitch of Rin's fox tail was the only indication of her agitation. "I've been waiting to talk to him. A lot has happened." The kitsune turned to Suzume, a question in her golden eyes. Suzume could give her the insight she needed to approach such a subject with Makato.

"No kidding," Suzume mumbled under her breath.

Rin picked up a few sticks to avoid asking straight away. But the more time that passed the harder it was to ask her question. What if Suzume said she should give up on her hope of reuniting with her husband? Makato, though he looked like her husband, had a manner that was so different from Hikaru's it was difficult to see her husband inside him. What if everything she had held onto all these years had been for nothing? Her thoughts took a similar path as she wandered farther from Suzume. Maybe now wasn't the time to bring up the subject to Suzume either.

As she added sticks to her bundle, the bushes to her right rustled. Rin's ears swiveled and her head snapped up. A few yards away from her, Suzume was frozen in place, her entire body on alert. She was much closer to the bush and whatever was behind it. A yokai could tear her apart before Rin could ever reach her. After Suzume's fight with the centipede, the dragon had asked the kitsune to watch the priestess and Rin had been so lost in her own thoughts she'd let Suzume wander away. Suzume reached slowly for the staff on her back, which was tied next to the bundle she carried. The leaves on the bush started to tremble and Rin shifted into her kitsune form, preparing to lunge and protect her.

The bush burst apart, and Suzume knocked her entire bundle of wood apart as she drew her staff. She held the staff in front of her, ready to defend. Rin launched herself into the air, landing between Suzume and the thing coming from the bush. She came nose to nose with Makato, who looked up at her bared teeth with wide, terrified eyes.

From the corner of her eye, she saw the deer he'd been hunting bounding away through the underbrush.

Suzume, who had fallen onto her rear, was shouting expletives.

"Are we in danger?" Makato said as he turned in place looking for an attack.

"You scared me! Why did you sneak up on me like that!" Suzume snapped at the priest.

He looked at the ground sheepishly and then grinned up at Suzume. "I scared you?" He laughed a short bark.

It was a painful echo of Hikaru, down to the coy smile and the sound of his laughter. Rin transformed back into her humanoid form, but she might as well have been invisible. His attention was wholly focused on Suzume, who glared at him with arms crossed over her chest. Rin was searching for connections because he looked so much like him, but any connections she found were more like ghosts of the man she remembered.

"Did it get away?" Tsuki asked, emerging from around a nearby bush.

Makato looked back at Tsuki and his smile fell flat. "It did." His response was terse and quick.

Rin who had basked in his brief smiles, saw the shutters close on his expression and could see the way he hid his feelings behind an unfeeling mask.

"What are you doing out here?" Suzume asked Makato, arms still crossed over her chest.

"Tsuki and I were hunting: the dragon's orders." A small smirk pulled at the corner of his lip.

Suzume shook her head, a similar smile echoed on her face. Rin's head swiveled between the two of them. Perhaps she was imagining it but she felt like there was something going on between them. *Don't be ridiculous, of course they understand one another, they both have Kazue's soul inside them.*

"Did you think we were yokai?" Tsuki asked, looking at the scattered remains of what had previously been Suzume's wood bundle.

Suzume looked down at the mess she had made. "Even if you were I could have taken you on." She held up her staff in a defensive pose.

Perhaps it was meant to be a powerful gesture but to Rin she looked like a child who was playing pretend. Makato looked her up and down, a quick glance which Rin caught. He saw her looking and blushed, turning away from her as he cleared his throat. "Have you fought a lot of yokai?" he asked her.

"Let's just say our Suzume is a bit of a magnet for yokai," Tsuki said before coming over to ruffle Suzume's hair.

She slipped out from beneath his grasp and swung at him, but the strike missed and Tsuki danced out of her reach.

While Suzume chased Tsuki, trying to get revenge for him tousling her hair, Makato was staring at the ground with his brows furrowed together. Unnoticed from the sidelines, Rin scrutinized his expression, looking for further hints of Hikaru or memories of his long past life with her. Was he trying to recall his own past?

"I guess you'd know about that seeing as you have Kazue's soul in you too," Rin said as she approached him from the side.

Makato did not lift his head, and instead knelt down to pick up the sticks Suzume had dropped. Rin squatted down to join him, and they reached for the same stick at the same time, their hands brushing against one another. As soon as their hands touched, he jerked his hand away and stood up abruptly. Rin felt as if someone punched her in the gut.

"Excuse me—" he started to say, pivoting to turn and walk away.

She couldn't let him go, not yet. "I wanted to talk to you — if you have the time," Rin said in a rush.

He turned just enough so she could see the silhouette of his face. More than anything she wanted him to recognize her. The longing that she'd kept at bay for so long threatened to overwhelm her and she fought the urge to reach out and take his hand. It was too soon to put any expectation upon him. She knew that much from watching Suzume and Kaito.

"I've been wanting to talk to you too," he said, a small frown furrowing his brow.

Rin stood up, not sure where to begin.

"Should we walk?" he asked, gesturing to the forest at large.

"Would that be okay? Isn't Tsuki watching you?"

"Are you afraid you can't trust me?"

Rin shook her head as she walked over to him. *I can't trust myself with you.* Memories of long gone days flooded through her mind, of similar walks in easy silence, assured in the affection of her life mate. She had known from the start that Hikaru's life would be limited and she had been prepared for his eventual death. But his death had come suddenly and without warning and though she told herself she could be patient and wait for his rebirth it had been a long couple of decades. The only sound that passed between them was the crunching of the leaves that carpeted the forest floor under their feet.

It was Makato who broke the silence. "You said in my past life I was someone named... Hikaru?" His mouth fumbled over the word as if it was unfamiliar to him. Another blow to her hope that he'd remember her from his old life.

Rin nodded, she couldn't get words past her tongue. It felt as if it was filling up her mouth.

"And you knew that I could heal the dragon, before I did," he added.

She nodded again. Words caught in her throat.

There was a long pause and then he said, "My memory isn't very good. I know some things without knowing where I learned them, like my spiritual powers. Memories filter in and out. If I concentrate, I can remember where I grew up, but I cannot remember my mother's face or whether or not I had siblings..."

Rin turned to face him, and he looked up at her with eyes so much like Hikaru's it made her chest hurt.

How desperately she wanted to touch his face, to lay her head against his chest and listen to his heartbeat to convince herself that this wasn't all a dream.

"Hikaru and I..." she hesitated. What if she was wrong? Or what if he rejected the idea the way Suzume so adamantly denied any connection to Kazue?

"I don't want to raise your expectations about me..." he said looking directly at her.

"Go on," she managed to choke out.

He laid his hand over his chest — the shape of his splayed fingers, his tanned skin and calloused hands, they all reminded her of Hikaru. Maybe she was looking for connections that weren't there but she could have sworn his hands were scarred in the same way Hikaru's were. "I've been searching for something for a very long time. And I hoped it was you, and I'm sorry to say this but I just don't remember you."

Tears threatened the back of her lids as she shook her head to dispel his protests. "I don't expect you to remember me."

"That's just it. I do remember the dragon, I can see Kazue's memories so clear." He hesitated.

Something felt like it had a hold of Rin's lungs and was limiting her ability to breathe. "Oh."

"What I am trying to say is, I don't think I'm Hikaru's reincarnation."

Rin forced a laugh. "Oh, is that all?" She lightly slapped him on the shoulder, in the same way she would have with Hikaru. But even as she did, it felt wrong. She had no right to touch this man. "Well I am glad you brought it up, because I wanted to say I don't feel burdened just because you're similar to him. That's all in the past after all."

He was looking into her eyes, searching perhaps for some sliver of memory that linked him to her.

"I am sorry," he said

She shook her head. "Don't be."

Just then Tsuki and Suzume rejoined them, coming back in their direction. Suzume was scolding Tsuki for some prank he had played. Makato turned immediately to look at Suzume and his entire face lit up. Rin could see it on his face, she was nothing to him. She took advantage of his distraction to slip away, retreating into the forest to be alone. And it wasn't until then that she allowed herself the luxury to cry.

As the tears streamed down her face, Rin slid to her knees, her hand covering her mouth to stifle her sobs. Behind her she could hear Makato calling out to Suzume and laughing. There was no place for her in his new life it seemed.

"You're much too beautiful to be crying."

Rin's entire body froze as she looked up at Hisato's smiling face, his hand outstretched to her. "What if I could fix this problem of yours?"

Rin growled at him, seconds away from transforming into her kitsune form.

Hisato held up a finger and as if by some spell of his she was frozen in place, unable to move. "Makato is Hikaru. All that he needs is to remember. Help me and I can return him to you."

"At what price?" she snarled.

"Straight to the point. I like that." He grinned.

Rin, still frozen in place, could not look away. She glared at him, willing him to answer.

"Kill the dragon for me and I will return your husband to you."

She laughed, mockingly. "I wouldn't betray Kaito, no matter the price."

"Is that so? Are you certain that the dragon feels the same?"

Rin bared her teeth at him in response.

Hisato laughed, his maniacal smile off kilter on his face. "Consider it. When you are ready, I will be there for you."

He bowed before stepping through a portal and leaving Rin who, once free from his spell stared at the place he had been.

TWENTY-EIGHT

"Where are we going exactly?" Kaito asked for what may have been the third time in the past fifteen minutes.

Suzume tried her best to ignore his question and pushed a branch out of her way, which whipped backward toward the annoying dragon behind her.

Kaito combated her cold shoulder by complaining in a whining voice, "Why aren't you telling me anything? I deserve to know where we're going."

Holding her head up in the most regal pose she knew, Suzume forged forward ignoring him. As the new leader of the group, Suzume had decided they'd wasted enough time at the dilapidated shrine. She was anxious to start the hunt for the missing eight gods and the other pieces of Kazue's soul. If she could find anything related to Kazue it would prove to Kaito that she was not only a good leader, but a better leader than him. She could just imagine the look on his face when she presented him with an artifact, or better yet, if she freed one of the missing Kami.

The only problem was Suzume was not sure where to go next. They had no leads, and what resulted was hours of aimless forest wandering. Almost immediately Kaito had questioned and challenged her leadership. Suzume had deflected each of his questions with place-holder answers: the ones he was characteristic of using against her.

Things like: that's for me to worry about. Or a more childish, I don't have to tell you.

Kaito had taken to the role of group dissenter and was complaining as often and loudly as he could.

"I'm tired. When are we taking a break?" he said in a high-pitched whine that she was certain was meant to be an impression of her.

Suzume grit her teeth together as she said, "We just stopped five minutes ago."

"But I'm injured, don't you even care about me?" he said in a screeching voice that sent chills up Suzume's spine.

Don't let him get into your head. This is just a test.

But after two days of wandering and Kaito's complaining and overall frustration at their complete lack of progress, Suzume's patience was wearing thin. She had sent Naoki out to look for leads. That had been two days ago, and he had not returned yet. *Perhaps he's not as bound to me as we thought.*

"You look angry," Tsuki said as he walked backward in front of Suzume, his arms folded behind his head.

"Brother, really," Akira scolded.

Suzume turned her head and ignored his question instead pretending the identical trees they were passing by were of extreme interest. Oh, is that a tree and look another tree, just like the million other trees in this never-ending forest. Why did none of this seem familiar? Shouldn't having a piece of Kazue's soul somehow guide her? Kazue only seemed to manifest when Suzume's life was in danger.

Tsuki exhaled in over exaggerated defeat. "I don't know why you two can't seem to get along."

Suzume, her tone dripping with fake sweetness, replied, "I get along with everyone. Some people just aren't very trusting." The last word was cast out loud enough that it echoed back at her from the treetops.

Tsuki raised a single brow in response. "Honestly, you two should kiss and get it over with."

Kaito scoffed loudly and then said, "I'd rather face a bloodthirsty yokai than kiss her. She's yucky!"

Unable to resist any more of his taunts, Suzume spun around and narrowed her eyes at him. "No one said you had to follow me."

Kaito crossed his arms over his chest. "You're right, I'd probably be safer on my own than under your leadership." He drawled the last word to indicate exactly how he felt about her being in control of the group.

Suzume's face flushed and sparks leaped along the ends of her hair as her temper rose. It wasn't that she expected him to welcome her leadership, not at first. She had just thought that after a while he would just go along with it. He was weak and in no position to lead. It had been naive of her to think that Kaito would be cooperative in any way.

Tsuki covered his mouth with his hand as he looked between Suzume and Kaito. Even then it could not disguise the pure glee in his expression. Kaito stood with hands crossed over his chest and a smug look on his face.

Everyone had stopped walking to stop and stare at the two of them. None of them took her role as leader seriously. Akira and Tsuki had orchestrated this to get what they wanted. But she knew she could be a good leader. With her frustration, the fire built up inside her, rising with her temper. It sparked along her fingertips, like popping embers in a fire. She would like nothing better than to burn that damn dragon to a crisp.

"And we were better under your leadership how? It was your idea to go into Daiki's camp and look where that left you." Suzume nodded toward Kaito.

Tsuki whistled, his gaze swiveling in Kaito's direction, waiting for his rebuttal.

"I think this is enough," Makato said, sheepishly inserting himself into their argument.

"The sexual tension is thick enough to run a knife through. Don't ruin this," Tsuki said as he slung an arm over Makato's shoulder.

"You've been in charge for less than forty-eight hours and we've walked several leagues in a circle. This is the tenth time we've passed that same tree." Kaito nodded toward a nearby tree with a distinctive crook that resembled a seat.

Suzume stared at the offending tree, realizing now why the trees all seemed so familiar. She wouldn't let this be a triumph for Kaito; she had to grab a hold of this situation.

"That was intentional. I was trying to be considerate of your condition. I know how sensitive you are about being weak, and I didn't want you to think we were waiting around for you. Should I not have?" She raised an eyebrow, mocking his weakness.

Anger flashed in Kaito's eyes. She braced herself for the pressure of his spiritual power which he would normally use against her. Sparks would fly between them and then someone like Rin would intervene before they killed one another. But this time his spiritual power didn't weigh down her chest, and his ice didn't clash with her fire.

"You think so?" he asked, his voice strangled, as if he was struggling to breathe.

It wasn't until Makato placed his hand on her shoulder that Suzume realized she had been unfurling her spiritual power and weighing it upon Kaito, who with his own spiritual power sealed was finding it difficult to breathe.

With some difficulty, she suppressed her power once more and Kaito gasped for breath. Suzume's eyes grew large, realizing their reversed position. She was more powerful than him right now.

"You rest here and let me worry about where we go next." She tossed her hair over her shoulder, not waiting to give him the satisfaction of a retort and instead spun on her heel and marched away. She could just imagine the scowl that was following her. As much as she wanted to look back and see it, she didn't want to ruin this powerful image as she walked away, leaving Kaito gasping on his knees while she took control.

It didn't take long before her confident stride slowed into an ambling slow walk, and the reality of their situation came crashing down around her shoulders. Kaito was right. She had been unintentionally walking in circles. She continued down the animal trail she'd been following through the forest, and found the familiar landmarks again, an oddly shaped boulder, a burnt decaying tree. A creek she had just passed that morning. Suzume slumped down into a squat. *How do I recover from this?* There was no easy way to admit this sort of mistake, not on her second day of being the leader of the group.

Makato followed her and she stood up again as he approached, not wanting to be seen squatting in the forest like some sort of peasant. She turned toward the forest, pretending she hadn't seen his approach. She raised her hand to shield her eyes as if she were surveying the trees, looking for their path.

"Something the matter?" he asked.

"Nothing is wrong," Suzume snarled. Why couldn't she have her moment? All she wanted to do was prove to Kaito that she was his equal. Now all she had done was make an even bigger fool of herself.

Makato blinked at her a few moments, then said, "I think you'd feel better if you confessed your feelings."

Suzume growled and threw her hands up in the air. "There's nothing for me to confess. I don't care what Kaito thinks. I am descended from the gods. Leadership is in my blood. I am more than equipped to be our leader. He just thinks I can't do it because I am human." The force of her anger seemed to shake the ground beneath her and her voice carried farther than she had intended it to.

Kaito was nowhere in sight, but she was certain he had heard her anyway and was mocking her for her failure.

Makato stared at her wide-eyed. "Ah. I see."

Suzume growled in frustration and returned to marching but this time instead of following the same animal trail, she changed directions, pushing through the underbrush. Makato hovered at her shoulder, perhaps waiting to force another embarrassing confession out of her.

When she realized she couldn't shake the priest she said, "I don't need your help. I know where I am going."

"I do not doubt your leadership abilities. There was something else I needed to discuss with you."

Suzume's steps fumbled, and distracted by the priest's topic, she tripped over some brush under foot. She was tumbling forward before she realized it, but before she could land on the ground Makato caught her around the waist.

The trajectory of Suzume's fall was too much for him it seemed because instead of saving her from a fall, they both went tumbling to the ground. Makato managed to maneuver himself to land on the ground first and Suzume ended up on his chest. Their noses almost pressed together.

Suzume leaped up and off of him within a few seconds, brushing her clothes off. Makato climbed to his feet with a sheepish smile.

"Sorry about that," he said, rubbing the back of his neck. His face was turning a bright red.

"Be careful next time." Hostility came as a natural defense in this sort of situation. She hated herself for it but she looked behind her to make sure Kaito had not seen. *I don't care if he sees. Let him see. He doesn't own me.*

Makato cleared his throat. "There's something I wanted to talk about." He glanced around, perhaps fearful they'd be overheard, and once he was certain there was no one listening he said, "Perhaps it's time to leave the dragon behind."

She blinked at him for a few minutes, not sure she understood his suggestion. "Like we go ahead and look while he waits behind?"

Makato shook his head. "No, I mean, we go on our own. Without him."

"I'm not leaving the others."

"Akira, Tsuki and Naoki have all agreed to join us," he said.

"What about Rin and Kaito?"

"I think it's best if we part ways."

"Why?" Maybe she'd been too quick to trust Makato.

"The dragon is dangerous; can't you see that?" Makato asked with a frown. "He has had control of you all this time."

"He didn't control me. I chose to stay with him."

"Do you have feelings for him then?"

"Of course not!" Suzume shouted, and this time her voice echoed back at her from the treetops.

She was saved from any more discussion by the arrival of Rin and the others who had found where they were standing in the middle of the forest. There was an odd expression on Rin's face as she looked between Suzume and Makato. Before Suzume could think too much of it, she saw Naoki trailing the group. *Finally, now I can figure out where to go from here.*

"Naoki, you're back. Have you found anything?"

He nodded and Kaito snickered.

Suzume ignored the dragon and said to the swordsman, "Don't leave me in suspense." Suzume gestured for him to continue. The others fanned out, creating a half circle with all eyes trained on him.

"There are rumors of a creature guarding an island to the north of here."

Suzume stared at him, waiting for the rest. But after a few seconds of silence it was apparent he had nothing else to say.

"That's it?" Suzume asked.

Naoki nodded again.

Kaito cackled in delight. "I'm impressed. Is this why we've been wandering in circles for two days? So you can have Naoki hunt for rumors?" He shook his head, wiping away pretend tears. "You've really impressed me, princess. I don't know what we'd do without your guidance."

Her head was pounding so loud it sounded like drum beats. This couldn't be the end of it. She wasn't going to let this chance pass her by this quickly.

"Two days and that's all you heard?" Suzume asked, imploring Naoki with her eyes. There had to be something, some yokai who saw Kazue in this area five hundred years ago and knew where she'd hidden the missing gods.

"There is nothing else."

The flames were licking up her arms, her spiritual power was fueled by her anger and frustration. Knowing Kaito was watching her every move, Suzume could not let this defeat her. She may be in over her head but she wasn't going to let anyone see that. She would make this work.

"Then we'll investigate it," she said.

"How exactly do you plan to get to the north from here?" Kaito asked. Arms crossed over his chest, a smirk tugging at the corner of his mouth.

"We'll head north, of course."

"If we head directly north, we go right into Namahage territory. They're fierce and territorial warriors."

"Then we'll go around their territory."

"That will take weeks. Do you have that sort of time to waste?"

Suzume balled her hands into fists, it was the only thing keeping her from slapping him hard across the face. "I thought I was the leader here?"

"Are you? I can't tell."

This was her challenge. Make a decision, waste weeks going around on what might be a false lead. Or head straight into yokai territory. *I've fought plenty of yokai. How bad can it be?* "We're going north, through their territory."

"Are you sure this is a good idea?" Makato asked.

"Are you challenging me now?" Suzume spun on him.

Makato took a step back to avoid being burned. The fire had escaped her entirely now. "No."

"Anyone else have any complaints?" She looked at the assembled group, all but Kaito were watching her uneasily. The Dragon glared back at her in defiance.

"Be my guest, I'm eager to see where this goes."

"You'll be eating your words when I have the artifact in my hand." She turned and started marching in the direction that she thought was north.

"That's not north," Kaito shouted.

She blushed and adjusted.

"Not that either."

Suzume growled. "Makato, can you navigate?"

He nodded. "You lead the way north then."

"This is going to work out great," Kaito said as Makato took the lead, ushering them toward a mountain peak. Suzume kept her eyes glued forward, that was the only way she was going to be able to get through this without making a complete idiot out of herself.

TWENTY-NINE

ach time a twig snapped underfoot, Suzume reached for her staff. The tension in the group was palpable. It had been her decision that had led them into these mist-covered hills. Each way she looked she saw shadows looming in the fog. A fanged creature with rows of dagger-like teeth turned out to be nothing but a group of gnarled trees. A massive figure brandishing a club was only a group of boulders.

She was jumping at shadows, quite literally. Kaito's warnings had spooked her despite her decision to go her own way. The rest of the group seemed on edge as well. Rin remained in kitsune form, her head swiveling this way and that. Naoki's hand rested on the hilt of his sword, and Kaito's eyes continued to scan the fog, searching for a yokai attack. Only Tsuki wasn't taking this seriously.

"I've heard the Namahage kidnap virgins from villages to force them to serve them." He waggled his eyebrows at Suzume.

She rolled her eyes in response.

"Good thing we don't have any virgins with us," Kaito said.

"What are you insinuating?" Her power tingled just beneath the surface of her skin in response to his insult.

"Well, according to the general, you have a reputation." He gestured toward Suzume as if that reputation was obvious.

Suzume sputtered, unable to find the right words to respond to his insult. Makato placed his hand on her shoulder with a shake of his head that was meant to say 'don't let him get to you.'

Kaito was always trying to get a rise out of her. And it was true Suzume had many suitors when she lived at the palace and she enjoyed flirting. But she had never gone any further than that. And even if she had, that was none of his damn business. His comment crossed the line.

"Do you have something you want to say?" Suzume snarled.

"Me?" Kaito said in a falsetto. "Not at all. Weren't you leading us through the mountain?"

"Well, you see, I was just worried about you. The Namahage might mistake you for a maiden," she said in sickly sweet voice.

Kaito bared his teeth at her. "What was that?"

"Should I have Rin watch over you to make sure they can't kidnap you?"

She did not wait for his response and instead spun around, stomping ahead of the group, reclaiming her place at the front.

Tsuki gave a low whistle. "She's out for blood today. We should all watch out."

"Shut up," Suzume said, her voice was like a whip crack across the group. Fire crackled along her skin, giving weight to her outburst.

Tsuki took a visible step away from her, as did Makato. Silence followed her shout and all she could hear was the hammering of her own heart like the beating of a drum. The fire grew in strength with her temper. It was never far away lately. She had even less control over her emotions than ever before. Naoki's warning that Kazue would consume her rang through her head.

"Suzume." Makato started to say something but she held up her hand to silence him.

"Now that I am in charge, we need to get a few things straight. No more teasing." She looked at Kaito darkly. "And do not question my decisions. If any of you don't like it then you can leave."

There was no reply, everyone was staring at her. Kaito scowled. The drumming in her head was getting louder and louder. It was so loud she thought her head was going to explode out of her.

"What none of you have anything to say now?" She asked, throwing out her arms. The flames rose even higher, brushing against the nearby foliage and sparks rained down upon her.

"Something is coming," Naoki said, his voice low but it sent a ripple through the group.

The drumming she thought was inside her head was actually coming from the forest around her, and the ground beneath her feet vibrated with the sound of it. The group closed into a circle, weapons drawn. Suzume held her staff crossed in front of her but it was no use, the others had closed in around her forming a protective barrier, before she could even get a chance to join. Even Kaito, who was still recovering from his wounds, was on the outer circle.

"I told you this was a bad idea," Kaito snapped at Suzume.

"Then let me deal with it." She tried to push her way out of the circle they'd put around her but she was only shoved back.

Before she could voice her frustration, the yokai spilled out from within the mist. Dozens of figures in red masks and grass capes. They stamped their feet in time as they closed into a circle around them, easily outnumbering them five to one. They wielded knives as big as Suzume's forearm with gleaming sharp edges. They did not attack straight away, just filled in a circle around them as they stamped their feet.

"What are they doing?" Suzume asked.

"I'm not sure, I've never encountered yokai quite like this," Makato said.

"Their strength is in numbers," Kaito said. "They move together as an unstoppable force. Stand back and let us take care of this."

Suddenly the stomping stopped. One of the red-masked yokai stepped away from the group and approached them.

"You have trespassed upon on our land, if you wish to leave unharmed you must pay the price."

"I am the great dragon, your master, there is nowhere I cannot tread," Kaito said in a thundering voice, reminiscent of the powerful yokai he had been. But it lacked the pressure of his spiritual power. And if she could sense that, surely these yokai could as well.

"You are an impostor. The dragon was defeated centuries ago. We serve no master now."

"I don't think they're going to listen," she said, unable to keep a bit of gloating out of her voice.

Already she was forming a ball of fire in her hand, as soon as she got the chance she would unleash it upon these creatures. Kaito held up his hand to silence her and she scowled at the back of his head.

"I have been returned. If you do not leave now I will unleash my wrath upon all of you."

"All who cross our land must pay tribute. Give us the one who is kissed by fire, and you may leave unharmed." He pointed his enormous knife in Suzume's direction.

"Why me?" Suzume squawked. Must she always be the target of every yokai she came across?

"You cannot have her, this human belongs to me," Kaito said.

The yokai shook his head. "Then you will pay with your blood."

They swarmed forward, crashing against the outer ring of her protectors, while all she could do was stand ineffectively in the center. Fire burned in her hands, but she could not unleash it without risking burning her friends. Chaos surrounded her, and yet her gaze kept drifting to Kaito, who despite having his spiritual power sealed, fought gracefully, swinging his blade, pushing back his opponents with relative ease.

Makato, to her left, was rapid firing arrows that were imbued with glowing green spiritual power at the approaching yokai. Fire leaped along Suzume's skin, itching to be released. Suzume clutched at her staff and scanned around her, waiting for her moment.

The yokai were relentless in their approach, pressing closer and closer, leaving few openings for Suzume to use her fire. The others closed in around her, making the space in which she occupied claustrophobic.

Tsuki was laughing as he swung his sword at the nearby yokai, and three of them came at him at once. He lunged forward, chasing after them and exposed a space for a few to come through.

Giant hands reached for Suzume and she fumbled to fire a ball of fire. It skimmed off them like water on a duck's back. Unprepared for their resistance to fire, Suzume froze. Everything Tsuki had taught her about fighting seemed to escape her mind entirely and on reflex she swung the staff around wildly. Suzume stumbled backward, knocking into Makato and throwing him off balance as well. One of the yokai would have impaled him on his blade if it hadn't been for Rin's quick pivot as she snatched Makato off the ground and picked him up by his collar and hoisted him out of the battle.

But the ring of protection around Suzume had been shattered, the group was divided, and Suzume was left with only her staff and fire that could not burn her opponents. *Why did I think going through the mountains was a good idea?*

Her gaze swiveled all around as she swung her staff in a circle around her. When the staff collided with solid flesh, it jarred her arms and caused them to lock up. Her fire leaped to her defense, racing down her arms to ignite the staff, and when she spun around a trail of fire followed. But the yokai were not deterred by her fire, rather they were encouraged by it. More of them stopped fighting, all of them gravitating toward her.

Suzume looked around in desperation as the enemy closed in on her. She brought her staff into her chest, the flickering flames on her body and her staff no longer held comfort. As she looked around Kaito caught her eye across the battlefield. He'd turned away from his opponent and was headed in her direction. And in that moment he looked away, one of the yokai came up from behind and he was too slow to react as the blade sliced along his side. The gash was deep, and bright red blood welled up along his torso. She saw him stumble and fall before the crowd blocked him from view.

Something inside her stirred, awoken by his plight, and it pulled energy from those yokai around her and from Makato, just a few feet from her. It even pulled from the sunshine falling on her skin. She felt it growing inside her, building to a crescendo.

Makato saw what she was attempting to do, or maybe a more accurate description would be felt. He shouted her name but it was lost in the drumming in her ears, the swirl of power that was overcoming her. She was losing herself in it. Her body moved without instruction, striking at her foes and knocking them down.

But just as she felt it building inside her, the power burst apart, evaporating on her skin and fizzling out. But she had felt it, tasted the power, and she wanted more.

"Don't try to use your fire. It's too dangerous." Makato was beside her panting, the specters of vines were wrapped all over his body.

"Why did you stop me?" She shoved him hard, her flaming hands catching onto his haori and he had to pat the fire out before it spread further.

"If you give into her, you may never escape her. Remember what happened last time. She took over your body."

"Then what am I supposed to do then?" Suzume shouted, and all the frustration poured off of her in the form of fire. Apparently not all of the power had dissipated. The fire scorched the earth and forced Makato and anyone else within her proximity to move away, and quickly, unless they wanted to be burned.

This feeling of terror that kept grabbing onto her, choking her, was a disease. This is why she didn't let people in. She couldn't trust anyone. Makato wanted her power for himself. She could see it now.

Pushing the idea that Kaito might be hurt and bleeding from her mind, she let the fire consume her. Her body was encased in flames. There was no need for paltry barriers when you were a living inferno. But the fire had only temporarily pushed back the yokai. Now they were closing in with no other obstacle in their way because all of her companions had fled from her, terrified of the power she could wield. It was better that they feared her. She didn't need them to protect her. Suzume spun in circles, waving her staff around, fire dancing in her eyes and through the air, creating waves of light.

All around her was the crash of blades and the stamping of feet as the creatures worked in almost perfect harmony.

Her attention was scattered between the stamping feet, her desire to check on Kaito that she could not suppress, and the roar of Rin somewhere behind her. She couldn't concentrate, and could not manifest that same power she had moments ago, not without Makato's power. He had shielded her from it somehow. The fire was already dying down, leaving her in a faint red glow. Six of the yokai rushed toward her as one, swinging large knives.

Makato called out her name, but it was lost in the stamping of feet, the clang of metal. All she knew was three of the creatures were standing in front of her and three behind. *I'm not giving up yet.* She held her staff in front of her, crossed in front of her body, poised for defense.

The creatures stamped their feet, and the others around them joined in the rhythm. The fighting stopped as they shifted, circling around Suzume, cutting her off from the others. They did not try to attack her or grab her. They simply closed in around her, and she turned around and around until she made herself dizzy waiting for an attack that would not come. Makato rapid fire shot arrows at their backs. A secondary circle formed around the outer circle that fought off Makato and the others, blocking each blow with their large knives.

Rin loomed above their heads, trying to claw and bite her way through to no avail. Somewhere on the perimeter she knew Makato, Tsuki and Naoki would be doing the same, though she could not see them over the creatures. *And where is Kaito?* Better not to think about it. She should be worried about herself right now.

"Offering, offering, offering," they chanted. Their voices melded together into one long song, rising up as one voice.

"I'm not going to be your offering!" she shouted and as she did the flames leaped up along her hands, racing up and down the staff.

Then one of the creatures broke away from the rest, approaching her.

She held her staff in front of her as if the piece of wood could stop him. It grabbed a hold of the staff and yanked it from her hand. Her holy fire did not touch its flesh. The fire only rolled off it as if it was nothing.

"You, who have been kissed by fire, have been chosen to serve the Lady of the Flame," it said in a deep rumbling voice that seemed to echo across the forest.

"You've got the wrong girl. I don't serve anyone. You should be serving me."

The creature gestured behind him and two more figures broke free of the group and stepped forward to grab a hold of her. They each grabbed her hands, and paid no mind to the flames dancing across her body. Suzume kicked and thrashed against them, but it was no use. Even as her fire burned their grass capes, they persisted by pinning her arms to her side so she could not strike at them.

"Let me go!" Suzume shouted, her voice her final defense.

To the left, a space was opened between the rows of creatures, and one holding her flanked by two others, ran at surprising speed through it. Over its shoulder, she saw Naoki break free of a ring of the creatures, giving pursuit but as soon as he broke free, a dozen more surrounded him, preventing any rescue.

THIRTY

They traveled through the forest at lightning speed, past countless trees, until the terrain started to change. The trees eventually thinned and she could see the ground was covered in boulders. After a while, they reached what appeared to be a village. It was a collection of huts made up of circles within circles. In the center was a space covered in flattened earth and in the middle of that was a pile of wood and kindling, which she assumed was meant to be a bonfire. *It's the wrong time of year for a bonfire festival though...*

She was brought to a hut in the outermost circle. It was larger than the others. One of her three captors opened the door and the one carrying her dropped her inside. The space was sparse: nothing inside but a fire pit at one end filled with yesterday's ashes. She ran over to the door, hammering upon it.

"I demand you let me go," she shouted.

Two Namahage outside her door ignored her demands and spoke together in low rumbling tones. She persisted in hammering on the door for much longer but found the only result was bruised hands.

After several fruitless minutes, Suzume slumped against the door, her head against her knees. *Why do these sorts of things keep on happening to me?* All she had wanted was to prove that she could be a good leader. *This is your fault, Kazue. If your power didn't draw in every yokai within a five-mile radius.* Of course Kazue made no comment. Suzume wasn't even certain she could hear her. But she had felt that feeling again, the one where she had briefly blacked out and Kazue had taken a hold of her body. If only there was a way to harness that power without giving into it entirely. Maybe then she could escape this predicament.

Suzume glanced around the room in which she had been left. She had to get out before she was rescued or else she would really lose all credibility as a leader. For a moment she considered burning her way out but that was just as likely to result in her being trapped inside a burning building without an escape. Her fire didn't work against her captors so she just had to come up with a different plan.

Hours passed and Suzume was coming up empty for a brilliant escape plan. She must have dozed off waiting for inspiration to strike, because the next thing she knew the door to her prison opened and Suzume was knocked to the ground. She leaped up and raised her hands, prepared to fight. But the person that entered was a young woman, her eyes downcast, carrying a bucket and a bundle of fabric.

Suzume ignored her and rushed to the door, but the guards were faster than her and slammed it in her face before she could even attempt an escape. Her escape foiled, Suzume rounded on the girl.

"Who are you?" Suzume asked the girl.

The girl did not respond as she crossed the room and set her bucket down near the empty fire pit.

"What is going on here? Are you mute, do you speak a foreign language?"

"You, who are marked by fire, have been chosen to serve the Nama-hage," she said in an empty and detached voice without looking up. She grabbed a pitcher hanging on the wall and filled it from the bucket.

Suzume laughed. "Is this a joke? I don't serve." She enunciated each word as if she was speaking to an imbecile.

"You must be cleansed before the feast. Please take off your clothes," the girl said quietly, apparently unperturbed by Suzume's rudeness.

"What feast? What is going on here?" Suzume demanded, arms crossed over her chest.

"You who are marked by fire must serve the Namahage," she repeated.

Suzume snorted. What was it with yokai? Either they were trying to eat her or they were trying to kidnap her. She supposed she was lucky this wasn't the eating type of yokai.

Suzume crossed her arms over her chest. "Like I said, I don't serve anyone."

"Please don't make this difficult," the girl said as she grabbed a hold of Suzume's sleeve.

"Let go of me!" Suzume shouted.

They struggled for a moment and Suzume found the girl was deceptively strong, despite her meek voice and posture. Suzume's fire, already close to the surface after being manhandled, blazed as the girl grabbed a hold of her. When she knocked her aside, a few sparks blasted between them burning the hem of the girl's sleeve. The girl was knocked to the ground and cowered at Suzume's feet.

"Please spare me. I did not mean to bring you displeasure." She pressed her hands against the ground, her head in the dirt.

Suzume looked down at her hands which were sparking with flames. *Why against a human?* Normally it only manifested when she was in real danger, not in a petty argument with a poor excuse for a servant. Sure she was angry about her situation, but not that angry.

The girl was still groveling and mumbled, "Please forgive me, I did not know."

Suzume wasn't sure how to react. She was not averse to being groveled to. In fact in her old life it had been a pretty common thing. But having someone fear her because of her power felt strange. Having this girl tremble before her didn't make her feel powerful, it made her feel like a monster.

Suzume reached for the girl, unaccustomed to friendly gestures. The girl lifted her head and Suzume saw her face for the first time. Burn marks marred the right side of her face, leaving it pink and contorted. She swung back and away from Suzume, apparently seeing her friendly gesture as a threat. Suzume's hands were still flickering with flame and the girl screeched and catapulted herself backward, patting out a small fire that had been ignited on her clothing from Suzume's stray sparks.

"Forgive me, forgive me! You are the first who has come here with such power. I thought... " the girl trailed off. The girl's hands clasped together as if in prayer. As if Suzume was a god.

The girls they brought here were probably all like this one, scarred by fire, but the difference was Suzume's skin breathed fire as if she was a living flame.

"It was an accident, stop acting like I'm some sort of beast!" Suzume snapped. Though it must have been difficult to believe when she was acting like a living torch and her frustration at the situation was only making it worse. At this rate she was going to burn down this entire building.

She took a step toward the girl in a failed attempt to calm her, but she only screamed louder. The door behind her opened and a Namahage filled it. He looked from the screaming girl to Suzume who was lit up like a brazier.

He gestured for the girl to exit and she walked out, clamping her mouth shut as she scurried away. Suzume and the Namahage were now alone together and the creature stared, backlit by the dying light outside. The low light made the mask it wore much more terrifying, bright red and tipped with terrifying fangs and dark beady eyes.

She wasn't going to let these creatures treat her like a servant. Using her haughtiest voice she said, "You dare insult me with this pitiful servant? Bring me a more satisfactory supplicant." Suzume always found her words much more powerful than her fists.

The creature did not respond and instead marched over to her. She backed away to the wall, hoping her internal fire would stop him when he got closer to her. Sparks danced along her flesh as he grabbed a hold of her arm, but he did not hesitate to grab onto her.

"Let go of me!" she shouted.

The creature ignored her words as if they were a minor annoyance, just like the sparks that would normally repel any other yokai. He dragged her out the door and into the ring of huts beyond. He brought her to the center most circle, where two yokai sat. Unlike the others the man to the right had a blue mask, with long fearsome tusks that jutted out from the front and the hair falling behind it was white as winter snow. Dark eyes watched her from behind the mask, making the hairs on the back of her neck stand on end. This must be their leader.

She turned toward him, prepared to give him a piece of her mind. Before she could a girl who would not look Suzume in the eye handed her a bottle of sake. Suzume caught a glimpse of burns along the girl's forearm as she handed her the bottle. Then the Namahage who dragged her out pushed her toward the leader.

"You serve the chief," the Namahage behind her said.

"I will—" Suzume prepared a retort.

But a very large blade against her throat cut it short. "Or you die," the Namahage said.

"My pleasure," she said behind gritted teeth. A plan was already starting to formulate in her mind. Using brute force against these creatures wasn't going to work.

Suzume plastered on a fake smile. In the White Palace, she had often poured sake when she entertained guests or when someone important came to visit her mother and Suzume was summoned to be a pretty decoration. The goal was always the same, charm the head of any group and a world of possibilities would open to you. Whether information or an influential vote, it didn't matter, the method was always the same. This was different of course, the air was charged with hostility and she could not control the fire within her from reacting to the presence of so many yokai. But if she could sway their leader then she'd gain control and that's exactly what she needed.

She approached the leader's table and poured sake into his glass with all the elegance and poise of a woman raised in the White Palace. Her gaze flickered up to the chief. His dark eyes pinned her in place and she could feel energy emanating from him. It drew her to him. Her own spiritual energy seemed to hum inside her, like someone anticipating a meal. She felt that same sort of mouthwatering sensation that spread across her entire body.

Then someone reached up to cup her rear. Suzume jumped out of her skin as she spun around to face whoever it was that dared to touch her.

More of the boorish creatures had entered the ring and had taken a seat behind her.

"Sake for me as well," he held up his cup for her to fill.

She debated whether or not she could get away with dumping all of the sake on his head but he patted the large knife set down on the table in front of him and she held her false smile in place as she poured for him as well.

"That's a good girl," he said patting her bottom again.

Suzume jerked backward and out of reach before he could attempt it again, or something worse. She clutched the bottle so hard she thought it might shatter. These were definitely not the genteel courtiers she was used to. Down the line she poured for each Namahage in turn. They seemed to think the fire that she spouted was some sort of novelty. About halfway through she gave up on elegance, as they groped and grabbed forcing her to slosh the contents of the bottle, spilling it on the table.

Once Suzume was finished filling all their glasses, more girls, some obviously burned some not so obvious, entered carrying bottles of sake and took over refilling for the Namahage. Suzume was relieved of the duty, but still hovered around the edges of the feast pretending to be serving. The chief had not called for her again, and after seeing one servant girl smacked hard for attempting to approach without being called, she knew that wasn't the way.

She could try and run away; the Namahage were getting drunker by the minute. Their voices rose as they sang, wrestled, and carried on. Now would be her best chance for escape. Except the chief kept watching her, no matter where she was she felt his eyes on her. He would not call her to him and allow her to use her charm against him but she seemed to have captivated him. That was a good start, she supposed.

"You should be serving," said a rumbling voice from behind her.

Suzume looked around. A group of the Namahage had stopped their carousing to glare in her direction. They had removed their masks to drink, and their faces were almost human except for their blood red eyes.

"I am." She held up the jug, which sloshed, exposing her for how little sake she had poured.

"You serve or you die, offering," he said. raising the blade high above his head.

The sparks were dancing along her skin, so whatever happened she was ready for it. Suzume dropped the jug of sake on the ground. Liquid splashed on the earth and pieces of pottery scattered. She held up her hands in a last moment of defense and then she felt something like a pop that exploded out of her chest, at the spiritual gateway near her heart. Red energy slammed into the Namahage's chest. He froze in place, and for a moment his eyes rolled back in his head. Then bright red and orange energy burst out from his mouth and returned to Suzume. The Namahage crumbled to the ground, folding over himself.

When the power hit her it seemed to sizzle inside her veins, and her mouth tasted of ash and fire. It spread throughout her like a wildfire: igniting all of her senses, exciting and intoxicating. She had a taste of this power before when she had taken it from Makato on accident, when Kazue had taken over her body. But this was different, instead of closing awareness she felt an increase in it. She could feel everything around her: the bonfire at the center of the clearing, down to the very core of the embers, the heartbeats of all sixty-seven Namahage who surrounded her, and more than anything she felt the power of the chief. He was a bright beacon of energy, a blazing hot fire that drew her like a moth to the flame.

The Namahage had risen, surrounding her with their blades drawn, ready to attack. The women were like dim candles in the dark as they shrieked and ran away from her, but they did not matter. Suzume held out her hands, which were burning balls of flames. Every inch of her was made of burning flame. She had become the living embodiment of flame. But the energy of the Namahage she had absorbed, which had burned hot and fast through her, was already fading away. When she looked at the Namahage in front of her she did not see yokai that were a threat but a chance to gain even more energy. A chance to gain even more power.

She raised her hands up to unleash her fiery fury upon them, to drain them down to the last, saving the chief for her dessert. Then the blue masked Namahage pushed his way forward and stood with his hands raised in the air. Suzume hesitated, wondering what he would do next.

Then he fell to the ground in a deep bow. The group followed suit, and row by row the Namahage bowed to her.

Suzume lowered her flaming hands to her side and looked at the Namahage.

"What is the meaning of this?" Even her voice had taken on a strange, powerful edge, echoing with power.

"You have returned to us at last, mistress." The blue masked Namahage said. Looking up at her, he removed his mask to reveal the face of a handsome man with dark red eyes. "The lady of the flame."

Thirty-One

They moved through the forest too slowly for his liking. The limitations of his fragile human body were reinforced by every ache and pain, and how he lost his breath when he tried to run or leap over obstacles that he would have before. The others were making adjustments to their path, taking longer roads around with fewer obstacles, and slowing down so he wouldn't have to work so hard and it only increased his anger and frustration. He felt smothered, but showing his anger was its own version of weakness, something they could use against him further. So he pressed forward, following the trail Naoki had set out for them.

According to the information Tsuki and Naoki had gathered from the local yokai — lowly creatures that he would not even bother himself to acknowledge had he come across them — the Namahage had been running amuck since he had disappeared. They were terrorizing local villages and kidnapping young women, spiriting them away to their village in the mountains. Where this village was located no one could say. Naoki had pinpointed a cluster of spiritual energy that he believed to be the Namahage village and that was where they were headed.

The forest was dense, and uninhabited by nothing more than low-level yokai. When he had ruled, Kaito had been aware of the Nama-hage but they'd always been under the control of their ruling deity, the Lady of the Flame, and they'd never given him much trouble. So much had changed while he had been sealed, and it only resolved his desire to regain what he had lost when Kazue sealed him. After wandering for hours, not seeing anything other than animals and trees, it was a shock to find two women wandering alone in the forest.

Their group saw them before the women noticed them. Their clothes were that of peasants but they carried no bags marking them as merchants, nor did they carry any baskets as if they were foraging. The girls kept glancing around themselves, as if they expected something to leap out from the trees.

Makato waved to them and greeted them. "Hello."

The girls clutched onto one another and tried to hurry past but did not run, though Kaito could see the terror plain on their faces. *They've seen yokai before. They know not to run.*

"Don't go. We just wanted to ask you some questions," Makato said, his hand outstretched toward them.

"Stay away, yokai!" One of the girls screeched and broke from her friend before running off into the woods. Her other friend turned to do the same, but was not as lucky because she stumbled and fell.

Naoki caught up with her first and he blocked her route to escape by standing over her. She looked up at him with wide terrified eyes, which darted toward his naked blade. Makato ran over, inserting himself between the girl and Naoki, and shook his head at the legendary swordsman. Naoki nodded and sheathed his blade.

Makato crouched down beside the girl, extending his hand to her. "You don't need to be afraid, we're friends."

She stared at him without speaking. "We're searching for the Nama-hage village, do you know where it is?"

She shook her head. "I won't go back there. You cannot make me. She set me free."

Makato held up his hand in a placating gesture. "No one is going to make you do anything. We're trying to find our friend who was taken by the Namahage."

The girl looked from Makato to the yokai. Kaito had his arms crossed over his chest, eyes narrowed. If the girl didn't answer soon, then he was going to make her talk.

Her gaze lingered on him for a second, and he scowled back at her. She swallowed hard and tore her eyes away from the angry dragon. "She may have already returned to her village. Those of us who chose to leave were given permission to do so. But a few remained to serve the Lady of the Flame."

Tsuki snickered and the girl looked at him with bulging eyes as if he had just roared at her.

Makato rested his hand on the top of her head. "You've done enough. Go back to your family."

The girl leaped up and scurried away from him. Makato turned to face the others and that was when Tsuki could no longer suppress his laughter anymore.

"The Lady of the Flame? I wonder who that could be?" Tsuki covered his laughter behind his hand.

Kaito only shook his head. "Suzume has likely awoken something dangerous. We should hurry."

As they continued up the mountain, they encountered more girls with similar stories. The Lady of the Flame had returned and taken control over the Namahage. She had ordered those who wished freedom to take it. It should have put him at ease that whatever Suzume had unleashed was magnanimous, but he had this sinking feeling. Nothing involving Suzume was ever that simple. She attracted trouble.

They found the village in the dying light of day. The ring of huts was silhouetted by fading sunlight trailing behind the mountains that cast the entire village in a golden glow. Despite his weakened connection to his spiritual power, and by extension his ability to sense spiritual pressure, a divine presence vibrated in the air as if he had walked into a shrine. Perhaps Suzume had awoken the goddess of flame. It would make their jobs a lot easier if she freed one of the eight. Having a Kami on their side might be what they needed to stop Hisato.

Just thinking of the fight ahead made him tired. The dragon's limbs ached in ways they had never done before and fatigue was a new and unwelcome feeling. Coupled with the crushing exhaustion, a warm trickle of blood dripped down his side from his most recent wounds which he'd refused anyone to look at, instead insisting he was fine.

They all had likely reopened and were bleeding through the bandages. The wounds had not healed at all. And coupled with the new wound the Namahage had given him, they were not even healing as slowly as a human's would. The wounds were killing him slowly, like a knife being thrust into his gut inch by painful inch.

They surveyed the village from a distance. Kaito was surprised to find there were no guards on patrol. It was strange in itself, surely the secretive Namahage would post guards? Kaito reached for his sword, finding comfort in the weight of the steel. The others were similarly in defense mode. Rin had not transformed from her true kitsune form since their fight with the Namahage, and took up her guard beside Kaito. It bothered him that she felt it necessary to protect him, in the same way it annoyed him that he had to rely on a weapon to defend himself.

"Someone should go in and investigate," Makato said from his crouched position.

"It won't be you," Kaito snarled. He still didn't trust him. He didn't like how Suzume kept looking to him for guidance.

"What do you suggest, we just rush in there, weapons drawn?" Akira drawled, scowling at the dragon.

"I don't have a death wish. Rin can sneak in quietly and take Suzume out."

"Wouldn't Naoki be better for that?" Makato suggested.

Kaito only scoffed.

"It's not your decision. You're no longer in charge here, remember?" Akira said, pinning Kaito with her dark eyes and challenging him to argue.

"I never gave up my control of this group," Kaito said standing up, which turned out to be a mistake. As soon as he did, Namahage came pouring out from behind the buildings as if they'd been waiting all this time to reveal themselves.

Kaito held up his sword, the pain in his side forgotten, as he prepared for battle. The Namahage had them surrounded in a matter of moments. Dozens of red-masked faces stared at them blankly. Kaito turned, looking for an opening, but if he attacked, he'd be overwhelmed in moments.

The group broke apart, and a blue masked Namahage stepped into the circle facing Kaito.

"The Lady of the Flame is expecting you," the Namahage said.

The Namahage in the circle behind him stamped their feet together, repeating "The Lady of the Flame" their voices melding together into one.

Their group exchanged a look, not certain what to make of this situation.

"I don't give a damn about the Lady of the Flame, where is Suzume?" Kaito growled at them.

"Lady of the Flame," the Namahage chanted as they stamped their feet in unison.

Kaito pointed his blade at the blue masked Namahage who had not reached for the overlarge knife at his belt. "The Lady of the Flame was sealed by Kazue five hundred years ago," Kaito said.

"She has returned to us," the Namahage replied.

"Maybe we should go with them," Makato said as he placed his hand on Kaito's shoulder.

Kaito knocked his hand away and rushed toward the Namahage, his blade swinging. The fool should never have exposed himself this way. Take out the leader and everything else crumbled. But before Kaito could land even a single blow, the chief of the Namahage had drawn his weapon and knocked Kaito's sword from his hand. It flew across the circle landing at the feet of one of the nearby Namahage.

"Take them," said the leader of the Namahage.

The remaining Namahage broke rank, rushing forward to capture them. Being this greatly outnumbered and as weak as Kaito was any struggle was futile. They were brought to the center of the village where a large bonfire glowed with golden flames. The Namahage led them to what could only be described as a throne. The woman seated upon it wore an ornate golden headdress and a flowing golden kimono in a multitude of layers that were draped over the edge of the throne. She concealed her face with a golden fan, which she peered at them over the top of. She was attended by at least half a dozen Namahage, who knelt on each side of her throne.

As soon as he saw the goddess, he rushed toward her throne, "What have you done with my priestess?" he growled as he charged, but the Namahage kneeling at the foot of her throne leaped up to block him.

The woman rose from her seat and waved her hand. All but two Namahage who grabbed onto each of Kaito's arms stood back. The goddess looked at Kaito over the edge of her fan. "Nice of you to join us at last." Though he knew the voice, he refused to believe it was true.

Suzume lowered her fan and smirked at Kaito in triumph.

"You've got to be joking. What are you wearing?" He forced a laugh but his intuition told him something wasn't right. This was Suzume's face and voice but something was wrong here.

She scowled, chasing away the idea that she was possessed by something. Only Suzume would have that reaction. She turned her head away to hide her anger. "I am the Lady of the Flame, you should show me some respect," she said, affecting a haughty tone that she usually reserved for telling people she was the emperor's daughter. It looked like Tsuki was right.

"How did this happen?" Tsuki asked before biting his knuckles to stop himself from laughing.

Suzume settled herself back into her throne, but had not given the command to have the Namahage release Kaito.

"I have fully come into my power, isn't that obvious?" As she sat down, a previously unseen girl rushed forward to straighten out the folds of Suzume's kimono.

"Alright, enough playing around. It's time to go," Kaito said as he elbowed a nearby Namahage in the ribs, catching him by surprise and forcing him to let him go. Kaito crossed the distance between them before the Namahage could intervene. He was inches from Suzume when she held up her hand. The Namahage who had been chasing him remained behind, while Kaito looked down at her full of her own smug pride.

"This isn't a game. I've found a way to stop Hisato," she said, glaring at Kaito and daring him to refute her.

"With them?" Kaito gestured to the Namahage who were murmuring angrily behind him.

Her gaze flicked toward them and then back to Kaito. "Not the Namahage, the holy purifying fire."

Kaito snorted in disbelief. "You think you can control the divine fire of the gods?"

"Do not speak to the Lady of the Flame in such a way, phony dragon."

"Phony?" Kaito sputtered.

Suzume laughed and hid it behind her sleeve.

"I have tamed the holy fire. I am the Lady of the Flame."

"The Lady of the Flame is one of the eight. You're a girl who has gotten a big head. Now get down from there."

Suzume shook her head, as if he was an ignorant child.

"You insolent creature, how dare you!" said the Namahage chief who had approached from behind and grabbed Kaito by the shoulder. "Bow before the Lady of the Flame and show the respect she is owed."

"I bow to no one." He knocked the Namahage's hand aside to turn and face Suzume once more.

In response, the Namahage struck him in the back of his knees, forcing Kaito to the ground. He collapsed in front of Suzume and stared up at her.

Who did this wench think she was?

Suzume stood above him, flames rose up along her hair and danced in her eyes. "I am more powerful than you think." Suzume held up her hand and the flames from the bonfire rose up into the air where they transformed into a bird that rose into the sky and glided over the camp. The Namahage stamped their feet as the bird cawed and swooped directly toward Kaito.

He lifted his arms, preparing to guard but before it could strike him it burst apart into a shower of golden sparks.

Kaito stared at the space where the bird had been, blinking in surprise. How was it possible that Suzume's power had grown so much in such a short amount of time? He turned back to look at her face, but when he looked into her eyes he did not see the spoiled princess, only the reflection of fire that continued to flicker in her eyes. Something intent on destruction.

"When Kazue conquered the Lady of the Flame she took her power for her own. A power which she left to me," Suzume said to Kaito. "I am the Lady of the Flame."

"Enough." Kaito once again tried to approach her but this time when the Namahage went to reach for him, Suzume held up her hand to stop them. So when he approached her makeshift throne they were almost nose to nose. "I let you pretend at being the leader. But the game is over. It's time for you to remember your place."

She raised her hand and slapped him hard across the face. Kaito reeled backward nearly knocked to the floor. Fire burned inside his flesh, creeping into him, burning him from the inside. But the feeling was only fleeting. When he looked at Suzume again, her eyes were wide and she was staring at her hands. The moment was fleeting and she turned her face away from him.

The chief of the Namahage was standing beside Suzume. "You should be punished for this."

"Take him from my sight. I do not want to look at him," Suzume said with a flick of her wrist.

Kaito pressed his hand against the place where she had slapped him, then looked at her seething. This had gone too far. "You can't just walk away from me. I'm not done talking!" He leaped to his feet, but the Namahage grabbed him and dragged him away.

The dragon growled obscenities and made threats that fell on deaf ears until the Namahage brought him to the hut where he was thrown inside and the door was slammed shut.

THIRTY-TWO

Kaito slammed his fists against the door until they were bloody and he kept hammering even past that. They could not lock him up, he was the dragon. But even so his energy was not limitless and exhaustion forced him to stop. He slid against the door, slumping onto the ground. The wounds across his torso had reopened and were bleeding freely. He ripped open his haori to inspect them. There was a large gash on his side where the Namahage's blade had taken a chunk of him.

The fabric of his haori had fused with his skin from the matted blood. As he peeled it away, he hissed through the pain. In his long life he had never feared death. His kind were immortal, even severe wounds only temporarily disabled them. His spiritual energy would have revived him, but cut off from the flow of power there was no way to heal.

Footsteps approached from outside so Kaito scrambled into a standing position and waited for the door to open. His hands flexed like claws in front of him, though he could not produce real claws. *I knew she couldn't hold out forever.* The priestess wanted to play at being powerful, but the game was over. The door swung open but it was not Suzume who entered. Instead the priest, Makato, walked in with his head bowed, carrying a bowl of water and bandages.

"What are you doing here?" Kaito snarled. He looked past the priest, but all he could see were the rows of huts. The priest shut the door, cutting off his view of the outside. He'd come alone.

Makato carried his items to the center of the room, the bowl and bandages balanced on his arm.

Kaito marched over to him and shoved him hard on the shoulder. "Answer me." Water sloshed out of the bowl, but the priest's balance kept it from spilling, or from dropping the bandages.

Makato turned toward Kaito, his eyes blazing. Then he turned away just as quickly and in a calm voice said, "She asked me to come and treat your wounds."

"Is this some sort of joke?" he asked as he balled his hand into a fist. If he didn't restrain himself he was going to strangle the priest. Not that it sounded like too much of a bad idea in that moment.

Makato ignored his question and continued to set out jars of salve which he removed from pockets in his hakama. Kaito growled as he paced around the priest who did not respond to the dragon's hostility.

"You can go back to that spoiled brat and tell her to let me out this instant."

"I can't do that," Makato said, looking up to meet Kaito's angry glare for the first time.

Kaito stopped his pacing and faced the priest who was staring at him. "What was that?"

"Your wounds are spreading; do you want her to find out how weak you've become?" He nodded toward Kaito who was covered in blood, hair disheveled. He must have looked more like a wild animal than the powerful ruler he had once been.

The dragon kicked over the bowl of water to show the priest what he thought of his help. The water spread out, creating a thick river of mud beneath the priest. Makato looked at the destruction without expression.

"I don't need your pity," Kaito growled.

"Will you at least let me bandage your wounds?" he asked without raising his head. He remained kneeling on the ground, the water soaking into the fabric around his knees.

Kaito threw his head back and laughed. "I don't need your help either."

"You haven't changed at all," Makato said under his breath.

The words sent a chill down his spine. There was an echo of Kazue, long gone but never far away it seemed. It was easy to forget that this man also had a piece of Kazue's soul inside him.

"What did you say?" Kaito said, his words thick and rough.

Makato turned to look at him. His eyes had changed subtly, no longer dark brown but more of a hazel. "Once you came to the shrine covered in blood, you refused treatment, and collapsed onto a futon and would not rise for two days. On the third day you got up and left. You never said where the wounds came from, or where you were going or when you would be back..."

The memories were fresh as if they'd happened the day before. Kazue in tears, begging him to stay. Each time he left her he never knew if he would return. *This is the end of it.* He told himself every time in those early days. *We cannot continue this.* Once he left for a month straight, fighting some battle or another, telling himself that it was a passing infatuation. It wasn't until it was too late that he realized it was so much more than that, which made leaving her that much harder. For so long he had fought to have her by his side. Clinging to the hope that soon he would find peace to be with her. But it had never happened. Kazue had turned on him in the end and he had fallen victim to his own damned heart.

"How do you know that?" he growled.

"You know why."

"Get out!" he roared as he took a swing at Makato's head. The priest dodged his attack easily, and instead grabbed a hold of Kaito's wrist, forcing the dragon to look him in the eye.

"I never had these memories until I met Suzume. But they're getting stronger all the time. Each time she takes some of my spiritual energy a new memory surfaces. Do you know why?"

Kaito knocked him backward and Makato skidded back a couple steps, his hands up in a defensive pose. But just that little bit of effort had stolen the breath from Kaito's lungs. He leaned upon his knees gasping for breath.

"Your condition is getting worse. I can heal you."

"At what cost?" There was a painful stitch in his side that he clutched. Blood rolled down his side and dripped onto the ground.

"Leave."

The word rung in his head. A threat, a promise, an escape. He couldn't decide which. Ever since he had been woken from the stone, he'd been trapped in these memories. Every time he looked at Suzume he thought of her. And as Suzume's power grew it was getting harder to distinguish the two. And that scared him. Would he let his heart betray him again, and fall prey to the same mistakes all over?

He had to mentally shake himself. That's exactly what the priest wanted. It had been his plan from the start. He needed Suzume to find the artifacts to stop that bastard Hisato.

"Do you think I don't see through your plan?" Kaito bared his teeth at the priest.

"You have to let her go, before it's too late."

Kaito made another ineffectual swing at Makato's head in response. The priest simply sidestepped out of the way. With too much momentum and not enough counterweight, Kaito tumbled face forward and crashed onto the ground. The dragon climbed up onto all fours but could not find the strength to get up. He coughed and blood splattered onto the ground in front of him.

"Don't you see? You're destroying her, the same way you destroyed Kazue."

Kaito was trembling. Like a weak mortal. Like a human. What Suzume had done to him was worse than what Kazue had done. At least Kazue had put him to sleep. He was living in a waking nightmare. He could feel his body decaying around him, despite his attempts to pretend it wasn't happening. He was dying.

"What do you want from her?"

"That's not for you to worry about."

Kaito struggled to his knees, that was the best he could manage. His head rolled back onto his neck like a limp noodle. It would be better to let her go, to free himself of this burden. The priest was staring at him, waiting for an answer. A slow smirk pulled at the corner of the dragon's lips.

"Swear to me you won't hurt her."

"I will protect her with my life."

Kaito wiped the blood from his lips. Bright crimson stained his skin. How many times had he seen his own blood? Of all the battles he had fought and won, this priest had brought him to his knees where so many other enemies had tried and failed. He had to respect that. But the fool's one mistake had been offering a chance to reverse what he had done. As soon as he was back to his old strength he would rend him into pieces.

"Then return me to how I was."

The priest squatted down and began to draw a circle in the mud, followed by a series of complicated symbols. He was familiar with the human methods of channeling their power. Their inferior bodies were not as strong as that of a yokai and therefore they had to depend on their songs and circles.

"It was me who sealed your power," Makato said as he worked.

"I know," Kaito grunted, watching him work with narrowed eyes.

"Why didn't you confront me?" He stopped to look at him, his fingers stained with mud, a slight furrow to his brows.

"Believe me I've wanted to kill you from the moment I realized. But..." he couldn't say the rest. That knowing Kazue was inside him had held him back. That even now she held sway over him.

Makato lowered his gaze back to the circle on the ground. "I was ordered to kill you, but I couldn't do it." He looked up at Kaito for a moment. "I didn't understand why at first, but now I know. It's Kazue, she still loves you."

"Are you saying you're in love with me?" Kaito raised an eyebrow at him. He'd had stranger lovers in the past. But somehow he couldn't see this priest having any real affection for him.

The priest shook his head. "That's not quite it." He stood up to admire the circle he had drawn. "Do you know why Kazue sealed you?" Makato asked as he squatted down to make a couple of corrections to the markings on the ground.

"Because she didn't want me to stop her from becoming immortal."

"That was part of it."

Makato stood, then gestured for Kaito to come stand in the circle. The dragon climbed to his feet and each movement tugged at his wounds, sending fresh ripples of pain through his body. As he inched closer to the circle, he paused. Could he really trust the priest?

"What is this?" He pointed at the markings on the ground. Some he recognized, having seen the human scribbles before. Others he did not.

"The circle will enhance my power and help me reverse the seal upon your spiritual power."

Kaito hesitated. This was too easy. This man could not be this naive. "Why are you doing this?"

Makato met his gaze and when he looked into his eyes they were green. "Because Kazue wants me to."

A chill ran down his spine as he looked into Makato's eyes. The shape and color of them were all wrong but it felt as if Kazue was looking back out at him. It may have been his imagination. Perhaps he was so desperate for any sign of her that he was looking for her in this man's gaze. *Then let this be our final goodbye. Perhaps once I kill him, your soul will be free again.*

Kaito stepped into the circle. The moment his foot crossed over the line he felt a tingle on his skin. Even before the spell was invoked, the circle had power. Once he was in the middle of the circle Kaito crossed his arms over his chest. The gooseflesh had risen all over his body and the hairs were up on the back of his neck.

"What now?" Kaito looked down once more at the circle on the ground. It glowed faintly, illuminating his feet and the bottoms of his hakama.

"Aren't you going to ask me what Kazue's other reason for sealing you was?" Makato asked.

Kaito rolled his eyes. He supposed he could give him that much at least. "What was it?"

"She planned on using your spiritual energy to make her son immortal."

As he said this, pain shot up Kaito's leg from the ground. The markings on the ground were a vibrant green now. The priest sang an incantation. His voice was different but the words were the same ones that had haunted Kaito's dreams for five hundred years. Makato's voice rose to the rafters. It was the song of sealing, twining its way around him.

"You bastard!" he roared. But already the spell's effects were upon him, lulling him to sleep, even as his mind raged against it. He shrunk downward, his vision growing dark. Soon he knew nothing at all but silence and darkness once more.

THIRTY-THREE

"When are you going to let the dragon go?" Rin demanded.

Suzume flicked open her golden fan and waved it in front of her face. She had been expecting this, although she hoped the moment would have lasted longer. Peering over the top of her fan, Suzume considered the best way to answer the kitsune's question.

"Do not speak informally to the Lady of the Flame," Tohru, the chief of the Namahage said. Chastising the kitsune for Suzume. *How convenient.*

The chief was never far from her side since the Namahage had crowned her the Lady of the Flame. Being made their ruler reminded her of her life at the White Palace. The Namahage carried her everywhere in a palanquin and every comfort was seen to before she could even ask. They asked nothing of her but pampered her in every way possible.

And she was absolutely bored out of her mind. She had not remembered how incredibly aggravating it was to not be able to so much as cough without three different people hurrying to bring her something to drink. The only reprieve she had from the mind-numbing monotony was imprisoning Kaito.

She figured she'd let him sweat it out for a day and then she would free him, after giving him a taste of his own medicine of course. It was only fair. How many times had he forced her to grovel at his feet? If he didn't think she was a good ruler then she would show him what sort of ruler she could be.

The kitsune was ruining everything. Rin's lips twisted into a frown as she grit out a "my lady" with a bow that was almost passable as polite.

Suzume waved her hand in a dismissive gesture, playing at the magnanimous ruler. "He will be freed as soon as he bends the knee to me," Suzume said, using her most contemptuous voice.

"Don't you think you're taking this a little too far?"

Tohru stamped his foot, "Do not question the judgments of our lady." Suzume covered her smirk with her fan. Rin couldn't ruin this for her, not with the Namahage's support. To them she was a goddess.

"Well if you're not going let him out then I will." The kitsune transformed into her massive true form and leaped over the heads of a pair of Namahage who tried to apprehend her.

"You can't do that." Suzume stood to better shout at her retreating back, losing the regal composure she had been affecting. When the kitsune did not respond Suzume gathered up the layers of robes she was wearing to climb down the steps after her. But she had forgotten just how heavy the formal garb was and she struggled to make even a few strides before Tohru was in front of her with hands out stretched to stop her.

"My lady, you should not trouble yourself with this. I will fetch her," Tohru said, bowing.

"Just bring her back to me," Suzume said with a frustrated huff.

Tohru rose up from his bow and with a few sharp commands sent two Namahage to chase after Rin. They disappeared behind a row of huts in the same direction Rin had gone. Kaito was being held in the huts that used to hold the serving girls, on the outer ring of the village. She'd set Namahages to guard him just in case. They should be enough to hold off Rin long enough for reinforcements to come. But Suzume had also seen Rin fight and when she was determined she was unstoppable.

Suzume sat, the weight of the multitude of layers forcing her down. But her agitation was rising. She rapped her fingers along the edge of her throne. If Rin let Kaito out before he bowed down to her, he would win. It would only prove that she had no control at all and this had all been a farce. Not that she wasn't a fraud. She knew very well she wasn't a goddess and she had no intention of ruling over the Namahage. But she wanted Kaito to believe that she was capable of that much at least.

After a few minutes one of the Namahage returned with Rin pulling at his grip. She had transformed back into her humanoid form, but continued to snap and snarl like a wild animal. The second Namahage carried a body slung over his shoulder.

Suzume scooted toward the edge of her seat. *Were Kaito's wounds worse than I realized? Maybe I shouldn't have locked him up.* Tohru saw her leaning forward to get a better look and made a small shake of his head. Suzume scowled at the barbarian yokai for correcting her behavior. She was a princess. But the other Namahage were watching her. Her control over them was tenuous at best. It wouldn't be long before they realized she was an impostor. And despite her desire to rebel against Tohru's instruction, she leaned back in her chair, placing one hand on each arm. Her nails dug into the wood, pushing back her nail beds painfully.

"What is the meaning of this?" she said, resuming her regal tone in order to mask the real fear that she had accidentally put Kaito in danger. She flicked open her fan and waved it over her face so no one would see her expression.

"Kaito is missing," Rin growled.

Suzume's stomach seemed to drop out beneath her. But she took a deep breath and schooled her expression to indifference. This had to be a trick. Something he and Rin had concocted to make her look like a fool. "Who is that then?" She nodded her head toward the body the Namahage was holding.

The Namahage flopped it onto the ground. As he did, it was clear it was not Kaito but Makato. His head slammed against the ground with a loud thud. Rin broke free of her captor and went to kneel beside the unconscious priest. She gently placed his head on her lap and stroked his face. A large lump had already started to form on his forehead, there was purple bruising around his eye, and his clothes were torn and bloodied.

"What happened?" Suzume said, standing once more without meaning to.

"We found the guards knocked unconscious and this man was inside, there was no sign of the prisoner," the Namahage who had been holding Makato reported.

A rapid series of thoughts ran through her mind. Kaito had found out about the seal. Broken the seal. Then taken revenge against Makato. And he would come for her next when he realized she had known and had done nothing to reverse it. Suzume looked around, expecting Kaito to soar in from the sky any minute raining ice spears down upon them all.

Makato groaned and opened his eyes. He squinted into the light of day and looked about with unfocused eyes.

"Makato, what happened?" Rin asked. She held his face between her hands, forcing him to look into her eyes.

Suzume took a step toward him, intent on interrogating him herself, but tripped over the voluminous layers of her kimono and stumbled down the steps instead. She was saved from eating dirt by Tohru's arm around her waist. She turned her head to look at her savior, and when their eyes met she felt that same draw of his power. It was tempting to try and draw from his power, like sneaking a treat before dinner. Suzume shook herself of the thought. When she blinked and looked away the impulse was gone and he had propped her back up on her own two feet. He bowed his head to her in a symbol of servitude, but his gaze lingered on her longer than seemed appropriate.

Suzume turned her attention to Makato, who had sat up and put distance between himself and Rin. "What did you do to Kaito?" she said, her voice coming out so fierce and powerful she hardly recognized it.

"The last thing I remember was going to visit the dragon," he said as he pressed against the lump on his head with a wince.

"Why would you disobey my orders and visit him?" Her words were like a whip crack. Had she been wrong in trusting Makato? What if he and the dragon had worked together to make a fool of her? She looked around again expecting him to jump out and laugh at this joke.

Perhaps the dragon had never really been injured and this was all some elaborate prank.

Makato looked at his hands, which were folded in his lap. "I was worried about the wounds he sustained while we were fighting the Namahage and I wanted to treat them."

She inched closer toward him, fire leaping to her skin, and she brandished her burning hands like a weapon. Makato looked at her hands and then into her eyes. She could see his fear reflected there. She didn't care. This power could protect her from anything.

"Then what happened?"

Makato held up his hands in a sign of surrender. "I don't know, the next thing I remembered was waking up here."

"The dragon must have attacked and then fled," Tohru said.

"But he was weakened by the seal." Suzume stood in a defensive pose, prepared for the dragon to leap out at her any moment.

"He must have broken my seal," Makato said sheepishly.

"Then where is he now? Find him!" She shouted to the Namahage who leaped to do her bidding. Suzume watched them go with little satisfaction. She felt like there were eyes on her from all angles. The dragon was watching her laughing, mocking her for her naivety to think she could trap him.

"Do you think he's going to leap out at you from the shadows?" Rin said, her voice accusatory.

"Why shouldn't I be worried? You know his temper," Suzume shot back.

"Because he wouldn't hurt you, and he wouldn't have left you behind. There's something going on here," Rin said.

"Are you saying I did something to him?" Suzume's voice rose a few octaves.

"You know that's not what I mean," Rin replied, her voice somewhat softer now.

But Suzume was beyond reason.

"The real reason he left is because he could not stand to see me grow more powerful."

Rin shook her head. "Don't be foolish-"

"You dare challenge me?" Suzume said. The flames were rising higher along her body, moving to engulf everything in flames. The Namahage stamped their feet and began chanting as one.

Rin looked at Suzume with wide, terrified eyes. "What have you become?"

"Leave. Join the dragon." She pointed away.

Rin glared at her with a defiant look in her eyes for a few more moments before transforming into a kitsune and leaping away.

Once she was gone, Suzume felt the fire die out of her and she collapsed back into her chair.

"I want to be alone now." There was a flurry of activity as the Namahage rushed to do her bidding. She rose up from her throne as the Namahage brought her a palanquin. Two of them carried her on their backs and brought her to the hut that she had made her own.

It was the largest hut in the village but lacked the refinement of her room at the White Palace. But it felt like a luxury nonetheless to have soft pillows and blankets. Even a table. Although the table was not much more than a tree stump. When they reached her room, she stepped off the palanquin. A rug had been rolled out to prevent her from stepping on the dirty ground.

Inside two of the serving girls were fluffing pillows and pouring tea for her to drink. The tea was served up in a crude sake cup and was nothing more than a weak imitation of real tea. She had taken these trappings of a fake ruler and convinced herself it made her a ruler. But Kaito had dashed that in one swoop.

Suzume flopped down on the cushion in front of her makeshift table. The things that earlier today had brought her happiness suddenly filled her with rage and Suzume knocked away the tea the servant was pouring, spilling it on the table.

"Leave me," she shouted. The servants bowed before scurrying out. Everyone left, except for Tohru.

"My lady, can I speak?"

Suzume leaned forward on the table, resting her head in her hands. Rubbing her forehead, she said, "I told you to leave."

He did not obey her command however, and she jumped up slamming her hands onto the table in front of her. "Did you not hear me?"

He was kneeling down on the ground, his head almost pressed into the dirt. "You seem dissatisfied with your role here, my lady."

"I am. I don't want to rule over a bunch of savages in the middle of the woods." She picked up a nearby pillow and threw it across the room. It made a dissatisfying projectile as it fell limp against the far wall.

She had been so angry as of late. It twisted around inside of her, coursing through her veins and erupting as fire along her skin. Nothing she owned was free of scorch marks any longer.

"Might I make a suggestion, my lady?" Tohru asked, once more not lifting his head.

"What? Speak then!"

"When the original Lady of the Flame was defeated, the priestess Kazue bound her into stone."

"Yes, I know that," she said, arms crossed and glaring at him.

"After many years we have recovered that stone." He opened his large hand and resting on his palm was a large obsidian stone. He approached Suzume with it and as it drew closer she felt the power within it. It called out to her. Begging her to take it. The draw was more than even the power in Tohru. This had to be one of the missing eight Kazue had sealed. She had found it. And without the dragon's help!

Her hands practically itched to get a hold of it, a real triumph, one that he could not deny her. Suzume reached to take it out of his hand but before she could, Tohru pulled it back. Suzume jutted her lips out like a child deprived of a sweet.

"This stone will give you even greater control of your fire. You would be even more powerful than the dragon."

"I already am more powerful." She jutted her chin out, but kept glancing toward the stone.

"Yes, my lady." He dipped his head in acknowledgment. "But with this and the Sea Stone, you would be even more powerful."

Suzume whipped her head in his direction, now he had her attention. "What is the Sea Stone?"

"It is like this." He gestured toward the stone containing the Lady of the Flame. "It is all that remains of the Lord of the Sea's power. I believe that is where the dragon is really headed."

Suzume tapped her chin in thought. The Sea Stone was likely the same artifact Naoki had heard rumors about, and it was just as likely one of the missing eight. *Of course he would know about an artifact and not tell me.*

"Show me that stone." She held out her hand to Tohru. He offered it up to her and she greedily snatched it from him. As soon as her fingers closed around it, the power shot through her and filled her with a tingling sensation. It was euphoric. And she wanted more of it.

THIRTY-FOUR

In her room back at the palace, Suzume had a painted screen depicting the ocean. It had been a gift from a suitor. She had loved looking at the white-capped waves, the blue that was somehow deeper than the sky, and the power the ocean seemed to possess even if it was just captured in the painting. Looking at the real ocean struck her with its majesty and the power she had felt captured in the painting was dwarfed by the raw power of the ocean even from this distance.

It was massive. That was her first thought. Even from a distance she could not quite process how large and flat it was. It seemed to go on forever in all directions. She had never felt so small and insignificant until she was staring at it. The ocean seemed to reach beyond the horizon to a place where only the gods could dwell. And it was dark blue, a color unlike any she had seen before in person with such intensity even the paint looked faint in comparison.

Makato stood to her left and smiled at her. "Is this your first time seeing the ocean?"

Suzume tore her gaze away from the view to look at Makato. His gaze was fixed on the horizon, and she saw that same sense of majesty that she had felt reflected in his own gaze. Was that just how the ocean made everyone feel, or was this some residual emotion of Kazue's welling up in both of them? That thought soured the moment and Suzume replied with some venom.

"Yes. I never saw anything beyond the walls of the palace until recently."

He turned to look at her. "It might have been better if you never left at all."

He didn't elaborate and she didn't really want him to anyway. He was wrong. For so long she had thought that was what she wanted. But as her power grew, she could only see her desire to return to that stifling place as childish fantasy. She was becoming more than she ever could have been at the palace.

The four-day journey here had been uneventful. The Namahage's intimidating presence kept yokai away and Suzume's urgency to get to the Sea Stone as soon as possible had kept them moving at a quick pace. The dragon and Rin had not made an appearance, which in her mind only reinforced her belief that he had gone in search of the Sea Stone as well.

They had stopped only momentarily along the rise of a hill but soon they were descending down a narrow pathway. This stretch of land was filled with rolling low hills and thick vegetation. The ocean was so large she could see it even from a distance and in almost every direction they were surrounded by it. Just beyond the crashing waves, she could see an island in the distance. The ocean divided the land in two as if the gods had cut them in half.

Beyond this shore was where the Sea Stone was hidden, she could feel it. There was a niggling feeling at the back of her mind. It called to her. She had been here before. Or at least, Kazue had.

"How do we get across?" Suzume asked.

"A boat would be easiest, unless you wanted to swim," Tsuki replied with a mischievous grin.

"Thanks. I figured as much." Suzume rolled her eyes at Tsuki. "How do we get a boat?"

"That's probably the best place to start." Makato pointed at curls of smoke rising on the horizon. It appeared there was a village nearby.

They headed in the direction of the smoke, but before they got too close to the village Suzume ordered her Namahage to wait behind. Tohru protested but she managed to convince him when she agreed to bring Naoki and Tsuki along for protection. And since they could conceal their presence they would not intimidate the humans the way the Namahage would.

The village itself was not much larger than maybe a couple dozen shabby huts set back a little way from the shore.

Older villagers gathered around a central bonfire while children ran around playing some game only children knew. A group of women sat in a circle in what could be graciously called the village center. The women surrounded an elderly woman with entirely white hair and more wrinkles than seemed possible. The men were conspicuously absent. The old woman had to be their matriarch, because when Makato and Suzume approached, the women around her stopped what they were doing and looked to the old woman to greet them.

They must have looked like a strange pair: Suzume in peasant's clothes along with an armed warrior.

"Hello, grandmother," Makato said, addressing the old woman with a bow.

The old woman's face was so wrinkled the folds on her brow nearly obscured her eyes entirely. Her skin was tanned and weathered with numerous cracks and valleys. "We do not often get visitors to our village, what brings you here?" the old woman asked, her voice was high and reedy.

"We are looking for a boat to take us to the island." He gestured toward the unseen island beyond the bay.

The women gasped and murmured to one another behind their hands while avoiding looking at Suzume and Makato. It was as if Makato had insulted the old woman.

The old woman's eyes narrowed as she stared at Makato. She set aside her sewing and crossed her hands in her lap.

"No one sails beyond this bay, or any bay along this coast," she said.

"Then how does one reach the island to the north?" Makato asked.

The old woman shook her head, the loose folds of her skin swayed. "That stretch of water is cursed, every good fisherman for miles knows that. Any who try to cross fall prey to the umi-bozu."

"Omi-bowsu?" Suzume asked. She'd never heard of such a thing. Of course there were many horrifying creatures she'd never heard of.

"OOH-mi BOW-zoo," Makato said correcting her mispronunciation without turning to look at her.

She scowled at the back of his head but his gaze was focused on the old woman.

"The Umi-bozu is a dangerous monster which hunts these waters. I saw it once when I was a girl, big as a mountain, dark as night. Any ship that tries to cross is taken by the monster."

"I've heard of these," Akira whispered in Suzume's ear. "If there is one nearby we must be careful."

Suzume dismissed her concern with a wave over her shoulder. The old her would have thought it nothing but villager superstition, but she had seen stranger things since she left her walled palace. It was very possible some monster stalked just beneath the crashing waves waiting for a careless fisherman to come their way. But even if there was, she felt confident she could defeat it now that she had control of Kazue's fire.

"I'm not worried about that," Suzume said. "Where can I buy a boat to get across?"

The old woman looked out to the sea beyond. "You would be wiser to not waste your time. Our boats are our livelihoods. No one will part with it for a fool's journey."

Suzume was about to make a smart remark when Makato placed his hand over her mouth and forced her into a bow to the old woman along with him.

"Thank you for telling us." He pulled her away before she could say anything else.

Once they were out of earshot, Suzume broke free of his hand. "That's it? How are we supposed to get across?"

Makato shook his head. "We keep looking. There's bound to be someone willing to help."

She sighed heavily. She never thought finding a way across would be the hard part.

Despite the old woman's warning, they went to the shore to wait until the ships came in. As the first ship came ashore, Makato flagged them down. Two men operated the tiny dingy, which hardly looked watertight to Suzume. As it brushed against the shore, Makato approached with a bow. The fisherman's weathered face was painted with suspicion as he watched Makato.

"Excuse me, we are seeking passage across to the island beyond, would you be willing to take us?" Makato asked.

The man stared for a moment without answering before turning back to gather up the line on his ship as if they were not there at all.

"We're talking to you!" Suzume raised a fist, prepared to use force to get an answer, when Makato put a hand on her shoulder.

"Don't, it's not worth the trouble."

"I hope the umi-bozu sinks your boat," she muttered a curse under her breath as she glared at his back.

They repeated the process several times with similar results each time. One fisherman spat in their direction, giving her the impression of what they thought about their question.

"That bastard." Suzume did not hold back her curses this time. "Do you know who I am? I should call my yokai army down on your head."

The man who spat at her glared at her. His face was leathery from the sun and his hair was streaked white.

"You should get your wife under control. Beat her if you must," the fisherman said to Makato.

"Beat me? You'll regret that once I'm done with you," Suzume snarled and Makato and Tsuki had to physically restrain her from flying at him.

Suzume's anger rose to the surface. That was the last ship, and they still didn't have a way across. Kaito had probably flown across. Flames erupted all over her body, fueled by her anger. The fisherman saw and took a terrified step backward. The flames burned Makato's hand who was not as quick as Tsuki to let go when her temper was on the rise. She felt the pain in her hands as she stared down at her palms sparking with flames, growing into a blaze. Her anger was a white-hot poker in her gut, closer now than ever before.

The other fishermen along the shore stopped what they were doing to stare at the girl on fire. Suzume looked around at the collection of their faces, old men beaten by the elements, afraid of legends of a monster. She'd fought worse. But now she had their attention.

"You see what I am capable of? Give us a boat or pay the consequences."

Her threats had the opposite effect and the fisherman gathered in a circle around her and Makato, carrying a mix of makeshift weapons, spears meant for bringing in nets, and clubs made out of broken pieces of wood.

"What sort of monster are you?" the fisherman she had almost burned asked.

"Your worst nightmare!" Suzume snarled. Balling her flaming hands into flaming fists. The power came so much easier when she was angry, but she could use that anger to teach them all a lesson.

"Get it together. Now is not the time to lose control," Makato said behind her. He did not attempt to grab onto her this time.

"And why not? We wasted an entire day looking for a boat. We've done it your way, now let's do it my way." She threw her hands up preparing to shoot fire at the nearby villagers.

Naoki grabbed her by both shoulders, forcing her to face him, despite the fire dancing along her flesh. She glared at him and attempted to yank her body away, but he held fast onto her, despite the fire that was running up his arms.

"This is not you."

"You don't know me." Her voice rose an octave, giving away her lie.

"You don't need to become a monster to be powerful."

She knocked his hand aside, not willing to listen to his good advice.

"They brought this upon themselves."

Suzume turned to face the fishermen, raising up her fiery hands and pulling energy into her from all directions. She would burn every last one of their ships. Perhaps that would teach them to scorn her.

But before she could draw all the power into her she felt Makato's energy wrapping around her, suppressing her fire. She spun in place to face him, teeth bared in a snarl.

"What do you think you're doing?

Makato grabbed onto her wrist, this time refusing to let go. She felt his power flow into her and like dirt thrown onto a flame, his power attempted to smother the flame that was burning up inside her. She couldn't break free of his grip before the fire was put out and all the anger drained out of her completely.

"They're humans, just look at them."

Suzume blinked. The rage was already starting to dissipate and when she looked at the fishermen she didn't see terrifying men brandishing weapons but instead frail old men. The one carrying the harpoon looked like he would blow over in a strong wind. *Was I really about to murder them all? What is happening to me?* She had been blinded by her rage. It was like she became a different person entirely.

"Both of you need to leave this place now. You're not welcome here," said one of the fishermen who had stepped forward. But Suzume could see his hands trembling.

Naoki stepped in front of Suzume, sword drawn. They all took a visible step backward as Tsuki joined his father.

Makato held up his hands. "Please, we don't mean you any harm."

"We don't want any trouble. Just leave us in peace," the old man at the head of the fisherman said.

"And we don't intend to harm you. In fact we can assist you. If one of you will loan us a boat, we can rid you of the umi-bozu."

There was a ripple of murmurs that ran through the group.

The fisherman glanced toward Suzume and then the two armed men in front of her.

"We're going to exterminate an umi-bozu?" Tsuki asked under his breath.

Suzume's gaze slid toward Makato, wondering what he was thinking. It seemed against his nature to be this reckless. His gaze was fixed on the fisherman who continued their debate.

After a few minutes of furious deliberation, the spokesman took a step forward.

"We will give you a boat only if you promise to leave this place and never come back."

Makato bowed to the old man. "Thank you."

"Don't thank me. No one crosses that water and makes it back alive."

Thirty-Five

The sea was dark and endless. Suzume stood at the bow looking toward the ocean. Now that she was looking at it up close, she was beginning to have second thoughts. The fisherman's ominous words continued to ring through her head. Would Kazue's power even be enough to defeat the umi-bozu? Behind her Makato unfurled a sail riddled with holes. It stank of must and Suzume crinkled her nose at it.

"Do you know how to sail a boat?" she asked him.

Makato pulled a line tight, tying it around a piece of wood at the back of the ship in a way that inspired some confidence. "In theory; I've read about it."

"So not really." That gnawing anxiety continued to scratch at the back of her mind. Perhaps they shouldn't try this. But if she changed her mind now, it was like admitting Kaito was right. That she didn't know how to lead.

"Are we even certain this thing will even stay afloat?" Tsuki asked as he kicked gently against the mast. Debris rained down on their heads. Suzume made an umbrella out of her hands to keep any of it from landing in her hair. Who knew what creeping crawling creatures or moldy fragments were hiding in this ship.

"My lady," a voice shouted to her, the sound almost stolen by the wind. Suzume frowned and searched for the source. Tohru waved to her from the shore. The Namahage refused to get on the boat, not that there was room for them. They were afraid of the water it seemed. Not that they would admit it. Even now they hovered far up the beach well out of the reach of the waves that were slapping onto the shore.

Suzume waved back at him. She was glad for an excuse to be rid of them. The Namahage had served their purpose. They'd brought her here, and she had no more need of Tohru's overprotective attentions.

But the Namahage shouted for her once more. With a frustrated exhale, she moved toward the back of the boat, thinking she could hear him better if she got closer to shore. He held something in his hand, which he was waving at her, beckoning her to come to him. But she couldn't make out what he was saying over the thundering of the waves. They'd already pushed off from the shore and the boat bobbed in shallow water. But even so she wasn't jumping into the freezing water for no good reason.

As Suzume squinted to better see what Tohru was holding, Makato did something and the sail pulled taut. Suddenly they were jerked forward and farther away from the shore and any hope of hearing what the Namahage wanted to tell her was lost. All Suzume could do was watch his form shrink on the horizon. *I'm sure it was nothing,* she thought and turned her attention back to the open sea.

Once they were on the open water, the rocking of the ocean swayed the boat, and just to stay upright Suzume had to hold onto the side of the boat. The Namahage's last request was quickly chased from her mind.

They veered back and forth across the bay, zig-zagging their way toward the open ocean. The jerking motions had Suzume's stomach turning over and she felt that morning's breakfast threatening to make a second appearance. But it wasn't until Makato tried moving the sail and almost knocked Tsuki overboard that Naoki took over navigation and Makato was exiled to the front of the ship with Suzume. For a while he simply stared out at the ocean without speaking.

"You don't need to worry," he said, breaking the silence.

"Who said I was worried?" Suzume said with a toss of her head. The wind caught her dark locks and unfurled them behind her like a flag.

Now that Naoki was piloting her stomach had settled.

Makato nodded down toward her white-knuckled grip on the edge of the boat. Suzume released her hands but only a little, she still felt like she might tip over with the force of the rocking of the ship.

"Is sailing supposed to be this unpleasant?" she asked.

"They say you'll get used to it after a while."

"How long is a while?"

"Some accounts say days?" The uncertainty in his tone was not comforting.

"Great. Let's just hope this dingy can get us to the other side in one piece for now." *Or we don't have to face the umi-bozu.*

Getting out of the bay seemed to take an eternity. The boat moved painfully slow. A steady spray of water soaked Suzume's clothes to the skin, and no matter where she moved on the tiny vessel she could not avoid it. Then the wind blew, making the water like ice against her skin.

Suzume shivered, her teeth chattering as the breeze blew through her water-soaked clothes. For a while the only sound was water lapping against the sides of the boat and the sound of her own teeth chattering. She made the mistake of looking back to where they had come from, and it seemed too close for how long they had been on the water and their destination much too far away.

But she was too cold to even complain. She rubbed her arms up and down, trying to keep herself warm. At least being cold distracted her from thinking about what might lurk beneath the dark surface.

"What will you do once you get the stone?" Makato whispered into her ear. He looked over his shoulder toward Tsuki, who was leaning against the mast, and then to Naoki whose gaze was trained forward, one hand on the rudder.

Suzume clutched her arms tighter around herself. "What else: become stronger."

There was a long pause. "What if it isn't enough? What if it only leaves you wanting more?"

"I won't make Kazue's mistake," Suzume scoffed. This was all to prove to the dragon that she was strong.

Makato did not comment and the silence that fell afterward was only punctuated by the slap of water on the side of the boat. After a few minutes Makato said, "I used to think I wanted to get my memories back, but now I'm not sure. Sometimes what we think we want isn't what will make you happy."

"Not for me. I'm never going to be helpless again." Though she had found a somewhat dry spot, she got up to walk away from him and headed back to the front of the ship. She didn't need his advice.

As Suzume looked out onto the water she saw the mouth of the bay approaching. Hills slid into the water on both sides, like two arms embracing them. No one spoke as they approached it. Suzume held her breath, waiting for something to rise out of the sea and try to stop them, but they sailed out without incident.

Beyond the break it was much quieter. The distant roar of the crashing waves faded away as they skimmed across the ocean surface. In the distance, the island loomed.

Looking at it from here she felt an even stronger sense of nostalgia. Kazue had been here, perhaps she too had sailed a ship out to the island to hide the Sea Stone. They were on the right track, she was sure. And once she had the stone, then she would look for Kaito. *I cannot wait to see his face once I show him the Sea Stone.*

Water dripped down onto her forehead. Suzume looked up to find dark gray clouds gathered overhead. *Great. Now it's raining.* Curiously the wind died down, and the sails went slack. Naoki adjusted the rudder and moved the lines without any success. They were dead in the water.

"What happened?" she asked, but got only confused looks and shrugged shoulders in return.

A bad feeling was creeping its way up her spine. She turned back to the front of the ship. There was what looked like the beginnings of a wave a few leagues in front of their boat. She squinted to get a better look, it seemed to be growing in size, swelling up to almost the same width as their boat.

"Draw your staff!" Makato shouted as he drew his bow and arrow.

"What's going on?" she said as she pulled her staff from its sheath. As soon as she did, the fire encased it without telling it to. "Is that the umi-bozu?"

"It looks like it! Hold on!" Tsuki shouted as he too drew his own sword.

The wave came toward them, growing in size, but not cresting. As it approached them it was almost the same height as their ship. *The fire stone, I need it.* Suzume patted her clothes searching for it but it was nowhere on her. It was then she realized what Tohru had been trying to give her. *I left the fire stone with the Namahage.* She groaned aloud.

Makato looked at her with a raised brow, but she only shook her head in response.

Before the wave crashed into their ship, a dark shadow burst out from under the water. It rose up into the sky, looming high above them. Suzume craned her neck back to look at a pair of bright white eyes blinking down at her. Water dripped off its massive smooth head. The sea, which was calm before, started to churn beneath their boat, rocking it from side to side.

The creature plunged back into the water creating massive waves which washed over the boat, almost knocking the boat over. The force of the wave knocked the staff from Suzume's hand and sent it flying across the vessel.

Suzume spit out water and looked around. She wasn't the only one who had been bowled over. Everything was quiet. Water lapped against their ship. She felt a tingling along her neck that said the umi-bozu had not finished with them. Suzume scrambled to her feet and lunged for her staff.

"Where did it go?" Suzume asked once her staff was back in her hands.

Naoki had abandoned guiding the ship and had drawn his twin blades. Tsuki similarly had drawn his weapon.

"It's circling," Makato said ominously.

A chill ran up Suzume's spine as she turned her head in circles looking for the yokai. Listening for the monster. She thought she heard a splash to her left, but that may have just been the waves crashing against the side of her boat. She peered over the side just as the monster burst up from the left side of the boat. It rose up out of the deep, a large bulbous black mass. It seemed to go on forever, rising from the water and towering above them dripping water down upon them like rain. The ship rocked as it created waves with its arrival. It opened large eyes with small pupils and the whites of the eye were enormous, stark and terrifying against the black skin.

The fire rose up to her protection and she felt that familiar spiraling feeling once more. The flames were licking up her body, reacting to the immense spiritual pressure of the creature above them.

"Don't give into the power!" Makato shouted to Suzume, but he sounded as if he was a million miles away. She had no control over it even if she wanted. Suzume was doubled over, clenching the staff to her gut. *Not now. Not now.* She cried out as something electrocuted every inch of her body.

On the opposite side, a giant hand burst out from under the water and wrapped around the ship. Naoki lunged for it, hacking at it with his swords, but it merely bounced off the thing's slippery flesh. Makato ran backward, shooting arrows imbued with spiritual energy but nothing could break through the creature's hide.

The creature closed its grip on their ship, squeezing, and the boat creaked and groaned beneath the pressure. If Suzume didn't do something, the entire boat would be smashed. Suzume's hands burned with flame; Kazue was trying to take over her body.

Take control.

With sheer force of stubbornness, she pushed back Kazue's influence. The mere effort left her limbs shaking, but the fire remained and lighted her staff. She swung it at the creature's hand. When her flame got close it screeched and retreated, fearing her fire. Bits of broken wood flew with the quick retreat. And cracks in the bottom of the boat let water seep in at an alarming rate.

"The ship's going to sink," Tsuki shouted.

Suzume was staring up at the creature, whose massive hand was coming back down toward them, transfixed in place and unable to move. Her fire wasn't enough to deter it. She was nothing but a child in comparison to this thing's brute strength. Naoki grabbed her around the middle and pushed her out into the water and away from danger. They plunged into the icy cold water and she gasped as she hit, swallowing a large mouthful of saltwater.

The hand smashed into the boat seconds later, shattering it into pieces. Once she was in the water the fire was extinguished from her skin. And somewhere in their fall she'd lost her staff. But she wasn't worried about that and instead flapped around in the water trying to keep her head afloat. She was sinking like a stone. Makato shouted out for her, somewhere in the chaos. Waves were rising up, flowing over her head. The force of them was pushing her and Naoki apart.

Suzume went under, losing sense of place and time. When she surfaced she could see nothing but the monster with its giant hands reaching, searching, its white giant pupils scanning the water. Another wave rose up and she went under once more, only this time she didn't breach the surface again.

Invisible hands were grabbing onto her and dragging her downward. She quickly lost sense of up and down. There was only darkness and water pressing against her lungs, trying to pry her lips open. Something inside her was screaming, clawing its way out. She wanted to live. She flailed her arms, flapping about, but she couldn't find the surface. Her lungs wanted her to breathe, to take in air until they forced her to try. The air burst out of her in a shroud of bubbles. Her mouth filled with the bitter taste of her own death as she sank further and further downward.

Thirty-Six

The feeling of unease was growing inside Rin. Immediately after she had left the Namahage village, she'd followed what appeared to be Kaito's scent. But after a day and a half of trailing it, she realized she'd been walking in circles. Someone had led her on a wild goose chase. She knew Kaito wouldn't leave Suzume behind and this only proved it. And so she returned to the Namahage village to look for answers. But found it deserted. The doors to the huts swung on rusty hinges. A thick layer of ash and dust covered everything. It appeared to have been abandoned for years instead of a day at most. As Rin walked past the gathering space at the village center, she found old ashes and bones on the ground. *This isn't right.*

It took the rest of the day, but she found Suzume and the other's trail. She followed it for several days until she reached the coast. It led her to a fishing village set along a bay. That was where she lost the trail again. In her fox form, Rin hid among the sand dunes observing the villagers as they went about their day. But these villagers were not acting as normal humans would.

The pungent scent of fear hung on the air. Children did not run wild as children do but instead clung to their mother's skirts. The mothers scanned the horizon like frightened animals. Fisherman were not out on the water in their boats, but instead gathered in knots along the shore, their angry voices were like a hive of bees. Patrols of middle-aged men walked the perimeter of the village carrying makeshift weapons made up of rusty harpoons and bludgeons.

Rin got as close to the village as she dared and hid behind a pile of crates in order to listen in on a conversation between two of the patrolling men. Their eyes were constantly searching for something.

"Do you think she'll return?" One man asked another.

"I saw them sail off this morning. They won't be coming back."

"Doesn't it seem strange that that group showed up when they did?"

The second man shook his head. "You don't think that army man asking questions was one of their kind, do you?"

"They wouldn't dare. I think the emperor's army is looking for them. That's what they're supposed to do: protect the people."

"She seemed dangerous, fire coming out all over. It isn't natural."

"Maybe we should send one of the boys out with a message for the army. If the umi-bozu doesn't finish them off first, the army will."

"They won't get past that yokai. No one does."

The other man nodded his head in agreement. Then froze, squinting in Rin's direction.

"There's something over there." He nodded his chin in her direction.

Now was her time to flee. She retreated from the village amid shots and rocks thrown at her, none of which hit their mark. But she had heard more than enough. She knew of the umi-bozu, though she'd never seen one in person. They were elusive deep-sea yokai, almost never seen this close to land. Why would Suzume and the others be at the risk of an umi-bozu if they were only crossing over the other island?

Without a boat or a way across, Rin was trapped along the shore. She decided to search for some sort of vessel to try and cross as well. It could not be mere coincidence that Hisato and the emperor's army were nearby. She had to find the others and warn them.

As she made her way along the shoreline in search of a boat, she found not much more than piles of seaweed and broken shell fragments. Growing discouraged as time passed, she considered going back to the village and risk stealing one of their boats. That was until she noticed something lying on the beach up ahead. It looked like a massive pile of seaweed.

The wind changed direction and blew toward her. It was not seaweed but a person. Rin loped over to it. When she got closer she could see his face. Makato lay on the shore, limbs spread-eagle on the sand, face down.

Rin flipped him over. There was a cut above his left eye but otherwise he appeared unharmed. The beach around him was strewn with wood and debris. It appeared they had met the umi-bozu after all. Rin pressed her head against his chest and listened for the faint sound of his breathing. Rin let out a sigh of relief, but as she pressed her hands to his skin she felt the chill coming from him. She looked around the surrounding area. They were far from the nearest village and she doubted they would take him in anyway. She had to get him dry and warm fast.

Makato's eyes fluttered open and he squinted up at her. "Rin?" he croaked.

"Don't speak. You're safe now," she said, stroking his face to soothe him.

"I've done something terrible," he said. His voice slurred and he closed his eyes once more.

Questions rang in her mind, but they'd have to be answered later. Right now all that mattered was saving him. She transformed into her kitsune form and picked him up gently in her jaws. Like a mother fox with her kits she carried him away from the shoreline to a shaded area among the trees. She put him down on the grass and then went about making a fire.

Once the fire was blazing, she stripped him down to his undergarments and hung his wet clothes up on a tree branch to dry. Human bodies were so fragile. She knew that if he was left in wet clothes for too long he'd become ill.

She pulled him as close to the fire as she thought safe. Despite the fire's warmth he continued to shiver. She curled up next to him, sharing her own body warmth. Once she did, his breathing returned to normal. As Rin lay there with her arm wrapped around his torso, she was filled with memories of Hikaru. His smile, his laugh, and how it had felt to be in his arms. A single tear rolled down her cheek. Makato didn't want to be Hikaru. He had made that much certain. But she couldn't separate the two in her mind no matter how hard she tried.

She should go and search for the others, but it had been so long since she felt this safe and comfortable. She couldn't bring herself to leave his side. Even though Makato continued to push her away, Rin felt compelled to protect him. His resemblance to Hikaru made it that much more difficult to disentangle her own feelings about him. Perhaps Kaito was right and she was a fool for trusting him. But just for a moment she wanted to be close to him.

It wasn't long after that when Rin spotted someone approaching from the beach. She jumped up, prepared to defend Makato. Until she realized the one who was coming closer was Akira, wringing out her sleeves as she walked. Rin put distance between herself and Makato. She didn't want the siblings to tell him that she had been spooning him while he slept. A small blush crept over her face. What was she doing? She should have been out searching for the others.

"You have great timing," Akira commented as she approached.

"When I couldn't find the dragon I came looking for you. What happened?"

"We attempted crossing to the island but our ship was destroyed by the umi-bozu. The waves were so wild we were forced apart."

"We stuck together though," Tsuki interjected.

"Very funny." Akira rolled her eyes.

"Dry off by the fire." Rin gestured toward the fire she had made.

"Have you seen Suzume?" Akira asked.

Rin shook her head. "I was just about to go look for her."

"I hope she's alright, the last I saw her a wave washed over her and she never surfaced again." Akira looked out to the water, frowning.

Her words were like a dark premonition. "What about Naoki? Perhaps they're together?"

"We haven't seen him either."

"I'll go look for them now."

Akira bowed her head as a way of thanks. Rin gave one more look to the sleeping Makato before heading back down to the shore in search of Suzume and Naoki. Rin's thoughts continued to drift to her last fight with Suzume. She had not been acting like herself as of late. She knew Suzume could be selfish, but the fact that she had dismissed the idea of looking for Kaito troubled her. Could the priestess have something to do with Kaito's disappearance?

After hours of searching, she found nothing but more of the ship's debris. And as the time passed, Rin was losing hope she was going to find the priestess alive. Feeling discouraged, she headed back to the others to give them the news.

When she returned, Makato was awake and staring into the flames of the fire. When he saw her getting close he leaped up and came toward her. *He's probably worried about Suzume.* She braced herself to deliver the bad news.

"I'm sorry, I couldn't find—" but before she could finish her sentence, he grabbed onto her shoulders.

"What are you doing here? You shouldn't be here." He stood up and looked past her toward the ocean.

Rin laughed but her stomach churned. *Does he really despise me that much?* "I think you're supposed to say thank you for saving you."

A blush was running up his neck as he looked from Rin to Akira. He coughed into his hand. "Thank you," he mumbled.

Akira shared a look with Rin, a single brow raised in question. Rin shrugged her shoulders in response and turned away so they couldn't see just how embarrassed she was. It had been stupid to think even for a moment he could be Hikaru. What a past life promised didn't mean the next life had to agree to it.

Rin cleared her throat before saying. "I'm afraid I have some bad news. I couldn't find Suzume. And I'm afraid she didn't make it."

Makato's eyes grew wide. "How can you be sure? She could be anywhere."

"If she didn't drown, we would have found her by now."

Makato put his head in his hands. "This is my fault." He looked up at Rin, guilt plain on his face. "I have to go look for her."

Rin held up her hands to stop him. "You need to rest. You nearly drowned."

"You don't understand, if I hadn't interfered then none of this would have happened." He threw his arms out.

"You didn't summon the umi-bozu."

Makato was shaking his head, eyes trained on the ocean as if he could will Suzume to rise from the sea.

"We'll look for Suzume," Akira said.

"Are you sure?" Rin asked.

Akira nodded. "We are bound to her. If anyone can find her, we can." She sauntered down the beach, leaving Rin and Makato in an awkward stand-off: both of them standing by the fire, neither of them willing to look the other in the eye.

If only Rin had tried harder to stop Suzume, none of this would have happened. She'd seen the signs of her thirst for power. Her obsession with it had led to her demise. And now Makato blamed himself for it.

"This isn't your fault," Rin said, gesturing toward the ocean.

Makato did not respond and instead paced beside the fire.

"Why don't you sit down?" she asked.

He seemed to be deaf to her as he continued to walk around, running his hands through his hair and mumbling to himself.

"Perhaps I should go and help Akira." Rin motioned to leave but before she could Makato grabbed a hold of her wrist.

"You need to leave this place. Go back to your shrine and your people," he said, his voice so low she might have thought she was imagining it if he wasn't looking into her eyes and pleading with his gaze.

"What?" Her heart was hammering in her chest all of a sudden. She had never mentioned the shrine she and Hikaru had run together for centuries. No one knew about it but the dragon.

"I don't need you here," he said without looking at her.

"How did you know I had a shrine?"

He froze and looked at her wide-eyed. The only sound was the snap of the fire between them.

"Do you remember?"

He hesitated then said, "It was a lucky guess." He turned to walk away from her to head down the beach but she chased after him, grabbing onto his shoulder and forcing him to face her.

"Why are you lying to me? You do remember."

"I'm afraid!"

His voice echoed all around them. Rin's heart was hammering so loud in her chest she was certain he could hear it.

"Of what?"

"Hurting you."

The ocean thundered in the distance and the wind moaned as it rolled over the shore.

"You can't hurt me," she said softly.

He turned away from her again. "I'm not a good person, Rin. I've done awful things."

She walked around him, forcing him to face her. "What sort of things?"

"I've been killing yokai." The words were direct and sliced the space between them. Drawing a line in the sand.

Her breath caught in her lungs, keeping her from uttering a coherent word. "Oh." She exhaled.

"I'm a danger to you. Before you get hurt, please go." He ran his hands through his hair, a painful echo of Hikaru. Could this be him? Was all of this done to protect her?

"Just tell me the truth. Do you have Hikaru's memories?"

He looked up at her, meeting her gaze for the first time. "Yes."

Time stood still. For a moment she forgot how to breathe.

"Are you Hikaru's reincarnation?"

He paused. A couple of heartbeats. He inhaled then exhaled.

"Yes."

After waiting so long, dreaming of this moment, she could not hold herself back and she leaned forward and pecked her lips against his before pulling back. She wanted to take it slow.

"Then I don't care about the rest. We promised to be together. We promised to find one another again."

His eyes were wide but instead of running away, he grabbed a hold of her, pulled her closer and kissed her. It felt as if her entire body was set aflame. With the feeling of his arms around her, his lips against hers, she was lost in that moment for eternity. All of the suffering and heartache she had endured up until now: this moment made it all worth it.

After a few breathless minutes he pulled away and turned his back to her once more, pacing away. Even his reactions were similar to Hikaru's.

"You don't have to run away from me," Rin said with a smirk.

He shook his head. "You have to leave before it's too late. That is all I can do for you."

"I'm not like a human girl. I don't break."

"I know that. But—"

He fell silent and looked past Rin toward a group who were approaching their camp. Rin could see their long grass skirts and red masks from a distance. It was the Namahage. And at their head was their leader Tohru, who carried something in his arms. Rin frowned as they approached. Could it be?

Makato took a step toward them. "No." He choked on the words.

Rin looked from him to the Namahage once more. What the head of the Namahage carried was a body. Suzume's body.

Thirty-Seven

The Namahage laid Suzume's body on the ground at Rin's feet. Her dark, wet hair fanned out on the ground like tendrils. Her face was pale, nearly translucent, and her wet clothes clung to her body, silhouetting the shape of frail arms and legs. Her eyes were closed as if in sleep, but her chest did not rise and fall. Normally Suzume had seemed so animated and full of life. In death it seemed she had diminished to nothing but a girl. Her lifespan was nothing but a blink for a kitsune who lived on forever. *What will Kaito think?*

"You killed her," Tohru spat, pointing a meaty finger in Makato's direction.

Rin tore her gaze away from Suzume to look at Makato. He was frozen. His eyes transfixed upon the dead body.

When the priest did not react as the Namahage wanted, he marched up and shoved him hard on the shoulder. Makato fumbled backward, but did not lift a finger to defend himself. Instead he bowed his head in apology.

"I'm sorry," he said, his voice cracking.

"Do you think that is enough?" The Namahage raised his hand, prepared to strike at Makato. Before he could, Rin threw herself in between them. She transformed into her kitsune form and snarled at the Namahage.

"You stay away from him," she growled.

This was the wrong thing to do. A wave of anger buzzed through the Namahage. They raised their large cleavers and fanned out, surrounding the pair of them. Makato remained still with his head bowed in penance. *He has no reason to apologize. I know he didn't force her on that boat. She made her own decision.* Makato's guilt was the least of their problems at the moment.

"Did you plan this together?" The leader of the Namahage accused, jabbing his cleaver in Rin's direction.

"She was our friend, why would we try to kill her?" Rin replied.

"The stone would have protected her, but it was stolen out of her pocket and left on the beach. That man took it from her." He pointed at Makato with his weapon and behind him the Namahage rattled their own weapons. "I tried to warn her, but he stopped me from doing so. That's when I knew he was the one."

Makato fell to his knees, then folded forward into a deep bow.

"Forgive me. I did not mean for this to happen."

The pain in his voice tore at Rin, if only she could take that guilt from him. Instead she took out her frustration on the Namahage. "Even the stone could not have protected her. She went up against an umi-bozu, nothing can defeat them."

"She is a goddess, and with the right power she would have been invincible."

"But she's not a goddess, she is just a human!"

"See?" Tohru said, turning to look at the seething Namahage behind him. "Even now she insults our lady. What shall we do?"

Together the Namahage chanted, "Kill them. Kill them." As they closed in around the pair of them the only way out was to fight, but she couldn't do it on her own. Not while Makato still had his head pressed to the dirt.

"Snap out of it." Rin nudged him with her paw.

The priest looked up at her with red-rimmed eyes.

"They're right, this is my fault." He shook himself as he rose up off of his knees. "I must face my punishment."

She wanted to shake him. Now was not the time. The Namahage were drawing even closer. She felt the press of their bodies around them. All of her animal instincts were telling her to run, to save herself. But she couldn't leave him behind, not after she had finally found him again. The Namahage stomped their feet in unison, the vibrations of it shaking up Rin's body. They were so close now she couldn't even turn around without hitting one of them.

"I'm not leaving you. Either you fight or I die here protecting you."

Makato turned sharply toward her, his eyes wide for a moment. A transformation came over his face as he realized just how serious she was.

That was when the Namahage attacked. One of them had broken away from the crowd and swung his large blade at Makato. Rin swiveled, blocking the blow that would have severed Makato's head from his shoulders and instead took a deep cut into her thigh. Rin roared in pain.

A blind animalistic rage overcame her as she contorted her body to avoid another attack while snapping and clawing at the Namahage. They came toward her from all directions. As soon as she confronted one, another was attacking from a different side. Rin shot blasts of her kitsune fire at them, blanketing the Namahage in blue flame, but the fire only rolled off their backs.

Somewhere in the chaos, she was separated from Makato. Even knowing she was putting herself in danger, she searched for him. All the while, the bodies closed in around her. One blow, followed by a second and a third, brought her to the ground. They piled onto her, preventing any escape. But as they did, a dozen copies of Makato swarmed over on top of them. The Namahage wrestled with the clones of Makato and those that remained Rin shook off her body.

One of the clones came toward her and held out his hand. When her golden eyes met his green ones, she realized this was not a copy but the real thing. In a moment a silent understanding passed between them. A plan formed without a need for words. It was as if she was back in the old days with Hikaru.

The Namahage had destroyed the clones and were once more closing in. They were even angrier than before. Rin placed herself in front of

Makato, blocking him from the Namahage as he spoke a rapid chant under his breath.

Giant vines burst up from the ground, blocking the Namahage and leaving them their chance to escape. Rin started to flee but stopped when Makato didn't follow.

"What are you doing?" she shouted at him.

"Don't argue with me and run," he said, his gaze transfixed on the wall of vines.

The Namahage were already starting to break through the vines; the metal gleam of their weapons poked through the thick greenery.

"I'm not leaving without you," Rin said, standing by his side.

"Just go," he said and the vines burst out of the ground at her feet, wrapping around her torso and launching her into the air several yards away from the fighting.

Rin landed on the ground with a hard thud, but was back up in a few seconds. When she looked up again, the swarm of Namahage had converged around Makato.

"No!" Rin roared and barreled toward them.

She launched herself onto the far side of the group, tearing and rending flesh, with a single-minded focus on finding and saving Makato. The Namahage swarmed around her, overwhelming her with their sheer numbers. She was hit from every side and still she pressed forward until one last blow brought her crashing to the ground. Bloody and beaten, she looked up at the Namahage who raised his clever prepared to make an end of her. But before he could, a blade was shoved through the back of him. Just the bloody tip of a sword poked through.

The Namahage slumped forward onto the ground, revealing a blood-spattered Tsuki.

"Sorry I'm late."

As he grinned at Rin, another Namahage came up behind him screaming for blood. Tsuki spun around slicing his head off his shoulders, which tumbled onto the ground with a wet flop.

The Namahage circled around their new opponent while Rin scanned the crowd for Makato.

"What has them all riled up?" Tsuki asked as he stood back to back with Rin.

"They think we killed Suzume." He nodded. No more needed to be said.

At the same time they both attacked, taking on several Namahage at once. But despite Tsuki's skill and Rin's determination, they were greatly outnumbered.

"That's enough," a cold voice said, effectively dropping a bucket of cold water over the group.

Rin, Tsuki and the Namahage all froze in place, turning to see Tohru holding his knife to Makato's throat.

"Let him go," Rin snarled.

"Rin get out of here. It's a trap. Suzume isn't really dead."

Tsuki, who was closest to Suzume's body, knelt down beside it. He picked up her arm which pulled away from the body, but instead of blood and bone straw fell out of an empty sleeve. Her face which had seemed so life like before, now appeared to be painted on.

"What is this?" Tsuki asked, his brows raised to his hairline in confusion.

"I guess the game is up," Tohru said, but his voice had changed. It was no longer gruff but more refined and familiar.

Makato would not look at her but stared forward. "You promised you wouldn't hurt her."

"And that was before you disobeyed me. Did you think I wouldn't notice?"

"What is he talking about? You were taking orders from the Namahage?"

Tohru threw his head back and laughed, it was high and mocking. "I guess I have no more need of this." He pulled back his mask and tossed it to the ground, revealing himself to be Hisato.

"You were working for Hisato?" It felt as if someone had just punched her in the gut. This had to be a trick.

Hisato traced his hand along Makato's cheek. Makato would not look Rin in the eye but instead stared at the dummy of Suzume's body. "You are correct, he's given himself to me. And I've put his power to good use. Even you were fooled by my illusion." Hisato snapped his finger and the Namahage that were surrounding them disappeared in a puff of smoke, along with the straw body of Suzume.

"Why would you do this?" Rin asked Makato.

Even though he wouldn't look at her, the shame of what he had done was written in his expression.

"He did it to get back his memories," Hisato said with a shake of his head as if he couldn't think of a sillier thing to do.

"You're lying." Rin snarled and took a step toward them but Hisato only raised the blade to his throat.

"Don't test me, kitsune. I'm not afraid to spill blood."

"You wouldn't kill him, you need him," Rin said, taking a daring step forward.

Hisato dragged his blade against Makato's cheek as he cried out in pain. He might as well have grabbed a hold of her heart and twisted it.

Her voice shook as she spoke. "Please, just let him go."

"Well, that's the problem. Restoring what was lost comes at a heavy price. And he has not paid in full." He laughed as he flipped his hand and a black stone appeared.

"What is it he owes? I'll pay it."

"Rin, don't!" Makato shouted.

"Don't be a fool." Akira agreed, using her brother's face to scold the kitsune.

She ignored them all and took a step closer toward Hisato. "What did you ask him to do?"

Hisato waved his hand. "It's too late now. I will have to take my repayment from him." He turned Makato's face toward him as he scored a line of blood along Makato's neck.

"Wait." Rin held out her hand.

Hisato stopped and turned to smile at her. "Yes?"

"Whatever you think is a worthy payment for memories of a past life, I will give it to you." She held her head high as she looked at Hisato.

"It wasn't his past life he had to remember. But this life."

Rin felt as if the ground had just been turned to sand beneath her feet. This had to be a trick.

"But he remembers me from his past life." Her eyes darted between Hisato and Makato.

"Tell her what you learned, Hikaru," Hisato purred. His eyes were trained on Rin. Hearing his name it sent a ripple down her spine. This couldn't be real.

"Hikaru died."

"I'll find Suzume and give her the stone, just let Rin go," Makato pleaded with Hisato.

Hisato laughed throwing his head back. "Oh no. That will not return balance. Not now. More is required."

"That's enough," Tsuki said and rushed toward Hisato. Before he could land his attack, vines rose up from the ground, wrapping around his body, pinning his arms to his sides. Tsuki struggled against them.

"What are you doing? We're on the same side," Tsuki shouted at Makato.

Hisato had let go of him and Makato stood at Hisato's side. He was staring at the ground, his hands balled into fists.

"As you can see, Hikaru has chosen his side," Hisato said to Tsuki.

Rin felt as if the entire world had been knocked off its axis. Hikaru wouldn't have done this. He was good, he fought to protect the innocent. He wouldn't sacrifice another for his own ends. Unless it was to protect her...

She had to save him. She rushed forward, prepared to attack. She would destroy Hisato by any means necessary.

As Rin ran closer however, Makato put his hand out and a dozen copies burst in front of her, blocking her path and preventing her from attacking Hisato.

Hisato laughed. "You cannot win, kitsune. Now is your time to choose. The dragon or your husband."

Just then a vine burst up from the ground and impaled Hisato in the shoulder. He stumbled forward and the blow knocked the stone out of his hand. It rolled toward Rin. Blood seeped from his wound, but it was already knitting itself back together. The only evidence that remained was the bloody stain down his front and a matching bloody wound was opened on Makato's shoulder as well.

He turned to face Makato, danger glinting in his eye. "You will regret that," Hisato hissed. He opened his hand and a blade made of black material appeared there. He rushed toward Makato, blade arched to kill.

"Rin, run," Makato shouted, slicing his hand through the air, indicating she should go.

Hisato raised up the black sword, while Makato surrounded himself in copies. She could not even consider leaving, and instead she flung herself between the two of them. As Hisato's blade fell it sliced into her shoulder. White hot flames licked inside her body, contracting every muscle as she screamed in agony. The power of the attack was enough to force her from her true form to her human form.

Hisato stood over her panting, his blade held at his side.

"What a touching reunion, too bad it will not last."

Makato stood over her, his arms outstretched. "Let her go. She has nothing to do with this."

"A price must be paid." Hisato smiled.

"Then take my life for hers."

Hisato shook his head. "That is not enough, you are already mine." He turned toward Rin with a sly smile. He leaned down and picked up the stone. He held it in front of himself for Rin to see.

"Inside here is the dragon. I will give him to you but Hikaru remains here with me. Or you can join me and I will spare both your lives."

Rin looked at Hikaru. He reached for her hand and squeezed it. She leaned forward, pressing her forehead to his.

"I should have found you sooner." She cried, tears rolling down her cheek.

"I will find you again. I will always find you."

She nodded against his head, and then kissed him one more time before turning to face Hisato. *I'm sorry, my beloved.*

"I will join you."

Thirty-Eight

uzume woke up on something hard. *I'm getting really tired of being knocked unconscious,* she thought as she sat up and rubbed her pounding head. Water dripped nearby. Her clothes were soaked and were suctioned to her skin, just as her hair was plastered to her head and wrapped around her throat into her mouth attempting to choke her. She spit out the mass of salty, wet hair and then pushed the strands back on her scalp.

Looking around, she seemed to be in the courtyard of a palace. Her mind was in a fog. *Where am I?* The taste of the sea lingered in her mouth and a vivid memory of drowning came to her mind. *Did I die?*

If this was the afterlife, it was not what she expected it to be. The courtyard was vacant. A covered veranda surrounded the square courtyard, and a single set of stairs led onto corridors to places unknown. The light here was strange as well, gloomy and ethereal. *I can't believe I died.* She had always thought you found peace in the afterlife, but she only felt annoyed. Nothing in her life went right, so of course she would die without accomplishing her goals. *At least I don't have to worry about defeating Hisato now.*

She climbed to her feet, skin shivering from cold. She would have hoped dying would mean being freed of cold and pain as well. But that was just her luck, wasn't it?

"Hello?" She called out, but there was no response other than the echo of her voice reverberating back at her.

She shuffled closer to the stairwell leading onto the veranda. The courtyard was covered in smooth stones, and the column was painted blue, and upon closer inspection she could see a motif of waves and sea creatures decorating the columns and the walls. She ran her fingers along the fine details. It was very delicate and would have been completed by a master craftsman. She tilted her head as she examined it, she could feel each ridge of the carving, even smell the salt in the air. *I didn't think death would feel so much like living.*

Someone behind her cleared their throat and Suzume spun around to see a small man staring at her with blue skin, bulbous eyes, a wide mouth, and what seemed to be gills on the side of his head. Perched atop his head was a pointed hat, something that was commonly worn by high-ranking servants.

Suzume screeched at the sight of him. She threw her arms up in a defensive pose. "Who are you?"

"Welcome, my lady, we've been expecting you," he said with a deep bow.

"Am I dead?" Suzume looked at the man and blinked in confusion.

He chortled. "You've reached the court of the Lord of the Sea," he said and then with a blue, webbed hand pointed up the stairs. "This way, he's waiting for you."

Suzume looked around again at the strange palace, "But I drowned. Are you sure I'm not dead?"

The man smiled. "Quite certain. Though the pathway to get here might feel a lot like drowning." He gestured upward with a flipper-like hand. Suzume tilted her head back and almost fell over backward from the shock. The sky overhead was not sky at all, but a blackish blue ocean.

Silvery fish flitted by like a flock of birds, chased by even bigger fish with many pointed teeth, and then a large shadow passed overhead, its form hidden by the murky water. It sent a shiver of fear down her spine. When Suzume looked down again, the fish servant was heading up the stairs without her. She almost stumbled on the edge of her wet hakama in her haste to chase after him.

Confused more than ever, Suzume followed the man through a long hallway. The place reminded her of the palace on the mountaintop where Kazue's heart had been hidden. It looked like a human palace, but there was a strange aura to the place that left the hairs on the back of her neck standing on end. The blue man led Suzume to a pair of double doors, which were guarded by two yokai. They had the bodies of men but their heads were those of largemouth fish. They held spears with jagged points, which gleamed beneath the blue-green luminescent light of torches behind them. Suzume looked at them from the corner of her eye as she walked into the room beyond.

The room was packed with even more strange creatures: a group of small men covered in red hair and wearing skirts made of seaweed sat around a low table drinking sake, while a woman with long strands of dark hair and eyes black without pupils watched Suzume walk by without blinking. Further along was another woman whose upper body was of a maiden but her lower half was a snake which coiled around her. In her arms she cradled a bundle that looked like a baby. When Suzume tried to peek at what she was carrying she hissed and yanked her bundle away from Suzume.

Suzume stumbled backward and nearly fell into a trio of ghost-like apparitions with skeletal bodies draped in tattered white robes. Suzume almost went through one of them. When she got close to them she felt icy and she shivered. They turned their heads in unison to look at her and she held up her palms toward them before chasing after the servant who continued walking without pausing.

The fish servant walked very quickly for someone who seemed to have very short legs. This strange place was beyond anything she had seen before. Mixed among the strange yokai were humans as well, fishermen with tanned, weathered skin and receding hairlines. They were drinking sake from cups filled by beautiful maidens with strange colored hair and fish-like appendages.

At the far end of the room, on a single raised dais, was a man in a gradient of flowing blue kimono. There were too many layers to count. The colors ranged from light blue to a blue that was almost black. His long hair was gray like the sky during a summer storm, tied half up and the rest falling down his back and pooling on the ground behind him. As she drew closer, the color of it shifted to a sky blue. It continued to transition as the sky does throughout the day, from gray to dark blue. His skin glowed faintly in the blue-green light cast by the torches that were placed behind his throne.

The servant stopped in front of the Sea Lord's dais and bowed low. Suzume, not certain how one addressed a powerful yokai, bowed as well, as if she was looking upon the emperor himself. It was strange, she had expected power to emanate from him the way it had from the leader of the Namahage, drawing her in. But she could feel none of his spiritual power, though at a glance he looked very powerful. It was as if there was a void of nothing sitting before her.

"You have arrived at last, Suzume."

Suzume looked up, frowning at the yokai. "How do you know my name?" she asked. It was never a good sign when they knew your name.

"We've been waiting for you, for a very long time," he said as he motioned for Suzume to sit on the cushion beside him to his right. On the other side was a little girl with dark hair and large eyes. When Suzume looked at her she felt a spark of power but the feeling was fleeting, so she couldn't be sure she hadn't imagined it.

"Why me?" she asked, taking a seat cautiously. As much as she liked to think of herself as powerful, drawing the attention of yokai was always dangerous and there were a lot of them in this room right now.

"My daughter Ai dreamed of you." He gestured elegantly toward the little girl beside him.

The little girl waved at Suzume. She wore a multitude of layered kimono as well, hers more pinkish like the inside of a shell and a dusky violet like the sunset over the sea.

"She did?" Suzume asked, brow raised skeptically. This was starting to sound an awful lot like a yokai trick.

"For five hundred years my people and I have been trapped by the umi-bozu, unable to leave our kingdom, but now that you have come to save us at last..."

Just the memory of that monstrous creature made her stomach drop. Going up against that thing once was more than enough. It was pure luck that she had survived the first time, a second time would surely kill her. She didn't even have her staff. It had gotten lost when she'd been thrown overboard. How could she gracefully wiggle her way out of this without upsetting them?

"See the thing is..." she began.

"We sensed your power the moment you rode out on that boat. We have not seen such a strong spiritual energy since the priestess who trapped us here."

Suzume sighed and rolled her eyes. *Of course this is Kazue's doing.* The hall had turned silent and every eye was turned watching her now. All of them had the same expectant look upon their faces. *I can't defeat that thing. But I can't let them know that.* What are they going to do if they found out?

"You must be tired from your long journey—"

"If I do this, what do I get?" Suzume interrupted him. Perhaps if she asked for something ridiculous, they would just let her go. It was a long shot but it was worth a try.

The Lord of the Sea did not seem perturbed by her outburst at all. Instead a slow smile spread across his face. "What is it you desire?"

Suzume considered him for a moment. There was only one thing she wanted, but there was no way he could get it for her.

"I want the Sea Stone," she said, leveling him with her gaze.

He pressed the tips of his fingers together. "You ask a large price."

"You're asking a lot of me too. That thing nearly killed me once already." *And when you refuse to get it for me I will refuse to help and instead negotiate to get out of here.*

"Very well then, I shall give you the Sea Stone once you defeat the umi-bozu."

Suzume almost fell backward on her cushion.

"Are you sure? I mean how can you even get it. Didn't Kazue hide the stone?"

A small smirk pulled at the corner of his lips. "I am not completely without resources. If you can free us, I will pay any price." He clapped his hands and servants rushed forward carrying platters of steaming food. "Now please eat and enjoy yourself." He snapped his fingers and a trio of fish women brought forth instruments and began playing a haunting tune.

The scent of food was mouth-watering but she had suddenly lost her appetite. The others in the room had returned to their meal or drinking. Now that she had made her promise to help them they had all lost interest in what she was doing. The servants prepared her a platter heaped high with broiled fish and vegetables along with a serving of rice. Suzume pushed the food around her plate without eating.

As she did, however, she felt eyes watching her. Suzume peeked out the corner of her eye to see the little girl, Ai, staring at her. Her large, dark eyes were unblinking.

"Do you mind?" Suzume said, gesturing to her food.

"No, thank you. Ai, is not hungry," the girl said.

Suzume sighed dramatically. "I would rather not be watched while I eat."

"Ah." The girl nodded, but did not move away.

Suzume sighed and set down her chopsticks, completely giving up on pretending to eat. "Can I help you with something?"

"You have a strange aura. It is as if there are two separate souls inside of you. Why is that?"

Suzume cleared her throat and didn't look the girl in the eye as she said, "I'm just that powerful."

The little girl nodded. "Ai heard stories of a woman who split her soul into pieces and hid the fragments inside the bodies of others. Did something like that happen to you?"

Suzume sniffed. "I've never heard anything like that."

"That woman was very powerful as well. She was the one who trapped Ai here."

"Oh?"

"Ai hates her."

Suzume shoved food into her mouth, hoping it would give the girl a hint to leave her be. But the child seemed content to continue prattling on.

"If Ai ever finds that woman she will punish her for what she did."

Suzume swallowed past a lump in her throat. "What would you do if you met her again?"

"Ai would make her feel the pain Ai has felt trapped for centuries..." Something in the child's eyes glowed dangerous and looming. But just as quickly she laughed, high and child-like. "Would you like to see Ai's dollhouse after you eat?" she asked.

The shift was so sudden that Suzume was left with food dangling on its way to her mouth.

"Uh, sure."

"Great." Ai came around the table and grabbed onto Suzume's arm and dragged her to her feet.

Suzume's meal was left uneaten as she was dragged out of the room and down the hall. The child led her to a room at the end of a deserted hallway. When they reached it, Ai threw open the doors and gestured for Suzume to follow her in.

Inside was a perfect replica of the palace in miniature. Suzume looked at the dollhouse with a nod.

"Very nice."

"Ai has complete control of it," she said, picking up a doll which looked to be a replica of the man who had greeted Suzume when she arrived.

"That's great," Suzume said distractedly.

"You asked papa for the Sea Stone, but do you know what power it really has?"

"I think that's between me and your father," Suzume said with a smile. She didn't have time to entertain the child. She had to figure out how to get out of here before she had to face the umi-bozu.

Ai did not smile back and once more Suzume saw that dangerous glint in her eye.

"That woman came looking for the Sea Stone too. When papa wouldn't give it to her, she trapped us here."

Ai slammed the doll down into the dollhouse and at the same time there was a knock on the door.

Suzume nearly leaped up into the air from the fright of it.

"Come in," Ai shouted in a sweet child's voice.

The door slid open and the servant, the same that Ai had been playing with moments before, was kneeling outside the door.

"My lady, we found this." He held up Suzume's staff.

Suzume stared at the man. *It's just a coincidence, nothing more.*

"You can take it. You're going to need it," Ai said without the saccharine sweetness, but something that sounded much older and much more dangerous. She had to remind herself that this wasn't any regular child, but a yokai child.

Suzume walked woodenly toward the servant who presented the staff. She grabbed a hold of it with some reluctance.

"That is an interesting weapon," Ai said, appearing at Suzume's elbow.

"Not really. It's just a piece of wood," Suzume said.

"It looks a lot like that woman's," Ai said, and her large round eyes met Suzume's gaze.

Her throat felt too tight to answer and all she could manage was a slow nod and a noise which sounded like a squeak.

"Ah." Suzume forced out the sound.

"Good luck fighting the umi-bozu, you're going to need it." Ai patted Suzume's arm before sauntering out of the room.

Thirty-Nine

Suzume was shown into the courtyard, where the entire palace had gathered together to watch her fight the umi-bozu. Before she had gotten onto that damned boat, she had been more confident in her abilities, but now she wasn't so sure. Her own power wasn't enough and without any other power source to draw from, she might not be able to defeat it. *Could I draw power from it?* She hadn't tried taking energy from her enemies, and she wasn't even sure how to do it. It always just sort of happened.

While Suzume fretted over escaping her likely demise, the Lord of the Sea was looking radiant. There was a smile on his handsome face as he held out his arms in a grand gesture.

"Suzume, as a show of faith, I have brought the Sea Stone." He gestured toward the servant holding the stone. "Do as you promised and you shall receive your reward."

To his left a servant held a tray on top of a small pedestal on which an opalescent stone rested. It was a swirl of pink, blue, and purple.

Suzume stared at the stone. She could feel the power emanating from it, the same way she had felt near the Flame Stone. If she had that she would be able to defeat the umi-bozu no problem.

But it was guarded by four very fierce looking guards and she was not certain she could get past them before they impaled her with one of their spears. Now would be a good time to admit she had no idea what she was doing.

"What is that doing here? I thought Kazue hid it?" She asked. She couldn't take her eyes off it.

"The priestess' spell bound us to this stone. And this place." He gestured toward the palace. "The only way to free us and get the stone is to defeat the umi-bozu."

Suzume licked her lips with anticipation. The stone's draw was undeniable, she had to have it. No matter what the cost.

"How do I get to the surface to fight it?" Suzume asked, tearing her eyes from the stone with great difficulty.

"The creature dwells just beyond that gate."

Suzume turned toward the gateway he had mentioned. The courtyard ended in a single torii arch, which led into a fog-covered landscape of darkness. It did not bode well for her chances.

"If I'm going to do this, I'll need the stone first." She held out her hand.

The Lord of the Sea laughed. "Do not worry, you shall have your payment soon."

"We are counting on you," Ai said, looking Suzume in the eyes and reminding her once again of the darkness she saw lurking in her gaze.

It was worth a try. Suzume swallowed past a large lump in her throat before nodding her head and turning stiffly toward the gateway. *I might as well get it over with. I can do this. I have Kazue's power. I am getting stronger.* Despite her pep talk, her head and limbs felt heavy as she marched over toward the archway that led into murky mist beyond. She inched forward, step by step. When she reached the barrier, she hesitated. Once she crossed over there would be no turning back. *This has to be one of the stupidest things I've ever done. Just for a rock?*

With one last look over her shoulder, she saw Ai out in front of the others. She was the only one who seemed to have any definition at all. When she looked back she felt that same lure of power, the promise of greatness. Ai waved at Suzume to continue, and with a final deep breath, she stepped through the archway. Once she was past it, she felt no different. Mist surrounded her on all sides, so thick she could hardly see beyond the reach of her arms.

A pathway led further into the fog, lined with more red torii arches. Their bright colors were like lanterns in the fog. She continued down beneath them. *Maybe this is the way out and I won't have to fight anything at all. There's nothing here.* As soon as she finished that thought, the ground rumbled beneath her feet. A shadow slid past her, just beyond the arches. Suzume reached for her staff and the weight of it gave her some comfort as she moved on.

The pathway ended a few feet later. Her flames came easily now. She could sense the creature just out of view, watching her, waiting for its chance. She stepped beyond the edge of the pathway and then turned in a circle, trying to pinpoint its location. That's when the yokai burst from within the mist. It showered her in sea water, raining cold drops down upon her head. The creature's bulbous black head and large white eyes stared down at her unblinking.

Before it could attack, Suzume shot a blast of fire at it. The umi-bozu screeched in pain, reeling backward, retreating into the water with a splash. Her fire burned away the fog, and she could see she was surrounded on all sides by water held back by an invisible source. The creature stalked overhead, floating like a shadow, circling around her. Suzume kept her eyes trained on it, hand clutching her staff. Fighting came easier now. It took little conscious thought, as if her body knew what to do without being told.

I knew Tsuki was teaching me the hard way. Now that I have control of my powers it's easy. The power coursing through her body was intoxicating. There had been no reason to worry. Her body felt alive with sensation and power consumed her. She was unstoppable. The umi-bozu swooped around behind her, but Suzume anticipated this and shot another ball of fire at it. The creature retreated before she could land her attack and the fire smoked and sputtered against the ocean, boiling it. The umi-bozu avoided that area afterward, though it continued to hover around her.

It's afraid of fire. Sensing its weakness, Suzume repeated the process again and again, chasing it as it swam away from her flames and the boiling water. All the while it was running out of places to go and falling into her trap.

With each blast of her fire, however, a strange dizzying sensation overcame Suzume. At one point she lost several minutes. Her body continued to move without her, and she was a hundred feet from where she had been last without any memory of how she had gotten there.

However it had happened, she had the umi-bozu cornered at last. It lunged at her from out of the water. Her normal impulse would have been to cover her face to avoid being hit, but her body instead spun the staff, twirling it in front of her, making a shield of fire. One of its giant black hands reached for her but pulled back in fear of the flame. Suzume leaped backward like a puppet on a string as the creature attacked once more, but she shot more fire in its direction.

How is this possible? Suzume wondered as she flipped out of the way, her body performing acrobatics that she had no idea how to do.

The umi-bozu brought its hand crashing down, blocking her escape. Suzume mentally reared back but her body had other ideas.

A song erupted from her lips, rising to the sky without her involvement, and a rain of fire fell down upon the monster. Suzume heard the sizzle of its flesh and an unearthly scream as the creature was burned by fire. *How am I doing this?* This wasn't her. She didn't know how to make fire come from the sky. She wanted to stop, but her feet would not obey her commands. She'd lost all control over her body.

The umi-bozu thrashed about as it was burned and then it fell forward, propping itself up by its arms. Dark, unblinking eyes bored into her. Then it opened its mouth to reveal rows of razor-sharp teeth. It screeched a high-pitched sound and rushed toward Suzume. It ran in an unhinged gate, on all fours and much too fast. And yet Suzume did not flee. *Run! Get out of here!* She screamed for her body to obey her, but it refused to listen to reason.

It was closing in fast, and just as it was about to bite her head off Suzume lifted up her hand and she felt a tug, or rather a push, as her energy was forced into the creature in a burst of fire. Flames licked up its body, traveling over its smooth, bald head and then down its long, dark body. The umi-bozu flailed its arms around, thrashing, splashing water, which crashed down upon Suzume. But even when submerged, nothing quenched the flames. It opened its mouth in one last horrified scream before landing a few feet from Suzume, collapsing into a pile of black goo.

Suzume panted out panicked breaths while staring at the remains. Her knees gave out from beneath her and she collapsed onto the ground. Her entire body was shaking. Suzume looked down at her hands, which she had control over once again. *What just happened. What did I do?* She looked at the smoldering black mass nearby and crawled back to get away until her head hit the torii arch. Her breathing was a ragged staccato. *It was like I had no control over my body at all. Did Kazue take over my body again?*

It took a few minutes before she felt confident enough to stand, but once she did she hobbled back to the courtyard where she had left the Lord of the Sea and his court. When she returned however, she found it deserted.

"I killed the umi-bozu, now you have to give me the Sea Stone. That was the deal," Suzume shouted, her voice echoing back at her.

She marched up toward the stairs and rested her hand on the banister. She pulled it back quickly, staring at the layer of grime that had been transferred onto her hand. The entire banister was covered in it when it had been polished to a shine just an hour before. *What is going on here?* Suzume continued on to the audience hall. Water dripped from the ceiling and puddles gathered along the ground.

"This isn't funny. I almost died to destroy that thing," she said just to fill the silence. It was too quiet all of a sudden.

There was no response but the constant drip of water. Everything smelled damp and brackish. The grand double doors of the audience hall were not only unguarded, but they were hanging off their hinges.

Suzume stepped around one of the broken doors and inside. Tables had been knocked over and scattered debris littered the floor. At the head of the room, one lone figure sat staring up at the empty throne. Ai looked even smaller in the wide-open space empty of all other occupants.

"Where is everyone?" Suzume asked. An uneasy feeling had begun to claw at the back of her mind.

"Ai knew it was you," she said, keeping her back turned to Suzume. "Ai sensed you as soon as you left the bay. And Ai knew it was my chance to finally get my revenge."

"What are you talking about? Where is the Lord of the Sea?"

"You know where he is. You sealed him away and killed the others." She turned around to face Suzume. Gone was the angelic child and in its place, was something much more horrifying. Her eyes were completely black, with white pinpoint pupils. Her long dark hair resembled tentacles rising from her head, twisting and swirling behind her.

Suzume held up her hands in surrender. "That wasn't me, it was Kazue."

"Do not lie to Ai," she shouted, her voice shaking the rafters.

"I did what you wanted. Now give me the Sea Stone," Suzume said as she reached for her staff. Not that she expected her request to be granted. As soon as her hand wrapped around her weapon, flames erupted all over her body, encasing her in flame.

"Ai will make you pay for what you've done to me!" she roared as she came rushing toward Suzume.

Immediately a song came to mind, though she did not know where she had heard it before. Without even meaning to it was wrenched from her lips, filling the chamber with its notes. The song was cut short when one of Ai's tentacles swiped low, knocking Suzume's feet out from under her. It sent her flying through the air where she collided with a far wall.

It should have knocked the wind out of her, or at least stunned her for a while, but once more Suzume's body moved without her command. She charged Ai once again, swinging the flaming staff like a sword, slicing through the tentacles which fell to the ground twitching of their own accord. But whenever she cut one away, it only grew back.

Ai laughed. "Ai has grown stronger since you were last here, Kazue. And today Ai will destroy you."

Dozens of tentacles twisted and writhed as they shot toward her. Suzume leaped out of the way, rolling on the ground just out of reach. Her entire body trembled. She wasn't sure if it was fear or that she had reached her limit. Whatever the reason, the fire which burned hot in her gut felt like it was also petering out.

"That's what you think," Suzume said. An idea was already forming in her mind.

Suzume ran across the room, dodging the tentacles with more skill than she felt herself capable of. Hiding behind the overturned table, Suzume concentrated on the song which had come to her before. In the past Kazue had given songs of protection which had saved her life. While she concentrated on the song Ai's tentacles slammed into the table before picking it up and throwing it across the room.

Standing to face the child-like yokai, Suzume held her staff in front of her, the song on the tip of her tongue.

"I will make you suffer for what you have done."

She smirked in response. She could feel the power of the song in the first note. It vibrated up from her throat and spread outward, filling the entire room with its melody. Every inch of Suzume was aware. She could feel the flow of spiritual energy in the room: Ai's and her own twirling cores of power, and remnants of yokai who had been here long ago. Like shadows of the past clinging to the present. The song encircled them all, drawing it inward and pulling it to Suzume. She took it all in, the energy filling her with bright hot light so powerful it felt as if it would burn her from the inside.

It surrounded Ai and then she was suspended in the air, her back arched as the song drew all of her spiritual energy from her. *This is what Kazue did. This is how she became immortal.* The power slammed into Suzume, almost knocking her off her feet. She gasped as it entered her. Flashes of images passed through her mind so fast she could not even process them. And then as quick as it started, it stopped. Ai came crashing to the ground, falling into a heap. Suzume held up her hands. In one she held a flame and in the other a ball of water.

Forty

Suzume woke, eager to test the limits of her new power. She threw back the covers and sat with a jug of water in front of her. With one hand held out in front of her, she concentrated on bending the water to her will. But it remained stubbornly still. *Why isn't this working?*

When she concentrated on making a ball of flame appear in her hand, fire lit there with little effort. Suzume glared at the jug of water as if it was the one responsible for her power's lack of cooperation. Just then the door to Suzume's room slid open and Ai came in carrying a tray. Suzume scooted back, watching the child-like monster with narrowed eyes.

"What are you doing here? I thought I killed you." Suzume reached for her staff, which she had left lying next to her. After she had drained Ai of all of her spiritual power, she had disappeared. Suzume had assumed she was gone for good and had spent the next several hours looking for a way out of the underwater palace. After hours of searching without success, she had found the best room she could and collapsed into sleep.

Ai bowed her head as she set a tray down beside Suzume's futon. When she looked up again there was a defiant look in her eye. "Ai is one of the first thousand children. We do not 'die'."

Suzume blinked at her in confusion. "I drained you of all of your spiritual energy though."

Ai tilted her head to the side in confusion. "You almost did. Unlike Kazue, you do not know how to harness your powers adequately. So Ai has reverted to this." She gestured to the tiny body.

"Then, what, are you back for revenge?" Suzume looked at the tray of what looked like food. Why would she feed her after trying to kill her the day before?

"Ai would, but all of Ai's strength has not returned yet." She glared at Suzume in accusation.

"Then how did you regenerate?"

"There are healing pools in the palace," Ai said, arms crossed over her chest and a tiny, haughty tilt of her head.

"Then is that why I cannot control the power anymore?" Suzume asked, sounding too much like a petulant child. But she didn't care, she liked feeling in control. And the rush of Ai's energy had been intoxicating.

"Of course you can't." Ai scoffed. "Without a vessel your human body cannot maintain a yokai's power. It is no longer in you."

"Where did it go then?"

Ai waved vaguely. "Into the stream of all energy."

"And what sort of vessel would contain that kind of power? Would the Sea Stone work?" Suzume asked, leaning toward the girl with interest.

Ai cleared her throat. "Yes. It would."

Suzume leaned back. She had been so eager to learn about this new possibility, she had not even considered why Ai would help her. "Not that I'm complaining, but why are you telling me this?"

"Because you asked."

Suzume scrunched up her face in confusion. "Yesterday you tried to murder me. Remember?"

Ai sighed and then turned to look at Suzume. "Do you not even know what it means to take the power of a yokai?"

Suzume shrugged. "I get stronger."

Ai shook her head. "It means they become bound to you. Even when the energy fades, a trace of Ai remains with you. Ai cannot disobey you, no matter how much Ai wishes she could." She huffed as she turned away from Suzume.

"If that's the case then give me the Sea Stone." Suzume held out her hand, expecting Ai to produce it from thin air.

Ai shot to her feet, and her tiny hands were balled into fists at her side. "Ai has been trapped within these walls for five hundred years, do you not think if Ai had the stone Ai wouldn't have used it to escape?"

"I saw it, in the courtyard with the others..."

Ai waved her hand and suddenly they were transported into the audience hall. It was filled with light, music and the perfume of food. Yokai gathered around in the exact same arrangement Suzume had seen when she arrived at the palace, chatting amongst themselves as if Ai and Suzume were not there at all.

"This was my father's palace before Kazue captured him, locking him in a stone and forcing me to guard over his prison."

The Lord of the Sea sat on his throne, smiling down at the subjects that surrounded him. Ai reached for him but when she touched it, the illusion burst into a cloud of mist. Ai hung her head for a moment before turning to face Suzume once more.

"What you saw was a memory. Nothing more," she said to Suzume.

"Then where is the Sea Stone?"

Ai pointed upward.

Suzume followed her finger and stared upward. "In the ceiling?"

"It is on an island just off the coast."

"So all I need is a boat then?" Just the idea of being on the ocean again made her stomach flop uncomfortably. Once this was all over she swore never to step foot off of dry land again.

A crooked smile spread across Ai's face. "Kazue's wards prevent all boats from approaching."

"I already killed the umi-bozu though."

"It is more than that. There are other protections in place, deadly waves, and illusions."

It would be so much easier to just forget about the Sea Stone, go find Kaito and admit she wasn't as strong as she pretended to be. But the memory of the power lingered. It wasn't for pretend like with the Namahage, or Kazue using Suzume's body. This had been her power. She had to get it back.

"I demand you show me how to get there," Suzume said, meeting Ai's gaze.

The child shook her head before standing up.

"If you wish," she said and headed toward the door. Suzume had to leap up to chase after her. Ai led her back to the courtyard where Suzume had first arrived.

"I hate to break this to you but I cannot swim." She'd already explored every inch of this courtyard the night before and she had found no signs of an exit.

Ai ignored her to whisper something into her hands. A bubble formed between her chubby fingers and when she opened them it floated upward and into the water. Suzume watched the bubble rise up with a single raised brow.

"What is that supposed to do?" Suzume asked, her voice dripping with skepticism.

"Shhh." Ai pressed her finger to her lips. With her petite stature, cherubic features, and high voice it was a much more childish action than Suzume was sure she intended.

After a few impatient moments of waiting, a dark shadow flew over-head. At first glance Suzume thought it was the umi-bozu returned from the dead. But as it got closer it became apparent it was not the giant monster, but a large sea turtle which floated through the wall of water to land in front of them.

It approached Ai and rested its head in her tiny child-like hands. As Ai whispered in its ear, it nodded its head.

Ai turned back to Suzume. "He will take you to the island."

"So I'm, what, going to ride on his back?" Suzume looked at the turtle dubiously.

"Precisely." Ai's smile was wide and mischievous.

"How do I know this is not some sort of trick?"

"If Ai wanted to kill you, Ai would have done it while you slept." She smiled, revealing rows of jagged, sharp teeth.

Suzume took a step back. *Perhaps my chances are better with the turtle.* With some difficulty she climbed onto the turtle's back. Then a thought occurred to her.

"But what about breathing—" she couldn't even properly form the question before the turtle shot off like a rocket.

She clung to the lip of its shell as it zoomed through the sea. All around her was a blur of white foam and bubbles. She held her breath for what felt like an eternity, until her vision started to go dark around the edges. Her lungs burned, threatening to expel what was in them and swallow sea water instead. Memories of her near drowning were vivid in her mind, tightening her chest with panic. Before she could give in to the feeling, they broke the surface and Suzume gasped for air. Never before had she been so thankful for the luxury of breathing.

They had arrived at a larger island and a small outcropping of rocks off the shore. The entire scene felt familiar to her. This had to be the place. The turtle skimmed across the ocean's surface before riding the waves into shore on the larger island.

"I need to go there to those rocks." Suzume pointed in their direction.

The turtle only blinked large, liquid eyes at her in response.

"Can you understand me? I need to get the Sea Stone."

It only shook its head. She sighed in exasperation. It looked like she was on her own from here. Suzume slid off the turtle's back and onto the shore. Once she did, the creature shuffled backward into the waves. She watched it go, wondering how she would get back when she had the stone. Then she shook her head. That was a problem for later. First she had to get the stone.

Suzume headed toward the smaller island. The closer she got, the more obvious Ai's warning became. The rocks were far offshore, much too far to swim even if she knew how. Large waves crashed over them, pummeling them relentlessly. Even if she could find a boat, those waves would capsize it as soon as she left the shore.

Feeling frustrated, Suzume sank down onto the sand and glared at the island, willing inspiration to strike. An hour or more passed and the sun was starting to set. She still hadn't come up with a solution. She squinted in the direction of the island, trying to avoid the reflection of the light on the water's surface. It was so intense she had to shield her eyes from it. As she did, she noticed something strange just beneath the water's surface. She stood up and peered in that direction. A thin track of rocks connected the beach with the island. The rocks were winding and slick with water and waves continued to wash over them at regular intervals, but this had to be the way across.

Standing along the edge of the shore, she felt uncertain. What if it had just been a trick of the light? Water crashed against her ankles and already the pull of the ocean was trying to drag her back down into its depths. She had to fight the urge to turn back around. *I can do this.* With a deep breath she inched forward onto the slippery rocks. She scooted along the rocky pathway, her hands clenched tight and clinging onto her clothes as if they would anchor her if a strong wave came to wash her away. The level of the water rose to her calves and she struggled to fight against the current. Panic clawed at her insides. Her heart was beating rapidly in her chest. The further she went, the deeper the water got. Waves rolled over her, filling her mouth with salt water as she got to a depth around her waist.

She flailed her arms in an attempt to maintain her balance and just then another wave rolled over. It pulled her under and her feet came out from beneath her. She kicked her arms and legs wildly until she found her footing once more. She gasped for breath, gulping in air as if she would never feel her lungs expand again. Then with a desperate drive to get off the island, she hurried the rest of the way across before she changed her mind and headed back to shore.

Back on solid ground once more she fell to her knees and gave her trembling limbs a moment to recover. When she looked up, she spotted the weathered wood of a torii arch forming an entry to a pathway. The pathway wound through a series of jagged rocks. Most likely the stone was hidden at the top of that path. It looked steep and slippery. Waves crashed over the little island and even now she was being sprayed with sea water. *I guess I have to climb.* She sighed and then started her ascent.

The climb to the top of the rocks was much more difficult than she had expected. The rocks were slippery and she lost her footing. When she fell backward she tore open her sleeve and scraped a shallow gash onto her arm. Suzume swore and hissed in pain as she stopped to look at the wound. Since it was superficial, and it was almost dark, she grit her teeth and kept on going. Climbing took forever it seemed and as she looked back to check her progress, she discovered that she had only gone a few feet from the start. *How is that possible!* Suzume growled in frustration and plopped herself down on a nearby rock where she wrung out her soaking clothes while she thought. Ai had warned her about illusions. Suzume had seen a pathway and taken it, not thinking about it, but perhaps there was another way up.

She decided to start over though it pained her to do so. Back at the bottom, she skirted the edge of the perimeter. As she went around, it became apparent that the island looked the same from all sides, except one. On the back facing the ocean was a sheer cliff face leading up to the shrine. Apart from being difficult to climb, it was under constant attack from the ocean. Suzume craned her neck to look up at it. *There's no way I can climb this.* It was completely dark now, the only light came from the half-moon in the sky. She had to be a complete moron to even consider this. Despite her own admonishments to herself, she inched closer to the ledge. Just then a wave crested the rocks behind her and the force of the water pressed her into the wall.

When her skull hit the stone, stars danced in her vision. Suzume had to lean against the stone for a moment as her head spun. When the world stopped turning, she pushed back and scooted along the ledge once more. Sea spray burned her eyes and she had to close them to protect them. It left her to fumble blindly against the stone, searching for some sort of chink or hand hold. Instead her hand found open air. Suzume opened her eyes and saw her wrist disappearing into the wall. She scooted closer just as another wave slammed into her, but she was prepared this time and braced herself against the wall. When the ocean receded, she scooted closer and found a hole disguised by the smooth stone just large enough for her to slip into.

Inside the hole was a tunnel carved from stone and leading upward. Suzume looked up at the stairs with a sigh. *Great, more climbing.* When she reached the top, she was panting and bleeding. She reflected on how far she had come from the pampered princess she once was. Her hands were black and muddy, a combination of her own blood and the thick mud that seemed to cover this island. If Kaito could see her now, he wouldn't be able to call her helpless. She grabbed a hold of the torii arch which separated the hidden stairs from a short walkway that led to the shrine. She took a few gasping breaths, her lungs burning from exertion, before she stumbled across the walkway to the shrine building itself.

The inside of the shrine was weathered and decayed and barnacles clung to beams and floorboards. What appeared to be bird's nests were in the eaves. Bird droppings covered the entire floor in a white splatter. She took steps carefully, afraid her foot would go through the wood or she'd step in animal feces. Crabs scurried across the ground in front of her. She kicked the discarded shells and seaweed out of her way. *This might be another illusion but I don't want to step in it just in case.*

In the center of the shrine was a single pedestal where Kazue had left the Sea Stone. This was it. She had done it all on her own. *I cannot wait to see Kaito's expression when I show him my power is equal to his.* She smiled just thinking about it.

Suzume inched closer. But instead of feeling the draw of the power she had when she was near the Flame Stone, she felt nothing. She looked down onto the pedestal and her stomach sank. It was empty. The Sea Stone was gone.

FORTY-ONE

Suzume stared at the empty pedestal. This couldn't be real. She was convinced that it must be an illusion created by Kazue. She ran her hand over the weathered wood, but only managed to get a splinter in her finger. She hissed as the wood pierced her skin and she felt the anger rising up inside her like a glowing ember someone was blowing on. Outside the wind howled, rattling the rafters of the temple. Suzume grabbed onto the edges of the pedestal. It burned beneath her touch as the flames rose up inside her in response to her fear and anger.

She grabbed the pedestal and threw it across the small shrine space where it collided with the far wall, smashing into a million pieces. She stood there for a moment just panting for breath, anger rolling around inside her. The stone was gone. Maybe it had never been here at all.

She threw her head back and growled, letting all her frustration out in that single guttural reaction. After everything she had done, and it was not even here!

From behind her someone clapped slowly. She knew before she even turned around who was standing behind her and the rage just continued to build.

Suzume spun around to face Hisato, who was leaning against the door to the shrine smiling.

She lunged for him without thinking. Fire was filling her, threatening to consume her. She was letting herself lose her consciousness to the power. Hisato had not attempted to dodge her, but let her grab onto his shoulders. She felt the burn in her own skin, and yet she didn't let go. There was a reserve of power inside her, begging her to take a hold of it and turn it into a blaze of destruction. Just as she had drawn power from Makato, the Namahage, and Ai, she could use it to consume Hisato as well. She might not get the Sea Stone but she could destroy him.

"How much longer are you going to keep wasting time like this?" Hisato asked, seemingly unaffected by the fire that scorched his flesh.

"Until I've destroyed you," Suzume said through gritted teeth. The burn on her own skin was almost unbearable. It was also the only thing keeping her from getting lost inside the desire to destroy.

Hisato knocked her back with a flick of his wrist, as if she was nothing more than a gnat. Suzume flew through the air and slammed into the far wall. As she lay crumpled on the ground, Hisato stalked closer to her.

"As much as your adorable attempts to stop me amuse me. I grow tired of watching you waste time on this pointless quest." He gestured toward the empty pedestal.

Suzume climbed to her feet, and blood trickled down her forehead from an injury on her scalp.

"Where is the Sea Stone?" she said in a growl.

He threw his head back to laugh. "It's gone. It has been missing for centuries. Did you really think objects of power would not fall into the hands of those who seek them?"

"What did you do with it?"

He waggled a finger in front of her. "Don't blame me. It is inside another body, just like yours."

"You're saying the missing gods... they're inside people?" Suzume clutched at her own chest. "But the Flame Stone... I saw it."

"Oh, my dear Suzume, you are so charmingly naive." He paced around her, circling her as he normally did. Suzume spun slowly in a circle, watching him and waiting for her moment. As he paced Hisato continued to talk. "When Kazue split apart her soul she did not merely rend it into pieces, she bound her power with that of the eight. She combined her mortal soul with theirs to make herself a god."

Suzume felt like the room was spinning around her. If a piece of Kazue's soul was inside her, and that was bound to a god, that meant this fire wasn't just Kazue's soul. It was a god's power. Which was why the Namahage had thought of her as the Lady of the Flame because the Lady of the Flame was inside her.

Hisato laughed all the harder. "The Sea Stone to hold the water of her soul; the Wind Stone to hold the air of her soul; the Earth Stone to hold the earth of her soul and the Flame Stone to hold the flame of her soul..." he trailed off, looking at her.

"Why did you do this to me!" she shouted.

Hisato folded his arms in front of himself. "What makes you think it was me who did it?"

"Who else would it have been?"

"Who indeed," he purred as he stopped and faced her, a wicked smile turning at the corner of his mouth.

Suzume's hand flexed as she prepared to create a ball of flame which she would fling at his head. Even if it burned her as well it would be worth it to get the upper hand for once. Then suddenly he was right beside her, hand around her throat, pressing her up against the wall. She gagged as he stared into her eyes, his intense gaze boring into her, searching her face. Maybe he could read her thoughts or perhaps he did know her as well as he claimed.

"I know you. You will not kill yourself to stop me."

"Try me," she gasped.

He laughed again before shaking his head. He released his grip on her throat enough to allow her to breathe, but he continued to pin her to the wall. His hips pressed against her abdomen and he placed his arms on either side of her, leaning on the wall. His face took up all of her vision, she could look at nothing but him.

"I'll let you in on a little secret, Suzume." He leaned in, his hot breath fanning across her cheek as he whispered, "The moment you were born, so too was I reborn."

"That's not possible," she said. If she could keep him talking he would remain distracted and she could attack him.

He pulled back so he could look her in the eye once more. His eyes darted over her features. "When Kazue sealed her soul fragments away, so too did she seal me away. And it would have remained that way if the stones had not been used to create you and the others."

Suzume focused her energy on growing the fireball in her hand. But it was difficult again, as it had been before. She couldn't even force a single spark.

"Don't even try. You never had control over it. Only what I gave you."

"You're lying," Suzume spat at him.

"You think you can kill me, then go ahead. I will not stop you." He stepped back, arms out wide, giving her an invitation to do what she had wanted to do for so long.

But even when she focused all of her attention on making a spark, nothing happened. She didn't even feel warm.

"What have you done to me?" she asked.

"On your own, you have no power. Kazue has been protecting you up until now. But her greed is great. She craves life, and she will not let you use it if it will risk destroying her."

"No." Suzume screwed her face up, looking at her hand, willing even the smallest of sparks.

"You've been her puppet all this time."

"I am no one's puppet." Since her fire wouldn't obey her, she grabbed the staff and swung it at Hisato. But he stepped out of her attack with ease, laughing all the while.

"It does not have to be this way, Suzume. You can take the power for yourself, just as Kazue did. You can become just as powerful as her."

"I'm not going to make Kazue's mistakes," Suzume said, panting for breath. She felt as if she had been running for hours.

"But you already are. You've been stealing energy from those around you just to make yourself stronger."

"It was to stop you."

"Then does that make it right? How are you any different than Kazue, who only used her ability to make herself immortal."

"Because I am doing it to stop you!" she said, hands balled into fists.

Hisato turned his hand over and revealed an obsidian stone, the Flame Stone that the Namahage had given her. "As you know the real Flame stone is inside you. But what is trapped inside this stone, is a yokai. You could easily take his spiritual energy and use it against me. But if you do, you will kill the yokai. What will you do?" He threw it toward her.

She caught obsidian stone and as soon as it was in her hand, she felt the rush of power. Flames erupted all along her body, igniting into an inferno.

"Where do you think your power comes from, Suzume? Nothing comes without a price. Everything must remain in balance."

This has to be a trick. He's trying to fill me with doubt so I won't use the power against him. And yet she hesitated as all the pieces began to fall into place. She rolled the stone around in her hand. If she sacrificed the life of another for the greater good, did that make it right?

"You see the truth now, all the power you gained was stolen from others. What will you choose?"

This was not a time to second guess herself. "I choose everything."

A ball of fire formed in her hands, growing to a massive size, almost double the size of her body. It pulled from the stone, draining it of every last drop. All the while a voice inside her head seemed to egg her on, urging her to do this.

Hisato laughed as she built up her power. It wasn't until she flung the ball of flame at him that he leaped out of the way. It still collided with him, and the recoil flung him and Suzume backward as if an explosion pushed them apart. Suzume felt the fire all over her body and inside her, burning every fiber of her being. Suzume arched her back and screamed as it coursed through her.

Hisato stood over her, his haori burned and revealing a gaping hole where her fire had torn his flesh apart. But as she watched the flesh was reknitting itself. In a few moments it was nothing but pale, pink, scarred flesh.

"We are alike." He smiled down at her.

Suzume climbed to her feet as the pain started to recede and she grabbed her staff which had been knocked out of her grasp. She swung it at Hisato's head. "I am nothing like you."

He leaped away from her attack. "Don't you want to know who the yokai was that you've killed."

"Does it matter?" She couldn't seem to catch her breath. There was a painful stitch in her side and her skin stung from the burns.

Hisato came up close, wrapping his arm around her and pressing the palm of his hand to her lower back. His face inches from hers.

"The yokai in that stone was the dragon."

Hisato snatched the stone out of Suzume's hand as she struggled to get it from him. He sang a song, and the stone burst apart in a bright light. Kaito's body floated on the air in between them before coming to rest on the ground.

Suzume turned to look at it but she refused to believe it was true. This had to be another illusion. She knocked Hisato away, but she did not have the strength to stand on her own two feet and instead crawled over to where he lay. She cupped his cheek which was ice cold to the touch. His entire body was covered in dark marks that wrapped around his face and arms.

"This is your fate. You were destined to destroy him."

"You tricked me!" She turned, eyes blazing. But the fire was gone, and she had nothing left to defeat him with.

"I told you the consequences and you chose your own power over the life of another. Just like Kazue."

"You bastard." She swung at him, but he only stepped away from her reach and she fell forward onto the ground.

"Join me, Suzume, and I will save him."

Suzume turned to him with anger in her gaze. "I would never join you."

"Then watch him die."

Hisato waved his hand and a portal opened up behind him. He stepped through it and as he did the reality of her situation settled upon her shoulders. Her chest felt tight like something weighed down upon it and her entire body was trembling with fatigue.

"I have to do something," she said, looking at Kaito's face and then to the island where they were trapped.

Rin said water can heal him. But she felt so tired she couldn't stand, let alone drag him to the water. Suzume cast around for something to carry water in, anything. She found a seashell the size of her palm. It was the best she could do given the circumstances.

Using her staff like a crutch, Suzume climbed up onto unstable feet. She could hardly stand, let alone walk more than a few inches at a time. She held the shell in her cupped hand. As she made her way down the tunnel she had to lean on the wall so she wouldn't tumble and break her neck. Her foot slipped and she fell down anyway, tearing her pants at the same time she broke the seashell she was going to use to bring water to Kaito.

Her hand was cut by the sharp edges of the shell. She looked down at her bleeding flesh and then to the end of the tunnel. The ocean thundered, echoing around her. She glanced back to where Kaito lay dying. This was all her fault. If she had broken the seal on his powers when she found out. If she had not tried so hard to be more powerful than him...

She drooped her head in defeat. She no longer had the strength to lift it and an extreme exhaustion fogged up her mind. Even if the shell hadn't broken she wouldn't have been able to save him. Tears rolled down her cheeks as she slumped onto the ground, face buried in her hands.

Just then she heard footsteps. She could hardly lift her head but saw that a man walked toward her. His face was hidden in shadow, but there was something about the way he walked that was familiar. But her mind was in such a fog that she couldn't place who it was. He probably wasn't real at all. This might all be a dream.

The man stopped right in front of her.

"Am I too late?" he asked. Kneeling down beside her, he scooped her up into his arms.

"It's my fault. He's going to die." That was the last thing she knew before she lost consciousness and exhaustion overwhelmed her.

FORTY-TWO

Suzume shot straight up, gasping for air. *Where is Kaito?* Through blurry eyes, she scanned her surroundings. Across from her Naoki sat with his back against the wall, one knee bent and his arm slung over it. He looked out through the door leading to the ocean. It was the closest to relaxed she'd ever seen him. But it didn't explain what he was doing or where she was.

Her gaze shot past him toward Kaito who was lying on the ground a few feet from Naoki. The swordsman had propped up the dragon's head and crossed his arms over his chest. He was so still it looked like he was dead. The very thought sent her stomach twisting with panic.

"We need to bring Kaito to the water, it's the only way he'll heal," she said as she attempted to crawl toward the dragon to help.

Naoki stopped her with a hand on her shoulder. "You need to rest," he said as he nudged her to lie back down.

How could she relax with Kaito in this state? His skin and hair were translucent. She could almost see the ground beneath him. His entire body was striped with black markings even darker than before, as if they were sucking all the color from him. Kaito's cheek bones were too angular, as if someone had shaved off part of his face.

"He's dying." She lunged forward, grabbing Naoki's hand as he tried to turn away from her. She did not care how pathetic she sounded. Because the truth was she was desperate.

"There's nothing I can do." Naoki met her gaze as he pushed her back to lie down.

"Then let me try. Just tell me what I have to do."

"No!"

Naoki had never raised his voice before. Since she'd met him, he'd hardly shown any emotions at all. It shocked her into silence, but it was quickly chased by anger.

"You have to obey me." She raised her voice as she puffed out her chest, like the spoiled princess she had once been.

Naoki stared right back at her. "It's no use."

His words rang with a dire finality. She shook her head, her hair whipping from side to side.

"Why not!" Her entire body trembled with the force of her anger and sadness.

Naoki did not respond at first. He turned to look at Kaito lying on the ground, his gaze lingering there for a moment before he turned back to Suzume.

"Because humans cannot create life, they can only take it."

Anger flooded her, filling every space, chasing out any trace of sadness. "This is his fault." She pointed at Kaito. "If he had just admitted he was hurt. If he had only trusted me." She shouted the words as if the very force of her anger would bring him back. "What am I supposed to do? Watch him die?" She grabbed fists full of the fabric of her hakama. She wanted to tear them to shreds, but she didn't have the strength.

Naoki stared back at her without answering. It only added fuel to the fire.

She climbed up onto shaking feet. Naoki tried to come closer to her to offer a hand or to make her sit down again, she didn't know which. She smacked his hand away. "You think this is my fault, don't you?" she shrieked. "I never asked for any of this. I just wanted him to see me and not Kazue." Hot tears threatened her eyelids but she refused to cry. Not over the dragon.

She turned away from Naoki to face the wall and leaned against it, resting her head on her arm. The wall was covered in holes, barnacles, and salt from the sea. It was a dirty place, just like she felt dirty for using Kaito's power to gain her own.

"You made a mistake." His words felt like a physical blow. She looked up toward the ceiling to stop the tears from flowing.

"If I got stronger, if I became more than human..." Then she would really become like Kazue, just as Hisato had said. Perhaps she would forget all about Kaito and become consumed by her need to become a god.

The only sound was the wail of the wind as it blew through the rafters. In the distance she heard the waves crashing against the island and the mournful cry of a bird.

"I don't want to see you make the same mistake," Naoki said, his voice gruff.

"That's how it started, isn't it?"

"Yes."

That single word was the final blow. Suzume's knees collapsed beneath her and she sunk to the ground. She pounded her fists against the wall. She'd tried so hard to untangle herself from Kazue, to prove she wasn't the same, and all she had done was follow in her footsteps. History was repeating itself. None of the power she had gained was real. It had all been an illusion, a symptom of Kazue's heart taking a hold of her.

She kept hitting her fists against the wall until her arms were too tired to go on. She leaned her head against the rough wood. Kaito was going to die and there was nothing she could do about it. *If you ever loved him, then tell me how to save him.*

There was no response from Kazue, not that she expected there to be one. She was long gone. All that remained was her ambition. If she had a god in front of her right now, she would drain them of all their power to bring Kaito back. Suzume sat straight up. *I don't have a god, but perhaps the next best thing.*

She spun around to face Naoki. "We have to take him to the Lord of the Sea's palace. There are healing springs there."

Naoki held his hand out without a word and helped her to her feet. She could stand, albeit a little shakily. Naoki gathered Kaito into his arms. The dragon looked so small, nothing like the larger than life figure she knew. It was difficult to believe this was the same person. Suzume averted her gaze. She couldn't look at the shadow he had become.

They went down the tunnel to the shore. From there, Naoki shifted Kaito's body onto his shoulder. The swordsman balled his free hand into a fist and when he opened it again a ball of light appeared. The ball took on the shape of a bird which flew up into the air before diving down into the waves. Suzume fidgeted, crossing and uncrossing her arms, and pacing in a small circle as they waited for a response.

After a few minutes two sea turtles broke the surface of the water. They blinked up at Suzume and Naoki with large black eyes. Despite her first harrowing ride to the surface, Suzume climbed onto the turtle's back without hesitation. Naoki placed Kaito on the other, taking a seat behind him. The dragon's head lolled back onto Naoki's shoulder. Once they were seated, the sea turtles dove beneath the waves and shot through the water in a flurry of bubbles and sea foam.

When they arrived in the underwater palace Ai was waiting for them, her small chubby hands on her hips.

"Ai sees you failed," she said with a tone that indicated she had not expected any better. Then her gaze drifted over to Naoki and Kaito. "Who is that?"

Suzume leaped off her sea turtle. "I need to use the spring you mentioned. He's badly hurt."

Ai scowled as she crept closer to inspect the dragon. As she did, her expression changed, transforming from scornful to concerned. "Kai?" With shaking hands, she cupped his cheeks, turning his face one way and then another as her dark eyes scanned his features. Then she turned to look at Suzume and her eyes were entirely black with white irises once again. "What have you done to him?" She growled.

Suzume reached for her staff, but before she drew it Naoki was between them with his sword drawn and pointed at Ai.

The child-like yokai looked at the sword with disdain. "You dare threaten me, swordsman?"

"We don't have time to argue," Suzume interjected.

Ai shot daggers at Suzume with her eyes and then looked back to Kaito. She sighed heavily.

"Ai cannot make any promises." With a wave of her hand a giant bubble formed in front of her and it drifted downward, encasing the dragon. He floated on the air just behind Ai. "If he dies, you will pay the consequences." A tendril of hair rose up from Ai's head, giving a hint of the dangerous yokai that lurked beneath her child-like appearance.

"Let's just worry about saving him first," Suzume said, hands on hips, trying to give off a confident aura.

With a huff, Ai turned, guiding the bubble up the stairs and into the palace. When Ai's back was turned, Suzume let go a breath she'd been holding. She could only hope the spring could save him. Naoki was waiting for her. She squared her shoulders and followed after Ai like the princess she was. They were led down a series of twisted corridors, down dusty hallways, which seemed had not seen the light of day in centuries, and down a staircase encased in stone that ended in a passageway with a ceiling so high it disappeared into darkness. At the end of it were double doors made of carved granite, with a motif of two ocean swells about to crash into one another. Ai waved her hand and the doors swung open and the bubble floated in before her.

The room was bigger than Suzume could imagine, filled with hundreds of pools of different sizes. Some with steam rising off them, others with rolling waves, yet another with lily pads like a pond. Ai directed Kaito's bubble to a pool with fingers of frost creeping out from the edges. Very gently she lowered his bubble into the water. Once he was submerged the bubble popped and Kaito was left floating on the water's surface.

Ai knelt down beside the pool, her face transfixed upon the dragon. "Ai thought she was the last," she said softly. She reached out to touch Kaito's face but her short arm could not reach him and she pulled away quickly.

"You know him?" Suzume asked in an accusing tone.

Ai spun around as if realizing Suzume was there for the first time. "Kai was one of the most powerful of the first children." She looked back at Kaito once more, her expression wistful. Then she frowned. "Until he let his love for a human destroy him." She turned her scowl at Suzume, clearly she blamed Suzume for that.

"Why do you call him Kai?"

"Because it is the name I gave him. He was mine before the priestess. He belonged to me." She crossed her arms over her small frame.

It was difficult to imagine this child and Kaito in some sort of romantic relationship. Suzume crinkled her nose. "You were lovers?" She choked on the words.

Ai laughed bitterly. "I did not always look this way." She turned to look at Kaito again. "But he was not my lover, as you so crudely put it. He was my protector."

Suzume raised a brow in confusion. "Kaito, a protector? Are you sure we're talking about the same person?"

Ai spun around with her tiny hands balled into fists as she glared at Suzume. "My father made him for me. He was the Lord of the Sea's greatest creation."

Suzume shook her head in confusion. "If your father made him, wouldn't that make him your brother?"

"You are a foolish human." Ai shook her head, mocking Suzume's actions. "The first children do not have siblings. We were not born out of litters like humans."

"Are you calling me a dog?"

Ai ignored this as she said, "But if it is easier for your simple mind to understand, then, yes, we are siblings of a kind. I was one of my father's first creations. And Kai was one of many dragons created by the Lord of the Sea to serve in his kingdom. They were made to be warriors, guardians, and protectors of the rivers, lakes, and streams. But Kai was different. He was meant for greater things. Until you ruined his life." She pointed an accusatory finger at Suzume.

Suzume crossed her arms over her chest. "I didn't do anything." Except steal his power to attempt to defeat Hisato. But it wasn't like she was going to admit that to her.

"I do blame you. I know him and he never would have done this unless it was for that human woman." She said the word human as if it was something foul.

"He loves Kazue, not me."

"You are Kazue, if in another form. None of this would have happened if it weren't for you."

Suzume raised her hand up, a ball of fire growing in her hands. As she did, Kaito's body contorted, and the black marks along his body grew thicker.

Ai's head swiveled toward the dragon and then toward Suzume. "Even now you are taking from him."

Suzume dropped her hand to her side, the fire extinguished almost immediately. But there was a painful throbbing in Suzume's chest and she clutched at her clothes. It lasted for several seconds and then subsided.

"You did this to him." Ai took a few steps toward Suzume, her hand raised as if she would strike her. But as soon as she got within striking distance, Ai's hand froze in place unable to move. She glared at Suzume. The priestess' influence remained over Ai. She could not hit her.

"How is this even possible?" Suzume asked. Ai was trembling with anger. With gritted teeth, Ai turned and waded into the icy water. Her head barely cleared the water's surface as she stood next to the dragon, hands hovering over his body.

"There is a link between your energies. If you use your powers it will steal from the dragon." She narrowed her eyes at Suzume.

"Can the spring fix it?" Suzume asked, ignoring Ai's jab.

Ai rested her hands on Kaito's chest. "While the link remains, he will not be able to recover."

It felt like she had been punched in the gut. Kaito could not die. It was not possible. There had to be some other alternative.

"But you said the spring healed you when I took your energy!"

"This link is tied to a seal of his spiritual energy. It is controlling the flow of energy both in and out. Until it is removed, he cannot heal."

"I can fix this," Suzume said, though she could not say how.

Ai waded back out of the pool, but her kimono was dry even as she stepped out of the water. "If you even try, it would kill him. You cannot stop yourself from drawing from him."

It hurt her pride to ask, but she was running out of options. "Can you break the seal?"

Ai shook her head. "In my true form, perhaps. But my power has also been sealed. The only one who can free me is Kazue." She glared at Suzume, bringing them all back full circle.

Suzume pressed her fingers to her temples. There had to be a way to save him. *Think.* If only Kazue was here. Perhaps she could tell her how to use her power without hurting Kaito. And then it hit her. There was someone.

She turned toward Naoki. "We have to find Makato."

FORTY-THREE

The ice around the edge of the pool left her knees damp and a chill had crept into her bones that would not leave her, no matter how many layers she wore. It was tempting to try and use her fire to get warm. If only it wouldn't kill Kaito if she used it.

"You're wasting your time," Ai said from behind Suzume. She did not need to turn around to know her cherubic face would be pulled into a sneer.

"Don't you have anything better to do than bother me?" Suzume asked between chattering teeth.

"It would be Ai's pleasure to see your weak human body succumb to the cold."

Suzume rubbed her palms against her arms in an attempt to get warm. The chill reminded her of when Kaito would lose his temper and ice would cover everything. "I'm a lot harder to kill than that," Suzume said as another shiver shot up her spine.

"There's a hot spring over there, go ahead and warm yourself." Ai gestured toward a nearby spring. Steam rose off it in a most enticing way. But doing that meant losing the battle with Ai. Until Naoki returned with Makato, she would stay by Kaito's side. It was the least she could do.

"Y-you'd like it if I did that," Suzume said with a cold stutter.

"This does not make up for what you've done," Ai said as she reached into the pool and splashed icy water onto Suzume.

Already at the edge of her patience Suzume stood up and shook off the water on her clothes. Sparks bounced off her hands. A few errant embers landed in the ice along the edge of the pool, melting into tiny pools.

"What are you doing, trying to kill him faster?" Ai snarled. She waded into the water and Suzume stood on the edge, prepared to dive in as well just to prove to Ai that she was more dedicated than her.

But as soon as her foot touched the water her entire body reacted. Flames shot along her leg, encasing it in flame. Kaito's body spasmed at the same time. It took all of her self-control to douse the fire before it did any more harm. Ai reached Kaito and ran small hands over his body, while Suzume held her breath in anticipation. There was no visible change in his condition, but Suzume felt the clock ticking all the same. Without control over her temper or her powers, she was at risk of hurting Kaito every moment he stayed like this.

"This is your fault," Suzume and Ai said at the same time and Ai exited the pool.

The two of them scowled at one another, hands on hips, neither one willing to admit they were wrong. Just then, footsteps echoed through the chamber. Naoki must have returned with Makato, but if Suzume looked away before Ai she would win. Ai's lips turned up at the corners in a smile. She could see Suzume's dilemma clear on her face.

"The swordsman has returned; don't you want to see what he has to say?"

"I will once you look away."

"Ai would gladly do so, as soon as you do." She gestured with her hand for Suzume to go first.

"I've found him," Naoki's said.

Unable to resist the temptation any longer, Suzume turned her head toward the swordsman. As she did, Ai whooped in triumph. Her annoyance at losing was quickly replaced by concern. The swordsman was alone. She peered around his shoulder as if Makato would be hiding behind his back.

"Where is he, then?"

"There is a problem." Naoki's expression gave nothing away.

"Ai should have known you would fail," Ai said scornfully.

Suzume had to close her eyes to suppress the fear and anger that were threatening to unleash the fire within her. After a few calming breaths, she felt certain she could think without bursting into flame.

"What sort of problem?" But her jaw wouldn't open all the way to let the words pass.

"They've been captured."

"Ai told you you could not save him," Ai taunted.

Suzume flipped her hair over her shoulder, pretending everything was going exactly to plan. "Then let's go rescue him." She marched toward the door but before she could pass the threshold Ai was there small arms outstretched as if they posed a real obstacle to stop her.

"Why are you trying to stop me. Do you not want me to save the dragon?" She raised her eyebrow in question.

"Ai is trying to save him. If you use your power, it will kill the dragon."

"I'm not going to use my powers."

"What are you going to do then?"

Suzume looked past Ai to the pool where Kaito remained. Staying here worrying wasn't going to do anything to save the dragon. Makato was her only hope. Naoki couldn't do this alone; if he could he would have rescued him already. This was a trap set by Hisato, she knew that much at a glance. But while she had been sitting here watching over Kaito she'd had a lot of chances to think. And she'd come up with the beginnings of a plan.

"You'll see when I'm done." She pushed past Ai and into the hall. Naoki came strolling after her, not saying a word.

"If you hurt him, Ai will find you and kill you herself," she shouted after Suzume's retreating back, but the priestess ignored her.

Suzume and Naoki left the sea palace on the backs of sea turtles who brought them to the shore. Naoki led the way to a large encampment.

It appeared Hisato had brought the emperor's army as back up. Looking at the sheer numbers of what they were up against, her stomach gave a nervous flop. She couldn't use her powers and this plan was full of holes. She and Naoki hid behind a sand dune watching a patrol of guards marching along the perimeter.

"Are you ready?" she asked Naoki after she'd gone over their plan perhaps for the dozenth time. A part of her wanted him to try and stop her or tell her this was foolish. But he did not question her, perhaps because he was bound to serve. Whatever the reason, they were going forward with it.

Naoki crept out from behind the dune and stalked over to the guards. The guards did not have the sight, and did not realize Naoki was there until the first guard was knocked unconscious. The second guard saw the first fall and came over to investigate. He looked around before kneeling down to shake his comrade, calling his name before he too was struck over the head with the hilt of Naoki's sword.

Turning to wave, he signaled Suzume to join him. She ran from behind the dune toward the first row of tents. Since she didn't have the luxury of invisibility, she had to be quick. Naoki's ability to sense spiritual pressure was their guide and he led her down rows of tents in search of their friends. At the end of an aisle, Naoki put out his hand and stopped Suzume in place. A soldier carrying a pair of buckets on a pole walked by whistling tunelessly. They watched him go past for a moment before Naoki gave the signal to move forward.

Down the next path there was a gap between tents that Suzume had to cross. Naoki went first but just as Suzume was preparing to follow, a group of half-dressed soldiers, bare chests glistening with sweat, walked between them, chatting and laughing together. Suzume pressed her back against the edge of the tent as they passed. Naoki had not realized she'd fallen behind, and had disappeared around the corner. They had all almost passed, when one straggler dropped a towel he was carrying right next to Suzume. She held her breath, praying he wouldn't see her. The man bent over to pick it up, and as he did, he paused.

He stood back up and turned to point at her. "You! What are you doing there?"

Suzume turned and ran back down the way she had come, taking flight. The soldier followed after her. She ran to hide, hoping if she kept making erratic turns she would lose him, but she only got turned around instead and bumped into the soldier who approached her slowly, his slimy gaze going up and down her body.

"Don't be afraid, little bird, are you lost?"

"Don't come any closer." Suzume brandished her staff at him, holding it in front of her and using the defensive pose Tsuki had taught her.

"You shouldn't play with weapons. You'll get hurt. Give it here."

"You think I don't know how to handle this?" she asked with a scoff. Fire sparked faintly against her skin. *No, get it under control.*

The man stalked closer. Suzume dropped her staff down toward the ground. "That's a girl," the man said with his hand outstretched as if he would take the staff from her.

When he got close enough, Suzume swung upward with her staff, catching him in the groin. The man reached for his crotch before folding in half and collapsing to the ground.

Suzume leaped over his incapacitated form. "I told you to stay back," she said.

"You wench! Come back here," he wheezed.

I need to remember to thank Tsuki for teaching me that move.

Naoki came running toward her, weapon drawn, but when he saw her self-satisfied smile and the man on the ground, he sheathed his weapon and turned the other way. There was only the faint shake of his head in response. But she might have imagined it. After several more minutes without any more close calls, they arrived at a tent with two guards waiting outside. Naoki made quick work of them, and once they were lying on the ground he held the tent flap open for her while he surveyed the camp around them.

Inside the tent was sparse, nothing but a dirt floor and a single occupant whose head was lowered, arms tied behind his back. As she entered, he lifted his head.

"Suzume?" Makato asked. His face was covered in bruises.

"Shh, I'm here to rescue you." She hurried around behind him and fumbled with the ropes that bound his hands to a post. "Where are the others?" she asked.

"I don't know he took Rin and the others," he said as Suzume teased the knot loose. Naoki stood just inside the door, his hand on the hilt of his sword, his head tilted toward the outside, listening for the soldiers.

"Naoki can find them." She pulled the last knot free and Makato's hands came loose.

He shrugged off his bindings and then turned to embrace Suzume. "I thought you were dead," he said, his voice thick with emotion.

She pushed him away, unaccustomed to such intimacy and also fearing that being too close to him would awaken Kazue within her and hurt Kaito.

"Now's not the time to be sentimental. We need to get you and the others out of here."

He nodded in agreement.

Naoki led the way out of the tent down a series of twisted pathways. All the tents started to blur together and Suzume lost track of which was which until they reached a tent that looked no different than any of the others. Naoki looked around the corners, but it appeared unguarded.

"Why aren't there guards?" Suzume asked.

"There's a barrier," Naoki replied.

"How do we get past it?" She wondered aloud.

"It won't allow any yokai inside," Makato said with a frown. "It was made to keep yokai in."

Suzume looked to Naoki, his gaze was focused on the barrier. She couldn't use her spiritual power, and leaving Naoki here was an unexpected complication to her plan. If Hisato wasn't guarding Makato, he had to be in there.

"Is it safe?" She asked Naoki.

He nodded. "I can sense their presence within." He turned to look at her. "Keep your guard up."

Suzume took a deep breath and then to Makato said, "Let's go."

Makato led the way. As she approached the barrier she could feel the tingle of energy. Makato held out his hand, testing the interference, but his hand passed through it with only a slight shimmer in the light to indicate there was anything there at all. He went through, and pulled back the tent flap for Suzume to enter.

She hesitated. With her luck she'd react to the barrier and hurt Kaito in the process. Makato held his hand out for her.

"Come on, it won't hurt you."

Suzume closed her eyes. *You can do this.* She held her breath as she walked through. Apart from an odd tingle up her spine she didn't feel anything at all. She ducked beneath the propped up tent door. Inside was dark, no light permeated except what came through the open door. When Makato dropped it, they were both plunged into total darkness. She had to fumble around with her hands outstretched in front of her to find her way around.

"Rin? Tsuki? Akira?" Suzume whispered. Her grasping hands found nothing at first then her hands bumped into something soft and fleshy.

"I think I found something," Suzume said into the dark. Outside the tent Suzume heard a roar. "What was that?" She swiveled in the direction it had come from. There was a loud crashing sound just outside, followed by grunts and running feet.

But Makato did not reply. Then a light flickered as a match was struck and a brazier was lit. Golden light filled the room revealing not a prison tent, but the general's tent. What Suzume had taken for a body was a plush cushion. She dropped it to the ground and turned to see Makato blocking the entrance.

"I knew it was a trap. Come on, we have to help Naoki," Suzume said, motioning to move past Makato but before she could he held his arm out to stop her. His eyes were not looking at her, but looking past her.

"What are you doing?" She scowled at him.

"I'm sorry Suzume, I didn't want to do this. But I had to protect her."

"Protect who?"

The animalistic roar thundered outside once more, and Suzume scowled toward it before realization dawned on her.

"I'm sorry." Makato shook his head once more.

Behind her Hisato laughed, and she spun around to face him.

"How did you find me?" she asked.

"What a silly question for a smart woman such as yourself, Suzume," Hisato said, strolling closer to her. She grabbed onto her staff, holding it out in front of her. "The emperor has ears everywhere." He placed his hand on Makato's shoulder and smiled at him. Makato looked like he was going to be sick and all the color had drained from his face.

"You used the emperor's army to find me?" Suzume snarled.

Hisato tutted. "Not his army. Though they do have their benefits." He laughed at his own joke. "No, I only needed one man to report your whereabouts to me." He grabbed Makato's chin and shook his head from side to side.

Suzume stared at Makato, eyes wide. "You were spying on me?"

Hisato clapped his hands together. "Oh, how delightful. You really didn't know? Why else would the emperor's right hand join you?"

She ripped her gaze away from Makato to instead stare at Hisato. "Do you think I am going to fall for that? Makato is hardly older than me. Why would the emperor rely on him?"

"Makato is much older than he looks." He paced around the pair of them.

"What is he talking about?" Suzume asked Makato.

But Makato would not meet her gaze. "He is not human, but a half yokai. And he's been helping the emperor rid the world of yokai for the past twenty years."

Suzume turned to look at Makato, her eyes darting over his face. "So what?" She jutted her chin at Hisato. She knew the only reason Makato had led her here was because Hisato had manipulated him into it. He'd done the same to her before. It didn't matter what he'd done in the past.

"That's not all he's done. Most recently he's been looking for something very precious to the emperor."

"And what's that?" Suzume spat.

"You."

FORTY-FOUR

"The emperor exiled me and all of my siblings." Suzume scoffed. Hisato was trying to distract her, get inside her head.

Hisato's smile got wider as he strolled over to the desk and plucked a piece of paper off of it. "It was my error to send her away. Had I realized how vital her return was to you..." Hisato lowered the paper. "If he sent you away, why is the emperor so desperate to find you now?"

"He's not." But her confidence wavered. The evidence was staring her in the face. She remembered reading the letter Daiki was writing to the emperor. She'd seen it on his desk and remembered Daiki's taunts about her being valuable to the emperor. What if everything she believed was a lie?

"Why don't you ask Makato." Hisato motioned toward the priest.

Makato stared at the ground as he replied, "He's telling the truth. The emperor ordered me to spy on you."

"Then why was I sent away?" Suzume threw her arms out.

"To hide you from him," Makato replied, looking up to meet her gaze. It looked like he was trying to tell her something but she couldn't be sure what.

She shook her head. "Even if I was to believe you, what would the emperor want me for?"

"For his war," Hisato purred, as if the very idea delighted him.

"What war? The empire is at peace."

"The war against yokai," Makato said softly. "He is determined to destroy them all, just as Kazue was."

Suzume felt as if someone had picked her up and had shaken her around and then set her back down on her feet again. She was left reeling. The emperor fighting against yokai? Never in her life had she even had the slightest inkling any of this existed. And the emperor not only knew but was planning a war against yokai?

"How long has this been going on?"

"The war has been raging for five hundred years," Hisato said, taking a few steps closer to Suzume. "I told you I needed you to return balance. The humans have grown too powerful, it is up to us to return it to the way it was." He was standing in front of her to obscure her vision so all she could look at was him.

"And how do you plan to do that exactly?"

Hisato leaned in close so he could whisper in her ear, "We destroy the humans."

Suzume had to swallow down on the protest that rose up in her throat. She looked into Hisato's eyes; his dark bottomless gaze would swallow her whole if she let it. "Have you forgotten I am human too?"

Hisato laughed as he cupped her face, rubbing his thumb along her cheek. "You have never been human, Suzume. From the moment you were born you were something so much more."

Suzume leaned into his touch. "What am I?" she asked.

"Does this mean you've decided to join me?"

"Suzume, you cannot be considering this?" Makato shouted in protest.

"You know what I can give you. Limitless power, everything you've ever dreamed of. Just take my hand, Suzume."

She looked down at the hand Hisato offered. Makato ran toward her, grabbing her around the middle, trying to force her away from him.

"Don't do this. You don't have to give in to him."

She wrestled against Makato for a moment before knocking him backward with one quick blow to the solar plexus. Air escaped him in a whoosh as he was left doubled over behind her.

"Don't try to stop me," she said and turned back toward Hisato. She grabbed a hold of his hand.

"You've made the right choice." Hisato wrapped his hand around the small of her back, pulling her close to him.

Their bodies flushed against one another. Suzume's heart was hammering in her chest as Hisato dipped his head down to press his lips against hers. As soon as they did, lightning shot through her body. It ignited every fiber of her being. His arms clung to her, holding her in place, preventing any escape. Then his power poured into her, and like water from a jar it filled every inch of her. And it burned. It scorched her down to her very core, to the point she thought she would rather die than feel this pain. Suzume cried out in agony. Her eyes felt as if they would burst from her skull.

And then the memories flooded through her: flashes of images running all together, blurring into one unrecognizable stream. All that remained were the spells, songs of power, of binding and unbinding. But just as his thoughts and memories had flowed into her, so had her own thoughts flowed the other way. They were united, without any way to say where one of them started and the other ended.

Hisato pushed her away, breaking their connection. He was panting for breath and his hair was a tousled mess. Even with the connection broken his dark energy continued to course through her like thousands of needles scraping on the inside of her veins.

"I should have expected such a clever trick from you, Suzume." He pushed his hair back on his head. Once more that evil smirk slipped onto his face. "But you will not be able to save him, even with my power."

"Watch me," she said equally gasping for breath. When she had gone over her plan in her head she had not thought it would hurt quite this much.

"Perhaps I should give you a taste of real power."

A dark mass uncoiled from him, blacker than night, it shot into her stomach. The pressure of it squeezed at her heart and every breath was a struggle. When the pain became too great she could not keep it inside her. Her body rejected it as it was destroying her from the inside like a canker in her gut, gnawing away at her insides. It brought her to her knees and she doubled over, preparing to retch.

Hisato stood over her. "Have you had enough? Perhaps you'd like some more?" He grabbed her shoulders, forcing her to face him as he filled her with even more of his dark energy. Suzume threw her head back and screamed. Her entire body felt as if it was being undone, ripped down to her seams and ground to dust. "You wanted power, well I can give you power, Suzume. More than you could ever have dreamed."

She had to fight it. If she could bend it to her will the way she had used Ai's power, she could stop him. Fire purifies. That was what Makato had said. With sheer force of will, Suzume grabbed onto Hisato's wrist, wrapping her hand around it.

Fire sparked along her fingertips.

"If you use your power, it will kill Kaito."

Suzume hesitated, afraid of the power inside her, afraid of what it could do to Kaito, but also fearing for her own life. He would destroy her, she could see it in Hisato's eyes.

Just then vines burst out of the ground, wrapping their way around Hisato. Suzume looked up as Makato ran over to her.

He held out his hand to help her to her feet. "Come on." He dragged her toward the door.

Outside Rin, Tsuki, and Naoki were finishing off the general's army, leaving a route for their escape.

"I thought you were working with Hisato."

"That's what we wanted him to think," Rin rumbled. She loomed well above Suzume's head in her kitsune form. Suzume was glad she was still on her side.

"It was Rin's idea. She knew he'd try and lure you here," Makato panted as they ran down the rows of tents.

Rin shot a blast of flames in front of her, clearing their way of tents and soldiers. Just when they thought they were home free, Rin and Makato both stopped. Makato doubled over while Rin was brought to her knees.

"What's wrong? We have to go."

Rin lifted her head and growled. "Run."

Before she could follow through with the command, she was surrounded by a half dozen copies of Makato. The clones surrounded them all: Suzume, Tsuki, and Naoki as well.

"What's going on here?" Tsuki asked, raising his sword up and his eyes scanning the copies. Rin had gotten back to her feet and was stalking closer to them, closing in.

Rin unleashed her flames upon them, showering them in fire. Naoki and Tsuki fought the copies while Suzume hid beneath a barrier that burst around her without her meaning to. She tried to destroy the barrier to avoid doing any more harm to Kaito but it remained stubbornly in place.

From behind the fighting crowd, Hisato approached. The group of copies moved out of his way so he could reach Suzume.

"Did you think I did not anticipate your betrayal?" he said, looking to Rin and Makato. "You belong to me now."

With a flick of his wrist, Rin lunged forward to attack Naoki. The swordsman held up his blade only to have Rin bite down on it, blood dripping down the sides of her mouth. The other copies of Makato surrounded Tsuki. All that was left were Suzume and Hisato.

"I can see now you will never listen to reason. You leave me no choice."

Hisato stalked closer to her and she swung her staff to defend herself but he knocked it out of her hand. She backed up to get away from him. Each step he took toward her sent pain rippling through her body, and it only grew stronger the closer he got.

Out of sheer desperation, she grabbed onto his shoulder. Fire sprung from her hands and made its way up Hisato's arm, sinking into his flesh. He pulled his arm back and snarled at her. She felt the pain echoed in her own body and she clutched her arm which felt as if it was on fire.

Whatever spell Hisato had on Makato was broken and he managed to shout, "You have to get rid of his energy before it kills you."

Hisato's breathing was heavy, and the sleeve of his haori had been burned off as he stood up to face them.

"I have been patient with you, Suzume. But now it is time I take your power for my own."

The song Hisato sang had no real notes, it was nothing but agony. She thought it hurt to have his dark energy forced into her. Having it and all of her own spiritual energy ripped from her body had to be a hundred times worse. It felt as if someone had the end of a thread and was pulling it, unraveling it, and with each pull she lost more and more of herself. It started with old memories, things she would not even miss, then more recent, the face of her mother and siblings, then her friends. Until nothing remained but her name, and even that he tried to take from her. She clung to it, desperate to maintain herself if nothing else.

Before Hisato could complete his task, everything stopped. Suzume was lying on the ground, a shimmering red barrier surrounding her. Everything came back in a tangled rush, for a moment all she could remember was the intense pain, but then time and memories trickled back in.

"You think you can stop me, Kazue? It is too late for that." Hisato stalked around the outside of the barrier.

Suzume looked at her hands. They were calloused, dirty, and scarred, they were not the hands of a princess. She massaged her temples. *I am not a princess anymore. I am a priestess.* Suzume stood up inside the barrier. She knew what she had to do. Outside the barrier Makato's copies were keeping Tsuki and Naoki from reaching her.

The copies might all be identical but Makato shown brightly in front of her, a beacon in the dark. She lunged for him, just as the barrier collapsed. She grabbed onto his hand and as soon as they touched she felt the power spark within her. It shattered Hisato's spell and Makato's copies disappeared one by one. He turned to Suzume, understanding in his eyes. The power was flowing through both of them now, building upon one another. They were growing stronger together.

A song was ripped from her throat, as if it had been burning inside her desperate to get out all this time. It vibrated through the air, echoing around her and Hisato who turned to face her.

In his hand Hisato had a black sword dark as midnight, ready to rend her in two. Suzume continued to sing, letting the notes give her strength. Her voice melded together with Makato's. The song took its shape, using Hisato's very energy against him. He froze in place, doubled over in pain as the song's effect took hold.

He looked up at Suzume through the curtain of his dark hair and smiled.

"You are not strong enough to stop me."

The song was already starting to lose power. Suzume felt the fatigue overwhelm her as all of Hisato's and Makato's energy faded out of her. He stalked closer to her with his hands out, as if he would take her into his arms. But already he was reaching for them both, preparing to take their spiritual energy as his own.

Just as she felt the first pull of his power, however, a blade pierced through Hisato's chest from the back. Hisato looked down at the bloody point which dripped onto his haori. He turned to look at Naoki and then at Suzume surprising her with a smile.

They had so little energy left, but she could not let this chance pass her by. And without needing to tell Makato, they switched the song to one of binding. If she could not destroy him, she would seal him away. Not even two notes had left her lips before Hisato opened a portal behind him.

"I think we've played enough for today." He stepped through the portal, leaving Suzume to collapse into a heap on the ground. "But I will see you again, soon." His voice echoed around inside her head even after he was gone.

She stared at Hisato's bloodstain on the ground. She had found a way to wound him without harming herself but it still wasn't enough.

Naoki came over and placed his hand on her shoulder. "You've done well."

"But he still got away."

FORTY-FIVE

The sea turtles were waiting to bring them back to the underwater palace. As soon as they landed in the courtyard, Suzume flew off the back of the sea turtle and hurried up the stairs into the palace. She ran down the hallways and down the stone staircase to the long corridor leading to the springs. Her heart was beating rapidly as she passed through the double doors. Ai was standing by the ice pool with her head bowed. Suzume scanned the pool, but Kaito was missing.

"Where is Kaito?" Suzume demanded as she stomped over toward Ai, her hands shaking.

Ai turned to face her, tears streaming down her face. In the palm of her hand was a single tear-shaped pearl. "He's gone."

"What?" Suzume froze in place. Her last footstep echoed around her. Everything felt as if it had slowed down. Suzume stared at the empty pool, a layer of ice covered the surface. There was not even a trace of the dragon left. Distantly she heard shouts, but they were muted as if her head had been put underwater. *I'm too late?*

She felt a hard slap against her face. Suzume whipped her head to the side and saw Ai standing in front of her. Her anger burned in her eyes, strong enough to overpower any spell that might have otherwise held her back. Naoki grabbed Ai by the shoulder, yanking her away but the child-like yokai fought against him, her hair turning into dozens of tentacles which twisted around his arms and neck attempting to strangle.

"This is your fault. You swore you wouldn't take his power and you did it anyway!"

Suzume stared back at her without seeing. *I killed him?*

As Ai tried to wrestle her way free of Naoki, Tsuki and Makato joined in, grabbing a hold of her and pulling her away from Suzume. Tsuki wrapped Ai up in his arms and she beat tiny fists against his chest. In the process, she dropped the pearl. It rolled on the ground, stopping a few feet from Suzume who squatted down to pick it up. It was cold to the touch and perhaps the size of the tip of her pinky finger.

"He's yokai. He should be able to reform," Rin said as she placed herself in front of Suzume, making an additional barrier between the angry yokai and the priestess.

"Not now, not anymore!" Ai screamed. Tears were running down her face but she sagged against Tsuki's embrace, small hands clutching at his haori. "Ai is all that remains now. They're all gone."

Makato approached Suzume, holding out his hand for the teardrop-shaped pearl. "May I?" he asked her.

Suzume clutched the pearl to her heart, reluctant to let it go. Strangely, no matter how long she held onto it or how tight, it remained ice cold.

"Just for a moment," Makato said coaxing, Suzume to cooperate.

With reluctance, Suzume opened her hand to reveal the stone within. Makato did not try to take it from her, but examined it while tilting his head from side to side, a frown on his face.

Then he turned to Akira who had taken control of the body she shared with Tsuki. She and Ai had sunk to the floor and Ai rested her head in Akira's lap as she stroked her hair. The little yokai sniffled, tears still running down her face. "In the legends, the dragons were formed from the teardrops of a goddess. Is that true?"

Akira shrugged. "That was before my time."

Naoki stared at the teardrop. "It is true. The Lord of the Sea created them from the teardrops of the Lady of the Moon. They were her bitter tears of imprisonment."

"Is this one of the teardrops?" Akira asked, looking down at Ai as she stroked her hair in a motherly fashion.

Ai gave another loud sniffle. "He has returned to the teardrop he came from. Nothing can bring him back but the Lord of the Sea's power." She sobbed loudly and buried her face in Akira's lap.

Suzume closed her hand around the teardrop, all that remained of Kaito was in this. "The dragon's essence remains, though it is faint. I can reverse the seal which kept him from taking back his energy. But..."

"Don't waste your time," Ai spat as she lifted her head to glare at Suzume.

Makato bowed his head in shame. Rin came over and placed her hand on his shoulder. "We have to try," she said.

They shared a look, a silent exchange only they could decipher. "This is my fault. I will try to make it right." Makato lifted his head up to face everyone in the room.

Ai's tiny fists were clutching the front of her kimono and tears stained her cheeks as she sat up. She looked very much like a hurt child in that moment. Lost and alone. She cried, "A half-yokai would never have enough power to reverse this spell."

"You're right. I can't do it alone." Makato knelt down so he was at eye level with Ai. "Will you help me?" He held his hand out for her.

She glared at his offered hand. "Why would I trust you? You're just like her. You'll only hurt him." Ai jutted her chin in Suzume's direction. Suzume felt too numb to even argue. She clutched the pearl tighter in her hand as if keeping it close to her would somehow reverse what she had done.

Makato glanced in Suzume's direction before returning his attention to Ai. "Because I want to save him as much as you do."

"What do we have to do?" she said, her voice small and cautious.

Makato smiled and then tussled Ai's hair. "I'll need a few things."

It turned out all that was needed was charcoal and a bowl of water. Suzume hovered nearby, full of cautious hope, as Makato drew a complicated circle on the ground. The strange markings, while foreign, seemed intimately familiar to her. It surrounded the ice pool. Once the circle was done, he placed the bowl of water on the outer-most circle.

And then he came for the pearl. As he approached her, she clung to it tighter, not wanting to let it go. Makato stood in front of her, meeting her eyes. Suzume looked down at her hand and slowly uncurled her fingers, before titling it into Makato's awaiting grasp. Makato carried the pearl ceremoniously in front of him. Ai was already wading in the ice pool, the water up to her ankles. Makato carried the pearl over to the pool of water and placed it into Ai's awaiting cupped hands. Very carefully, Ai transported it into the center of the frozen pool. Makato stood in line with the bowl and Ai in front of him, making a line to the center.

Ai held the pearl above her head as the level of the water reached her neck. Once she'd gone as deep as she could, Makato lifted his hands to the heavens and a song flowed out of him. The song of unbinding, the same Suzume had learned from Hisato's memories — or perhaps they had been Kazue's. The hairs on the back of Suzume's neck stood on end. She could feel the power coursing around her, like the torrent of a river. The power was a temptation, one she could not resist. If she closed her eyes she could take that power for herself and become stronger with it. The very thought terrified her.

The urge was so strong she had to leave the room or risk doing more harm in the process. Suzume wandered away from the spring pools, up the stairs, and out into the courtyard. There she plopped down onto the steps which led into the palace and dropped her head into her hands. But the memory of that desire remained. All of this had happened because of her thirst for power. Even now she felt like a slimy eel was writhing around inside her gut. *He is going to recover. He has to.*

Some time passed; it felt like an eternity but perhaps it had only been a few minutes. Either way when she heard footsteps falling on the landing behind her, she did not even lift her head to see who it was. She couldn't face the truth, whatever it might be.

"I've broken the seal," Makato said.

"Good." Her voice was thick with emotion. She exhaled a breath she hadn't realized she was holding. Not wanting Makato to see her in such a vulnerable position she stood up, intent on running away. It was what she was best at. But Makato grabbed her by her bicep and kept her from leaving.

"There's more we need to talk about," he said.

When he touched her she felt the draw to take power from him, to use it to her own ends, to awaken the flame. She wrenched her arm away from him and started down the hall. "I'm not in the mood."

"It's about your father... the emperor."

Suzume's footsteps faltered. Since Daiki had first taunted her with the idea she'd been running away from the truth. She refused to confront it. But there was no use running anymore.

"Then what Hisato said was true?" she asked, keeping her back to him.

"Yes." He exhaled the word.

Suzume nodded her head. "Then that's all I need to know."

She took a few more steps and then he shouted, "Wait."

"I don't blame you for what you did." *Because I did worse.*

"There's more. You heard what Ai said. I am not human. I'm a half yokai, a hanyou."

"So what?" She didn't care if it sounded harsh. She was ready for this conversation to end. She didn't even have the courage to look Kaito in the face to confront what she had done.

Makato ran his hand through his hair. "Kazue's soul was fused with mine. But we remain separate. You were born this way, you—"

Suzume turned around to face him. "Kazue wants to take over my body, I already know that."

Makato bowed his head, listening to her chastisement. "I don't think who we are is an accident," he said, then he raised his eyes to meet hers.

"So?" she asked, her words like the crack of a whip.

"I think someone is trying to bring back Kazue from the dead."

Suzume gave a bitter laugh and shook her head. "Do you think I care about that? I'm done with Kazue, her quest, and every other way she ruined my life." She turned to storm away.

"The dragon's not improving," he said, stopping her in her tracks once more.

She balled her hands into fists at her side. Already she could feel the fire welling up inside her, threatening to take control once more. But if she did that, then she would really lose Kaito. *Maybe I have already.*

"I don't think he can recover on his own. He's lost too much of his energy," Makato continued.

"Then what do we do?" she asked, but her voice came out barely above a whisper.

"I think it's time to let him go," Makato said, reaching out most likely intent on comforting her.

Suzume knocked his hand away and took a step back. Her eyes narrowed as they darted across his face. "Are you saying I should just let him die?"

"He's already gone, Suzume. This is why you were sent to the shrine, not to free him but destroy him."

"You're wrong," she shouted as she stomped her feet. She knew she was acting like a child and she didn't care. She knew he was right, their powers had always been in conflict from the moment they met. And whether it was some plot by unknown figures or destiny's design, she didn't want to believe it.

Makato shook his head as he looked down at his feet. "I feared this," he said under his breath.

"Feared what?" She glared at him tossing her head. She could put up a strong front but on the inside, she was terrified.

He jabbed a finger in her direction. "You're falling in love with him."

Suzume balked at the notion as she shook her head. "I am not in love with him."

It was Makato's turn to shake his head. "Everyone can see. It's written on your face."

"That's not true."

"Then why risk your own life for him?" he said, his voice raised.

Suzume only shouted back, "Because this was my fault!"

Her words echoed back at her. It was the first time she had said it out loud. They all thought it, she knew. But no one had the guts to say it. Makato wouldn't look her in the eye, only confirming her suspicion. He ran his hands through his hair as he sighed.

"Believe me, I know what you're going through."

Suzume scoffed. "I doubt it."

"I betrayed the woman I love because I thought that was the best way to protect her. But I only put her in greater danger."

Suzume crossed her arms over her chest and looked away from him, not willing to admit he had a point. "You didn't sentence Rin to death though."

Makato sighed again. "I don't want to let him go either. The part of me that's Kazue cannot bear to see him like this. But I also know we cannot keep waiting for a miracle."

Suzume balled her hands into fists so hard her nails broke the skin of her palms. "This can't be it. There has to be something we can do."

There was a long stretch of silence, where she expected Makato would tell her that there was no hope left. But he made no such denials.

She turned to look at him, sudden hope blooming within her. "Is there a way?"

Makato turned his shoulder to her as if he would walk away without answering, but she grabbed him and forced him to face her. "You have to tell me."

"It's dangerous, and there's no guarantee it's going to work..."

"What is it?"

He looked anywhere but at her. "We have to take the energy you took and put it back inside him."

"Then let's do it."

"It's not that simple."

"What, are you afraid I'll hurt him again?"

"Not you, Kazue."

She thought once more to the warnings she had received about how her power would consume her and of Hisato's taunts that Kazue's soul was what had been protecting her all this time. When Hisato had tried to kill her, Kazue stopped him. There was no guarantee this would work and even if it did, it might kill her in the process. But if she didn't do this Kaito would die.

"We have to try," Suzume said.

FORTY-SIX

They returned to the spring room. Rin stood by one of the pools, staring into the water. Naoki was leaning against the far wall, while Akira and Ai were speaking together in low tones. Akira was still stroking the back of the child-like yokai. When Makato and Suzume entered everyone looked in their direction.

"How dare you come back here," Ai hissed.

"There's one more thing we'd like to try," Makato said, holding his hand up to stop Ai from shouting more obscenities at Suzume.

Ai glared but made no comment.

"We're going to try a ceremony to bring Kaito back, but it requires a lot of power. I will need representatives for air and water in addition to Suzume's fire and my earth.

"I will stand in for air." Naoki stood up, hands crossed over his chest.

Suzume could not look him in the eye. She didn't deserve his help.

Makato looked to Ai who was standing back, arms crossed over her chest.

"This will not work," she snarled.

"We have to try at least," Makato said, pleading with her.

"How do we know Suzume won't drain us all of our spiritual power?" She nodded toward Suzume.

"She won't," Makato said in a tone that left no room for argument. "We do this now or lose the dragon."

Ai scoffed but made no further protests.

"Everyone join hands," Makato said, pulling everyone into the circle he'd drawn on the floor. Suzume could see the pearl floating on the surface of the ice pool. It glimmered faintly, as if the small spark of Kaito's life remained within it.

Everyone joined hands. Only Suzume hesitated. Even before any spells were invoked, she felt the draw to take the power. She had already stolen from all of them, it would not be difficult to do it again. The pathways were made. Suzume stared at her hands, afraid of the power she had no control over. Power that had already hurt so many.

"Suzume?" Makato said, drawing her attention.

Suzume shook her head. "You'll have to find another fire." Suzume turned and ran from the room. She ran as far as she could without leaving the palace. In the end she ran all the way to the courtyard and through the torii arch she had gone through to fight the umi-bozu. She kept going until she was lost in the mist, unsure where she came from or where she was going. She sunk down. *I can't do this. All I am good for is destroying.* She pressed her forehead against her knees.

"What is it that you're afraid of?"

Her head snapped up. She had not even heard him follow her. "I'm not afraid of anything." She glared at Naoki.

"Then why can't you be the fire?" he asked her. There was no judgment in his expression, just an honest question.

It was a loaded question all the same: on the one hand she could expose herself and her fear to another person and on the other hand if she lied and said she could not do it, he would see right through her.

"I can't do it. I never had power of my own. All I've done is take from others," she said, her voice hardly above a whisper.

"That is the nature of fire. It cannot exist without consuming others. It needs both air and wood to form. But it also creates heat, for warmth, for food, and for protection..."

She scoffed. "And it destroys those things to give that."

"In life we must give up one thing to receive another. Alone fire can be destructive, but when it works with the other elements it can create too. A pot cannot be made without being forged in flames. New trees cannot grow without the old dead being burned away."

"What if I can't control it? What if I hurt more people?" Suzume asked in a whisper. She'd never exposed these fears to anyone. But here in fog, shrouded from anyone's face, she felt she could speak her fears.

"I won't let you."

She snorted in disbelief. "No one has been able to stop me before."

"And you've never learned to trust before."

Suzume stared at the ground for a moment. She'd never been this raw in front of anyone else before but Naoki had a way of bringing these things out of her.

"Why should I trust you?"

"Because I have faith in you."

She turned around to face him and saw he carried none of his usual weapons. His expression was blank as usual but she saw a hint of openness there.

"Why? What have I done to earn that?"

"You're different. And you're trying to do better."

Suzume looked away once more. The fear of her power was real and palpable, but maybe if she could lean on someone else for once, perhaps she could balance the excess of fire in her soul.

She stood up. "Let's go."

The two of them returned to the spring room, where the others were still gathered around the frozen pool. When Suzume entered, Ai rolled her eyes. Suzume marched past her, ignoring the look she gave her.

Suzume resumed her position. Makato looked at her giving her an 'are you ready' look. She nodded her head in response. He held out his hand to her and Suzume took a deep breath before grabbing onto his and Naoki's hands. The moment their hands touched she felt their energy spark against hers.

Makato started to sing and as he did the feeling only intensified. Energy flowed through the four of them, collecting in Suzume. It pressed down upon her chest and made it difficult to breathe. Something deep inside her slithered and moved about in her stomach. It wanted that power for itself, it wanted to drain the three others to make itself even more powerful. But before she could give in to the feeling she was filled with reassurance, the earth of Makato's soul was fuel for her flame, and the air built it bigger, but water dampened it before it could grow out of control. The four elements were in harmony. She was not just destruction but part of a greater whole. The balance of life.

Ai joined Makato's song, making their combined power greater, and then Naoki joined. Suzume should have joined them last but her throat felt dry and the words would not come. As their spiritual energy passed through her getting stronger through their connection so too did the feeling of unease grow inside her. She was terrified of what she might unleash by accident. The others continued the song, the power was growing stronger and building between the four of them. She felt it coursing through her veins using her as a conduit. The song fell over the pearl Kaito was trapped in.

"Suzume, you have to sing," Rin said from behind her.

Suzume shook her head and closed her eyes, the fire was rising up in her, overwhelming the others, taking too much and sharing too little. Her fear was stronger than their trust. She was going to burn someone. She was going to hurt them all. She had no control over herself, and she could not stop this feeling. She tried to jerk her hand away to retreat before it was too late, before the darkness consumed them all. But she could not pull away and she was spiraling, losing control, disconnecting from herself drifting into darkness.

And then suddenly it stopped. She was lost in darkness, floating. She swayed back and forth, drifting with the tide. When she opened her eyes, she was out on the endless sea. The sky above her was a swirling kaleidoscope of colors. Clouds moved overhead as the waves rocked her to sleep. She closed her eyes once more.

When she awoke again she was a tree, deep roots reaching outward, connected to a network of other living things. Her thoughts were slow and endless as time, looping into one another. Ancient and new at the same time. Her branches reached higher and higher into the sky, brushing against the clouds.

She burst from the treetops, taking flight on the wind, drifting lazily as a cloud on a summer day. When a strong breeze blew she was sent tumbling from the sky, careening toward the ground, but before she could crash into it she was turned into a white-hot blaze. Scorching, consuming, leaving nothing but devastation in her wake. Suzume was back in her own body and she ran from the fire which continued to chase her, hot fingers reaching for her, burning her clothes and enveloping her until there was nothing left but darkness, complete emptiness.

Suzume looked around into the darkness. "Hello?" Her voice seemed to echo back at her. She was alone in this endless void.

Where am I? She looked down and she could see her hands. She could feel her body, she pinched her arm. "Ouch." *How did I get here?*

"Did I not tell you? We are connected," a familiar voice said in her ear.

Suzume spun in place. Hisato stood next to her, a beacon in the endless darkness.

"How did you bring me here?" Her own voice echoed back at her.

Hisato shook his head. "I did not bring you anywhere, we are inside you. I am a part of you."

Suzume looked around at the tunnel of darkness. "This can't be inside me."

"The darkness in you is growing, Suzume." He sounded as if he was behind her but when she spun around he wasn't there.

"This has to be a trick."

"It's no deception. Just like Kazue, your darkness has grown out of balance. Your selfish quest for power has led you here. And all that your power touches will be tainted by it."

"No. You're lying."

"You are meant for me, Suzume, because we are the same. We both desire more, we need more. Don't you remember how it felt to take my power from me? How good you felt to consume the energy of others?"

She shook her head and covered her ears. This was all a trick. She knew it.

"You are not a good person. The more you use the power, the bigger it becomes. It is not Kazue who has been trying to consume you, but your own greed. Your own desire for destruction. It was not Kazue who was evil. But you."

"NO!" Suzume screamed and she woke on the ground covered in sweat and panting.

Naoki was at her side, looking down at her. Suzume looked around bewildered. "Where am I?"

"The ceremony is complete."

Suzume sat up quickly but her head spun as she did so.

Kaito's body floated on the surface of the water, eyes closed and not moving.

"Why hasn't he woken up?" Suzume asked.

Ai who had been kneeling at the water's edge turned to scowl at Suzume. "Because the ritual was imperfect."

"Are you saying this is my fault?" But she knew deep down it was. What Hisato had said about the darkness within her, it had stopped her from performing the ritual as it should have been.

"You hesitated too long," Ai said, arms crossed over her chest and chin tilted haughtily.

Suzume deflated a little. Perhaps none of them suspected what really lurked within her. Snakes were battling in her stomach; her own foolishness might have doomed him anyway.

Naoki brought Kaito to a room. All they could do was wait and hope he recovered. While waiting for Kaito to wake up, Suzume could not stay still and started pacing the floor of her room. But the space was too small and she decided to walk the halls instead. As she wandered she had no particular destination in mind and yet, without meaning to, she found herself standing in front of Kaito's room. She stood outside the door, wanting to go in, but fearing to find out that she had caused his death.

Just as she turned to walk away, the door slid open. Suzume looked over her shoulder to see Rin standing there, bags under her eyes.

"Did you want to see him?" Rin asked, gesturing to the room beyond.

"No, I was just passing by," she snapped, but the Kitsune could see right through her.

Rin raised her brow.

"Don't blame yourself for him not waking. If we had drawn any more energy from you, it would have killed you. Makato did it to spare you."

It didn't make her feel any better. She was not sure she had a right to be spared. Suzume cleared her throat. What Rin likely didn't know was, it had been Suzume's fault he had become as weak as he was. "Great." She half choked out before half turning attempting to leave.

"Maybe if you sat beside him it would help." Rin's words halted her in her tracks.

Suzume kept her back to her as she said, "I doubt it."

"He did it all for you."

Suzume sighed heavily. She supposed she could sit beside him for just a few moments. It couldn't hurt, could it?

Rin stepped out of the way so Suzume could enter. Inside the room was bare except for the futon where Kaito lay. She could not make her feet move beyond the threshold as she stared at his immobile body. His wounds had healed, except for the shiny pink scars on his previously unmarked body.

There was a certain hush to the room as if raised voices were forbidden and would impede his healing.

"I'll leave you alone for a few minutes," Rin said.

Before Suzume could protest, Rin slid the door closed behind her, trapping her inside with the sleeping dragon. Something coiled around Suzume's heart, grabbing on so hard she wasn't sure she was breathing properly.

Don't be stupid. You're just worried about him because he almost died. But it wasn't just the fear of him almost dying, it was relief at seeing that he was healing. That she would still be able to fight with him and still see him smirk when he teased her.

Suzume closed her eyes. *Don't be an idiot. Don't let him worm his way into your heart. Do you want to end up like Kazue?* But no matter how much she told herself these things she still couldn't break this spell. She was frozen there, half terrified and half relieved. *Just a few more minutes*, she kept telling herself. *Just a few more minutes and I'll leave.*

A few more minutes turned into a few more and Rin did not return. Suzume's legs hurt and she was weak and tired from the ceremony. She took a few steps into the room, and decided she would sit down for a few minutes. She would watch him sleep for a little while and sneak away before he ever woke and found out.

Kaito moaned in his sleep and she jumped up, torn between running before he caught her and wanting to check and make sure he wasn't injured. In the end, she rushed over to his side, kneeling by his bed, searching him for open wounds or other signs that he was injured or in need of assistance. As she searched his face she realized it was the first time she had properly looked at him in a long time. The color had returned to his tanned face, the scars were fading, and he was back to the same arrogant bastard she knew. But when he slept, he seemed so innocent. It was hard to believe he lived to torture her. She reached out tentatively to stroke his cheek, to convince herself that this was indeed not a dream.

As she did so his arm snatched her, grabbing her and pulling her down onto his chest. Suzume pushed against him.

"Let go."

But he would not budge, and his arms wrapped tighter around her, holding her to him. She could hear his heart beating, felt his warmth around her, and smelled his scent which was comforting. The sparks didn't fly and she didn't feel his energy fighting against hers.

"If you're feeling well enough to play jokes, then I'm going," she said into his chest.

He did not respond. His breathing was deep and even as if he was in a deep sleep. She could not release herself from his grip without risking injuring him. It felt nice to be wrapped in his embrace. *I'll lay here for just a few minutes. Then I'll leave.*

FORTY-SEVEN

Kaito woke to the scent of her, the soft edges of her curves pressed against him, and her heart beating in time with his. Everything that had happened before was all just a bad dream, the five hundred years in the stone, all of it. Kaito nuzzled against Kazue's neck, relishing the feeling of her in his bed. But instead of melting into him, she tensed and then jumped away from him. The spell was broken as Suzume scrambled backward and away from him, brandishing a pillow at him like her staff.

Not what he had expected but almost as good. He leaned on one elbow and felt the slight pull of injuries, but otherwise he was back to normal. That empty feeling of being disconnected from his own spiritual energy was gone, the flow of water inside him had returned. He wasn't sure how but he was back to his old self. He also wasn't sure why he was naked beneath the blanket, but he wasn't mad about it. As he began to rise the blanket fell low on his hips, exposing his abdomen. Suzume's eyes drifted downward, skimming over his body.

"Looks like I got my night after all." *Too bad I cannot remember it.*

A comedic series of emotions crossed over her face. She opened and closed her mouth, preparing a retort, while fighting the embarrassment that was turning her face crimson.

"First of all." She held up her finger. "Nothing happened. And second of all." She held up her second finger. "You still owe me a rematch."

He chuckled to himself, she was fiery as ever. "What am I supposed to think when I wake up with you wrapped in my arms?"

She crossed her arms over her chest. "You grabbed me and wouldn't let me go."

He raised a skeptical brow. "Sounds like my kind of night."

"I just fell asleep," she corrected him.

"So I grabbed you and you just fell asleep..." He gestured vaguely with his hand.

"I passed out from a lack of air. You were suffocating me." She jabbed a finger in his direction. "I'm lucky to be alive!" She threw her arms out, tossing the pillow on accident and it collided with the nearby wall.

He laughed before leaning forward and the blanket, that was covering not much of anything, slipped further down and her eyes bulged in her skull.

"Was this your attempt at seduction?" he asked, creeping closer to her on all fours. "I have to say, I've seen better."

Suzume coughed and sputtered as she turned away from him to conceal her blush with her sleeve. She kept her gaze upward toward the ceiling to avoid his naked body, which was proudly on display.

"Clearly you're back to normal. Why don't you put some clothes on?" she said and turned around to walk out of the room as fast as her feet would carry her.

"Aren't you going to help me dress?" he called after her.

She stumbled before she reached the door, but she ran out without another word.

Kaito fell back onto the futon and laughed to himself. But as the humor faded, he realized he was in an unfamiliar place with no idea how he had gotten here. He sat up and looked around. The last thing he remembered was that the priest had sealed him. Anger bubbled up in him. Now that he was back to normal, he had a score to settle.

He stormed into the hall in search of answers. But it wasn't until he came out of his room that he realized where he was. It had been centuries since he had last set foot in this place and yet it felt like it was yesterday he had served the Lord of the Sea. Revenge could wait, he decided as he wandered the halls instead. The palace had fallen into disrepair, the paint on the murals was peeling. Water crept in through every crack, running down walls and pooling on the floor. A mildew stench permeated everything. The halls were too quiet, the hush was almost suffocating.

The palace of his memories had been teaming with life: servants, yokai, visiting kami, all filled these rooms with music and laughter. Now all that remained were shadows. *What has happened while I slept?* He stopped to stare at a mural which long ago he had passed hundreds of times without a second glance. Now he stopped and was absorbed in old memories. His creator, Lord of the Sea, stood amongst the waves surrounded by the dragons, Kaito's brothers and sisters.

Kaito stared at their figures rendered forever in paint. A hand reached out to touch them, his long-forgotten kin.

"Ai almost didn't recognize you, Kai."

It had been a very long time since he had been called that. Today was just a day for old memories it seemed. Kaito turned his head to face Ai who had strolled up to him, the elusive and beautiful daughter of the sea, and his one-time mistress. But she was not as he remembered her. Instead she'd taken the form of a child.

"Ai is that really you?" Kaito threw his head back and laughed. "What happened to you?"

Ai crossed her arms over her chest in a most child-like way, her face screwed up in anger. Kaito had to cover his mouth to suppress his laughter for fear of offending her. She tapped her foot on the ground, her chin up in the air waiting for him to beg forgiveness, he knew. And old habits were hard to break. Even if he had ruled over all of Akatsuki, she had been his mistress once.

"Forgive me, my lady." He bowed his head to her and she looked down at his subservient position with a little huff. With her signal he was able to rise again. "What happened here?" He gestured to the desolate palace.

"You know what."

She meant that as a dig at him. Well let her throw her fit. He did not control Kazue and he had not asked her to seek out the power.

"You expect an apology from me I suppose?"

Ai rounded on him, her pale face bright with anger. "You have no idea what I have suffered. For five hundred years I have been left alone here to watch my father's kingdom fall to ruin."

"And how is that my fault?" Kaito said with arms crossed over his chest. "Was I to know that the great Lord of the Sea would fall to a mortal woman?"

"You started this. When you let her capture your heart and taught her about our world. If she had not learned the power of our names." Ai stopped and took a deep breath.

"Do you take me to be a fool? I would never have taught her that."

"Then who did if not you?"

He scoffed. He did not need to answer to Ai or to anyone else. It had been a mistake teaching Kazue the power their names had over them. Perhaps if he had not trusted her as much as he had, then none of this would have happened.

"I am going to right the wrongs she has caused," Kaito said, ignoring her question.

Ai laughed mockingly. "How do you plan to do that? With that priestess? You make the same foolish mistakes all over again."

"Do not test me. I am not the man I was back then. I no longer serve you."

She did not flinch, though he knew how it would strike her at the heart to know she could not control him as she had long ago.

"The palace can be rebuilt, the kingdom reunited, but not by human hands," she said softly.

Kaito looked at her from the corner of his eye. Long ago, he had desired her, as had all those who saw her. Not only was she beautiful but a brilliant strategist and powerful second only to her father. But not any longer, he had surpassed those naive fantasies. He had risen even higher than her.

"What are you suggesting?" he asked, raising a brow.

She turned to face him now with determination in her gaze. "Together we can rebuild the kingdom that was lost. We could rule it side by side."

Kaito's own kingdom remained divided, his power weaker than it was before. If he went to her now, he could regain his kingdom and all the power he had lost.

She took a step closer to him, planting a hand on his arm. She came no higher than his middle and he had to look down to meet her eyes. She looked up at him through long lashes. "You wanted to save me back then. Well now's your chance, Kai."

Kaito smirked, his head dipping down toward her, his breath was hot against her neck.

"You never needed saving, Ai."

He stepped away from her. If he accepted her offer he would be putting a collar around his own neck and they both knew it. He returned to his hunt for Suzume, walking away from Ai and his past life and old memories. He would regain his kingdom on his own, just as he had obtained it the first time. He did not need her help.

The others had gathered in the main hall and their chatter carried beyond the doors. From outside Suzume's voice rose above the others as she scolded Tsuki.

"Give it back," she said.

Tsuki held something just out of reach, taunting her. Suzume smiled at him, reaching for the object. Laughter was in her voice as she scolded him. For a moment Kaito watched her, entranced by every movement she made.

Perhaps it was because he had just woken and his dreams of Kazue had put him under a spell, but he couldn't keep his eyes off of Suzume. He watched as she chased Tsuki around the room, but when she passed Makato his infatuation turned to rage.

He threw open the door into the main hall and the wall trembled beneath the force of it. Tsuki and Suzume froze in place upon his entry.

You could have heard a pin drop in the room. Everyone's gaze around the room shifted back and forth as if they were all afraid to speak.

"You!" he roared and rushed past Suzume and Tsuki to grab Makato by the throat and pin him against the wall.

Rin shouted for him to stop, but everything was coming back to him now. How this bastard had betrayed him. How he had tricked him back into the stone.

"How dare you show your face before me after what you did," Kaito growled.

Rin grabbed onto Kaito's arm as Makato sputtered for breath. His face was turning red and purple. He would watch the life drain out of him.

"Let him explain himself, please," Rin pleaded. But he did not hear her pleas. He would destroy the priest. He had sealed his power and then he had put him in stone; there was nothing else that needed to be explained.

"Stop!" Suzume shouted.

Kaito turned toward her, his grip relaxing only slightly on Makato's neck.

"You're defending him?" he growled.

"He had to do it."

Kaito laughed. "So I should just forgive him because he had a good reason?"

"He did it for me," Rin said, yanking on his arm again.

Kaito lowered him to the ground. Makato fell to his knees, gasping for breath. He looked at the three of them, arms crossed, waiting for an explanation. Not that there was anything they could say to change his mind.

"Master," Rin fell onto the ground in a deep bow, head almost pressed to the ground. Makato followed suit. Only Suzume remained standing, stubbornly glaring at him. "If you must punish someone, punish me. It is my fault he got mixed up in any of this."

"Rin had nothing to do with this. I'm the one who made a deal with Hisato."

He looked between the two of them, hand raised ready to strike them both. Rin raised her eyes to him.

"I told you not to be a fool," he growled.

"This is my husband, what other choice did I have?"

Kaito lowered his arm to his side. As much as he wanted to be angry at her, he couldn't. Because when it came down to it, he would have done the same. Even now, knowing Kazue was inside Makato kept him from killing the man.

"Leave."

"Master?" Rin said.

"You heard me! Go."

"What are you doing?" Suzume interjected, coming to stand in front of the pair of them. "He saved your life."

"After he tried to kill me. I cannot trust him, he has to leave."

"You're being unreasonable."

"Do not argue with me," he roared.

Rin stood up to face him, hurt and anger in her expression. "If he goes then I go too."

"Then go. Take your priest and leave my sight. I never want to see you again."

Rin glared back at him. They'd been friends for a very long time and perhaps she knew him better than anyone else. But he knew she would betray him again, and he couldn't leave himself vulnerable as he had been.

FORTY-EIGHT

Before Makato and Rin were to leave Makato asked to speak with Suzume. She'd tried convincing Kaito to let them stay but he wouldn't see reason. When she arrived at Rin and Makato's room, she knocked on the door and was ushered in from within. He and Rin were packing their bags. But when she entered Makato stood up to greet Suzume and offered her a seat.

Sitting down across from him, Suzume looked around the room. They had only just started to scratch the surface of what it meant to be part of Kazue and she didn't want to see him go. But she couldn't see another way to keep the group together.

"What did you want to talk about?" Suzume asked after a long awkward silence.

"I want you to come with Rin and me."

"Why?" Suzume sat up straighter, brows furrowed in confusion.

"There is more to what we are that we've yet to discover. Rin and I are going to the White Palace to search for answers and I want you to join us."

Home. To the White Palace. A part of her had given up on the idea of ever returning there.

"But the others..."

"Akira, Tsuki, and Naoki will follow you anywhere. But the dragon..."

It shouldn't matter if she left Kaito behind, all he did was irritate her. And now that he was healed it wasn't like he needed her.

"He won't let me go." The dragon would follow her to the ends of the earth she suspected.

"And that's the problem," Makato said with a sigh.

"What do you mean?"

"You asked me to save his life once. Well now I'm asking you the same. You cannot stay with him and have him live. Because you've taken his energy you're bound together. What if you lose control and..."

"I can learn to control it," Suzume said, though she didn't feel confident on that score.

"It's more than that," Rin interjected. "The dragon cannot separate the past from the present. And the more confused he gets, the worse it will be for the both of you."

Suzume scoffed. "It's not like he's in love with me."

Makato gave her a small smile and Rin shook her head.

"I don't have those kinds of feelings for him either."

They both just looked at her as if they thought she was a liar, or maybe they knew how she felt. Rin had waited for Hikaru's reincarnation and Makato had a piece of Kazue's soul within him. If anyone understood the complicated brew of emotions inside her right now, it was them. These foreign feelings were confusing her, clouding her judgment. Ever since she had slept in his bed with him her head had felt fuzzy and confused. As if she couldn't untangle her own thoughts. Kazue was the one who loved Kaito, not her. Suzume's only priorities should be herself, protecting herself from Hisato, and living to see another day. Kaito didn't factor into the equation.

"If we can find out why we are like this, then perhaps we can reverse it," Makato said, changing the subject.

More than anything she wanted to be free of Kazue's curse. And not long ago she had dreamed of nothing more than going back to the White Palace. But knowing what she did now, she wasn't sure she could return. She was different, and the palace was a different place than she thought it was.

"There you are," Kaito said as he threw open the door to the room. But when he looked at Rin and Makato, his expression changed.

Suzume leaped up as if she had been caught doing something she shouldn't have, which of course she hadn't. Kaito had no say over who she spent time with or how she lived her life. Makato placed himself between Suzume and the dragon.

"What's going on here?" Kaito asked with narrowed eyes.

"It's none of your business," Suzume snapped back at him.

"I've asked Suzume to leave with me and Rin."

Ice frosted over Kaito's gaze. "Do not test me, priest."

Rin stood up, putting herself between Makato and the dragon. "It is her decision."

The dragon's eyes narrowed further as he glared at the kitsune.

"She's right. It is my decision," Suzume interjected defiantly.

Kaito's head swiveled in her direction. "Is that what you want? To leave?" there was a note of something in his voice. Something that terrified her.

Not wanting him to see the fear in her, she glared back at him. "What if I do?"

She hated the hurt she saw in his eyes. It would be so much easier if he hated her, or resented her for what she had done to him.

"I won't let you go."

Ice hung on the air and clouds of vapor rose around Suzume's head as Kaito's temper dropped the air to glacial temperatures.

Kaito grabbed a sword he wore at his belt and pointed it at Makato's throat. The tip of the blade was mere inches from piercing the skin.

"This was your plan all along. You got into her head, and now you're going to bring her to Hisato aren't you?" Kaito said in a low growl.

The priest did not deny nor try to explain. He merely said, "You know that's not true."

The dragon pressed the tip of the blade against Makato's throat and a bead of blood rose up to the skin. Another couple inches and this blade would go through his throat and end the priest's life.

Suzume placed herself between the two of them, hands outstretched. "I don't belong to you."

He growled low in his throat, his eyes trained on Makato. "Leave now, before I really lose my temper."

Makato stepped back and pressed his fingers to the cut on his throat. Rin rushed over to check on him. She looked to the dragon, trying to catch his eye but he kept his hands at his side, gaze forward, pinning Suzume in place. There was nowhere to run now. They left the room, leaving Suzume and Kaito behind.

Suzume tried to follow, but the dragon grabbed her by the wrist, holding her in place. "Not you."

"Let go of me," Suzume said through gritted teeth.

"I won't let you leave. You're going to stay here at the palace. I've already spoken to Ai..."

"Stop!" Suzume held up her hands. Her anger boiling. Flames erupted along her fingers as she did so. "I'm not going to stay here like your pet?"

"How else can I protect you?" he roared.

Suzume was trembling, with anger and fear of herself. The fire was dancing along her skin again, broken free once more. There was a visible strain on Kaito's face. Though he wouldn't admit it out loud. She was still hurting him without meaning to.

"Do you think this is acceptable? How much longer before you destroy yourself or others?" He gestured toward her.

"I could learn to control it if you gave me the chance."

"I can't risk it. Not again!"

"Do you think I'm going to seal you like Kazue? Or perhaps grow mad with power? Cause I've done that already," she said, venom dripping from every word.

"That's not what I meant and you know it." His voice shook the air around them. His spiritual energy was uncoiling with his temper and pressing upon her lungs, making it difficult to breathe. It only made the fire in her grow stronger, encasing her in red flame.

She gave a false laugh. "Then what is this?"

He shook his head as if this was an argument they'd had a hundred times. "Hisato is trying to use you, your power, your body."

"So you'll hide me away like Kazue? Well you can see how that turned out." She gestured between them. This whole mess had started because Kaito had fallen in love with Kazue, because he had introduced her to the world of yokai, given her a taste of immortal life. Because he hadn't respected her and she had been driven to get more power. The same way Suzume had sought his approval.

"Why do you keep putting her between us?"

"Because she'll always be there like a wedge. Don't you realize that yet? Everything comes back to her, every bad thing that happens to me is because of some divine punishment for what she did. Even your desire to protect me is because you couldn't protect her." She panted as she shouted the words that she'd been holding in for too long.

"I don't want to see you hurt and that makes me the bad guy?" His temper was rising as well, blue scales flashed along his skin, and when he spoke two large canines protruded.

"I can protect myself."

"How do you plan to protect yourself when you have no control at all?" His words felt like a slap across the face. For a moment Suzume was stunned into silence.

Then she glared at Kaito. "Do you think Hisato is going to just give up on looking for me? He's working with humans, the emperor! This isn't over just because I hide away. I need to go to the White Palace, to figure out why I am this way. To find a way to learn to control this power." She swept her arm to the side as she spoke. Her tone rose as the flames burst up along her skin.

"You don't have to do anything. The artifacts are gone — I don't need you anymore."

Suzume stared at him in stunned silence for a second. "So you'll leave me here?" she shook her head. "Everything I did was to prove to you that I'm not weak," she said in a half-strangled cry.

"Just admit you need someone to protect you," he shouted back.

And that was it. He would never see her as his equal. He was always going to think of her as a weakling. And with that she came to a decision.

"That's what you think," she said softly, almost too low to hear. She didn't want him to see the hurt in her expression that she could not hide and she tried to brush past him, fed up with this argument.

He caught her wrist and held her. She didn't try to knock his hand away because a part of her wanted him to stop her. She wanted him to tell her that he believed in her, that he supported her no matter what choice she made. That he would join her on her quest to find answers.

"I hated that I couldn't be there for you. I hated that I felt helpless and couldn't protect you," he said, his voice just a low rumble.

The gooseflesh prickled along her neck. She wanted so badly to turn around and look him in the eye, to search for even the smallest hint that the person he was talking to was her, Suzume, and not Kazue. But she was equally afraid she would turn around and only confirm that he was talking to Kazue.

"I told you before, I don't need your protection," she said, still lacking the strength to break from his grip. The fire had died away and all that remained were the smoldering embers in her gut.

"Suzume." His voice was pitched low. He so rarely used her given name that when he did it felt so much more intimate.

"What," she snarled, trying to break the spell of his voice. *It's not me that's feeling this. It's Kazue. She wants to be with him not me.*

"Can't you just let me protect you?"

She took a long-ragged breath. Her heart was hammering in her chest, and he likely could feel the change in her pulse just from holding onto her wrist. She wanted to pull away to deny this draw he had on her. To pretend like it was her heart yearning for him, not Kazue's influence. Falling in love was for fools. Her head knew that but her idiot heart wouldn't listen. She'd been telling herself that for years. But then why couldn't she break away from his grip? She wanted to believe he was being sincere. *Stop it now before it's too late.*

"Come with me to the palace," she said, her final plea. "Help me find out who I am."

It was Kaito who let go of her wrist and Suzume pressed her hand to her chest, covering her beating heart.

"Please stay," he replied.

"Then I guess this is where we part ways."

Even a couple of weeks ago she would have jumped at the chance of being kept away from the fighting, secure and protected. Free of the burden of her destiny. She no longer had the luxury of forgetting. She had this power and for good or ill, she had to learn to live with it. She walked out the door, leaving him with his back to her. She had to walk away now before it was too late.

Acknowledgments

As I write this acknowledgment, I am overwhelmed by gratitude. The seeds that would bloom into the Dragon Saga germinated in high school. Though the final version looks nothing like the story I first envisioned, the earliest themes of elemental magic and a love that stretches across eons and tale of epic proportions remained. This book started out on Wattpad, where it gathered a small cult following of persistent, dedicated readers who spurned me to complete the first draft, which took me two years to write.

This series has been a decade in the making and I must heap praise upon my husband, Drew, whose always supported me as I've struggled with it giving me quiet encouragement and excitement over every story related triumph and comfort in the dark parts of the creative process. I also would be lost without my sounding board and best friend, Nicole, who is and will always be my biggest cheerleader.

This gorgeous edition you're holding in your hands wouldn't be possible without the support of my Kickstarter backers. I never thought I could see my words bound in such a beautiful fashion. Thank you a million times for helping me make my dreams a reality.

ALSO BY NICOLETTE ANDREWS

Moonlight Dragon

Empress Ascending (Newsletter Exclusive)

Dragon's Deception

Dragon's Temptation

Thornwood Series

Fairy Ring (Free)

Pricked by Thorns (Free)

Heart of Thorns

Tangled in Thorns

Blood and Thorns

World of Akatsuki

The Dragon Saga

The Priestess and the Dragon (Free)

The Sea Stone

The Song of the Wind

The Fractured Soul

The Immortal Vow

Tales of Akatsuki

Kitsune: A Little Mermaid Retelling (Free)

Yuki: A Snow White Retelling

Okami: A Little Red Riding Hood Retelling

Diviner's World

Duchess (Free)

Sorcerer (Free)

Diviner's Prophecy

Diviner's Curse

Diviner's Fate

Princess

<u>Witch of the Lake Series</u>

Feast of the Mother

Fate of the Demon

Fall of the Reaper

About the Author

Nicolette is a native San Diegan with a passion for the world of make believe. From a young age, Nicolette was telling stories whether it be writing plays for her friends to act out or making a series of children's books that her mother still likes drag out to embarrass her with in front of company. She still lives in her imagination but in reality she resides in San Diego with her husband, children and a couple cats. She loves reading, attempting arts and crafts, and cooking.

You can visit her at her website: www.nicoletteandrews.com or at these places:

- facebook.com/nicandfantasy
- x.com/nicandfantasy
- instagram.com/nicolette_andrews
- amazon.com/author/nicoletteandrews
- bookbub.com/authors/nicolette-andrews
- goodreads.com/nicolette_andrews
- pinterest.com/Nicandfantasy